The Divine Tragedy

LAUREN WANTZ

ISBN 978-1-950818-36-5 (paperback)

Rushmore Press LLC
1 888 733 9607
www.rushmorepress.com

Printed in the United States of America

CONTENTS

I am frightened of the church and state, I am frightened of all institutions because of what they have made me- they have made me insane, and made me alone by making me frightened of them. And what's worse, I believe it is a justified fear. A justified fear is much worse than an unjustified fear, for unjustified fears are more "regular," more accepted and even proliferated by society. Ogden Nash said "I don't belong to anything so nothing belongs to me." I belong to no institution and so society has made me its refuse, because institutions do not care for a person like me- they thought I aimed to destroy them before I even wanted to, and yes, now I do, just for their suspicion. In order to try to stop me they made me alone. I did not belong in society so I was free, and wedded to all the loneliness freedom implies, since institutions do not allow those who do not belong in them to be anything else when they are finally faced with the world than alone. I did not belong in the church because I felt sympathy for the devil. I did not belong in the government because I felt sympathy for those it so casually and carelessly leaves behind. I did not belong in school because I felt sympathy for those who had no drive towards success. I thought they were the intelligent ones, and besides, disturbingly I could find little difference between the university and the mental hospital. I do not belong in any institution because of this damned sympathy that has forced me to be unusual so I can feel it, thereby making me not a member of the institution that tells you what to pity and what to revile- it tells you to pity people who don't need it and revile everybody else. I couldn't live that way, I have always had to pity everyone. It's what I do for a living, it's all I am. I am everybody's fool.

I was created by two unusual parents. They were unusual because they used unusual platitudes, not the regular, circumscribed platitudes. But I was different from them because though they were strange they still tried to belong in some institution- the institution of marriage, though it had so desperately failed them, and they did pity and revile what this institution told them to, in spite of their odd platitudes, they were lucky that they were still platitudes. But I came out different. I could never listen to anybody except myself, not my parents or the institutions they were told was their duty to put me through. I could only ever know what I wanted, not what society wanted for me, which always seemed inimical to who I am. I wanted to live completely without platitudes, if it were possible. I wanted to pity everyone and revile only those my conscience told me to revile. The institution was one of these things.

My conscience told me to revile the institution because it tried to negate both freedom and responsibility, mainly, the responsibility of freedom. But being free has taught me this- freedom *is* responsibility.

PART 1

Treuga Dei

"I went to my room to get down on my knees and pray,
But the blues swept my spirit away-" Son House.

Cara Weisman ran as fast as she could, away from the certain death sentence of the church and the state, though there was no discernible difference between the two. She had broken the confession machine by putting her novel in it, she had confused it and then it had melted down. It was what was supposed to determine if she was innocent or guilty, but, because it was a machine, it was easy for her to out smart it. All you have to do to out smart a machine is *want* to out smart it. That was the problem with people these days, they didn't want to. For some reason a machine being more intelligent than them was a comfort to them. Cara didn't understand why. It was her worst nightmare, but people didn't realize all that it implied- they only realized that if the machines they used were smarter than them they could think less. But Cara *had* out smarted the machine, the goal of man in modern times, and now she would have to receive justice the traditional way- people would have to decide whether she was guilty or innocent and not the machine. That's why people were going to hate her, because she was going to undo their so called progress, their machine progress, their futurism, of course not their social prog-ress- that went with the machines, that went with the new dystopia, which, like all dystopias, called itself utopia.

So Cara ran and ran. She knew she didn't have much hope, the town she lived in, Kapporeth, was an incredibly small town so everyone lived and died in each other's ass. Cara mostly stayed away from everyone. She was a writer, which meant she had to work alone, and sadly, for the most part live alone as well. These people, this populace of the town of Kapporeth, they could not understand her. They did not understand why she wanted to destroy the world they lived in, to tear down civilization as it was, but in her mind it had already destroyed itself. She just wanted to deal the final blow, and not with force, but intellect- she wanted this modern world, this society, to one day bow down to her in realization that her caustic criticism of it was right. She wanted to knock everything down with words, tear apart kingdoms, empires, systems of government, simply with metaphors and allegories. She didn't think it would be hard. It was already weak, it was already held by the tenuous thread of people being willing to sacrifice a certain amount of freedom for security, but once she made people realize this security was false, surely they would take up arms with her, for their freedom that they bartered for nothing.

Cara didn't know where else to go, so she went back home. She walked in her small, frowzy apartment and stared at the security camera in her living room. Kapporeth was part of the carceral archipelago, the chain of nations under constant video surveillance. There was a security camera in every room in every house in Kapporeth. Cara always flipped them off. It was the first thing she did when she walked in her apartment. She took her shirt off, grabbed a beer and sat down half naked on the couch as she turned on the TV. She knew they would be here soon, the Holy Statesmen, the priests that held power in the government, would be here soon to arrest her. But she had put them in a difficult position. They had forgotten how to determine justice without the help of a machine. Doing it the manual way would surely be onerous for them. But Cara knew she was condemned, because it was true. She did want to ruin their so called Utopia, Utopia for themselves, a nightmare for everyone else. Cara knew these things happened all too easily. Nature allowed them, and human nature as well. Nature rarely resists humanity and human nature rarely resists itself, particularly in large groups.

Cara drank her beer and burped profusely as she turned on the television. She thought it was strange. Society barely let people these days be lazy, one always had to be working, and yet it supported and mass marketed technology for tools of human laziness, things like the television and the smart phone. But Cara supposed she knew why. Whether it was labor or idleness, the carceral archipelago was manipulating you either way- through labor you were working for them, through idleness you were being idle for them, because the idleness they made accessible to people involved not thinking, just as the hard labor did. 'I don't want to do either,' Cara thought. 'I don't want to work and I don't want to be lazy.'

She flipped through the channels numbly, doing what she just said she wouldn't do, then she stopped on the public access channel. They were interviewing Manuel Sanchez. "Oh good," Cara said, and relaxed back in her chair and burped again. She liked Manuel Sanchez. Once a slave, now a politician on the news almost everyday. He was trying to end Mexican slavery, which Cara supported. It was an awful thing they were doing to the Latin Americans in the country. Everyone who couldn't get in legally had to work for free, and those who did get in legally, they had to work practically for free, for less than minimum wage, which seemed no different than slavery to Cara. And still there were no laws for open immigration, even after the government of the carceral archipelago had duped these people into thinking there was a better life but instead giving them the same life, just in the midst of prosperity. Manuel Sanchez was trying to stop that. He was the last politician Cara could believe in, because he wasn't a priest.

The interviewer asked him questions. "People think you believe in nothing…"

"Well, nothing does certainly exist."

"But I mean politically."

"I believe in a few things politically," Sanchez tried to say as politely as he could. "I believe in what I call 'Historical determinism,' and coupled with that 'political indeterminism.'"

"What does that mean?"

"I believe Tolstoy was right. I believe history is fate, that it is beyond our free will, that it is determined, but politics on the other hand, politics are supposed to be our free will in the midst of that.

And with that we can have a little control over history, so long as politics represents free will…"

"But do you want it to be so lawless…"

"No one said anything about it being lawless. In fact laws are created by free will. I just believe politics shouldn't be so fatalistic. It has been fatalistic for too long. The almost now ubiquitous belief that war is inevitable, that's the determinism of history, but the indeterminism of politics should fight that. Our job in politics is to undo the mess fate has made, not collude with it."

"So you don't believe in lawlessness?"

"I believe in the lawlessness of fate and that it's humanity's job to fight that, not just in politics, but in everything. I'll tell you what I believe," Sanchez said as patiently as possible. "When I was a kid, my dad was in the military. He was your cliché drill sergeant kind of asshole. He fought for a country that had made his people slaves. And he would always tell me 'you have to decide if you want to be a leader or a follower,' and I always told him neither. He would say because of this I was an aimless, unambitious fool, but I tell you now, I am so happy, so content, not telling people what to do and not being told what to do. And if only everyone could be this way, civil anarchy could be possible, self- governing could be possible. I wouldn't have to be a politician, there wouldn't need to be politicians, and we could just fight fate as human beings, without ideology but unfortunately that is not the way people are. The masses like to be told what to do and a few sociopaths like telling people what to do. But I don't think this is how people naturally are. I think society has made them this way. I think society has made humanity i be many things it's not, for example, something that gives in to fate."

"You seem more like a philosopher than a politician," the interviewer said, for some strange reason, admonishingly.

Sanchez shrugged. "Yes," he said. "I am. But in ancient times all politicians were philosophers. I think that should happen again. I think to undo fate, which is the job of the politician, one has to first understand fate. And the only way we can do this is through philosophy. But you're right, I would have rather been a philosopher, and in many ways I am…"

"So why did you become a politician?"

"For a simple purpose. To save the world, to save it from the fatalism and defeatism certain pundits have swayed people into believing is normal. And to free my people. Politics, fighting fate, that's about freedom, or should be. Fighting fate *is* freedom. Giving into it is slavery."

'Goddamn,' Cara thought. 'This guy is awesome. He wants to save the world and I want to destroy it as it is, but we are on the same mission. If only I could get to him somehow, if only I could show him my writing. But I'm a nobody like everybody else.'

"Do you hate white people?" the interviewer asked.

"Certainly not."

"Then why did you say in an earlier interview on MFGBC that they were oppressing your people's culture?"

"Because they are."

"And why do you think that?" the interviewer asked, almost as if he was talking to a child whose behavior he was trying to correct.

"Because white people don't have a culture, so when they come across a group of people who do, they first oppress that culture and then try to adopt it as their own, flippantly, as means of compensation."

"What makes you think white people don't have a culture?"

"Because you don't need a culture when you rule the world."

Cara turned off the television and moved to her desk. After she had ruined the confession machine she had taken one of the typewriters they had there with her. That would be another major crime she would be charged with but she didn't care anymore. In the carceral archipelago life was a prison, so what was the difference if she went to a prison that openly called itself a prison, not a prison that called itself society. She sat at the typewriter, then checked the time.

"They're taking an awful lot of time," she said aloud. She thought she would be arrested by now by the holy police. If you offended the church you offended the state. Cara remembered that old law, that old law everyone had forgotten, the separation of church and state, but really it had never existed, an invisible God had always had a hand in government, the fate Manuel Sanchez said must be fought by politics, but the people had given up. They had given up their rights and their free will for the promise of certain comforts, religious and political, but they did not receive these comforts. Instead religion and politics as one had become completely resigned to fatalism, and the people along with it. Everyone was so much of a positivist they did nothing, believing that the chain of cause and effect could never change or be broken so it didn't matter what one did. By trying to escape the arbitrariness of indeterminism and anti-positivism they had only made life more arbitrary, more undetermined, by giving in completely to the fate no one was quite sure even existed. This way they had created fate- by doing nothing, they had created fate. That was what Manuel Sanchez meant. If you fight fate it won't even exist. And that's what people were so frightened of. Fate was a daunting prospect but a lack of fate was even more daunting because it meant freedom from a God that didn't care, from an invisible metaphysical scheme that wasn't looking. People thought that was too much freedom, even if it was the truth.

Cara sat down at her peculated typewriter. 'This may be the last chance I get to write,' she thought to herself. So she did. She realized writing, what most people thought was a chore, was actually one of the most proven methods to *defi le regle*, and Cara certainly wanted to defi le regle, she wanted to challenge every rule because, in spite of how objective rules tried to make life, she knew they were arbitrary as well. She wanted to be the ghost that haunted the regular, reminding it always that it was a lie. She wanted that to be her eternal life, as the phantom that haunted society for its inadequacies, even after death, and that would be how she would stay immortal, that would be the undying memory of her, as a kind of pestilence that never ceased noodging the standard order. And she knew the best way to do this was through writing. That was the most important lesson she had learned from history, from determinism. So she did it. She sat at the typewriter and wrote as fast as she could, doing something people never did anymore, something that was eternal but which stupidity and too much so called progress that abetted this stupidity had regrettably made archaic. But Cara knew it was eternal, and her task was to help make sure this eternal thing didn't die, though the task was trying to kill eternal things, the eternal folly of man. She wrote and she wrote, then she heard an odd voice.

"Tell me who's that writing: John the Revelator."

She looked around frantically. There was an old blues man sitting behind her, playing the Son House song. "Tell me who's that writing?!" he cried.

"Who the hell are you?"

"I'm Rhadamanthus," he said succinctly, and kept playing his guitar. "Do you know where you are?"

"I'm at home."

Rhadamanthus scoffed. "No you ain't," he said. "You've finally done it. You've finally wrote yourself into Hell. Tell me who's that writing! …These are the gates, the gates to hell…John the revelator!"

"I'm not a revelator," Cara said succinctly.

"Well, you're a writer, ain't you? You don't think they're the same thing? You don't think you're a lonesome prophet of doom hiding alone in a cave from the ones that wanna persecute you, drive you out? And I wonder Mrs. Revelator, do they wanna persecute you because you're a prophet of doom, or are you a prophet of doom because they wanna persecute you?"

"I guess both." Suddenly there was a frantic knock on the door and Cara sat bolt upright.

"That's right," Rhadamanthus said. "They're here for you. We're willing to hide you in hell. You have to go through hell, purgatory and then heaven, and we'll compensate you by hiding you there. It's what's called a 'treuga dei,' a divine truce, a treaty for your war against heaven and hell."

Cara froze but as she did she heard another knock on her door. The holy police were trying to destroy it with a battering ram.

"Tell me who's that writing…"

"Hush!" Cara admonished.

"Well, are you coming, or not? The way I see it, it's the only way you're gonna survive. I'm a blues man, Cara. I guess that means I'm a bit of a revelator, too, I guess that means I'm alone in a cave hiding from people trying to persecute me too, and I'm doing exactly what you're doing. I'm trying to punish them for this with words, with words and music, words and music that will at once hurt and nourish your soul. And you're trying to do the same thing. So come with me before they tear down your door and you don't get to finish the job. I am a harsh judge, people made me that way, but I can be kind to one of my own, a fellow revelator."

The battering ram slammed against the door one last time and it started caving in. "Deal," Cara cried. "It's hell here anyway," and she followed Rhadamanthus into the gates. Rhadamanthus cried with glees- "Tell me who's that writing? John the revelator. Tell me who's that writing? John the revelator, wrote the book of the seventh seal." .

Gershom Ben Yehuda sat down in his chair in the Knesset and sighed as he cupped his face in his hand, resting it on the desk. 'God, I just want it to be over,' he thought to himself. He had been Prime Minister of the great Eretz Israel for six months now, and he was already hating it, he was already feeling the tragic history and corruption of both Israel and Palestine sinking into his bones, the short sightedness of the Zionists. Israel had the strangest history. People like Hannah Arendt had helped the Zionists. Gershom wondered if she ever regretted it. Gershom was made Prime Minister after Netanyahu was indicted during the early emergency elections, when the society of Israel was crumbling, and he had tenuously tried to put it back together, shoddily, until it was an edifice still partially destroyed after its repair. Gershom wondered why he ever got into politics. He used to be a member of the Palmach, he was a revolutionary, not a politician. But he found both positions had moot results. When he was a young man in the Palmach he never imagined this, what Israel would become, nor did he imagine being Prime Minister would be so unrewarding as well, that he would have to try to undo so many almost insoluble mistakes, that he was at the head of the internecine, the internecine he had unknowingly caused as a member of the Palmach, which now as Prime Minister he would have to try to end. History has such long lasting butterfly effects, caused by macrocosmic accidents.

Gershom was distantly related to the great Eliezer Ben Yehuda, the man who had revived the Hebrew language after the war. Gershom wished he was more like his distant relative, that he had worked in language instead of politics. Language is not quite as blind, nor so irrevocable the effects of its blindness. Both Elie Wiesel and Albert Einstein had been offered the role as Prime Minister of Israel, and they had turned it down without even having to think about it. 'That's the problem with politics,' Gershom thought. 'Smart people don't want to partake in it. Smart people only have knowledge of it because they realize knowledge of it is a civic duty, but they would never want to be politicians, they are too smart for that, too idealistic, too pure. And geniuses, geniuses stay away from it like it's the plague. Perhaps it is the plague. God, I just hope Manuel Sanchez gets the vote in America, he may be the exception. I'm so tired of hearing about the two state solution. Sanchez wants something else for us.' There was a knock on the door.

"Come in!" Gershom cried flippantly.

His wife Hadassah peeked her head in, "The members of the Knesset are on their way." Gershom nodded his head silently.

"I think this is going to go well," Hadassah went on. "Kein ayin hara."

"I hope so. Did you hear what America wants? They want us to be at the seat of the Holy Government, because we are the holy land."

"Are you going to do it?"

"I don't know," Gershom said stoically. "The Holy Government…I think it's the same thing as the carceral archipelago. I think in Dystopia we always call things something else than what they really are. The Holy Government, it's built on lies, society itself…and I suppose society has always been built on a certain lie, the lie that man is civilized, but now it's based on more lies, the lie that the government is holy."

"So you're not going to do it?"

"I don't know," Gershom said again. "I may not have a choice. Manuel Sanchez is right, politics has had so little to do with choice recently. I can only hope his vision for that to change will come true, but everything is against it, the Holy Government is against it, and they run the world. The powers that be are against it…"

"They can be replaced by new powers," Hadassah said seriously.

Gershom sighed. "And then they will make the same monstrous mistakes, if not worse. Politics, it is so wrapped up in history, and therefore historical determinism. You idealists, I believe in you and I don't. I believe in the idealists, I believe in them as they are, but the world around them they wish to change, I am not sure if it's capable of that. And you know what the world does to idealists. It either corrupts them and if it can't corrupt them it martyrs them, it murders them, and that's the only way to be remembered kindly by history, to first be vilified, hunted, persecuted, and murdered by the masses. I don't know if I want to go out that way. I am not enough of an idealist...So I will be remembered by history as most politicians are. An inept, incompetent man who was given power blindly, and so had their hand in ruining the world."

"That's not true," Hadassah said. "You are better than that. Don't give in to the fatalism of history. Do as Manuel Sanchez says, use your free will."

"But what if my free will bends to the destructiveness of history?"

Hadassah shook her head. "That's not you," she said. "That's not your free will. I've seen your heart, Gershom, I've seen your weltschmerz, the way history disgusts you so much, the way it makes you so melancholy. That is your soul wanting to fight it. That is the part of you that *is* an idealist. I believe in you, Gershom. I believe you will do the right thing."

Gershom sighed and hugged his wife gently but for a long time, breathing in slowly the fragrance from her hair. "You always live up to your name," he whispered.

A man knocked on the door followed by a train of mostly men and a couple women who had to fight their way in tooth and nail. "The members of the Knesset are here, sir," the man at the front of the enfilade said.

"Good," Gershom said, trying to seem as calm and competent as he could, even though inside he was a mess of aporia, but if you let them see that...

Gershom sat at his seat at the head of the council of the Knesset while the others also took seats. Gershom cleared his throat. "Now," he said. "A man has requested an audience with us, his name is Yasser Al Haifa, the opposition leader of Palestine…"

"He's a terrorist," someone said immediately.

"That's not our thinking at this time," Gershom said slowly.

"An Israeli soldier was murdered at the border just last week."

"I don't believe Al Haifa had anything to do with that."

"What about the two state solution?"

Gershom barely concealed a groan. "I'm tired of hearing about that," he said. "I'm not sure it's a solution at all. Now, I have granted the man his audience. I was a member of the Palmach. I believe Al Haifa lives a similar life to the one I used to, opposition, but not terrorism…"

"Yes, but for the enemy."

"There is no enemy. They want the same thing we wanted when we came here after the war. They want their right to live in what might be their homeland too…If you look through the history of almost every single war, with the exception of perhaps World War II, bot sides have wanted the same thing- land, revanchism, and in noble cases, freedom. That's all the Palestinians want, the same thing we want, not to be oppressed by any powers or governments that perceive themselves as stronger than us…"

"You've gone soft, Yehuda," someone else said.

"Perhaps," Gershom said with a shrug. "But I have made my decision. I am letting this man have his audience. I believe he has every right. That does not necessarily mean I will grant him his wishes, I'm sure the world won't let me, but I will at least listen to him."

"Alright, alright," someone said. "Fair enough. But we'd like some terms and conditions," and the man pulled out a stack of thick papers and Gershom groaned aloud this time…Sometimes he missed the Palmach. Sometimes he missed being Yasser Al Haifa.

The nurse sat on her coffee break watching the news. It was almost six in the morning now. She would get to go home in a couple of hours, try to sleep before it started all again, before she had to touch the sick and the damned who were draining her compassion daily. People all have a limit on it. But she worked for KHC,

Kapporeth Health Corporation, the corporation that ran all the hospitals in Kapporeth and Kapporeth itself. All hospitals were a part of the Holy Government now. That meant every time you went into a hospital you had to hear some bullshit about how Jesus is going to save you. There were hospitals everywhere in Kapporeth. It was such a small, impoverished area that it was easy for people to get sick in, so it was easy to have several hospitals there. Hospital corporations made more money now than the president and the queen combined, and it all went to the Holy Government. There were never any laws about separation of state and medicine, nor separation of church and medicine, so now all three were combined inexorably. The Health Corporations were how the Holy Government made their money, behind the banner of healing and Jesus, a man who healed for free and thought the love of money was the root of all evil, whereas the Hospital Corporations made billions from healing people at exorbitant rates.

The Health Corporation was the Holy Government and the Holy Government was the carceral archipelago. It was all an elaborate prison. KHC was the only wealth in Kapporeth, and it was provided *by* the people, not for them. The nurse knew this but she tried each day to forget it- she tried each day to forget that her job, which was meant to help people, was plundering their pockets, that the ideal she had strived for as a youth was corrupted thoroughly by the powers that be, that life and death had become a business now, and one no longer saved a life for free. But the nurse knew she was not a part of this evil. The billions the KHC got every year out an impoverished city, she didn't even see one percent of it. She was just another part of this machine, like everyone else. She flipped through the channels dully. Again Manuel Sanchez was on television. As much as the interviewers and the Holy Government hated him, the people loved him, so they put him on TV. The nurse was sure they would do anything they could to crush him in the election though, because the people loved him. They didn't want someone the people loved in office. That would make their job harder, their job of keeping the carceral archipelago inn check and convincing people it was order, social harmony. And all the elections had been shame elections recently, the Electoral College now being used as a tool to keep the Holy Government in power. It was always a member of the Holy Police that won the election now. The elections were a scam. The nurse stared at Manuel Sanchez on the television.

"I believe it is immoral to tame someone," he was saying. "To tame the multitudes, that's evil."

"I don't understand you," the interviewer said back.

Sanchez shrugged. "I'm used to that."

"Hasn't the Holy Government maintained order this whole time?"

"There was a writer named Karl Kraus," Manuel Sanchez said slowly, as he always did. "He once wrote a statement that has shaped my entire political view, especially in the modern world. He said 'better chaos than order at the expense of humanity.'"

The interviewer gaped at him. "You're a radical," he spat.

Sanchez shrugged. "We're off topic," he said. "What were we talking about?"

"North Korea."

"Oh yes, our Treuga Dei with North Korea…"

The nurse turned off the television, and went outside to smoke a clandestine cigarette. All the other nurses frowned upon it. The Holy Government that controlled KHC had told them it was a sin. The nurse didn't care. There were much worse ways to be a hypocrite, and you have to be a little sick yourself to even want to heal. People who are sick in no way cannot even imagine illness. But the whole world was sick right now. Strangely it gave the nurse hope, hope that if it was so sick it would know how to heal itself, or be healed by some other sickness. Or maybe just one sick person like herself, some kind of diseased savior. But it would have to be its own savior, it's own illness, its own patient and its own doctor. In manners of a sickness of morality, a world sickness, a mal de seicle, what has to end the plague is that which began the plague, the people of the world that had contracted the disease by inventing it. The nurse shook her head. She didn't know how man, something she believed in her heart was good, otherwise she would never have tired to heal them, could come up with such evil. She didn't know if it was due to too much imagination or not enough.

She thought of something she had learned in college, in her logic class. That was the hardest class she had to take, because they talked about things the majority of people could not understand, even though they could often be very basic things about humanity. What she had learned from that class was that humanity didn't know itself, didn't understand itself, and that's why they committed so many atrocities, because they did not have enough imagination to have ever imagined themselves. And yet they did. Of course they imagined themselves, or how else would they exist? But they imagined themselves very unconsciously, almost flippantly, without realizing it and certainly without analyzing it. It was enough imagination to make one exist but not enough imagination to think of a reason why one existed. It didn't matter anyway. The latter, even if it had been imagined, would still be just that- imagination, a fantasy, a dream.

There was something she had learned in logic class, she was struggling to remember it now. It was something about how human beings made words. Oh yes, it was physei and thesei, physei meaning that words were created in conformity with nature, thesei meaning they were arbitrarily given by humanity alone. The nurse believed it was the latter simply because of hate words. Hate words, like hate itself, were arbitrarily given, and certainly not by nature, which feels no prejudice. That is the main difference between it and man. Those words were made by humanity alone, prejudice itself was made by humanity alone, without the influence of nature. It was thesei.

She finished her cigarette and went back into the hospital. She sprayed some perfume on herself quickly. Ever since the damn Holy Government, everyone had to feel guilty about everything. Everyone had to feel guilty except the Holy Government. And they were all forced to feel guilty about the most trifling peccadillos- war, and greater crimes against humanity were still generally accepted without conscience. So few people had a historical conscience, and so no conscience for the present either. It was all received with blindness.

She went back to work, for the Health Corporation, for the vampire that waits patiently in the dark to drain the blood of the ideal, making it as corrupt as anything else in a decaying machine-present society, the modern world.

Malin Genie

Cara awoke in Hell. Rhadamanthus was still with her, singing at smiling at her as he looked at her out of the corner of his eye.

"I lost faith in the lord!" he crooned. "So I started playing the blues./ Then I lost faith in the blues/ and when you lost faith in the blues/ ain't nothing to do but play the blues."

"Did you write that?" Cara asked.

"Yes," Rhadamanthus said coolly.

Cara looked around. It was mostly empty, she couldn't see anyone for miles. "I expected this place to be full," she said.

"Couldn't be Hell if it weren't lonely," Rhadamanthus said. "But keep going along, you'll find people. The one good thing about being lonely, the one good thing about Hell, is on the way you meet other lonely people, and they'll distract you for a moment, make you less lonely, until it's time for both of you to move on. That's the thing with lonely people, with the damned, you guys always gotta keep moving. You're not the staying type, even though you wanna be. Probably you guys feel that way, because you never met a staying type either. Staying types just aren't attracted to you guys."

Cara nodded. "I don't know if I was always a drifter or if I just became a drifter from so many people moving in and out of my life. I had to move with them. But I didn't get to move with anybody. All this time I had to move by myself."

Rhadamanthus nodded. "A lot of people like that in Hell," he said. "You won't be that lonely."

Cara sighed a long, forlorn sigh. "tell me, Rhadamanthus, if anyone knows you must know. Why? Why are we damned? The people here, me, why are we here? Did we really do something that wrong?"

"No," Rhadamanthus said. "Hell is arbitrarily given. It is *thesei*, of human invention, and human invention can be very cruel. I guess we're just trying to work in accordance with nature on that one. Nature is arbitrary, and I guess we want to be too. So we made a place like Hell, so we could be as free as chance, no rules, no guidelines, and no reasons."

"But human beings have always tried to fight that. They've objectivated everything…"

"All except cruelty. That's the one instance they don't mind being arbitrary, that's the one instance they don't mind being as blind as fate, because in that moment they feel like they are at last fate's author."

"There has to be other ways," Cara said in a pleading voice. "There must be other ways to feel arbitrary and free, like fate's author, without cruelty, without unusual punishment, without evil."

"Well, there's art, but most people don't have the stomach for that. You gotta be lonely for that."

Cara nodded. "Yes, I believe you do," she said. "Look, someone's coming!"

Rhadamanthus chuckled. "That's your guide," he said.

"What?"

"Well, you don't think you can really make it through hell, purgatory and heaven by yourself, do you?"

"I thought I had to do it by myself."

"In a way, but you'll still be needing a guide. I know your type. You get lost easily. And this whole metaphysical scheme of the afterlife…It's a labyrinth."

"Is it even real? Am I not imagining this whole thing?"

Rhadamanthus smiled at her a sickly, sardonic, impish grin. "You'll find out," he said.

"I'm an atheist," Cara said emphatically. "I don't believe in this shit." At last the figure in the distance came close to them. "It's you!" Cara cried.

The figure nodded. Cara turned to Rhadamanthus with a harried, alarmed look in her eye. "You knew about her?"

"She's existed as long as human beings have. And she helped, she helped create heaven and hell. You should feel lucky she is your alter ego. Most people don't participate in the making of heaven and hell, they just passively receive its outcome. And she is particularly unusual. The people who actually make heaven and hell, they usually do one or the other. She did both. She comes from both and she belongs in both. She is everywhere."

The Poet was now right in front of them. "Hello, Cara," she said.

Cara swallowed heavily. "Hello." She knew The Poet well, she had always been her alter ego. She looked exactly like Cara but she was so much taller, so much harder to reach, and for her whole life she had towered over Cara. It had intimidated her but it was always what she had aspired to be, The Poet, and Cara remembered with pleasure and pain all the times the two of them had at last fused together and created something as tall as The Poet, but Cara couldn't do it alone, she couldn't do it without The Poet, and even when they fused she was still so much taller than Cara, still Cara could not reach her, even when they were one. The Poet was a costume, a mask, something Cara had to put on when she couldn't face herself, and had to become something else, an entire entity. But it was strange. The Poet always showed Cara to herself anyway- when she couldn't face herself she only became more conspicuous and the only thing to do was try to be a poet, try to make this half martyr half monster that possessed so many personalities into at last a singular unit. The Poet looked down at Cara as she always did, as she looked down on the entire world.

"Welcome to hell," she said. "It's empty and full. It is just like any other void, and just as natural."

Cara swallowed hard and just nodded. The Poet would always intimidate her, even though she was her- she was the part of Cara that was intimidating, she was the part of Cara that Cara wasn't sure she could live up to, and she had already spent so much of her life trying, and she knew she would spend the rest of her life that way, too, then one day die, just hoping she had managed to do it, to measure up to The Poet.

Rhadamanthus looked at both of them and grinned again. "You know," Cara said. "For a blues guy you smile a lot."

"All blues guys do," he countered. "You two ladies go on. I have some business to attend to. Poet, guide her well."

"I always have," The Poet said proudly, "even counting all the times I led her astray."

Rhadamanthus laughed and just disappeared, as if he were never there. Cara wasn't surprised. She was sure this was all a hallucination anyway. The Poet grabbed her by the arm. "Come on," she said. "I'll show you around. I know this place well, and I guess you do, too, but you've never seen it with your own eyes, you've just carried it around inside you, like most people…"

"Isn't that the only place it exists?"

"In a sense. It's the place where it's born, at least, and when it gets to be too much, when it's too much inside you, then it starts to manifest outside of you, with your own deeds, your own actions. And with everyone on the Earth carrying it around inside of them, it's no wonder the human world is a mess. But fate has its hand in that. Take the holocaust…"

"I will never believe that was fated," Cara said sternly. "That was the result of human ignorance."

"And that's fate," The Poet said with a chuckle. "Don't you think it's strange? World War I had to happen for World War II to happen, and Germany had to lose World War I, and then the treaty of Versailles had to happen, and going back further, Franz Ferdinand had to be assassinated for World War I to happen. It is as Sanchez says, it is determined…"

"Then fate is evil. Can you really live with yourself, looking into the face of a holocaust survivor, and telling them it was fate? That it had to happen?"

"I didn't say it had to happen, it just did. That's fate, it is a long chain of accidents with accidents as the result. Fate has no reason. *That's* the reason that it happened. The reason was that there are no reasons, so atrocity is free, so anything can happen, so destiny can be as cruel as it pleases. People always think about the strange chain of events that happened to bring them to their lover, but they rarely think of the strange chain of events that has to happen for such a great atrocity, for a World War, for a horrible genocide of that magnitude to happen. It is the same chain of strange events. It does not always leave to love, to joy, sometimes it leads to death, to a tragedy partially of our making, in accordance with fate, that we cannot comprehend in spite of helping author it. I do not believe it happened for a reason either, but I do believe there was something much higher than human authority at work there when it happened, and yes, perhaps this thing is evil, or perhaps it is so indifferent to human beings it doesn't care, it finds us fungible. Listen, most people these days are optimists. *That's* why these things happen. People like to think optimism is good, but the truth is, by refusing to see evil in anything, one lets evil slip right through, and the optimistic attitude is the one that prevails in the occident. That's human ignorance, that's fate, the refusal to accept that evil exists, and the thinking that you reject, that everything happens for a reason. By trying to nullify tragedy they have only lent it more fury. You can't nullify tragedy simply by denying its existence. It takes a lot more effort than that, and that's what the optimist is trying to avoid. They would much rather adjust to evil and convince oneself it's happiness than to actually rid the world of it. It's lazy."

Cara twitched for a moment and lit a cigarette. "Well, I do agree with you there. And if the holocaust was fate's job then yes, I do find fate evil, and I do think fate must have no reasons either if that is the case."

"And capitalism these days," The Poet suddenly said apropos of nothing. "People get better health benefits if they have a better job. That means people are literally competing for life. Capitalism these days is social Darwinism. And the Health Corporation helps. Health care is capitalism and now and capitalism is a subtle form of eugenics, one where you do not leave behind the weak, but the person who makes less money. It's financial Darwinism, through the mode of the Health Corporation."

"Yes," Cara agreed again. "I don't understand it, though. The wealthy are only one percent of the country, surely they can't leave ninety nine percent of us to be left behind, to not survive, to die, particularly since it's our poverty that makes them rich. That's how capitalism works. And now that has seeped into health. It was bad enough when it got its hands on education, but medicine too?"

"That's the evil I speak of, the evil the optimist denies. I reject it too, as evil, but I cannot deny that it exists. My eye is not blind and turned away enough."

"Jesus this place is empty," Cara said stoically as she smoked her cigarette.

"There will be more people soon. That's what I'm leading you to initially, in this tour of hell. You are lucky you are a tourist."

"I feel guilty about that, about the fact that I get to leave."

"People like you and me," The Poet said, "we get to leave everywhere we go. We are tourists of the planet Earth."

"But we're not on Earth anymore."

The Poet smiled. "And Heaven and Hell. Look, there's people over there," and the poet pointed to a group of ten people sitting on several couches in front of the largest smartphone Cara had ever seen. It was the size of a monolith. The ten people were on their individual smart phones, too, staring at them numbly, their eyes beginning to hollow and drool falling from their lips. Cara could tell they hadn't eaten in a very long time. The monolith sized smartphone they were all gathered around was playing an advertisement.

"It's a rainy day outside," it roared. "It would be a good day to lie in bed and read a book, but who the hell reads books anymore?" the crowd chuckled without looking up from their phones. "The much more modern, socially acceptable thing to do is scroll through your phone looking at memes all day. We've made that easier for you!" A mild, limp hoot from the crowd that still did not look up from the phones, scrolling through pages of memes, being modern and socially acceptable- completely spiritually castrated, empty and all too happily nullified.

"Jesus," Cara said. "This is Hell."

"You wanted to go where the people were."

"Now I just want to be alone again. This is strange. This is certainly hell, and they're fucking enjoying it."

The Poet smiled sardonically. "Well, she said, "hell does like to pretend to be heaven."

"And they believe it," Cara said, disappointed in her generation, disappointed in mankind she had always tried to reach out to, had always searched for, only for them to disappoint her so thoroughly that she wanted to be alone again, even after all the trouble, the hardship, walking through hell, trying to find other human life. "Hell tells them it's heaven and they believe it just so they don't have to accept they are in hell…Optimism is easy to deceive and manipulate, yes, for it holds so tenaciously to the idea that hell is heaven."

Cara shook her head with disgust. "I want to get out of here," she said.

"Good," the poet said. "I wanted to show you, there are worse things than loneliness. Sometimes other people are worse than loneliness…"

"But I still feel sorry for them," Cara said. "I still want to help them, help them realize their heaven is actually hell, so they can get out of it."

"They won't listen to you. But you can try. It is time for us to do some writing," then the poet chuckled acerbically and smiled her at once bitter and idyllic smile. "Hell is the easiest place to write in."

Cara nodded. "Is there a typewriter anywhere here?"

"There's typewriters everywhere here, you just have to look for one, look for it like you looked for the people. Sadly, it will not disappoint you as much."

"Sadly, yes."

The Poet clasped a hand around Cara's shoulder and they moved on, away from the people, to just be alone and write again, an activity they were both tired of, it being the only thing they were born to do, and it demanding such loneliness, but it was less disappointing- loneliness was less disappointing than other people. At last they found a typewriter. There were several of them abandoned on the hills of hell. They had been replaced by that monolith sized smartphone, all internal reverie was. That's how it was. Everything had to bow down to the future or else be swept aside. Cara wouldn't though, she would not bow down to a future she found so dystopian, mindless and cold. So she would be forgotten instead. She would be alone in hell busying herself with a machine no one used anymore, still wedded to certain aspects of the past, when a philosophy text was not quite as rare as it is now, at a time when intellectualism was not as rare as it is now, at a time where at the very least people read a newspaper. But this time was gone, and Cara knew her desire for the past was a lie as well, that the past was just as rotten as now, but at least there were writers. That was her main problem with the modern world. Not enough people were inveighing it, so it ran too baleful and free, its scourge was kept untamed, no one was keeping it in check, so this hell that called itself heaven was all the more hellish, and with no one there to point out to others that it was actually hell, all the more people believed it was heaven, so they accepted it, so they did not try to change it. That was the terrifying thing about the modern world.

Cara sat at the typewriter. It burst into flames. Cara stood up and flew back.

"What is…?"

"Don't worry, it will stop soon," The Poet said coolly as she smoked a cigarette. Out of nowhere Rhadamanthus appeared just as casually as he had disappeared.

"I knew you two would go right for the typewriters. That's alright. I go right for the guitars."

"There are so many different ways to be creative in hell," Cara said absently. "But no one utilizes them. They're all too distracted by the giant phone." The fire on the typewriter at last went down.

"Go ahead," The Poet said, gesturing to it, and Cara sat down and began to write.

The Poet looked at Rhadamanthus and smiled. "Elle est un genie," she said.

Rhadamanthus hung his head and shook it doggedly from side to die. "Ne," he said. "Elle est un malin genie."

But Cara just ignored them and went on typing, creating a false world.

Confutatis Maledictis

The doctor sat in the break area. The news was on. Easter Sunday bombings in Sri Lanka. The doctor sighed. 'It wouldn't be a religious holiday without a massacre,' he thought bitterly. 'Christ must be somewhere weeping eternally. We took his message of love and we spit on it, after crucifying it of course. He is risen, and so many more dead in false remembrance of Him.' The doctor numbly poured more creamer in his coffee. The news went on, as it always did. A woman was talking about xenophobia. The doctor turned the television off. He had studied Latin and Greek, he had to. He knew the root of the word xenophobia. It came from xenos, which means stranger but it also means guest or host. It was the derivative of another Greek word, xenia, which was the code of hospitality. The doctor remembered a little of the Greek mythology he had learned. There was a man named Ixion. He had broken the code of Xenia so the Gods had forever put him on a spinning wheel of torture. The doctor supposed that xenia just meant it was one's duty to be hospitable to strangers. 'God,' the doctor thought. 'If the Greek Gods were still around, we would all be spinning on wheels. Our society does not teach you to be hospitable to strangers, it teaches you to be afraid of them. We have all broken xenia, and we will all go like Ixion for it someday.' He scoffed to himself. 'I don't even believe in one God, let alone many, so what am I saying? We'll get away with it like we get away with everything, because there are no Gods, so no one holds us responsible for our evil. And I think evil is the result of ignorance, and ignorance is the result of fear. Evil, if you really boil it down, is just being cold to strangers, it is just breaking the code of xenia. But since no one is there to put us on the wheel for it, the wheel keeps on turning, the wheel of history fueled on prejudice. So I suppose we did get punished. But not by the Gods. We invent our own sins and we invent our own penalties for them. We damn ourselves, though unknowingly. We commit the crime and then we unconsciously give the sentence. We punish ourselves by keeping the wheel in motion. We have invented the fate that rolls over us and leaves us either privileged or victimized.'

Cara finally took a break. She had been at the typewriter for hours because there was nothing else to do in hell. Nothing else than staring at a smartphone, and Cara had always found that abhorrent. It was a tool of culture industry and the carceral archipelago, it was a tool to at once control you and to know where you are, who you are, what you are doing. It was another security camera staring back at you. Cara didn't know why people liked it. She stopped writing and then The Poet finally removed herself from her body. Cara was relieved. Though she loved it when she and The Poet melded, it was difficult being so tall, especially when she was used to being more humble in height.

"What shall we do now?" Cara asked.

"I need to show you more of hell. We've just reached the surface."

"Why do I have to see it?" Cara asked. "Why am I obligated to see hell? So many other people don't have to."

"Because you're a poet. And besides, most people have to see it, actually only a few are spared it."

Cara hung her head. "Is it because I'm a poet or because I'm insane?"

"Both." The Poet put a hand on Cara's shoulder. "Don't take it personally. So you're insane, what does it matter? Anyone who's never lost their mind completely, it's because they aren't paying that close attention to the world they live in. I don't blame them, that's a survival mechanism, and that's all being crazy is, not having that survival mechanism. A reasonable person is just someone who when they have a thought that makes them depressed or uncomfortable, they put a kibosh on it, they no longer think about it, whereas an insane person cannot stop thinking about it. An insane person has to delve deeper into the things that bother them, the things that make it hard for everybody to live, not just crazy people, but everyone. An insane person just has to learn to manage to live knowing these things well, not being able to block them out, not having the survival mechanism of not looking too closely at certain things. That's the only difference."

Cara nodded and didn't say anything.

"We're going to run into more people," The Poet went on.

"I can handle it," Cara said. "It's not really them that disappoint me, it's not them that I hate- it's the giant smartphone I hate. I do not hate the puppets, I hate the puppet master."

"And who is the puppet master?" The Poet asked quizzically with a raised eyebrow. Cara did not respond. The Poet chuckled and went on. "That's the horror of a Godless universe," she said. "There is nothing at all for us to blame."

"Who wrote that?" Cara asked.

"We did."

"Oh yea," Cara said distantly.

"Over this hill here, there will be more people. What you see will probably disgust you, everything you see here will probably disgust you, but there's plenty typewriters along the way you can stop at and get the disgust out…"

"It doesn't matter how much I write," Cara said defiantly. "The disgust is still there."

"So you will have to write for your whole life. So what? What else would you do?"

"I suppose," Cara said succinctly. They got over the hill. There was a giant sculpture of Cicero having his tongue removed and what seemed like hundreds of people at the foot of it, all in line for something. Cara looked more closely. She watched the man at the front of the line. Another man was cutting his tongue out.

Cara screamed and The Poet went on smoking.

"It's the confutatis maledictis," she said. "The confounding, or the silencing, of the wicked. Come, let's get closer."

"This is evil," Cara said sternly. "Confounding the wicked is wicked."

The Poet grabbed Cara's shaking arm and led her down to the scene. They stood at the foot of the statue of Cicero getting his tongue cut out, and looked at the man who was cutting everyone else's tongue out.

"What do you want?" the executioner said stiffly. "Don't cut in line, wait your turn."

"I'm just a visitor," Cara said nervously.

The man scoffed. "That's what they all think, at first."

"Why are you doing this," Cara cried defiantly. "Why are you cutting their tongues out?"

"Because they are maledictis. That means the things they said when on Earth were abusive, spiteful or deceitful. Here in hell, a silver tongue gets removed. You know the scripture, 'it is not what goes in a man's mouth that defiles him.'"

"Well then they are already defiled," Cara said. "Why defile them further? You have a statue of Cicero. Cicero didn't deserve to get his tongue removed, it was not silver it was just pure. Maybe these people don't deserve it either."

"Trust me 'visitor,' they are maledictis, they have been defiled, and yes, I am defiling them further. But it's orders. Hell is silence, little girl, so big talkers have to have their tongues removed or else they will ruin the place with palaver. We have strict rules here and that's one of them…"

"No speaking?"

"No speaking in an inveigling, sycophantic, persuasive or abusive way, yes. Many people are in hell because they get fooled, fooled by these people you see before you, so I cut their tongues out. I rid this place of their wicked language that defiled Earth when they inhabited it."

"I dislike people who speak like that as well, but where I come from there's a little thing called freedom of speech…"

"Where you come from!" the man screamed, and cut out another tongue. "Your imbecilic planet Earth. What kind of naïve fool are you?" he asked and turned towards her with fiery, passionate and embroiled eyes. "When you came here, you really thought your rules applied? You're in hell, little girl. There is no justice in hell."

"But wasn't it created for divine justice?"

"No," the man said emphatically while his next victim screamed as he removed their tongue. "It was created for punishment. That's what you little thinkers on Earth think, that the two are the same, but they're not."

"I know..."

"No, you don't know. Wanna know why there's no justice in hell? Because man was made in God's image and hell was made in man's image. It's based off your Earth. Hell, it's a thing that's always in the back of the human mind, and it takes more control than most humans are capable of to keep it there, to not leak it out into the world around you. In your world you think justice is punitive, so in Hell justice is punitive as well. In hell justice is not about rewarding the good but punishing the evil so harshly, that in turn our punishment is evil as well, our justice is evil. And we learned that from human beings. This is what people on Earth want, to see everyone who's ever hurt them tortured eternally. But not themselves, of course, though they've hurt people, too. The human vision is narrow. It still believes in an eye for and eye, a tongue for a tongue, it still believes that is justice."

"But what about the harrowing of Hell?" Cara asked. "Didn't Christ shut this place down?"

"Indeed he did," the man said. "But humans demanded it be reopened. They like the idea of people being sent here. Then they get sent here for that. They get sent here for confusing justice with cruelty."

"Well if you're so against it, why are you participating in it?"

"I could ask you the same question. If you're so against hell, why are you visiting it? If you're so against hell, why are you in it?"

"Because I haven't figured out how to create a heaven yet..."

"Just like all the other human beings. You are participating in this narrow vision I spoke of, a vision that can only see damnation, not salvation. Even when you guys invented Christ, you could only be saved if *he* was damned. On the rare instances you can conceive of heaven it always needs a sacrifice."

"Well, doesn't it?"

"If the sacrifice is the brutal torture and murder of an innocent human being, I'd say heaven isn't worth it. I'd say that is a false heaven, built on humans' barbaric notion of so called justice."

"It's interesting to hear morality preached by a man who cuts out tongues for a living."

"I'm just doing my job, the job human beings built for me. If I could have chosen I would have done anything else. If I could have chosen I wouldn't be in hell, just like you, but we are here and we don't want to die, we want to survive at all costs like everyone else, no matter how awful hell is, so we participate, so we play a game even though we despise its rules. We play by the rules so we can still live. We all participate in hell. That's why it exists."

Cara hung her head. "I suppose you're right," she said. "But I don't do this. I don't cut people's tongues out."

"No, you just tongue lash people with your writing. You are an admonisher too,"

"Yes, but…"

"I know. You're a peaceful admonisher, so you're better than me. But I can feel your scorn, too, your self righteous scorn, which you think is justice too because of your twisted human head, like all twisted human heads, which have lead humanity to believe scorn is morality."

The Poet walked up to them, smoking yet another cigarette. "Enough of this," she said.

The man who cut out the tongues suddenly got a sickly smile on his face and turned to Cara. "You're a cynic, aren't you?" he said.

"At times."

"Do you know what they used to do to cynics?"

"Yes," Cara said. "They cut their eyes out."

"I might have to do that to you."

"What? You're the one that's been cynical. Besides, no one even knows what cynicism is. People mistake cynicism for wisdom and wisdom for cynicism."

He smiled his sickly smile more, wider, exposing putrefied and vellum colored teeth. "That's very cynical of you," he said.

"Or perhaps she's right and it's wise," The Poet interjected.

"Who the hell are you?" the man asked then looked at her for a moment and stopped. "Oh yes," he went on. "I know you, you've been here many times but you never stay. You're The Poet."

"Yes."

"You're a cynic, too."

"I'm wise," The Poet returned curtly. "I should be. I am ancient. I am old as humanity itself…"

"And humanity still isn't wise, so why should you be? And besides, every time you fall in love you are a drunken ass. You can feel only intensely. When you're high you can only be much too high and when you're low you can only be much too low. You think that is wisdom?"

"Perhaps it is."

"No. Wisdom is somewhere in the middle. Wisdom is the grey area humanity can never get to, because grey is not a striking enough color for them. It must be either black or white or red, the color of war and the color of peace, because peace is never attained, and when it is, it is at a sacrifice, it is paid for the blood of martyrs."

"That's very cynical of you."

"No, it's wise."

The Poet sighed. "If you have to take anyone's eyes out," she said, "take mine. I've been around much longer than she has been and garnered a much larger confusion of cynicism and wisdom. Besides, I think what made me a cynic was that I've seen too much. It might be nice to see nothing at all. Then I'll become like everyone else- I will only be able to see phantoms, I will only be able to see what isn't there, not what is. I'll be able to see God that way. I'll be able to be an optimist."

"Fine," the man said. "We will spare this child. And you're right, she is a little naïve, standing up for the maledictis…"

"Well," The Poet said. "They have no one else to stand up for them."

"She scorns them when they're alive, but suddenly when they're in hell she thinks of them as victims."

"Everyone in hell is a victim," Cara said sternly, but the man put up a wary, defensive hand.

"I don't want to hear it," he said. "I don't want to hear your supposed moral purity. There is no place for that here. I have to take The Poet's eyes. I will be glad to. After all these times, hell has never made a mark on her."

"Actually, hell has marred me much more than a mere blinding. All this time it has given me an excess of vision, and that's madness."

The man turned to her and prepared his knife. "No!" Cara yelled. "Please don't! She 's done nothing wrong!"

The man sneered his ugly, unctuous sneer with the putrefied teeth behind it and held up the knife dangerously. "She has done something wrong," he said. "Poet," he went on, "I'm taking your eyes out, for you have committed a crime against the world's morale. You have committed the crime of seeing evil."

"Even if it really is there?" The Poet asked.

"Even if it really is there," the man said, and then he lunged towards her with the knife and began gouging her eyes out. The Poet did not scream, she just stood there and passively let herself become blinded. She had said she wanted to be like everybody else. Cara threw herself on the man's back but he shoved her off with his shoulder blade. It was already done anyway. The Poet was blind.

The man put himself back facing the line of the maledictis and looked at both of them, The Poet with two large hollows in her face with blood raining down from them, and Cara who was shaking and had blanched to the color of a great white void. The man gestured toward them. "Get out of here," he said.

Gershom sat once again in the midst of the Knesset. 'I feel this is all I do,' he thought to himself.

"Why can't we be the seat of the Holy Government. After all, we are the holy land!"

"The problem is," Gershom said. "No one really knows whose holy land it is."

"Well of course it's ours," the man cried. "It's our ancestral homeland, it's…"

Gershom waved him off with a lazy hand. "I'm still thinking about it," he said. "I don't know yet. I feel like maybe the separation of church and state was a good idea, and maybe that's the whole problem with Yisroel, that it's become more holy than a land, more holy than a government, because religion is at the seat of all our politics…"

Another man cleared his throat and talked. "What are we going to do about hamatzav?"

"I told you. I'm speaking to Al Haifa next week."

"How's that going to help? The two state solution…"

"I know, I know," Gershom almost groaned. "We're working on it."

"Netanyahu, just before he got indicted, named a street here after Donald Trump, just before he got impeached and the holy government took over. But their work together was never finished, and that street has been one of the most violent on the Israel Palestinian border. Just last week Palestinian protesters died…"

"Israeli police killed them," Gershom said wearily. "I know."

"And then Israeli soldiers were murdered there by Palestinians. The bombings in Sri Lanka, what if we're next? These people are terrorists. How can we fight brutality without brutality?"

Gershom was about to riposte when there was a large commotion in the hallway. His secretary came crashing through the door. "Prime minister," she called. "The war on war people," she cried. "They're ere and they're destroying the building."

"Great," Gershom said gloomily. "More terrorists."

The group that called themselves "The War on War," was a small terrorist group that never was called a terrorist group because thy were domestic, and not ethnic. They sprung from the youth groups that called themselves "The Alt Socialists," and "Antifa." They thought they were revolutionaries, but really they were just the fascists of the left. They fought war by pipe bombings, burning down buildings, and many other war like acts. It was sad to Gershom. The alt socialists were always insane, but Antifa had initially good intentions, and then together they had turned into this. That always happened with revolutionaries.

"What should I do?" Gershom asked.

"Get them out of here, they're destroying the building."

Gershom got up wearily and walked into the hall. The War on War people were waging war, as they always did. They were rifling through his desk and destroying everything in it. Gershom saw one young kid with a pipe bomb he was about to throw into the wall.

"Stop!" Gershom screamed at him, but it was too late. The kid threw the pipe bomb and there was a loud salvo right before an incredible ringing in the ears that only lasted a few moments but which Gershom thought would go on forever. 'It's only the traumatizing memories that last like this,' he thought. 'The ones you do want to stay forever, they leave as quickly as they have begun...when I met Hadassah..."

Then suddenly Gershom reared back. "Hadassah!" he cried. "Where is my wife?"

Then in the midst of the confusion another kid found him and grabbed him by the collar and pinned him against the wall.

"Stop war," he said. "Or I'll slit your throat."

"That's a very bellicose act," Gershom said matter of factly, rage boiling inside him. "I swear if you hurt my wife..."

The kid got a knife out of his pocket and pressed it against Gershom's throat. "End this war..."

"I have nothing to do with the war."

"Of course you do, you're a politician..."

"You need to talk to an oil magnate. I'm simply trying to keep my country from falling apart..."

"It deserves to fall apart."

"No it doesn't," Gershom said. "*We* deserve to fall apart, and we have. My country, though, it deserves much more than I've ever been able to offer it."

"Then resign!" The boy yelled.

"I wish I could." Gershom slumped against the wall as another pipe bomb was thrown. He remembered vaguely something he had read, something in Hugo. He had said sin always happens in darkness, so one should not blame the sinner but the one who created the darkness. But who created the darkness? God? He probably did not exist. We created the darkness, we created the darkness we cannot help but to sin in. We were the only thing to blame, because we were the only sentient thing in the universe. And we were in this darkness we created, unable to do anything else but sin. So who was to blame? The sinner or the one who created the darkness? They were both the same, but they were so different. It was the few who created this darkness, the ones in power, people of Gershom's title, and the rest were the sinners. The rest were lost hopelessly in the dark that people like Gershom had half knowingly and half unwittingly created. But still Gershom felt it was a collective guilt. We had damned ourselves, we had placed ourselves in darkness, so we could sin. And Gershom didn't know who was responsible for this darkness, he did not know what to blame. He wanted to blame the darkness itself, but it did see m like something human had invented it. But it wasn't the humble sinner. But it was the humble sinner. It was all of us. Everyone had helped create this darkness so we could spend life groping blindly in confusion. But none of us had wanted it. None of us had wanted the darkness, either, but we could not help but to create it. So we were guilty for creating this immense confusion but innocent for being confused within its confines. We were not to blame for being sinners, we were to blame for creating a world where sin was the easiest way out of it.

The ringing in Gershom's ears finally stopped. He looked around. It seemed many were injured, but none dead. Gershom was relieved. It could have been worse. But he did not know who he was and who the War on War people were. He felt for a moment the War on War members were the blameless sinners and he was the one that created the darkness, and they knew this, and that was why they hated him, that was why they were doing this. People like Gershom had turned them into something they weren't, villains, terrorists. Gershom knew now he would never make a good politician because he was too capable of feeling guilt. The War on War members at last got tired of their own recklessness, their own sin, their own adrenaline rush, a pseudo light in the darkness, but it was so much more difficult to find a real one.

"You've heard our demands," the leader said to Gershom.

Gershom nodded humbly, docilely. "Yes," he replied weakly.

And then The War on War members simply absconded. The other members of the Knesset were behind a portiere all shaking with fear. At last they came out. Gershom smiled wanly at them. "As if we don't have enough problems," he said.

"You did nothing!" a member of the Knesset cried.

"There was nothing to do. These people are literally kids, they have not learned yet you cannot wage war on war, you have to wage peace on war, but this is much more difficult, and something dear usually has to be sacrificed for it…A sacrifice that could start another war." Gershom slumped against the wall. "I am very tired," he said. "Where is my wife?"

"She's with security. They protected her."

"Oh good," Gershom said absently. "Someone get me some wine," he said. "I need it for my impossible, messianic task that is so hard to fulfill because I am not a messiah. I will need it to turn blood into water."

CHAPTER 4

Merces

Cara and The Poet walked warily through Hell. Their arms were interlinked, now that The Poet was blind, and yet still it was The Poet that was guiding Cara. As if reading her mind, The Poet smiled and turned to Cara. "Let the blind lead those who can see but can't comprehend," she said.

"Comprehend what?" Cara asked doggedly.

"Hell."

Cara shrugged and lit another cigarette. "I don't think anyone can comprehend Hell," she said. "Especially the people inhabiting it. Us, watching at a distance as we always do, that's the only reason we have such a vague idea, that's the only reason we're poets, and have a *mens divinior*, by not taking part of the human."

The Poet chuckled. "You're getting better everyday," she said. "And I suppose you're right. I suppose human beings can't imagine many of the things they've imagined, cannot comprehend many of the things they've invented. They cannot comprehend god or the devil, war, hell, many things that are implicit to their nature. So it is our job to come up with such a vague idea, as you put it, to try to explain it to them. The job of the poet is to explain people to themselves."

"They don't want to know," Cara said miserably.

"The majority of them don't, yes, but there are a few. There are a few people like you and me who will work hard for their vague idea. You see, people are beset by the things they have invented, they have become addictions, dependencies. That is because of the hollow feeling they feel inside of them when they don't know themselves. You have struggled with addiction before, yes?"

"Yes."

"And why do you think it was?"

Cara shrugged and drew on her cigarette languidly.

"It is because," The Poet continued, "at that moment in your life you could not confront your existential angst, your hidden and almost unbeknownst, even to yourself, grief at being born human, in other words, at being born alone. That's all addiction is. It's an escape from the void you have a faint feeling for, and a steadily stronger realization is there. Many people will do anything to escape that. Even you, a writer, someone whose job it is to know that, even you picked up a bottle and tried to forget it. Drugs, alcohol, they're just synthetic forgetfulness, for when you cannot erase bad memories on your own. And the bad memory, I think, essentially, is partially knowing the void you came from."

"And that's why I'm smoking a cigarette right now?" Cara asked sardonically.

"Well, what would you do if you were not smoking a cigarette? You would be doing nothing, which would make you uncomfortable because doing nothing brings you closer to nothing. And so you smoke instead. The action of drawing the cigarette to your mouth, inhaling the smoke and then exhaling it, is a mind numbing task that keeps your mind off what you would feel if you were doing nothing in its place. Our American society is particularly bad about it. We Americans, I think we are afraid of nothingness more than anyone in the world, because we are constantly surrounded by it. Everything in our culture is nothing, but we must pretend it's not to survive. So we over indulge in it. So we work all day everyday, even when we get home, we do something all day to forget we're doing nothing all day, that our culture is an abyss. And society supports it. It uses our noogenic neuroses, our anxiety, to keep us so hard at work, to make us slaves. And all we get for it is our occasional smoke breaks."

Cara laughed and stomped on her cigarette. "I suppose I'm smoking so much because I'm in hell."

"Exactly, and one has to forget they're in hell to survive in hell. We can't all just kill ourselves. I've noticed that it's in the worst of times that the life instinct is the strongest. The problem is that during those times *society's* death instinct is just as strong. Truthfully, society knows it's a prison, because it is even a prison to itself. Its barbarism always has to be clandestine. So it is suicidal, and it tries to drag the people down with it. But like I said, when the terror of death is actually upon you, your mind cannot help but to fight it, the life instinct rings louder than ever, particularly in times when suicide would almost seem rational. We want to live the most when we know we are going to die. That's why you want to survive hell, that's why you don't simply kill yourself here, and not just here, back home, too, in the midst of this invasive dystopia, the carceral archipelago- all your worst fears have come true. You wish to die more than ever and that is why you will fight to live more than ever. So you will elect to forget, forget that you're in a dystopia, forget that you're in hell, so you can survive it..."

"But that's how they get away with it!" Cara cried.

"Exactly," The Poet said. "They use your strength to survive such a terror to propagate the terror."

"Then I should just kill myself?"

"No. You should remain surviving at all costs, but without the forgetting. Always remember what you are surviving and maybe one day you can end it, and live free. Maybe we can all live free. Maybe you, Cara, can end hell."

"I would like to," Cara said with a trembling voice. "But I doubt I have that strength."

"You do, you just haven't been recognized for it yet. Keep writing, keep inveighing what needs to be inveighed, and you will get there. The only reason it's so hard to be a writer, particularly a good one, is that non creative people have always decided the fate of creative people."

"I've always hated that," Cara admitted.

"Now, the next thing I have to show you will probably disturb you, too."

"I'm used to it," Cara said. "Many traumatizing things have happened to me that I have to carry around with for the rest of my life, only to go trudging wearily into the future with all that weight, so the future can only add more pounds to my burden, but you're right, I don't want to die. And that's why I have to live the way I do 'one day at a time,' as they say, because the past still haunts me and the future is a ghost as well, just a ghost I haven't seen yet, so I live in the nonce, without retention or protention, without memory and without anticipation, simply in the seconds as they melt away instantaneously, in a present like any present that does not really exist, so I do not really exist, since it is the only time I can live in, and it is more fleetingly than love, which is the bulk of my collection of bad memories, loving things that cannot possibly love me, loving things that are either dead or rotting, so I cannot think about it. The past is the only time that truly exists. The present and the future are just passing phantasms, protention is actually impossible, in spite philosophy's efforts at it, in spite of philosophy's impossible efforts to undo the chaos of time simply with the mind. All that exists is the past, and I cannot think about the past. I cannot think about the past if I ever expect to finally get to the passing phantasm of the future. I have to at once shoulder my burden and pretend it doesn't exist, thought it is the past, and therefore, the only thing that exists."

Cara said these last words mournfully, with a sorrow that made The Poet's soul quake against it, especially now that she was blind, and could feel unseen things more than what most people could. That man had damned her. Her lack of vision had only made her inner vision more acute, and how can someone live like that, with inner vision but no outer visions, with only introspection and introversion, never extroversion, attached to nothing but what was inside of her, nothing outside, no real world, only an inner one? She sighed.

"I can't wait to get out of here," she said.

"Same," Cara agreed, and lit another cigarette, for she was one that didn't mind anymore when addiction won, especially here.

"Every time I'm here," The Poet said eerily, "I am only here for a few moments but it feels like an eternity every time, and it is so easy to remember when I at last do escape it, much easier to remember than my memories of heaven, happiness never being potent enough for my mind to retain. I need to sit down."

Cara gently placed The Poet down on the ground. "Give me a cigarette please," The Poet said. Cara did so.

The Poet felt the cigarette in her hand and smiled. "You and your cheap cigars," she said fondly. "I must apologize ahead for what I am about to show you…Come to think of it, I should apologize for many of the things I've shown you. I think I've shown you too much, but you must forgive me. I have no choice. I have to share with someone all the things I have seen, the idyllic bliss and the unnamable horror that haunts one for so long simply because one obsesses over trying to find a name for it, in a futile attempt to make sense of it."

"It's ok," Cara said. "I signed up for it. I wanted to be you."

"You are me."

Cara nodded. "And I strived for a long time to become you. It was difficult, and when I finally achieved it I was happy my only regret is that you are all I have, and only you will guide me through hell. There is no Beatrice waiting for me on the other side."

They walked around some more, until finally they found what The Poet had to show Cara, though even ow she was not sure why she had to show her these things, she did not like showing her these things. Cara was almost like her daughter, and she wanted her to be content and safe in the world, but she knew for them to be one, that would have to be a stark impossibility. And Cara was right, this was what she wanted. It is always a shame when we get what we want, but Cara had always wanted to be a writer more than anything, and she would take in any contingency that fell under that title, and one of them was knowing hell. The Poet stopped her in her walking. "We're here," she said glumly.

Cara could hear a distinct wailing amidst what looked like only the shadow of trees. "The suicide forest," The Poet added.

"I've been here before," Cara said, trying to sound self assured but there was a quivering in her voice. She hoped she would never have to come back here. This was the place she feared most. The Poet lead her through the shadows of the trees and there she saw several people tied to these umbra like trees, each with another large monolith sized smartphone in front of their faces. They were all wailing and begging for mercy. "What are they looking at?" Cara asked The Poet.

"They are doomed to watch all their family members commit suicide from missing them so dearly after they have died."

"Did they?"

"No. It's an illusion. But they don't know that."

"That is cruel and unusual," Cara said firmly. The Poet just shrugged, wordlessly saying to her 'what do you expect.'

The wailing continued after all of them were trying to break their chains so they could kill themselves again, to make it end. "What happens if you kill yourself in hell?" Cara asked.

"You go to hell," The Poet said tacitly.

"It's not fair," one of the suicides wailed. "They called me a narcissist. I am not a narcissist. A narcissist is someone who steals their own soul. I didn't do that. I just murdered mine because I couldn't get it to shut up. I would have done anything not to listen to it anymore, not to listen to it constantly begging for something that does not exist, but I never sold it or bartered it on anything…" tears were falling out of the mans eyes. "I'm not a narcissist," he repeated. "I killed myself because I couldn't listen to myself anymore. I killed myself to escape myself. I never indulged in it, and I do not gamble with hate. Hate can only make someone sick…"

"Love can make you sick, too," another suicide interrupted.

"Yes," the first suicide admitted. "That is what killed me. But love is a sickness that heals. Hate can only make one rot."

Cara moved up to the first suicide cautiously, and reached out a hand and touched his face. "I understand you," she said gently. "And I do not think you're a narcissist. I do not think you're selfish. I know what it's like, when you have no control over your mind anymore. When your mind becomes the master of you, and not the other way around, often the only thing it feels one can do is kill it."

"Thank you, my dear," he said. "All these years in hell, and even on Earth, that was all I ever wanted, the three simple words 'I understand you.' To some of us it is even more dear than I love you. When people don't understand you, they are filled with scorn for you, for they hate anything, particularly people, that they don't understand, and that's really what killed me, the loneliness mired in censure, the disapproval, but more than anything, the misunderstanding. That's one of the worst feelings in the world, being misunderstood. It always boils down to this- being misunderstood is simply the state of being an innocent, perhaps even a good thing vilified."

"I tried it too," Cara said with a quivering lip. "And for the very same reason…"

The suicide smiled at her. "You're lucky it didn't work," he said. "All these years in hell, having to watch the people I love die over and over again, my biggest regret throughout the whole thing is that it worked, that I was successful, that I got what I wanted."

"I'm sorry," Cara said.

The suicide shrugged. "No going back now," he said. "I am too thoroughly corrupted by death. Maybe I always was, and that's why the living could not stand me. When I think of it that way, I don't blame them."

"Well, don't hate yourself anymore. You're right, hate is a sickness that can only make one rot, even if it is only hate for yourself. Besides, the one thing I've learned from hell is this- the judges, the jailers and the executioners are much more wicked than the accused."

Cara and The Poet continued walking, arm in arm through hell, a woman with no eyes who was leading the woman, who, like her before she had been blinded, had too many eyes. The Poet always felt she was showing Cara things she already knew, but which she simply had not thought about yet, but they were already in the ken of her mind, but which she hadn't stumbled on yet in the clutter of her intellect, which knew nothing and everything, just like any mind, the only difference was the Cara had The Poet to force her to stumble on these things, to force her to know everything, to demand that all human suffering, if she could not experience it all, she could understand it all. That is what knowledge truly is. The Poet smiled up at Cara.

"You were kind to the suicide," she said. "I think it made him happy."

`   "Well, if there's one thing I can understand it's that," Cara said. "It is also my greatest fear. But I understand it. That's what's so frightening about it."

The Poet wrapped her arm through Cara's. Cara smiled at her even though she knew she couldn't see it. "Mercy is a strange word," she said, and one could tell from the tone of her voice how exhausted she was. Cara often forgot how old she was. She seemed to be both the heart of youth and old age, she seemed to be the thing that glued eternity together, making it so it wasn't formless. "I believe it comes from the Latin word *merces*," she continued, "which means to pay. I suppose that means Christ was right, and we do have to pay for each other's sins. I suppose it means punishment is not the way, but pay-ment, payment in mercy, which is taking responsibility for mankind, its faults as much as it triumphs. I have learned very much from you, Cara. You are right in what you say. Hell is immoral. Punishment, particularly extreme punishment, is immoral. I suppose the point in mercy, paying for each other, is that we neither punish goodness or wickedness too much. We just pay for it. Christ, through carrying the burden of pity for all mankind, was able to nullify hell. Maybe with you, Cara, if you keep being so merciful to the damned, maybe we can shut this place down again, and then we never have to come back here either. All we need is to pity the damned. All humanity needs is to pity the damned- to pity prisoners instead of scorning them, and this world yet can be saved, and hell will just be an old bad dream, something archaic, something that is not necessary anymore once we finally realize it never was."

CHAPTER 5

Le viuex ami

The Bum lay down in the grass. It was raining again. He thought about all the people bitching about the weather. They had no idea. They had no idea what it was like to always have to depend upon nature's mercy, nature which is too blind to ever be merciful except on accident. He hated the rain but it made the grass feel nice, even though it was staining the back of his only coat. At least winter was over. He knew the hell of the seasons so much better than the average person. He knew the agony of the Earth as it cannot escape its constant rotation and repetition more than he knew the agony of the cycles of humanity, because he had escaped them, and the price to pay for that was to be completely alienated from them. To not be a part of the repetition, the routine, it was not be part of the human race anymore, who had taught themselves that this repetition was dignity. Anyone with a different cycle was strange. And the poor bum, he had no cycle at all. That meant he did not even exist to other human beings. He was something that one simply ignored because he represented all the social problems of modern society, which people were supposed to forget- he was a stark reminder that America was not the land of opportunity, that in one of the richest countries in the world, many people starved to death. He was a walking emblem of the fact that everything is not perfect, that "the American dream" had died. It had died in him. It had died in him by proscribing him from his fellow human beings, it had died in him by first killing him.

But he still had the Earth. He did not have human beings, so he had the Earth, the cruel and arbitrary, unforgiving Earth. He knew it much better than its cruel, arbitrary and unforgiving people. The Earth was somewhat more forgiving to him. It would put him through rain and sleet and hell, but at least it would not eject him. The bum laughed to himself as he lay in the rain and the cold grass that was smearing green stains all over the back of his only coat. 'The meek shall inherit the Earth,' he thought to himself, 'and that's what I've done. I've inherited the Earth. But it's not like Jesus said. I can go anywhere on this planet, there's nothing stopping me, but to inherit the Earth means to have nothing else but the Earth- no house, no family, no woman waiting for you at the end of the day with a hot meal. These people do not have the Earth because they do not need it. They already have everything else. But I've got nothing, so I've got the Earth. Because I am meek. At least God gave me something. He gave me this wet grass to lie on. All the people that remain in society, some of them want to kill themselves just to get away. I don't want to kill myself. It is too important to me that I survive, because surviving is all I can do. They don't know, those suicidal people in society, they don't know wanting to die is a luxury. If you're actually dying…Well, nevermind. I just wish they knew. I just wish they knew they're lucky to have a few chains. Just the right amount of chains on you is happiness. And happiness always escaped me, so I had to have freedom, no chains and therefore no comfort.'

He rolled over sleepily in the grass. The people "out there," as he called it, the people still in society, they worked all day and at the end of it were tired, but they had no idea, they had no idea what it was like to actually be exhausted. The bum knew he could kill himself, he knew even that society wanted him to, but he was too indifferent to himself now. He rolled over in the grass and went to sleep.

Gershom cleared his throat and shuffled his feet nervously. He was meant to meet Yasser al Haifa today. The meeting was not supposed to be today, but the Knesset had pushed it earlier. They wanted Gershom to make a bargain with al Haifa. They would meet some of his demands if he would deal with the War on War children. Yasser al Haifa was escorted in by a few guards. Gershom wanted to tell them that was not necessary, that it certainly wouldn't help their case if they treated him like a criminal. But al Haifa's golden brown face which had a deep set stoic dignity in it betrayed no emotion at all. He had a keffiyeh hanging on his left arm and his clothes were simple but well kempt, and he had a head full of dark volute like curls that seemed to conform around his brain. Gershom bowed deeply to him.

"As Saalam alaikum," Gershom said humbly as he bowed to him.

"Shalom alacheim," al Haifa said and returned the bow, then handed the keffiyeh to Gershom.

Gershom cleared his throat again. Al Haifa was indeed a commanding presence, commanding in his taciturn seeming indifference, in his mostly silent intensity. Gershom looked into his eyes. They were not stoic like the rest of the face. They seemed to be burning. "I appreciate you seeing me on such short notice."

Al Haifa shrugged. "It's no matter," he said. "For me sooner is actually better. That's the trouble with me and my people, Ben Yehuda, why we get violent, is simply that we have been waiting too long, and perhaps you might understand. Have you ever waited an agonizingly long time for something that should always be there, for everyone, for something that is your right as a human being? When you have to wait so long for something that belongs to you and all people of the Earth, eventually something snaps, eventually the fact that it belongs to everyone but it has been denied you, and people expect you to just sit and wait for it to return, it makes you insane."

Gershom swallowed nervously. "I do have some idea of what that's like," he said. "I think everyone in this holy land does."

"Then why are my people treated so, by people who know what it's like?"

Gershom was shaking as he began to light a cigarette. Al Haifa put a strong, firm hand on his arm. "Don't be frightened of me, Ben Yehuda," he said. "I am not like so many other terrorist groups. I said I understand why my people are losing their minds, but I do not believe violence to be an effective motivator, because if the Israelites fear of me ever becomes justified, why then, you guys win."

Gershom relaxed a little bit but kept smoking his cigarette. "You're right," he said. "What can I do for you? What are your demands?"

Al Haifa grabbed a chair and started to relax as well. "You have another cigarette?" he asked.

Gershom nodded and gave him a cigarette. Al Haifa seemed to relax at this too as he put his back against the chair he was sitting on. "My demands are very simple," he said. "Israel limits Palestine's water supply. I want that to stop. I want protesters no longer to be murdered. I want a measure of irredentism for out lost lands. In the British Palestinian Mandate Israel was given half of Palestine, but now it's much more than that."

Gershom nodded. "Your demands, I feel, are reasonable, but the…"

"The Knesset," Al Haifa finished for him.

"Yes," Gershom said miserably. "They're still trailing after the ghost of Netanyahu. But I will try, I promise. But there's one more thing…"

"An ultimatum?" Al Haifa asked.

Gershom sighed. "Yes," he said. "I'm sorry."

Al Haifa shrugged. "It's alright," he said. "I was expecting one. I have many ideals I would happily die for, but my mind is still grounded in reality. I am always reaching towards a sky I cannot quite get to, because the Earth will not let go of my feet, because realism will not allow much room for my idealism, and I have to fight to remain somewhere in the middle of the two, to realize the truth but still want to change it, to know my limitations because I want to break them, and to realize when they can't be broken. I am always being stretched between the two, trying to stay in the middle but often being bent from one extreme to the other, one of my limitations being that I am unable to completely mediate the two, that I cannot get the two to come to terms with each other. I often cannot stop them from being radically opposed." He stopped for a moment and scoffed. "It is just like this severely divided nation," he said. "I often cannot find room for my desires in the midst of the truth."

Gershom hung his head. "So it is hard to be an idealist?" he asked.

"Yes," Al Haifa said emphatically.

"I've never been an idealist," Gershom went on, "because I wanted to be in politics and often idealism is not welcome there. But realism isn't either, there is room for nothing but base cynicism. I am stuck between the idealism and realism as well, with neither of them in my grasp. I have never been an idealist but I always wanted to be one. Now that I hear you speak though I think perhaps I have made the mistake that many spoiled people make, envying something that is actually quite painful."

Al Haifa nodded. "What is your ultimatum?" he asked, changing the subject.

"We…The members of the Knesset and I, were wondering if you could take care of The War on War people."

Al Haifa nodded solemnly. "Yes," he said. "I can deal with those imbecile Americans. They think they are on my side, but in reality, they don't have the remotest inkling what my side is like. And if the world were the way I would like it, I would have no side at all, because I wouldn't need a side. Myself would be enough. If the world were the way I would like it there would be no sides at all."

"Yes, that would be nice."

"I spoke with Manuel Sanchez last week," Al Haifa said.

"You're going all over the world."

Al Haifa shrugged. "Sometimes when the world is not your home it's easier to explore it. If it doesn't own you then you don't try to own it, and the Earth silently appreciates that, and lets you explore it, so long as you remain an outsider, so long as you are never naïve and reckless enough to think the world is yours, that it belongs to you and you belong to it. That's the trouble with people these days, they don't realize that. They don't realize the world is much more free than we will ever be, in spite of our constant attempts to enslave it, it is impossible. We are only enslaving ourselves when we do that. I wish people realized that, too, that in our foolish desire to assert superiority we have only made ourselves inferior, we have only insulted and wounded humanity, insulted and wounded ourselves."

"You're of quite a philosophical bent, aren't you?" Gershom asked with what, to Al Haifa's great surprise, sounded like fondness.

"I did want to be a philosopher," he said, "but unfortunately the world demanded me to be something else, a sort of revolutionary, a hope my people could rest on for a moment, as if I were a port in a storm, and I like it, I really do, but I am often afraid…what if I am a false hope? What if I am a lying prophet?"

"I worry about that everyday, too," Gershom admitted, and it was good to finally say it out loud. "It is no fun to be someone who has stake in the world. People know that, that's why most of them elect not to."

Al Haifa nodded. "I spoke with Manuel Sanchez," he said again. "He's trying to lift the Holy Government and the Health Corporation's ban on abortion. He is trying to emancipate the Mexican slaves in America. He used to be one of them, you know, so he knows better than anybody… He said he would help me, too. I have faith in him. He could change this world. I could change this world. *You* could change this world, Ben Yehuda, if you finally face the fears that come along with being an idealist- you yourself said you wanted to be one."

"Yes, but…"

"Do you trust me?" Al Haifa suddenly asked Gershom with candor that was unnerving.

"Yes, I…"

"Then do me a favor," Al Haifa said bluntly. "Don't make Israel the head of The Holy Government. You would be colluding with the thing that has enslaved us all."

"I don't know if I have a choice."

"I'm begging you," Al Haifa said with his unnerving candor. "If you do, the consequences will be dire, particularly to the Palestinians, to me. I am very glad to meet you, you and Sanchez, because I can tell neither of you want to disappoint me. It is so rare that I meet any politician that even remotely cares if they disappoint me and me people or not. But if you do make Israel the seat of the holy government, it will disappoint me, Ben Yehuda." He grabbed Gershom's arm again. "You know," he said, "you very well could be an idealist, I know you have it in you. I know there is a good man waiting within you. Join Sanchez and I. All you have to do is face your fears. In fact, that's what makes any person good, in the end, is abandoning the comforts of fear."

Cara was stopped at another typewriter. That was the only way to survive this place, and she was glad that God or nature or what the hell ever it was governing this semi cosmic scene was kind enough to at least have placed typewriters sporadically throughout hell. The only thing that made her sad is that she was the only one that was using them. Everyone else had abandoned them for the monolith sized smartphones, not realizing they were a tool of hell. Cara wrote and frowned a little, then finished and turned to The Poet.

"What next?" she asked.

"I'm going to show you something else you will relate to."

"I relate to all of it," Cara said stiffly. "All the suffering in Hell."

"Yes, that's like I said. You will be able to shut this place down, so long as you hold onto your pity. Your pity will guide you through."

"I'm not Christ," Cara said sadly…

"You don't have to be, to carry the burden. He was the prototype to show us how to carry the burden, but one does not have to be him to do it."

"Is that what happens to people who carry the burden? Torture, a horrible death?"

"Maybe, but maybe not. The times have changed…"

"No they haven't."

"Follow me."

"How do you know always where to go here, even now that you are blind?"

"Because I'm blind," The Poet said stonily. "So I have this landscape memorized in my heart. Because I've carried the burden. Now, this way."

So Cara followed the blind poet blindly, as she had her entire life, which had made her become lost in the strangest places, and yet even when she was irrevocably lost, she was never lost, because something inside her was leading her the whole time, leading her through hell, and though this meant she had to explore the whole thing, that there was not one single stretch of it ignorance would spare her from, this thing inside her would also show her the way out, just as it had shown her the way in. She followed The Poet, and they walked for what felt like miles in the empty landscape of hell. Then they came across a small procession, much smaller than the groups they had already met, and that seemed to be part of their struggle that they were such a small minority.

"Are we there yet?" The Poet asked.

"How should I know?' Cara said lissomly.

"Well, how should I know?" The Poet immediately riposted. "Do you see a small group of people, in a line, going nowhere?"

"Yes."

"Then we're here. This is something you particularly will understand," The Poet said. "These are the old souls finally grown old."

Cara looked at them. They were led by a man with a small flag in his hand who was the most aged person Cara had ever seen. He looked to be about three hundred. He looked like a ghost, with a bent back and shaking, dry hands full of veins and hair so white you could almost not see it. He stopped and looked at Cara, with searching, slowly becoming blind eyes. "Who are you?" he asked.

"Who are you?" Cara immediately returned.

"I am Tithonus," he said, "leader of the old souls finally turned old."

"I've read about you," Cara said. She looked in the short line and suddenly started. Rhadamanthus was among them.

"Rhadamanthus!" she cried. "I thought you were just a judge."

"The judges face judgment, too," he said. "I am an old soul finally grown old. That means I am an *abnormis sapiens,* an unusually wise man, because I have always been wise beyond my years- I was too wise for youth, and now I am too wise for old age. The only thing that's left for me to face is death. You understand somewhat. You are a young old soul, but you are not an old soul grown old yet, but you can imagine…"

"Yes, I can imagine. So few of you…"

"Yes," Rhadamanthus said. "So few of us when we were young, so we thought old age might be different, but it wasn't. Our minds have aged past our bodies, so we are ready to die. Having once been born we had already lived too long."

"What are you walking towards?"

"Same thing we've been walking towards our whole lives, death. That's what made us different. In youth you run from it, then in old age you walk to it, but we have always been walking towards it, now it is just finally close, but it's always felt closer to us than it has to everyone else, because we never ran from it, because we never tried to escape it. That's being an *abnormis sapiens*, something that has always been old. That's all eternity is, always being old, ask Tithonus."

Ttithonus grunted. "These bastards have it easy," he said bellicosely. "They get to die. They're not really eternal, they're only eternal when they're alive. I have to grow old throughout all eternity. And it is not slow. Each day I grow older and older, and each day the days become too large a number, and I know that number will only increase, and with it my age- age without the satisfaction of death. It is like always having a disease that never kills you, but also never goes away. Old men are afraid to die. They don't know how lucky they are to get surcease from the illness, the illness of old age, of being closer and closer to death…I am always an inch away from death and yet I never die."

"Quit your griping," Rhadamanthus said coolly. "You asked to be eternal. We never asked to be eternal, we just were, and that meant we were always old- that meant we were always ready to die because the soul in us aged so much faster than the body…"

"I would do anything to die," Tithonus cried. "I'd do anything not to be old anymore!"

"So would we," Rhadamanthus countered. "And we have always been old. You were young once."

"You were young once, too, you just couldn't feel it in your soul, you just couldn't appreciate it because of being an *abnormis sapiens*, you couldn't appreciate it because you were eternal. You wasted the youth of your eternity in your premature wisdom…"

"There is no youth in eternity."

"And I was young once," Tithonus said with an air of nostalgia for something irrevocably lost. "But it was so long ago I don't remember it. I only remember being old."

"Aye," Rhadamanthus said. "Same here. I can only remember being old in hell." He got out his guitar and strummed some beautiful, crystal clear chords that rang out all through the emptiness of hell, "To be alone is to grow old/ and lord I was born alone/ you know you made me that way,/ so I can't remember being young,/ cuz I can't remember being with someone."

Tithonus sighed and sat down. All his bones creaked as he did and he almost screamed. The rest of the old souls finally turned old sat down with him. "Eternal youth!" he cried. "It does not exist. There is only eternal age, because youth is vainglory, and for the higher minds that sit among me, vainglory was never an option, youth was never an option because it is folly. They were too old to engage in folly, so the only thing they got from youth was madness instead, the only thing they got from youth was the beginning of aging. Most people each day awaken and forget they are getting old, but these men and women here, they did not forget it, so they got to it faster, they got to it in youth. And to me youth is not even a memory. It is completely gone from my mind. All that's left for me, since I cannot die, is old age. Rhadamanthus, I suppose you cannot die, either. You have to judge us all."

Rhadamanthus cackled and put his guitar away. "Yes sir," he said. "But I am not as harsh a judge as people make me out to be, as nature sometimes has forced me to be. I am just an old man with a guitar, casting aspersions on a world I was never really from."

"But I don't understand," Cara said. "Why are you in Hell for this? What did you do wrong?"

"Not everyone in hell has done something wrong," Rhadamanthus said. "In fact, most of us haven't. Hell is just a place to suffer, and yes, we suffer for sins, but not necessarily our own. We suffer for sin itself. And, in a way, we *have* done something wrong."

"What?"

"We have wasted with wisdom the only part of our lives we could have lived without it."

CHAPTER 6

Recuillement

The drug dealer sat in his hotel room, gun under the bed and waited. What he was waiting for he didn't even know anymore. Just a few more bucks to pay off the child support, and hopefully enough for himself as well, so he also could buy what he sold. 'You never get high off your own supply,' the drug dealers motto since drugs existed, which was at the beginning of human history. We have always needed to be inebriated. At first, in primitive societies, it was for spiritual reasons, but now it is for the opposite, it is for secular reasons- it is built to forget for a moment there isn't a god, no spirits you can communicate with, no matter how open your mind is, that all there is is a technocratic society with its agents of one numbing themselves to it, all too readily available, all frowned upon by the government that invented most of them. The stigma the drug dealer faced every-day, it was ridiculous. Every time he saw a 'shoot your local heroin dealer,' sticker on some asshole's SUV he had to turn his head in shame, and gently squeeze his gun in his pocket. He was just trying to protect himself, protect himself from the evils of the world the easiest way that has always been known to man. He was just trying to escape guilt. He knew that while escaping evil he was helping propagate it, he knew he was selling it by the gram, but it was a personal choice. The people who bought it were consenting adults, he certainly did not force it upon them. They were all only hurting themselves, because they liked to be hurt after a lifetime of it, and it became easily confused with love after first abusive parents and then abusive girlfriends. The drug dealer didn't care what people thought.

He was simply trying to survive, and one must do anything to survive. And he didn't believe hurting yourself was evil, only hurting others. Hurting yourself is just free will.

He just wished they knew, all the people who looked down upon him, that this was all an accident. He never thought about it because if he did his mind could not even delineate how the accident happened- somewhere in high school, he guessed, when he was intelligent but too broken to try to achieve in the facile game the institution presented to him. It felt like there was no other alternative. But still this accident was a thread so labyrinthine he could never find its beginning. He could not tell the accident from the substance anymore. That was how he knew he was truly lost, that this accident had a hold on him, just as much as the substance, that it had never been a choice but an inevitability of fate, that it was preordained, that the god that had abandoned him to this dirty hotel room and this dirty life had written this for him, so everyday he would have to face the shame. Other people didn't have to live like this, so why did he? Because he was a cornered animal who had to constantly wonder, 'how am I going to eat today if I don't? ...And 'how am I going to shoot up today if I don't?'

He had been pacing the hotel room. It was a dirty motel off the side of the highway, so lots of drugs were trafficked there, he was not alone, but he knew it was dangerous. He was afraid to sleep now. People were watching him, someone was always watching him. Anyone and everyone except God, that had brought him to this awful fate with his bastard predestination and then left him there, giving him no clue of how to get out of it. It was free will- he had wanted to hurt himself to feel good, but it was not free will- something both within him and without him made him do it, that strange and inevitable summer of his nineteenth year. He paced around the hotel room, waiting for a customer. He was frightened and he was paranoid. He wanted some drugs even though it would only make it worse, but it would make it better. It would make it better and worse. He didn't care anymore, he was going to get high off his own damn supply, he just needed to get high.

He shot up on the motel bed and turned on the news. American spies had spotted an Iranian ship loaded with nukes. The drug dealer was glad he was on heroin because he didn't care. The world could end tomorrow, it didn't matter anymore. His world was ending everyday, every time he had to shoot up so he no longer had to look at himself. Of all the things he had faced in life, and there were many, the one thing he didn't want to face was himself. He didn't want to know himself. He was always of a philosophical bent and he had started using drugs so that would end. He did the drugs because then he didn't have to face anything anymore, after a lifetime of having to face the hardest things, now he had to face nothing. He could pretend life was in a cloud. All he had to face now was his drug addiction, and the drugs could help him escae that, too, even though it heightened the addiction. He knew the truth, he just wanted to forget it, that the more you run from things the faster they chase after you, the closer they get to you. So he would just run more, with the breath of all the things he was running from on his neck, but he couldn't feel it anymore on heroin. It was like he was running simply by staying still, doing nothing.

For once he could watch the news without being scared. For once it didn't matter. He cracked open a beer and smiled to himself. "History is the folly of man," he said out loud to no one. "But I don't care. I have my own folly that demands a lot of me, too much of me to care about the world. I have my own folly to maintain each day, just like everyone else. They think they're better than me, but really they're just the same. They escape, too, they're just lucky enough to have not as much to escape from as I do." Then A customer knocked on the door and he was happy.

Manuel Sanchez sat in the lobby of the oval office, waiting to talk to the president. He was numbly reading a newspaper. The British Parliament had once again prorogued the decision on their measures to leave the EU, which they had left years ago. Sanchez sighed and threw the newspaper down in disgust. 'I am a fool,' he thought to himself. 'Thinking I can change the world, the world that does not want to be changed…'

A secretary finally acknowledged him and told him only a few more minutes. Sanchez was trying to undo the law the Health Corporation and the Holy Government had passed a year ago outlawing abortion. He was also trying to emancipate the Mexican slaves, because he had been one of them, and knew how awful it was. He knew how awful it was to be useful to a country that didn't look at you as a human being, that didn't even want you in the country, but kept you so long as you were useful- so long as you were useful and would work under minimum wage. Then they would kick you out as soon as they could, as soon as you weren't useful anymore, or if someone could prove you were illegal. They separated Mexican children from their families, it was no different than the first system of American slavery. It was treating people like cattle, it was treating people like they didn't deserve their ties of natural affection, and then obliterating them completely. Prejudice always amounts to basically this- it is telling a group of people they don't deserve to be loved.

And it is of course based on no facts, no rationale at all, and that's what makes it prejudice. It is telling a group of people they don't deserve to be loved but having no reason to feel this way about them, and usually people who suffer from prejudice, it only makes them love more deeply, and in fact that is why people are so prejudiced against them, because they can love better. Hate hates love. It envies it because it cannot feel it. The psychopath knows something is wrong with them. They know they are missing something essential to make them human, but it does not make them sad, they cannot be melancholy, it makes them envious and angry, it makes them hate, it makes them hate love because it is not within them.

Sanchez had been among Mexican slaves all his life. Their ties of affection were all the more important to them because they knew they could be severed at any moment, severed by the corruption and indignity of the world. And that was what made it real love. To love in the midst of prejudice, to love even when one is told they are forbidden it, that's *actually* love. That's what makes prejudice moot, the fact that it has told people to not love, and only made them do it more. That's where prejudice has failed, its main end, and it can drag us displaced all among the Earth, it can make us slaves, it can put us in prisons, detention camps and concentration camps, it can wage war over the entire Earth and its very heart, love, but it cannot ever actually kill love, nor stop people from loving. In that way it will always lose. It can try to turn us into animals but animals love as well. It cannot destroy the thing it aims to destroy, the thing it envies so much, and which it should envy as well. The more you are hated the more you love, as a defense, a defense against prejudice, and it is the greatest defense- prejudice is like a tyrant that is trying to nip a possible conspirator in the bud, as all tyrants do, and their paranoia is what destroys them, their suspicion makes itself come true, and they are finally destroyed by the people they were so frightened of, so frightened of they tried to control them, so frightened of them they tried to put them in chains, finding out at last, towards the end, that when they had broken them they had only become more baleful. Manuel Sanchez thought of all of this and smiled. There was hope after all. There was something in man worth fighting for after all. He had always known that, and he remembered the times that he had forgotten it were the darkest times in his life, the times when he was most alone. So it was imperative not to forget. It was imperative that we all remembered it. It was the thing that could save us, and Sanchez knew in this moment that it was what he was fighting for.

The secretary came back and at last let him into the oval office. The president was there, a broken man like Gershom Ben Yehuda, destroyed by his office, overwhelmed by the world he had tried to control.

"Sanchez," he said angrily. "What do you want?"

"You know what I want," he said.

"I know, I know, an end to Mexican slavery and to make abortion legal again. It's already been done, Sanchez…"

"The supreme court completely flouted the law of Precedence when they did that. Roe v. Wade…"

"I know, I know Sanchez, but it was before I was president, and besides, it was the Holy Government and the Health Corporation's decision…"

"I wonder what's the difference between the two," Sanchez said stiffly. "And if we can't overrule their 'decisions' then they are what I say they are, a totalitarian regime."

The president sighed. "Listen, Sanchez," he said. "The supreme court has delivered a writ of mandamus to the appellate courts to see if they can overrule the ban. Things are in motion."

"But I'm afraid both, the supreme court and the appellate courts, are just words now, and any writ of mandamus is just a formality. You know the laws of our constitution have been replaced now, you know the supreme court is just a front for a democracy that doesn't exist anymore. The Holy Government doesn't give a damn about the constitution, because it is church and state, and so they don't give a damn about the due process of law, about Precedence or any writ of mandamus…"

"If you know that why are you still trying?"

"Because I want an end to it."

"The abortion ban or the Holy Government?"

"Both. And to emancipate the Mexican slaves. It was the Holy Government that enslaved them, too. It enslaved *me*, Richard, you must understand why I hate it."

The president paused for a moment and put out his cigarette in the ash tray on his desk. "I hear you met with Al Haifa last month."

"So I did."

"He's a terrorist."

"No he isn't. Besides, Ben Yehuda met with him too."

"You can't change everything, Sanchez. There is a system in place, and it is not the best system but it works…"

"It works for you, but what about the slaves? What about the Palestinians? What about the thousands of women who have died from back alley abortions this year?"

"They're the minority."

"No, they're not, they're the majority, they're just not Caucasian so you call them a minority, but really they are most of the world. They are a majority whose voice has been taken from them, and so we call them a minority. And even if they were a minority, that doesn't mean it's okay to overlook them and exclude them from the rights of your system, which, as far as I can tell, has only given rights to itself, to the minority, not the majority."

The president smirked. "Have you ever read H.L. Mencken?"

"Yes, but what does that have to do with anything?'

"I remember a passage of his," the president said in a regaling tone. "He said having an idealist in politics was like putting virgins in a brothel- he said they would either have to get out of the brothel or stop being virgins... You're so called purity, if it's not a fake, has no place here, Sanchez."

Sanchez snickered. "Well, I've always thought it more important, to humanity itself, to be mournful but intelligent, instead of blissful and an idiot."

The president turned around in his chair, back facing Sanchez and glibly opened up a newspaper. "We'll make a whore of you yet, Sanchez."

Sanchez walked out of the oval office and slammed the door behind him. He sat back in the chair he was in while he was waiting, because his head was spinning with rage, and he couldn't stand anymore. He put his head in his hands and kicked the chair. "Goddamnit!" he growled. But he was an idealist, so he was always in a state of constant disappointment. He knew an unusual truth. He knew that the time he was born and raised was the necessary time for him to live, *because* he didn't belong in it, because it was so offensive to him. He had always felt, since a child, that he was made for this, that he was made to wage war with corruption, that the whole reason he was placed in these times where he was so out of place and so disgusted with the zeitgeist he never understood, and which was even offensive to his whole purpose in life, was because he was meant to change it. What else could he have possibly been born for, and in this particularly world? He tried to search for another reason, and all he could think of was love, and he realized it was the same thing, that his hate, his disgust, his restlessness, it was all love. What more was there to life? Nothing. He just didn't understand why he was met with such resistance, why the world wanted to be sick. He supposed the higher the ideal the more impossible fate tries to make it, but still he desperately believed, he *had* to desperately believe, because as he looked around he couldn't find a single other thing to believe in, and he, like most people, never had then stomach to believe in nothing, that it wasn't impossible, many people would just like it to be, and that was the well armed resistance he was facing.

He thought of something he had read in Shakespeare once. He was paraphrasing it in his mind, it was something like, 'the impatience that waits with true suffering.' Sanchez thought of that now. It was true. Suffering meant you had to wait for something that should have been yours all along, and that's where the impatience came in. And still one has to wait. Certain people have to wait patiently for things their need for is dire while other people are born with these things, and never had to struggle for them, because *no one* should have to struggle for them. They are the Earth's bounty to man, and it is only humans that deny it from other humans. And so they have them wait for it, like a starving man waiting to be given a piece of bread even though there is no line, the person with the bread is just toying with him, and telling him like an officious, patronizing mother, "be patient," though the need is so dire and there its solution is ready at hand, the hand will just not give it, the hand demands you wait for it, wait for your right to basic contentment, can readily give it but will not, then tells the starving man it is his fault for being impatient, as if anyone who is dying can be patient in trying to receive the last remaining rewards in life. The waiting of the Mexican slaves for freedom, the waiting of any oppressed group for the rights of man, was essentially waiting for love- waiting for love when one is completely starved of it, and needs it this very second, waiting for love in a world where the idiot powers that be have denied it, and keep us at the mercy of their whims instead.

More walking through hell, Cara still arm in arm with The Poet, the only person she had been arm in arm with for years, and she had been around all of Cara's life, in the form of ghost stalking her every ambition, in the form of a ghost she knew one day she had to become. 'It is good that we are mortal,' Cara thought, 'because death is what motivates our every activity. Without it I don't think we would do anything. And as much as I've trumped it up as so noble, so brave, I know deep inside the only reason I write is because I'm afraid to die.'

The Poet looked at her sideways. "What are you thinking of?" she asked.

"I hate when people ask me what I'm thinking of," Cara said tetchily.

The Poet laughed. "It's fine," she said. "I already know anyway."

"Is it possible to be in love in hell?" Cara asked.

The Poet raised an eyebrow. "Why do you ask?"

"I don't know," Cara said and she stopped and sat on the ground for a rest, dragging The Poet down with her. "I think perhaps maybe someday I'd like to be in love. And to be in love in hell…It seems like a good defense mechanism."

The Poet laughed and lit a cigarette. "hell is the easiest place to write in, so I suppose it must also be the easiest place to love in. It is hard, though. Love is a game…"

"No it's not," Cara said seriously. "It's a joke. It's the wit of a fool. It's a thrasonical vaunting of what we do not have."

"Yes," The Poet said, "it is a joke, but the wittiest joke ever known to man, and the most meaningful one. It is written by a fool, but a wise one, a Shakespearean fool. It is a satire, so it is a joke but it is also a tragedy, therefore it does have meaning…"

"You think there's meaning in tragedy?"

"Well, don't you?"

Cara sighed. "I did," she said. "But then I got to hell. After that it all seemed senseless."

"Well, it is," The Poet said, "but there is meaning in the absurd, as well, perhaps much more than in the rational. So, you want to be in love in hell? Do you see anyone you would like to be in love with?"

"No, actually I don't."

"Patience," The Poet said ominously, and with a smirk on her face.

"What if I get out of hell before I fall in love?"

The Poet looked at her curiously. "Isn't that what you want?"

"It is," Cara said stoically. "For whoever I love's sake, more than mine, but still…I feel like it won't be as meaningful anywhere else."

The Poet smirked at her again. "That's the joke."

They got up after each had their cigarette and started moving on from the spot quickly, as they always did, as they were trained by heartache to do- not linger anywhere so long.

"We're running low on cigarettes," Cara said.

"Don't worry, we're in hell. Addictions are more accessible here than anywhere else."

"Ok."

"Does that comfort you?"

"With great regret, yes."

"Ah," The Poet said. "We're almost here, I can smell it. This is another group of people you will relate to. These are the people you used to be, that year when you had writer's block and your mental illness had nothing to keep it within bounds anymore…"

"Who are they?"

"The catatonics."

Cara swallowed heavily. This would indeed be like the past. At last she saw them. They were not catatonic exactly. They were still walking, moving around, but only in a small circle, and one looked in their eyes and they were completely dead, hollow eyed and lost to something they could never hope to explain aloud.

"They are lost in thought," The Poet went on, "irrevocably lost in thought. They are so lost in thought they do not remember actions or words, and certainly cannot preform them. They are so lost in thought they do not even remember the thoughts they have, they are barely aware of the thing they are so lost in, but they *are* lost in it, too far along the road one should not travel to come back, because they are too unaware to make it back. They can only keep going in a circle, a circle of repetitive thoughts. They are so lost deep within themselves, they will probably never leave themselves again."

"How did this happen to them?"

"It was a defense against hell. You know that, you know this state of mind, this state of mind that is all mind and yet no mind at the same time. You know, this is what happens when you think often but do nothing productive with your thoughts. They consume you, you have absolutely no control over them…"

"Does anyone really have control over their thoughts?"

"No, but these people, they have let their thoughts run so loose that they have replaced their lives. They are lost in their minds. And their minds are gone. They are actually nowhere, lost inside a lost thing. Their minds are gone for them now being the only thing present. That's the thing about the human mind, it needs things outside itself. If it is only inside, it is gone, it is nowhere. These people are lost in a place most humans cannot get to, to a place they are not supposed to go, and no one is willing to walk into the same oblivion to save them. They can't anyway. You cannot get into another person's mind, especially when it is lost…"

"That's what makes insanity so lonely," Cara said, and The Poet was shocked that there were tears coming out of her eyes. "If you decide to live in your mind instead of the real world, you have to do it alone. No one will go with you, it is too much to ask of someone to go with you. And I think that's why people do it, is to get away from everyone else. It is the only way to actually be alone."

"Why would anyone want to alone so badly?"

"No one really wants to," Cara said solemnly "But sometimes one gets to a point in their life where they think they have to be, when finally, sadly, it is the only thing that makes sense, and it is the only place where you belong, in your own mind." Cara looked at the catatonics. They had stopped walking and were now just standing and numbly staring at nothing. Cara wished she could get their attention, snap her out of it, because she knew this way of living- it was actually hell. But she also knew that no one could get through to them now, the bastion they had built around themselves was now much to thick to penetrate. Cara knew that, just as one can only get trapped inside their mind alone, one can only ever escape it alone, too. Sometimes the recovery is just as lonely as the illness, because no one understands someone that has almost literally come back from the dead, someone who has seen the things human beings are never supposed to see, especially when they are alive. Cara's heart bled for the catatonics. She had been them before, she knew what it was like, and she knew it worked like everything else in physics and metaphysics, that it was much harder to delve yourself out than it was to delve yourself in.

There was a flower growing on the ground next to Cara. A strange thing in a place like this, but she supposed one could grow anywhere, perhaps especially in hell, and especially when one does not belong there. She smirked to herself with bitter sadness. 'No one belongs here,' she thought. 'Everyone's an outcast here.' She plucked the flower and gave it to the catatonic closest to her. The catatonic took it but with no recognition of what it was, and not being able to care either. They simply grabbed it and walked away. Cara did notice they were clutching onto it though, almost desperately, as a rare link to the living world that they had so renounced themselves from.

"Don't bother," The Poet said.

Cara was shaking. "Fuck off," she whispered.

"What? There is no hope for them."

"HOW CAN THAT BE?!" Cara screamed at her, then lowered her voice a little bit. "I got out of it."

Cara sat down again, shaking violently now. The Poet looked at her with her gouged out eyes. "You got lucky," she said.

"No I didn't," Cara said sternly. "I had to work very hard to get out of that. I had to do it myself. Fate did not lend a hand."

"It always lends a hand, even if you can't see it. It's often just easier to see its work in misfortune than fortune."

"There has to be hope for them," Cara cried. "Otherwise there's no hope for me."

"You're not one of them anymore."

"Why did you show me this? Why did you remind me?"

"Because I am your mind, and I can often be cruel to you. Unlike you I work with fate, not against it, and therefore must be cruel to you when fate is being cruel to you. I am sorry though. I shouldn't have reminded you, but it was a long time ago, much longer than it feels. And maybe I remind you so you will never go back to it. Maybe I remind you because if you hate me a little bit, you won't get lost in me again, without ever utilizing me. It was painful for me, too."

"I don't know which one started it, myself or my mind."

"They're the same thing."

Cara shook her head. "Not when you're insane. When you're insane there is duality between them, a schism. Your mind is a whole separate entity, and when you become lost in it," she said, gesturing to the catatonics, "your mind becomes a stranger to yourself and yourself becomes a stranger to your mind. So you don't know yourself at all, yourself or the strangely separate thing that is governing you. It's the same as how you're a separate person from me."

"I'm not, though."

"You seem like it. But perhaps I'm just going insane again."

The Poet lifted her off the ground, as she was able to do sometimes, after, of course, she had placed her there. "Cara," she said gently. "It will ever happen again, you don't have to worry. You are too wise now to let yourself be lost in the confusion of insanity, of having a mind that is a different person from you. The only reason it happened is because you are someone whose mind needs a heart, and that's all that happened, the two got disconnected, so your mind, without a leash, ran on its own. And it will always be impossible to tell if you cut the string or your mind did, but I'll tell you this, even if you felt at the time your mind had a will of its own, it didn't like it either. It was also lonely without the heart having it in safe chains, that's why it put you in chains instead."

"I wonder, though," Cara said. "Maybe my mind is supposed to have a will of its own."

"Yes, but it's not supposed to be contrary to your own."

"I did want to die at the time, though," Cara whispered. "That was my will."

"That is no will."

"So I had no will and neither did my mind. We *were* in agreement."

The Poet sighed.. "It's complicated, it's very complicated. Perhaps you listen to your mind too much, or your mind listens to you too much…Who cut the string? Who forsook the heart to dwell aimlessly in the mind? We will never know, and it is best not to think about it…"

"You've made me think about everything."

"I'm sorry and you're welcome," The Poet said stiffly, then interlaced her arm with Cara's, "let's go," she said. "All of your ghosts are here, and if we stay any longer, they will haunt you again. I know now that you have made it through insanity there are philosophical, perhaps almost even wise things you can say about it now, and I know that feels good, because it means you are not insane anymore, but if you dwell on it for too long, that wisdom will become confusion again. The past is always ready to destroy you again, particularly if you indulge in it."

Cara shrugged. "You're the one who brought me here," She looked at the catatonics again and a shiver went down her spine. The Poet was right, she could not look at them. All her pity went out to them, but if she pitied this condition too much it would become hers again, and she could not do that, not even for love, which, looking back, was what she had done it for the first time as well. There was not enough time to do it again. There had not even been enough time to do it the first time, but it was an inevitability of the trials of her youth.

"I'm sorry," The Poet said again. "I'm sorry I brought you here, but you should know, I'm not the one in control either."

"Then who is?"

"God only knows, if there is one. Come now, we must leave."

Etwas Uberhaupt

The Soldier sat bolt upright in his makeshift bed. All night he could hear bombs, all night he could hear war, there was no escape from it, not even in sleep, on the rare occasions he was able to sleep. 'Christ,' he thought to himself. 'I don't have time for PTSD, the trauma is not even post yet. I have to keep living it first.' He was an animal now, his only thought each day was to stay alive. He had never wanted to live so much in his life, and he had never wanted to die so much in his life. Some days he wished everything would die, that the damn nukes would at last go flying, that we could finally do what we have been threatening to do for decades after the A bomb was made, but which we were too cowardly to do and to cowardly not to do. We could only ever flaunt the end of the world, we could never actually deliver it, we do not have that kind of power, no matter what weapons we have, and everyone was like the soldier- everyone wanted to die and everyone wanted to live. But the soldier knew what the end of the world was like. He lived it every day, from hour to hour and rapidly increasing second to second, he saw the apocalypse that has been waged since the dawn of civilization against itself. And now sadly it had become a part of civilization, a supposedly irrevocable tool of society, a sacrifice we all had to make for some God we could not even see, and whom was only getting rich and fat off the profit of death. And most people in America didn't have to make the sacrifice, only the few who were desperate and unaware of their own finitude enough to voluntarily be expendable to society. But now that the soldier had seen the rest of the world, the way most people have to live in war, with it right in their front yard everyday instead of at a comfortable, even entertaining distance of their television set, it was hard for him to think they were the enemy, it was hard to think anyone was the enemy except war…But he couldn't think like that if he expected to live.

He had to try to not think at all, he had to break painfully loose all the obligations and all the comforts of affection, love, and the last and most regrettable, (but also the most important to abandon,) mercy. He had lived in America with all the painful inadequacies of family life, first a family where he was the son, and then, naively thinking his family would be different, the father, and it was not different. They were never enough for each other, they loved each other but this love was such an obligation that everyone in the household resented it. This was how the American dream actually turned out, being that it was built on success more than love, naturally the love we could find in it was disappointing. The American dream had failed the soldier .So he had to settle for this nightmare instead, because as much as he hated it, it seemed much more real. The blind, irrational hate they were all brainwashed with each day, had kept him alive more than the stale, almost forced love of the family, the dying heart of the American dream. War was fine. He would either die or he would live, and since he wanted to do both, either outcome was fine…But oh he wanted to live, but then again, for what? What was there to go back to?

He hated it. He felt like it was something wrong with him that was a sickness he had caught from the entire world, but now he felt this barbarity, this sickness of humanity, was the only truth about it.

The War on War group hid in the shelter. The Proud Brethren, a group of white supremacists that had always been against them, was outside at the rally with machine guns trying to shoot them. They had snuck in the shelter. There were shelters everywhere but one had to rent them and they were at an exorbitant rate- in other words, if the nukes ever really did drop, only the rich could afford to survive it. 'Cockroaches,' Manny, the leader of the War on War group in Kapporeth thought. 'Only they survive nuclear annihilation.' He rest his head against the wall of the shelter. It was underground, so the wall was mostly made of dirt and mortar, but Manny didn't care. The whole world was made of dirt and mortar anyway. But it was times like these he felt like he *was* the good guy, though recently he hadn't been so sure. He knew they were initially, but something had gone wrong. Their disgust with war had made them bellicose, their disgust with war and the times, with the white supremacists and the president, had turned them into domestic terrorists. 'We're just the Nazis of the left,' Manny thought bitterly and his head slumped against the dirt and mortar.

They could hear the Proud Brethren. "Where are those hippie Jew loving bastards!" one of them screamed. "I want to put a shell in all of them!"

"Calling us a hate group," one of them said. "It's the War on War idiots who are the hate group!"

"Yea, they hate war."

'We're not a hate group,' Manny thought to himself, 'we're a misguided love group, which can be just as bad sometimes.' He tried to suppress the sigh that was coming out of his mouth. 'Besides ideology,' he continued thinking, 'what's the difference between me and the enemy? And ideology is nothing. Ideology is a mask we all wear, it is just rhetoric disguised as some beautiful and hopeful truth when most of the time it is another lie. Either way, it is hiding a tyrant underneath it, underneath its mask with savior's words, but empty savior's words, a savior who reaches out their hand to you and there is nothing in it, and we know there is nothing in it, but we grab onto it anyway, latch to it tenaciously, just so we have something to grab onto. It's a far leap between ideology and idealism. We used to be idealists, when we were simply Antifa, but then we got corrupted, then we took up ideology instead, abandoned the real truth that is in idealism for the mask of the hollow savior of ideology.'

"Let's go," another member of the Proud Brethren said. "I don't see them anywhere here." Manny heard a shotgun blast and some giggling then all was silent. He finally let his sigh out.

"Al Haifa said he would help us," someone whispered.

"Al Haifa is in Palestine," Manny said tetchily. "Where he has his own problems."

"What about Ben Yehuda?"

"He's in the same land as Al Haifa but of a different name, and also has his own problems. Besides, the Boston faction took a plane there and attacked the Knesset, the fucking idiots. I doubt he'd be too keen to help us after that."

"What about Sanchez?"

Manny waved him off with a flippant, lazy hand and resumed his position with his head against the wall. He resumed his previous train of thought, thinking about the difference between ideology and idealism. 'It's seem so much easier,' he thought, 'to resign oneself to a pseudo truth than the real truth. The real truth is complicated, and comes with many caveats. A pseudo truth is hollow, and we like hollow things in this society, because they're much more simple, because we have been bred now to be consumers, and that's what consumers buy, is the pseudo truth, consumerism *is* a pseudo truth. That's everyone's piece of mind, a dulcet, sweetened lie with only a mixture of the truth within it- a bowdlerized version of it, like a flavored medicine, flavored with some untruth so it's easier to swallow, and because of this flavoring it gets rid only of the visible symptoms, not the disease. And the symptoms are still there, too, we just can't feel them as sharply with the guerdon of ideology, with the medicine of a pseudo truth, a drug like any other, something people are addicted to, a consumer habit, all that is hollow and unsatisfactory in this society, all the lies we are supposed to live and worship…Jesus.'

He lit a cigarette. Many of the others did the same thing. 'But I'm no different. I've picked up an ideology, too, I've given myself over completely to a pseudo truth, because it seems, in this world, there is nothing else to live for. I suppose I could live for a real truth, but then I would be living for nothing.' He held his cigarette an inch from his face and numbly inspected the small burning cinder on top of it. 'What am I talking about?' he thought. 'Living for a pseudo truth is living for nothing as well. A pseudo truth *is* nothing, but unlike the real truth it at least puts on the pretense of being something. Lies are more comfortable, they're easier to live for. To follow the real truth one must be pyshioplastic, which is a state, I do not think, man finds himself in naturally- that is man's nature, not to conform to nature. So we are ideoplastic instead. We form all our impressions of the world from the mind. We cannot get away from the thing inside our skull and back into nature. It is like physei and thesei…when we created language we created culture, and it was away from nature, and back deeper into the mind. That is why it has always been so lonely.'

"Do you think we can get out of here?" someone asked.

"I think so," Manny said. "We better get out of here before we're charged 3,000 bucks each for this place…Some members of the faction in Atlanta are supposed to talk to Al Haifa. Maybe he can help us, but I think Ben Yehuda is going to be of essence to the deal."

Someone groaned. "Really? We gotta make a bargain with Yehuda? Israel is everything we're against…"

"Shut up," Manny said curtly. "We'll do what we have to do."

Everyone nodded reluctantly and then they slowly filed out of the shelter. A hate group, a misguided love group, Manny did not know the difference anymore. It is natural to hate war. To hate war, injustice, oppression and inequality *is* love, and the War on War members did just that, they loved, but they were going about it the wrong way. They were loving wrongly, which regrettably, in the end, is the same as hating.

Cara and The Poet stopped for cigarettes in hell. It comforted Cara. It was like the comforts of the real world, but she supposed in many way hell was the real world, but it shouldn't have been. People had made it that way, but often Cara felt like suffering was the only thing that was real. She didn't know if it was just her sickness that made her feel that way or if it was the truth. She often couldn't tell the difference between the two- often she could not distinguish where delirium ended and reality began, because it was a strange transition, one that you didn't really notice much, it just sort of happened, and either way it didn't feel very real. Suffering, it was hard to delineate. Cara could not tell if it came simply from the head or if it came from reality, or if it was both, if suffering initially was bestowed upon you by the world and the head twisted it into disease. She couldn't figure it out. She couldn't figure out if suffering were delirium or reality, she couldn't tell if hell was only a dream or if it was truth, or if there was even any difference between dreams and the truth. She supposed she would never know, she supposed she would never know the truth about this, and continue just walking through the dream, the agony of suffering that could have been real or just a malfunction in the head, that could have been truth or merely the mind's skewering of it.

But she was happy to have her cigarettes. She supposed that was the only thing that mattered right now, being able to occasionally have the comforts most people could afford to have all the time. That was the only upside of being poor, of being destitute in hell, that one could appreciate all that was taken for granted in the "real world," which unfortunately to Cara would never fell as real as hell. The Poet, reading her thoughts as always, turned to her.

"You are comforted?" she asked.

"Yes."

"You know if you do fall in love, in hell or otherwise, you're going to have to give up many of your comforts."

Cara shrugged. "I don't mind at all," she said. "My comforts are what have made me lonely."

The Poet smiled at her. "At least you are aware of it," she said, and lit a cigarette of her own. "I have pity for people like you, you and your constant malaise, always being able to know what's wrong with yourself but never being able to fix it. And then the same problem with all of humanity."

"Yes," Cara said absently. "I find it hard to abide by the wisdom I'm able to so easily put into words, but not into life."

The Poet shrugged. "You're young, and bogged down in addictions, or 'comforts,' as you call them."

Cara grimaced at her. "Is there really any difference?" she asked. "Love is a comfort and an addiction, because people cannot live without it. They try to, because they know life would be easier, but they can't do it. Life is not supposed to be that easy. When it is that easy you are bogged down in addictions and false comforts, blearily through intoxicated eyes trying to tell the difference between the two. People who can't love, I pity them. I think their lives are easier because they can't love, but I do pity them."

"You and your blasted pity," The Poet said. "It only ever gets you into trouble."

"Yes, it does, but it feels like there is no other reason for me to exist…"

"And do you help the people you pity, or do you just right them down in your unnecessarily complex diary?"

Cara paused for the moment, and looked at The Poet strangely. "What's wrong with you today?" she asked. "You're the one that made me a writer, you have an unnecessarily complex diary, too."

The Poet sat down on the ground. "I'm sorry," she said. "This place is wearing on my nerves…And then the real world, it doesn't seem much different to me."

"No, me either, but I have been thinking about the real world, the state it's in, I don't think it's permanent."

"Really? You don't?"

"No. I think the fascists will always lose, I don't think they can ever hope to win. Love is much too strong…"

The Poet scoffed. "Hippie."

"No, hear me out. Fascists are able to get elected, to come into power, but they always face their doom in the end, because of the life and death instinct. Humanity is often dying for its own destruction, and they will elect any idiot catalyst who will help, because that's all fascists want to do is destroy the world, but people eventually snap out of it. Once they finally see the destruction they have unconsciously yearned for actually wreaked, the life instinct kicks in, love kicks in, because the life instinct *is* love, and it is too strong to even, in the end, be overcome by the death instinct that the fascist has been playing off of, let alone the fascist. No one is happy in the Carceral Archipelago. We many have accidentally helped put ourselves in this state, but we will constantly and fully aware get ourselves out of it, because the death instinct is unconscious, it is only half truly felt, but the life instinct we know in its fullness…"

"Do not underestimate unconscious things."

"I don't," Cara said emphatically. "I know the unconscious can motivate us actually quite powerfully, particularly towards destruction, but in the end, even when someone truly wants to die, when their survival is actually confronted, they will fight to live. And that's the situation we are in now, the situation we put ourselves in yes, but that means we can get out of it. We know we made a mistake, we know now the death we partially asked for is too painful, and now we want life, and not just for ourselves, but for everyone in the world. That's why the life instinct is love, especially since it manifests most in procreation."

"So does the death instinct."

"Well, they're very close, because life and death are very close, and particularly in procreation…"

"Particularly in love."

Cara sighed. "Yes, but it is the only hope of life we have. Hate propagates death, it sells it on every street corner to the consumers who have taught only to be stupid and don't know any better. But love, with its promise of rejuvenation, even though that has to be paid for with death, always gives life for free."

The Poet smiled at her. "It's so rare to see you this optimistic," she said. "I like it."

"Thank you. It is hard, it is hard for me to be optimistic, but that's one thing I know I can believe in, even though it's let me down so many times, every time it let me down, it was still worth it, it was worth it just to feel it, just to feel something. I have this problem where I'm either sad or I feel nothing, and some days it is easier to feel nothing and other days it is easier to feel sad. But I have this problem, I am happy one moment then in despair the next, and I vacillate between the two constantly. That happens to me a lot. Sometimes I think I'd rather just be sad all the time, instead of having to take the journey from bottom to top and then from top to bottom over and over again, it's exhausting, and to be happy all the time, that is much too much to ask from the world. Anything endowed with any amount of intellect can't be happy all the time, that is the price you pay for intelligence."

The Poet smiled again and clap a hand on her shoulder. "I am fond of you," she said, "because like Tithonus I do not remember being young. It's recorded in history but in my own mind I've for-gotten it. So I like watching you, you being a youthful poet, but I suppose no poet is ever young, or ever old. We are just like the world. And nothing is ever really a long time ago. This is comforting and discomfiting at the same time. I have something else to show you, something else you will not like."

"Great. Why will I not like it?"

"For the same reason you have disliked all of hell. You will be able to relate to it. Follow me."

Cara did as she was bidden, but she paused and thought for a moment. 'Why do I follow?' she thought to herself. 'Why do I follow a blind woman? I have never followed anyone in my entire life, not even someone I've been in love with. I've never lead anyone either, but I suppose that's because I've never been blind. But I have, and even still, I only listened to myself and my lack of vision. I do not need authority in my life, in fact, most of my energies have been spent avoiding it, so why? Why do I follow The Poet? I can't stop myself, though. She has some power over me. She takes me places I do not want to go, but I follow her because the promise of happiness, of hope, of the future are in her, in a woman who is full of such despair. I let her show me all the sides of the world I do not want to see because the reward she has offered me if I do it is love. I know it is.'

So Cara went on following The Poet, as she had her whole life, following at once a blind dream and a lucid nightmare, because it was the only hope she had.

They walked a few more feet, and The Poet groped around. There was a curtain in front of them. Once The Poet felt the fustian fabric she stopped and knew she was in the right place. "We're here," she said. "This is almost the last step in our journey. I have to put you through this one last bit of anguish and then I promise you will find love afterwards, and we'll be out of hell," The Poet turned her blind eyes towards Cara, and it still felt like The Poet could still see her, that even in blindness, she knew her face. "Keep doing what you're doing, Cara," she said. "Keep being an artist that is even stranger than all the other artists, because you do not take up their alternative but equally prescribed lifestyle. Keep fighting the times you live in, keep being so out of place in the world, do not conform to the things you do find so inimical, continue being brave and true, and for the time being, alone, and I swear to you, after all these years of bad luck, after all the loneliness and uncertainty of if and when love will come, you will achieve a so much more meaningful happiness than the hollow happiness of so many other people that grew older and gave up your fight, because you will have truly earned it. You have already truly earned it, but for people like you this happiness always comes late, because it is a happiness that you have to suffer for, because it is a true happiness, and only comes to those who have first known great misery. And I am sorry to say, you have a little more misery to go through, but keep looking to the future, applying your idealism to it, and I swear to you on my eternal life, yours will be too."

Cara smiled weakly. "Ok," she said. "What is my last task?"

"Remove this veil."

Cara swallowed heavily and walked up to the black curtain. There were strange words written on it in white ink, but Cara was able to read them. They were German, and she knew a little German. The first phrase written on it was "Etwas Uberhaupt," something at all, and under that it said "Laute der stille," the voice of silence.

'That's nice,' Cara though n a naïve and distrait way she did not understand. 'Silence does need a voice in this world.'

So she walked up and removed the veil, and an inexplicable horror was underneath it. It was nothing, absolutely nothing, but it drew Cara in, it sucked her in, and she could not look away from it. It was darkness like she had never seen before, and the horror was that she would never be able to explain it, she would never find a therapist that she could tell this to, she could never confess it to anyone at all, because it was beyond even her fertile imagination, and yet it was a fact of nature. Yet it was the thing that was always at the bottom of life. And that's where Cara was right now as she looked into this thing, the bottom of life, the most hollow and lowest ring of hell, the center of the Earth, and it would be such a long climb back up and there would be so many things she could not explain, especially this, the very bottom, the very bottom of existence, to know the absolute blank and dark nothingness whose contrast was what made existence possible- she was looking into the other side of existence, the side human beings are not supposed to see if they expect not to go mad, and that's what really hurt- after seeing this thing she could not only not explain, (and the things we cannot explain are the things that haunt us our entire lives, without the succor of being able to elucidate them,) she would be expected to stay sane afterwards, after having seen sanity itself, the only thing in the world or nature that is stripped bare and bereft of illusion, which, a human mind, needing illusion to survive, could not bear. But she stared at it and stared at it. There was something compelling about it, for everyone, for the whole human race though it is our biggest fear, but frightening things can often be compelling. Cara got the feeling the truth was in this, always waiting beneath it's veil of illusion. The truth was the voice of silence, the truth was something we could not hear over the noise of our own violence, but it was always waiting, waiting for the day when there was nothing left to say, when the obfuscation of words were at last no use to a person, there lurked the voice of silence, wanting to deafen you with the noise of the truth. Cara realized that this thing most people only saw when they died, but she was young, and already too wise for a young person, already an old soul, and seeing this…Well, she would never be the same again. She would forever be odd, enigmatic and cold, having known the great unknowable at such an early age, having already toured the empty landscape of hell in youth that was being shattered and wasted on it. But she had wanted to know the truth, and she didn't care what age she learned it at, because she was still young, and still with the heart of a fool in spite of all her anachronistic wisdom- she still had her naivete, the heart of her idealism even in the midst of the pessimism of her mind, and she realized now she relied on that just as much as her brain with its lack of enough dopamine to feel much hope. But she did hope for a world she practically had no stake in, because it had abandoned her voice and left her to hell, to the voice of silence, to the truth instead of the comfortable illusions of a society which Cara knew, in spite of its glittering mask, was rotting and decaying beneath.

The voice of silence dragged her further and further in, and Cara could not look away from it. She had been enlightened. She had found enlightenment in darkness, which is often the only place to find it in. The Poet, even though she could not see, knew Cara had been staring at it too long so she became alarmed and pulled Cara back to so called reality, but now and for the rest of time, even though Cara knew she had to fight it to be alive, this void with its hollow and infinite truth would be the only possible reality to her. Her senses were dulled and she did not know where she was. She looked vaguely at The Poet.

"Cara," The Poet said with shaking hands. "You're not supposed to be that attracted to it."

Cara shook her head back and forth and finally snapped back into reality, the world of illusions, of familiar noises and voices covering the voice of silence. Cara was shaking as well, and she looked at The Poet with eyes of hate that The Poet could not see.

"Why did you make me do that?!" she cried defensively. "After seeing that…No one is ever going to understand me again."

CHAPTER 8

Anastasis

The Mexican slave sat in his shoddy one room shack on the master's land and listened to the storm. It was a violent storm, and there weren't many fortifications in this room. Buckets were scattered everywhere collecting heavy raindrops from the roof. The slave sighed and turned over in bed. It would be a poor night of rest again as outside the storm raged, as it always did, with so many innocent people were caught in the middle of it. 'It's so strange,' the slave thought, 'what they do to me, how they lord over me, how they prevent me from being free. I feel throughout all human ages it has been proved over and over again that what any one group of human beings can do, all the other groups of human beings can do also. Inequality is not natural, it is man made because people were offended by and resented their lack of any real superiority over any man or woman.' He turned over again.

'I would be a philosopher,' he thought, 'if I weren't a slave, if only I were *allowed* to read and write. I know what so many other people forget in their busy lives, but I've got plenty of time, I've got all the time in the world: I've got plenty of time to remember that the universe is an artist, and artists die young and are immortal...I would have been a philosopher. I know so much more about God than a free man. It's not pleasant, though, to know that much about God. People don't know that religion isn't really a comfort. No one takes up God with real, true devotion unless they have been abandoned by human beings. I am so jealous of the free men, because they can believe in God casually- they only have to go to church once a week, the prescribed hour or two one thinks about God, and they don't really think about God, they let the preacher think about God for them, they don't know what it's like to really *need* God. It is awful to need God. It is awful to have nothing else to look to *but* goodness, because you have only seen the worst of human beings and been victim to this worst part of them, so you have nothing left but God. But the reason I believe so deeply in God is because He is what made us so equal, and one day he will make sure we are all treated equal, too, but then again, he already does, with death. Whether we like it or not we live equal and we die even more equal, all of us amounting to ashes to ashes in the end. You can take away a man's rights, but he will still be equal to you. That's why I'm a bad slave, that's why I get beaten so much, because I'm a philosopher, and this world doesn't even like free white male philosophers, let alone the voice of a Mexican slave. And when you're a philosopher you know all people are equal and free, so you can't really be a slave. I'm not a slave in spirit- my spirit has reached out to God too much for that to be true. It's a catch 22. You can't be a good slave if you're s philosopher, but you can't bear being a slave unless you take up philosophy.

'Suffering is really what makes us start to think, what makes us begin to delve deeply into the world around us, and if your suffering is a lack of freedom then even more so, but I suppose really all suffering comes from freedom- either not enough of it or too much of it. But I really have no freedom, so I'm one of the few people in America who know its true value, in this land of the free, freedom being the main tenant of America but which has never truly existed within it. That's the problem with America, and all the free people in it. They treat freedom like it is just a word. They treat God like He is just a word, instead of the word. They don't know. They don't know so many things even though they are supposedly more educated than me. They don't suffer so they don't think. All I do is suffer, so all I do is think. All I do is think, so all I do is suffer. I can't stop thinking. Thinking is my biggest rebellion, because I know they don't want me to think, and in many ways, my hard life would be a little bit easier if I didn't think so much, but that's rebellion for you- rebellion is thinking when they don't want you to think, so rebellion is suffering, too. Some people are punished greatly for thinking, but I don't care. They've taken everything else away from me, but they can't take that away from me. No matter how hard they try, they cannot turn me into an animal, they cannot stop me from being human.'

The storm outside made one final gasp of nature rebelling against itself, and perhaps humanity, too. The lightning made one more blinding flash and then the rain slowed- the anger of the Earth made its last gasp and then returned to its usual, more quiet melancholy. The slave turned over in bed again. The water drops from the ceiling began to slow to a halt and the slave quietly watched them fall until it stopped. He smiled to himself and at last settled in bed. 'All storms end,' was his last thought before sleep at last took over him.

Yasser Al Haifa lay on his back on top of the roof of his rather modest hovel in Palestine. He chuckled to himself. How strange it would be to the world, which was now paying so much attention to him, if they found out he was poor. He looked up at the dark Palestinian night. It was beautiful tonight. Al Haifa swore there was nowhere else on Earth that you see the stars so well, but then again, he did live in the holy land, and it was beautiful but it was mutilated, sliced into pieces along with the people's will as the whole world fought over its Godly inheritance. Israel and Palestine were beautiful, but they both drove people mad, just like religion itself, because people could not accept the beauty and the simplicity of it, nor the immense complexity and the mystery of it- they had to bend it to their own individual minds, to their own unique, and regrettably, typically weak will instead of leaving it where it should be left, in both collective understanding and imagination. Everyone wanted to be holy, and they did it in the most unholy way possible- they thought salvation meant damning others, that the only way to be holy was to have a high, false sense of morality over other people, and to subjugate those who were supposedly less holy. People thought the only way to be divine was to send others to hell. They had missed the entire point of religion itself, and instead applied it to their desperation, their desperate need to think they were good without having to do the work it takes to actually be good. Being good can come at many great costs and caveats, and people know this, that is why they try to take the easy way out to supposed goodness, through condemnation. But Al Haifa did not feel he was put on the Earth to condemn. It was unfair to condemn, because he knew only good people feel within them the conflict of good and evil.

Al Haifa pulled a joint out of his pocket and lit it as he gazed at the Palestinian stars. He had always loved the stars. He fancied himself an astronomer when he was a child, but his parents could never hope to have enough money to send him to school. He wanted to be an astronomer, a philosopher. He wanted only to do what he was doing now- nothing while he stared at the stars, but again, the world would not allow it. Truthfully he was like so many other women and men who were driven to think more about the world around them- he had intelligence, but no ambition. So how did he end up as he did, leading a generation of bedraggled, oppressed and angry young Palestinians as their revolutionary leader? It was never what he had wanted to, but he supposed it was philosophical, he supposed it did involve doing nothing while he stared at the stars, but he had never wanted to participate in the world this directly. He wanted to participate in the world, everyone does unless they are ready to die, and Al Haifa had in his life experienced long years of depression, just like everyone in Palestine did, being a belittled and oppressed nation whom so few people, particularly in America (though Al Haifa had never understood why it was any of America's business, but for some reason they were tied in this mess, too, as they always tried to insert themselves in any foreign ideological war,) were on their side, because so many people around the world were frightened merely of their race and religion.

But Al Haifa had gotten over his depression, and so, someone who never wanted to be a leader, someone who had never much liked playing the game of ambition, was now a leader of a strong but peaceful opposition group Al Haifa hoped he was not brainwashing, as the terrorists actually did, but also whose anger he had to keep in check. But it was simply because he was the first to have fought the despair and come out its victor. After that he knew he had to do something or the despair would come back, so he became a damned revolutionary, though it was the least practical application of his philosophical studies, as it was an activity that in the end could be very war like, and therefore contrary to philosophy. That's what Al Haifa was trying to stop from happening. He knew so many revolutions that were based on ideology, even idealism, that were some of the bloodiest events in history. He had been very inspired by Martin Luther King Jr. when he was a child. King's revolution was one of the world's few successful revolutions, and that's because it was peaceful, and the poor man had to pay for it with his life, but his legacy was something that would never die. That's what Al Haifa wanted to be like, that's the way he saw his revolution, and, contrary to American belief, many Palestinians were behind it. They were not all violent revolutionaries. Many were just like Al Haifa- they didn't really want to do this, but they had to, and they agreed with Al Haifa when he had held his first meeting for the opposition group, only about twenty people had come, but now there were hundreds, and he had said to them- "we are fighting immorality, and one can only fight immorality with morality. We cannot pluck out the eye of the man who has plucked out our eye, we have to let him pluck it out and then be kind to him, though it will only make him hate us more, it will also make him frightened of us, because we will seem superhuman in our morality, whereas he has always been weak in his, and the more frightened of us he is the more he will hate us, but to be loved by such a man means to be part of his hate. He will probably pluck out our other eye, but in the end, history will remember him as the blind man, and history will remember us kindly, not as terrorists but as saints. That's how we will fight, by refusing to fight, by being moral. Allah will reward us for our lack of destruction, He will have us win the war because we refused to take part in it."

He smiled now as he remembered the applause it was met with. He had been surprised by that. He kept puffing quietly on the joint. Police never came here, and they had bigger problems than marijuana. He kept thinking and looking at the stars, his favorite activity since he was born. 'It is strange,' he thought to himself. 'People in America. They watch the news everyday and they see the atrocity and they say 'how awful, what a tragedy,' but most of them support the system that allows these tragedies to happen.' Al Haifa sighed, never keeping his eyes off the stars, as he had his whole life, because he thought the stars were the ultimate resting place of mankind, and mankind's ultimate goal. He wished he wasn't resigned to the Earth and its imbecilic politics. In the stars none of that existed. Lifelessness was too wise for that.

The joint was running low, but he smoked the remainder of it. 'I suppose I can't blame the Americans,' he thought, 'this system, they are afraid not to support it, because not to support it would mean to be an outcast. I suppose they are oppressed too, oppressed by majority which has slowly become an ignorant mob. They are oppressed, too, but in such an insidious way that most of them don't notice it. I do feel sorry for them. I feel sorry for anyone that isn't free, and I feel sorry for people who are free, too, people like me, whose only recourse in life is the stars. But the Americans, this system that so subtly oppresses them and which they feel they must agree with to belong, they built it together, and now they feel they must conform to it or lose all that they believe in, because the alternative is to believe in nothing, and most people are not brave enough to do that, particularly in America, (and not even just America, the whole world,) where to believe in nothing is a taboo. But in America, even when people's beliefs are proved wrong and wrong again, they still feel they have to hold onto them, because that is all they have there, that is their only way to be part of the system that is a requisite to be part of society.'

The joint was finished. He flicked the roach off the roof and onto the ground. Now it was just him and the stars alone, the way he had always wanted it. 'I would have been an astronomer,' he thought again. 'I would have been a philosopher, I would have been a poet, because really, when you think about it, physics, poetry and philosophy are the only things that exist. Physics is the way the universe works, poetry is how we feel about, and philosophy is our real insight, and eventually, our wisdom into it. Politics only came after, and in opposition to the three things, counteracting the wisdom we learn from the stars and making it the tool which bad men, with no wisdom, conquer the Earth. But what physics, poetry and philosophy has taught me is that all people are equal and when people are not being treated equal it is an offense against nature, and must be corrected. I am working in politics, but also against it at the same time. I was born at entirely the wrong time and the exactly right time as well- I am a man put in his time and place for a reason, and nature has made me take up its errand to ensure all people are free, and though it was not what I wanted to do, it is what I have to do. I am trying to undo the deleterious effects politics has done on nature, and physics, poetry and philosophy are behind me, because they know there is a parity that exists behind all things, and I am trying to re—establish that parity which politics has so foolishly tried to disassemble because it has ignored physics, poetry and philosophy. And one day, when it's over, I can be lazy again. I can write my philosophy and observe the universe alone like I have always wanted to do, but first I must ensure that the Palestinians are free, because if they are not free neither am I, and I won't be able to devote myself to these essential 'three p's' if I'm not. And they have taught me equality is the only thing worth believing in anyway.'

Cara was quiet for the rest of the journey. She felt like she would be quiet for the rest of her life after that experience, that it had sucked her ability to talk away, because she realized sadly, if she couldn't explain *it* she wouldn't be able to explain anything, and no one can really explain it. So all of it is just empty words, even the words Cara had found most meaningful, they could not quite get at the heart of reality, the lifeless thing that always was underlying life, waiting to convert it back to death. But she supposed she could learn. If man had learned how to explain with clarity how the universe began, she supposed one day she could learn how to explain how the universe ends, about the small point in space at which creation is undo, just as it came out of a small point, as well. It was not significant, even as it grew. Everything in the universe was running away from each other- that's what Cara admired about the stars, that they were not only unafraid of being alone, they were actually afraid to be anything *but* alone. That was their nature, and humanity was an aberration of that. Cara could relate to both- she could relate to the stars desperate need to be alone and she could relate to being the sole aberration in that perfect scheme, known as life, because she was a part of it, no matter how well she knew that the universe was much wiser than the Earth, still she was an earthling. And her quest to explain the end of the universe, it was a quest to explain something no one wanted to listen to, as most of her life had been. Much of her knowledge, much of what she had discovered and learned, was dismissed flippantly as the ravings of a lunatic, as truth often was, when it did not conform to men's desires, which it almost never did.

The Poet snapped Cara out of her reverie. "It's almost over," The Poet said with relief.

"What is?" Cara asked absently.

"Hell."

"Hell itself?"

The Poet smiled. "Yes. Your pity will have nullified it. But there is one more task."

"What's that?"

"Meeting the devil."

Cara chuckled. "I've always wanted to meet the devil," she said. 'But then again, I know him well. Sometimes I know him better than God, because he makes himself so much more obvious, because evil, to humanity, is famous while good is always clandestine. But I can't make an judgments, because I have turned to him, I have turned to the devil when God was too busy or too hard to see. I have turned to the devil when it seemed I had no other recourse- no other recourse than self destruction."

"We all have," The Poet said gently, "some of us just can't admit it. But we have all done it. You're right, the devil, particularly in the modern world, is more accessible than God. But now you will actually meet him."

"And then what will happen?"

"We'll get to leave. I am too blind to lead you further, but I will go with you. Rhadamanthus will take us the rest of the way."

And then, on cue, Rhadamanthus appeared with his messy, stray hairs, clothes wrinkled and a battered old guitar at his side. Cara smiled at him.

"It's good to see you," she said.

Rhadamanthus did not smile but gave her a curt nod. "This last part of your journey will be long, though it is a short ride to the devil. But these are your last days in hell, of course they have to be long. My mother used to always tell me, the closer you get to the light at the end of the tunnel, the farther is the walk to it. But still you get there in the end, even though the last stretch feels longer than the previous miles, soon it will all be over. Come now, we have a long walk."

And the walk was indeed long. Rhadamanthus was right, it felt like years just these last few miles, it felt longer than the entire time they had been in hell. They were silent the entire way, except Rhadamanthus who played his guitar and sang occasionally. The Poet clasped desperately to Cara's arm. Cara looked at her with a bit of a sardonic smile.

"Are you afraid of the devil?" she asked.

"Yes," was all The Poet said, and the rest of the walk they resumed their long silence. By the time they got there Cara's shoes had worn out and beneath them her feet were blistered and burned from the heat of the bottom of hell. She removed her shoes and whined for a moment. She looked upon her surroundings. She was standing at the rim of a large pit.

"This is the devil?" she said wearily. "A hole in the ground?"

Then suddenly fire burst forth from the rim of the great pit and something, with a roar of agony, came flying out of it.

"Why do you disturb me?" the man in the pit said in anguish. Cara got a closer look at him now. He was covered in heavy chains all over his body. He was not large, he was actually quite small. Cara thought the chains were probably heavier than he was. "Who are you?" he wailed.

Cara stopped. "I was supposed to meet you," she said slowly. "Are you alright? Are you in a great deal of pain?"

The devil faltered. "Oh yes," he said dully. "You, you who have been walking through hell armed with only pity…You'll find that actually is a good weapon here."

"It's not a weapon," Cara whispered. "It is not meant to strike or defend. In fact, if anything, it makes me much more vulnerable."

The devil shrugged and his chains raised slightly on his body. "It can be used as a weapon," he said.

"I don't want to use it as a weapon."

"Well, what do you think you've been doing? You've been using your vulnerability as a defense mechanism this whole time."

Cara's whole body slackened as she conceded to this point. "It's alright," he said. "Anything can be used as a defense mechanism, and you need one down here. Mine was my lack of servility which has put me in these chains. You probably understand that, living in the world above that is not much different than my kingdom down below. You being different, you being a 'rebel' so to speak, you know what it's like to be free in a world that has abandoned freedom, and even discourages it, because now *with* freedom one is vulnerable. But you were smart. You used this vulnerability to protect yourself, and your pity, which has indulged the horrors of hell, has also kept you safe from them, at a distance…"

"One can't pity from a distance," Cara said stiffly.

The devil laughed. "What do you think you've been doing this whole time? You and your writing…"

"No," Cara said firmly and emphatically. "I pity the people in hell because I really have been through the things they have."

"And that's why you have to pity them from a distance, so you won't go through them again. And you're right, one can't really pity from a distance and it still really be pity. Then it is just a show, it's just like watching the news on Earth, the five seconds of moot pity and then going about your inane day because there is nothing left in the world to do anymore. It is a useless pity, and it wastes itself in an instant, pity at a distance."

Cara, feeling more tired than she ever had in her life, sat on the ground and stared into the distance. The devil continued. "I knew every person, including myself, had to be a slave to something, so I chose to be a slave to freedom. And so God put me in chains. You with your distant, moot pity, you who pities every possible human condition because you understand all of them, supposedly, do you understand this?"

"Yes," Cara whispered. "I do."

"Then listen. What they say about me is true. I am the thing that prevents people from ever being satisfied, I am what hollows them out, but it is only because I was hollow and unsatisfied and didn't want to be alone. So I have spread my inanition all over the Earth, I have given it to people like a disease, but only in the vain hope I could get rid of the disease myself. You, you who pities all of hell, tell me, do you pity me?"

"Yes," Cara whispered. "I hate you, but I pity you."

Then a great roar came from what seemed to be the sky, but was really the floor so to speak of the Earth, the top of the bottom, which was incredibly hard to climb to, perhaps even harder to climb to than the absolute top. Cara looked around wildly but the poet just smiled with satisfaction. "We've done it," she said. The devil smiled but also wept, more bothered by his chains than usual.

"Will He take me, too?" he asked pitiably.

"I'm sure He will. He takes everyone with Him."

"Who the hell are we talking about?" Cara asked, then she turned around and saw behind her a svelte, dark skinned man who was smiling at her humbly.

"There you are," the devil said. "Can you get these chains off me?"

"No," Christ said simply, as He said everything simply. "Only you can remove those chains, Lucifer."

"But I don't know how. I've tried so many times..."

"You will learn, especially once you leave hell," then he turned to Cara and put his dark, thin but almost alarmingly steady hand on her shoulder and Cara gasped at the pleasure of being touched by such a man. "You've done beautifully, Cara," he said. "You know in your heart the ultimate lesson of mankind, that in order to rid the world of hell one must take up the habit of mercy, that to rid the world of hell one must actually want it to be gone. You do not want people to receive cruel and unusual punishment, even if they deserve it. You do not even want the devil to be in these chains. That's all I want, that's all I had to teach human beings when I was one of them, when I was stripped of my Godliness and had it returned to me by the barbarism I tried to speak against, which naturally meant I had to become victim to it…"

Cara swallowed heavily. "Will the same thing happen to me?" she asked.

"It might," Jesus said ingenuously.

"You're really him," Cara whispered. "You're really Christ?" He nodded.

"I'm so sorry," Cara said with shaking hands, "I'm so sorry, for what we did to, what we're still doing to you. We're still crucifying you because we still don't understand you. That's what it is to be crucified, to be damned, to be condemned,it is just being misunderstood," she looked to the devil, "even he," she went on, "is just misunderstood."

Christ smiled at her and put his hand on her forehead. "You do understand me then," he said, and Cara felt her whole body shot through with ecstasy at the approbation. "And people like you, you can do it. You can take me and all the other condemned off the crucifix, you can take the whole world that has put itself on a crucifix because it does not understand itself off of it, you can free all the manacled souls in hell. That is what I tried to tell people when I was human, that because I was human too any human being, no matter how feeble they felt, could take up my errand. A few have, but in these times that are just as troubled as any other times, no one has stepped forward yet. That makes these times even more troubled than other times. And the great people, people like you who hide in the darkness until you know you must come out to take up my errand on the Earth and not just in your little room, you are largely ignored. And again, this makes the times more troubled. But do not worry, as I said before, 'this happens every generation…'"

"That's why I'm so tired of it all, because this has happened before and will happen again, what can I do? I make art that is relevant and that's why people hate it. No one makes abstract art anymore, and yet I feel it's applicable now more than ever. People have abandoned the past for their materialistic future and they do not wish to believe the past still applies. And because of that, because of ignoring the past, now almost every art form is dying. And I'm an artist. What am I supposed to do when my craft is so piercingly relevant that people, in their ignorance and their refusal to believe their times, which are supposedly the future, might be fatally flawed, deem it irrelevant just because I didn't create it with the help of a smart phone."

"It will change," Christ said, "this imbecilic, modern *paideuma,* it always does. People don't realize in the future there will probably be no technology at all. But you're right, it is dangerous when people confuse the present for the future, and completely abandon the past. That makes people ignorant, that makes them not only stop looking behind, but looking ahead, because they think everything that could possibly happen has happened already, and they are very wrong. It is sad to me, too, people's obsession with technology, but that's the only way they can feel the planet is making progress, but you're right, in its preponderance it not only leaves no room for artistic, cultural progress, but social progress as well, because the two are irrevocably linked. But we have talked enough. We must get out of here."

\ "Yes," the devil groaned. Christ smiled at him patiently. Then something strange happened. All the inhabitants of hell gathered around. Christ looked at all of them with a sweeping, kindly glance.

"Get on my back," he said. The inhabitants of hell did so, almost greedily, but they had been in hell for a very long time. Cara looked with amazement. He was so small and slender, but he could carry everyone. He even lifted the devil, with all his heavy chains, and also The Poet, who was no small weight on the world either. He turned to Cara. "Get on my back," he repeated.

"I don't know if there's room for me," Cara said, her voice trembling.

Christ gave her His patient smile again. "There's room for the entire world," he said. "it's is just like your back and the backs of so many and yet so few others who have demanded real progress. Come, get on."

Cara did so and was amazed to find there really was room for her. There were so many other human places that were so much more vast that supposedly didn't have room for her, but this slender back… Then they began their ascent out of hell, the ascent out of the descent. It was difficult for Christ. Though He was able to carry the weight, He wasn't able to carry the weight as if it were nothing- it showed on his face, the strain of it, and Cara supposed that was only natural, and that it was the thing that made Him brave, the fact that it was not easy, that the trials of mankind to those who can ameliorate them are still their trials as well, and they still feel them just like everyone else. Though they can lift it, they still feel the weight of all the people who cannot carry themselves but which is one's human and divine duty to carry them when they cannot, to not leave them behind simply because they have lost their strength, which is very easy to do in this world- it almost seems to be encouraged by the barely seen authority that warps people's minds to conformity and to this weakness. Someone has too liberate them, someone has to lift them out of hell when they have been told to not try to make the climb out of it. Cara smiled as they reached the floor that was the top of hell and ripped out of it. The devil cried with joy, and at last hell didn't exist again.

PART 2

Purgatory

"'It is not the liquor that is corrupted, but the vessel,"

Epicurus.

CHAPTER 1

Dachboden

The prisoner woke up in bed. The reveille had went off, it was breakfast time. The prisoner hated the prison but at least there was food. He would have never been a criminal if only there were food. He would have never stolen if only he didn't have to beg and in the midst of his begging there were so few people willing to give. He remembered how they all used to just walk past him, without even looking at him, the whole busy world that had only time to feed themselves, not those who were actually hungry. He lived in prison the same way he did on the streets, not day by day, but minute by minute, hour by hour, being happy for a moment when someone would give him a cigarette or a few dollars, those rare occasions that he had to live for, and the moments when he did get food, he would have to be happy in that moment, he would have to shrug off the thought that was naturally in his mind, and which whispered to him, 'you'll be hungry again tomorrow.' Who wouldn't have turned to crime? Who wouldn't have violently cried to a world that had forgotten them 'I am still here, and I will still leave my mark, and if you will only let me live as a villain, I will be a villain just to live, just so you will remember me again, even if you won't remember me kindly.'

He did petty crime. He robbed a few banks and houses. He had to get a gun to defend himself on the streets, where one could be attacked easily. He did have to hurt a few people. And naturally the longer he stayed on the streets of Dayton, Ohio, the heroin capital of America, the more likely he would use heroin, since he had nothing to live for anyway and the only reason he stayed alive was to spite a world that wanted him dead. The world didn't even want him dead, it didn't even care about him that much to spite him so, it simply just did not care if he did die, and it would be relieved if he did die, because people were taught he was rotting society to the core, when truthfully society was rotting him to the core by proclaiming him an enemy. He knew the real truth. They vilified him to veil their true feelings towards him- the reason they were relieved when he died is because it was one less person to take care of, one less person to feed and to clothe and god forbid to even love. The prisoner didn't understand why they felt this way, because they never fed clothed or loved him anyway. They were the lazy ones. They used their jobs as an excuse to never have to feel compassion, which was just a nuisance to them in their busy day. But the prisoner had all the time in the world, he had ten years that may as well have been eternity- he was punished for being a vagrant and condemned to this maddening, slow second ticking ennui that felt like several lifetimes, and all the wisdom you could learn from it- how to make a shank out of a toothbrush and a razor blade, how to smuggle cigarettes in your ass, how to do dope when the guards weren't looking, how to keep yourself from being raped in the showers- ancient, important wisdom of the most basic human need, survival.

He groaned as he got up, brushed his teeth put on deodorant and then stood outside his cell with his back straight like a soldier and waited for the guard. In many ways prison was more comfortable than freedom, because the prisoner had lived the worst freedom, the most lonely, desperate and ravenous freedom, but he realized that's why it all had happened to him- because he had loved freedom too much to belong anywhere in society. So society had called him anomic, and there was commination at every turn in his life- everything he did was supposedly wrong. So then he did do things that were wrong, just to satisfy society's image of him. We usually end up being what the masses tell us we are. This heartless *volksbildung* has made so many people with no compassion the seat of virtue, and so many people with compassion chandalas, at the very bottom of society, having to wait each day patiently and starving for its dregs, and the few people who notice them scorn them. The attitude in

America is one that is afraid of suffering, so it is banished so no one has to be reminded of it. The attitude in America says any who suffer it is because they deserve to suffer, and that anyone who is successful deserves to be so, even though it is really the other way around. The prisoner was smart enough to know this, and so he was condemned, and long before prison. He had been condemned his whole life, first to that freedom people look upon with scorn, then to prison.

The Al Asqa mosque was full. Al Haifa had convinced his opposition group to make the pilgrimage to the Dome of the Rock, or the Qubbat al sakhrah, in Jerusalem so they could hold a funeral for Abdullah Mahkmed Sarout, a Syrian rebel who was killed in combat a few days ago. People filed into Al Asqa slowly, as Al Haifa sat at the back of the room, staring idly at the inside of the minaret. Many people got down on the ground and prayed, but Al Haifa didn't. It was no secret among his friends. He was actually an atheist. But still he was happy with the turn out. Many people had come, many people had made the hegira to Jerusalem to commemorate Sarout. It had been a heavy loss for Muslims all over the world, especially ones in the middle east who were fighting terrorism just as much as the Americans were. Al Haifa remembered the first time he had seen Sarout on the television. He led one of the very first uprisings against Assad, and he wrote many songs for the revolution. Al Haifa sighed and put his face in his hand. He had never known the man, but it was a heavy loss because it was a loss to the cause.

At last Manuel Sanchez walked in. Al Haifa sighed with relief. "There you are," he said. "Care to go outside for a smoke?"

"Sure," Sanchez said and reached in to give Al Haifa a hug, to which Al Haifa smiled warmly at him and returned the gesture.

"Thank you for coming," Al Haifa said. They went outside, Al Haifa still staring dully at the minaret.

"It's a beautiful mosque," Sanchez said, trying to start conversation.

"They all are," Al Haifa said. "I never believed in Mohammed or Christ or any prophet. I even stopped believing in myself when I became a prophet, but ever since I was a child, the mosque has always been beautiful."

"You sound depressed today."

"Yes, a bit. I've been thinking a lot. You know, men like Ben Yehuda, they have been put in a position of power completely by accident, and so the populace loves them more. You and I, on the other hand, we had to force our way into it, with much resistance from the world, because we were not people, who, by accident, were born into enough power to change the world so casually as most politicians do. We, on the other hand, did not want power and we did not want to change the world as if it were nothing, as if it were our god given right to be known by history, but because we came out of the slime of poverty and anonymity to make a more lasting change, one that was not casual, but meaningful. And we are hated all over the world for it, for not being born into it all, for not acquiring the means to change the world by happy accident, but on purpose, and with a struggle. People hate power but they believe in it. They do not believe in idealism, though, they do not believe in people like us who want to change the world simply because we know it is the right thing to do. We don't think of it as the great privilege of our wealthy, powerful family but as our obligation from having been poor. And that's strange to most of the world now."

"Don't worry about it," Sanchez said tiredly. "Ben Yehuda has the capability of being a good man, but you're right, unlike us he doesn't *have* to be a good man, so yes, his life is easier. I know how you feel Yasser. All I want is equality for all people and because of that I am labelled an extremist. But you, being a revolutionary, and demanding the same thing, you have to be careful. You have to be careful that the people you have lead out of subjugation do not begin to subjugate."

"I know," Al Haifa said with a groan, and dragged with anxiety on his cigarette. "I wonder," he said distantly, "when all is said and done, what is the difference between a revolution and a civil war? I mean, both are an attempt to remove the powers that be, and both end with either new powers or the old regime remaining. I don't know how things are going to change, I only know they have to change, and every second of every day I know I might be the author of an awful tragedy. I never used to care how history remembered me. I don't do this for history, I do this for now, because I know now is the most appropriate time for this to happen. To liberate any group of oppressed people, the only time is every now, and that's a difficult position to be in. because now is naturally fleeting. Now hardly exists. It's such an insecure position, to not be able to know the future, to be stuck in the present and waiting for it to become the distant past, where you will be remembered as a hero or a tyrant. I don't want to be remembered as a tyrant," he scoffed," Hell," he said, "I don't even want to be remembered. It's a terrible burden. But the only time is now and someone has to do it, and it may as well be me because it could be anyone. But still, I have power now, power I had to wrest from the world by force, power I never wanted but knew I must have to set my people free, power I filched with good intentions, and that's exactly where power goes incredibly wrong, when you wield it with good intentions, when you meant to use it as a tool of compassion. Power doesn't like compassion, or to be used for it, so naturally it will corrupt it."

"It'll be ok, Yasser," Sanchez said slowly. "Compassion is the only thing worth fighting for, and our people have been *peculium* for too long…"

"But how can one have any compassion, if one must fight for it? And that's the tragedy of history, that one *must* fight for compassion, but it gets lost in the battle for it because it was a battle."

"I can't tell the future either Yasser. But we're doing what we have to do."

"We're pawns," Al Haifa said stiffly.

"Yes," Sanchez agreed, "but we knew that the moment we started. We're just trying to be pawns for compassion, pawns for mercy…"

"And that's what I'm saying," Al Haifa retorted glumly, "how can we achieve compassion or mercy as pawns?"

Sanchez smiled at him fondly and then cupped his cheek and patted it. "You poor thing," he said. "You should have been a philosopher."

"That's why I make such a terrible revolutionary."

Whatever you do," Sanchez enunciated clearly, "you cannot let your people know you are having such doubt. You are all they have to believe in right now, and if they know you don't believe in yourself, they will plunge into despair as well, and then nothing will get done. It will be just as much of a disaster as a revolution."

"I know," Al Haifa said wearily, "that makes it all the worse, that I must keep my doubt to myself. I don't understand why anyone would want to be a leader, why anyone would want power. Reason lives without it. But politics, the world, is not governed by reason anymore. I just must put on a show of sanity, and become all the more alone."

"You'll be alright. You're a tough man, and you've been through worse. The people who don't even really believe in leadership make the best leader. Our people have been kept as *peculium* too long," he said again. "And we both have a very simple message to teach: everyone deserves to be loved except those who cannot love."

"I don't decide who gets loved and who doesn't," Al Haifa said sternly. "And people who can't love *aren't* loved, they are merely admired for having a so much easier life, they are merely powerful. That's close enough for them."

"Who does decide who is loved and who isn't?"

"Pure chance," Al Haifa said glumly, "in other words, the exclusionary cruelty of man. Nature would have all of us loved, it's we ourselves who prevent it from extending to everyone, as it does naturally."

"And that's what we're fighting."

"That's what we're fighting. But you cannot force anyone to love you."

"No, but you can force them to give you the basic rights of all mankind. That's close enough."

Al Haifa smiled distantly and put out his cigarette. "Thank you, Manuel," he said. "For coming all the way out here. And you have made me feel better. I feel a little guilty. I drag you to Jerusalem and then I pour on you my doubts which are also your own, then force you to ameliorate a sickness that is also yours."

"That's what idealists do," Sanchez said with a smile. "I have to keep my doubts to myself, too, same as you, to 'ameliorate a sickness that is also mine,' as you put it."

Al Haifa smiled and grunted. "My mother, when I was growing up, always thought I was too morose as well. She used to say that I hate positivity, but that's not what it is. I don't hate positivity, I just hate the kind of so called positivity that involves trying to ameliorate everything with clichés. I think it's lazy and it doesn't work."

"I agree," Sanchez said. "You're right, it's not positivity, it's just a way of excluding the lugubrious because they supposedly threaten the optimism that is not really optimism but the act of ignoring all the problem's in the world, of sticking one's head in the sand about anything tragic, no matter how true it is, and shunning anyone who tries to talk about these problems, so, of course, anyone who tires to fix these problems as well, because these 'positive' people would rather pretend they don't exist. You're right. It's lazy and it doesn't work...It's fascinating the way people behave. They meet someone who wants to save the world and they call them a pretentious know it all and a freak. I suppose it's just what they've been taught, and all too readily believed, that the world doesn't need saving, even though it is desperately sick and begging us to stop taking optimism too far, to the point of refusing to look at sorrow."

Al Haifa nodded. "We should go back into the mosque. I know they're expecting me to make a speech. I need to be strong," he said firmly. "For my people, and if not them, for the memory of Abdullah Mahkmed Sarout."

"I'm very sorry," Sanchez said to Al Haifa ingenuously. "I'm very sorry about Sarout."

Al Haifa shrugged his shoulders. "I remember when I was a boy...he was my hero. But no matter. I do not have time to mourn. And anyway, he died for a reason. So few people get to do that."

After the anastasis Cara blacked out for what felt like hours. Finally she began to rouse and groped about in the darkness, as blind as The Poet. She felt with her hand a shoulder blade lying next to hers. "Poet?' she asked.

"Yes, it's me."

"Where are we?" Then suddenly a bright, white light shined in their eyes illuminating sanitized white walls behind them, just a sea of white.

"Welcome to purgatory," a tired, bored and uncompassionate voice said. Cara tried not to blame her. She supposed she was forcibly drained of all her compassion by the job she did just like the people at home. "First we must test you for any diseases, vet you and find you a place to go. You are currently in the new arrivals office," Cara looked around. There were thousands of people there, all pale and drained by the numb bureaucracy that surrounded them. The woman saw Cara look around and nodded to her curtly. "Yes," she said. "This will take hours, perhaps days. There is a doctor over there," Cara looked. The line for him was also incredibly long. "he will examine you and then you will come back here and we will vet you and perhaps give you a new name. Please note, all conversations here may be monitored for your security. Purgatory is the center of the carceral archipelago…"

"Purgatory is part of the carceral archipelago?" Cara asked, alarmed.

"It is the center of it," the woman repeated. "Our great leader needs to know what people are doing at all times. There are terrorists, spies…"

"Did the great leader tell you that?"

"It's a fact."

"Who is this great leader?"

"His name is Juno Moneta. You will be asked, when this process is over, to make a contribution to him…"

"I don't make contributions to tyrants."

"Then you won't get along well in purgatory. I don't have time for this shit. Get in line for your examination," and then the woman walked away.

Cara inched closer to The Poet. "I don't like this," she said, "I don't like this at all."

The Poet shrugged. "Is it really any different than home?"

They did stand in line for hours for the examination. At last when they got to the front of the line the doctor eyes them both curiously. "She is blind?" he asked Cara.

"Yes."

"And you, what's the matter with you? You seem strange. I can tell you're not normal. Are you mentally ill?"

"Yes," Cara said and sighed.

"Are you passive?"

Cara stopped for a moment. "…What?"

"Some mentally ill people are passive. We only let those ones into purgatory. You see mentally ill people can e harder to control than normal people, but the passive ones, they're ok. Perhaps you might even feel more at home here. We actually encourage passivity here. Now, answer the question, are you passive?"

"Yes, very much so."

"And what does that mean?"

"It means I've bitten my tongue so many times it has fallen off, and now I can't speak."

"Very good," the doctor said. "That's what we want. We like our people quiet, we like our people to bite their tongues. Now, you're not an artist are you? Mentally ill people are hard enough to control, let alone mentally ill artists. They've always caused a ruckus in an organized society. Are you an artist?"

"No," Cara lied.

"And not a writer? Writer's cause even more of a fuss. And your friend is blind. That's fine, too. We don't mind blindness…"

"You encourage it," Cara said under her breath.

"What was that?"

"Nothing."

"So you're not a writer?"

"No, I'm not."

"Are you unintelligent?"

"I suppose so."

"That's good. Intelligent people cause problems, too. Intelligent people," he scoffed, "they are never happy with anything. They find something wrong with every mode of human behavior, particularly if they're writers. I do feel sorry for them. Most people are able to survive a society like this by not looking too closely at it. An intelligent person looks closely at everything, and therefore, they can't really live in any society. I mean, they can, but they cannot survive it as well. It tears them down. I hope you are unintelligent for your own sake, even more than our society's sake, because an intelligent person is bad for society, but I think, even more so, society is bad for an intelligent person."

"That's awfully philosophical of you."

"You're right," the doctor said. "I shouldn't be philosophical. Then I will realize how rotten my life actually is, and how awful the job I do is, and how awful the world I live in is. I need to take my own advice. If I suspect to survive this society I can't be philosophical, and I am a human being. All I want to do is survive, even in this world. So I keep quiet, stay out of the way and do my job, just like any other supposed 'good citizen,' and I can't question too much if I hope to survive."

Cara softened a bit. She felt a little bit sorry for the man. She felt sorry for everybody in this world, just like she felt sorry for everyone in hell. "All is well," she said, "I am passive, unintelligent and not an artist, and she's blind. We should be able to get along in your society fine."

"Good," the doctor said, reassured. "Again, I only ask for your own sake," and he lowered is voice to a whisper and bent into Cara's ear, "this place," he said, "is a place where you have to keep your eyes down. This place is somewhere you have to conform to survive in."

"Most places, most *societies,* are like that now," Cara whispered back, and she saw the sadness in the doctor's eyes.

"We can't talk anymore," the doctor said. "I don't have time. No one has time anymore, not here. I have to do your physical examination now, please get undressed behind this curtain, then your friend next."

The doctor finished her examination and The Poet's and they were back I the line they started out in initially. They waited for another two days, with no food, shower or sleep until they at last saw the woman who had seen them initially, who had gotten to go home at some point during these two days, but even she was here in this waiting room for about sixteen hours a day. Cara just watched numbly as people were processed like so much *pecus,* and she felt nostalgic for hell, which happens to people sometimes. Then finally the woman vetted them, which took another six hours. At last they were allowed into purgatory. The woman gave them a huge stack of documentation which she stamped.

"Take these with you wherever you go," she said. "You never know when someone needs to see your papers. I've decided I will let you keep your name, Cara Weisman, and what's her name?" the woman asked, gesturing to The Poet.

"Virginia Woolf," Cara said off the top of her head.

"Like that old author?"

"Yes."

"I might have to change her name. Subjects are only allowed to read what's on the approved reading list, and I don't believe Virginia Woolf is one of them. We'll say she is your sister. Her name will be Virginia Weisman."

"Okay," Cara said, already bedraggled and without will and she hadn't even entered purgatory yet.

"You will both share a small two bedroom apartment in the town of Dachboden…"

Cara recognized the word. "The town of roof floor?" she asked.

"Well," the woman said, "that's basically what purgatory is, a roof floor. It is *le esprit de l'escalier*, it is just barely no longer the bottom of the ladder. Now, welcome to purgatory. You're very lucky you got in. Half these people we send back to hell. Praise the mighty leader, the tycoon, Juno Moneta!"

CHAPTER 2

Olam ha zeh

The starving artists schlepped all her paintings and grabbed her two dollars in quarters she had to scrounge the entire house for as her bus money and got on the bus with a heavy feeling throughout her whole body, throughout her whole soul. She sat at the very back of the bus, in a spot where the fewest people would be, and she grabbed her sketch book out of her heavy back pack and began to draw. She drew because she was hungry, and drawing was one of the few things that could distract her from that hunger. She was just at an art expo and not a single one of her paintings sold. There were so many other paintings in the gallery that probably took a lot less work than hers but which was easy to fool people into believing it was art. One man had sold a taxidermized cat for four hundred dollars. Another person had sold what was simply a desk with a science class skeleton glued to it, six hundred dollars. She had a long series of abstract paintings, all priced humbly at thirty dollars at the most, and none of them had sold. People had barely looked at them. People told her all the time, 'no one makes abstract art anymore. No one *likes* abstract art anymore. You're trying to resurrect a dead art.'

And she knew it was true, but she felt like the death of abstract art had been premature, and she wouldn't have tried to bring it back if modern art wasn't such a bullshit scheme, if it weren't highway robbery that involved fooling people, the opposite of what art was supposed to do- art was not supposed so obscurantist, the starving artist thought, it was supposed to be illuminating, it was supposed to be apodictic truth, it was supposed to be a way to help people understand what was difficult to understand, including the artist who made it. It wasn't supposed to be an act of sophistry that said, 'I know what art is and you don't, so I will dictate to you what art is and you will give me four hundred dollars for a dead cat.' But people love to be deceived, so that was modern art, deceiving the masses that begged to be deceived, giving them what they wanted, instead of forcing them to see the truth, instead of giving them what they did not want but which the artist knew they needed. It was not noble anymore. It had become another staple of capitalism, and it produced alienating and cold art without passion but which made a lot of money by being so irrelevant people thought it meant something.

The starving artist drew on the bus and the growling in her stomach became audible. 'Just wait,' she said to her own body. 'I think I can find enough change to buy a McChicken when we get home.' So she kept drawing to ignore the hunger and her stomach kept roaring rebelliously as she did it, and she kept trying to silence it with her mind, but it was hard to think with this hunger, too. The world had been particularly hard and cruel to her because she was very sensitive and always had been, and the world is lazy- it likes to break things, people, it knows will be easy to break, and it heaps up sufferings on the pair of shoulders not strong enough to carry them until these shoulders do become strong enough to carry them, and then it throws more suffering on the pile. That had been the starving artists life, and it had made her tougher, it had made her braver, but it hadn't made her any less sensitive. She still felt the injustice, the harshness of a world that had forced her deeper and deeper into anonymity until it had felt like she didn't exist anymore. The gnawing hunger was the only thing that let her know she was alive. If she ate she might go back to being dead again. She looked out of the window of the bus. An advertisement came on the speaker, 'get Narcan trained today, you could save a life.' The advertisements on the bus were always like that. It was 'come here for free HIV testing, pregnant and scared? Here are your options. Did you drop out of high school?' and things like that, all the problems of the poverty afflicted in America blasting on the loudspeaker. It was better than most advertisements, though. These advertisements were at least about something real, not about false happiness in rabid consumerism, not about how an ice cream come can change your life and erase all your problems, etc. The starving artist thought for a moment perhaps she would get Narcan trained. She did know a fair number of addicts, they crashed on her couch and some of them would steal her things, others wouldn't, but she appreciated the company, and she couldn't be around regular people. Regular people thought she was scum. She didn't have a 'real job,' and she probably never would. She didn't go to college, because there were as much opportunities being an artist with a degree as being an artist without one, and at least she didn't have all that debt. She sighed as she drew and her stomach howled. She wished she didn't have dreams. Dreams meant poverty, dreams meant isolation, dreams meant being on the bottom of the pile. People who didn't have dreams were so much happier, and yet her dreams were the only thing that made her happy. She had given them up before, and that was even worse. She had a job then, she was still poor but she could afford to eat, and she had never been more miserable in her life. There was no reason to get out of bed anymore- her job, a benumbing and cold factory job, was hardly enough to motivate her, and in fact each day she went in the future seemed dimmer and dimmer, like a candle slowly flickering out, so eventually she had stopped getting out of bed, and she lost her job and she was in this predicament again.

But after she had lost the job eventually the ennui of her depression was no longer tenable. So she started drawing again, and it was like coming back from the dead. 'Get Narcan trained today.' She remembered the time she tried heroin. She never would have if it weren't for that damn job and giving up her dreams. She only did it twice though. It made her vomit for days and feel nothing, which was what she had already felt at the time, so it wasn't that mind altering. It had just made feeling nothing feel a little more natural, like it was what one was supposed to do, that there was no other reasonable way to live. She put the sketchbook away because she still couldn't ignore the hunger. It had gotten too loud. But though this was bad, this gnawing hunger, this chasing after dreams that either ran as fast as flash or were invisible, it was still better than not having dreams, and a struggle like this, particularly one for food, will make you want to live more than anything, and that was all she needed right now, even more than food, just the will to live, just the ability to get out of bed every morning. Even if her dreams meant this struggle would never end, and that these dreams would never become realized, at least they got her out of bed everyday. At least they made her feel again.

It was the Sabbath. Ben Yehuda and his wife were in shul, sitting down patiently and with bemused faces watching the shammes scramble rapidly to get everything together. There was to be a new Rabbi, Ben Yehuda was interested to hear him. The last Rabbi had finally retired after many years, many years of studying Hebrew and the Cabbala and having to be the keeper of the mysteries of a culture so ancient that it was indeed thorough- he felt like no Rabbi, no matter how scholarly, could know it all. The congregants sat patiently and waited. Ben Yehuda sat with Hadassah and gently put his hand on her back. She looked up at him and smiled at him peacefully. For some reason the room seemed to be filled with nervousness. It wasn't surprising. They had the same Rabbi for years…At last the nervousness reached its peak when an asthenic, elderly and short man wearing glasses and a long tallith that seemed to consume his entire frame stepped up to the pulpit and mildly cleared his throat.

"Hello," he said, and everyone looked at him and it seemed he was the only person in the room that *wasn't* nervous, and though he was so small he was a strangely commanding figure. He completely ignored the Torah in front of him. "I'm here today to talk to you about Olam Ha- Ba." he said, and the room was less nervous. This was a topic they were familiar with, every Rabbi discussed it, this was just going to be a normal Shabbos. "Olam Ha- ba," he said, "the world to come, is an Olam Oneg, a world of joy, or at least that is the way we perceive it. We compare it often to Olam ha- zeh, this world, which is an Olam Nega, a world of plague. As you all know, written in Hebrew, Olam Oneg and Olam Nega are written the same. That is because there is not much difference between the two, one can so easily be the other." He stopped here and the room became nervous again. 'Where was he going with this?'

"I submit to you then," the Rabbi went on, "that if Olam Nega and Olam Oneg are the same, Olam Ha- Ba and Olam ha Zeh are the same world, and we do not know, our language is too shrouded in mystery, if this world is a world of joy or a world of plague. This is a grave matter indeed. To not be able to tell if the world you live in is a world of joy or a world of plague is even worse than merely thinking it is a world of plague, especially when it has so much potential for both, making both of these outlooks true. That is a difficult, oner- ous thing for the human mind. To be joyful or to be plagued with misery, either are easy to do, but to possess both at the same time, in one mind, this is the thing that is hardest to bear, that is madness, and madness based on truth, which is the worst form of madness to endure because it is not madness at all- it is a truth that could have been avoided, it's a truth that we lie about because this awful truth is our own doing, crafted by our own blood stained hands." at this he looked directly at Ben Yehuda and gave him a long, searching look. Ben Yehuda squirmed under his gaze, and everyone else in the syna- gogue noticed it, too.

"What if Olam Ha- Ba," the Rabbi went on, "is just the world we leave to our children?" and at this he stared at Ben Yehuda even harder, not in an accusative way, but in a challenging way, as if to say, 'what are you going to do about it. "I think this is the only clear idea of Olam ha- Ba that we can ever have, for we will never know for certain if there is a next world. Science itself has not even be able to determine if there even is another world at all, so let us make Olam Ha- Zeh an Olam Oneg, a world of joy, seeing as we can only ever know upon faith that there is an Olam Ha-Ba, and whether it is joyful or not we can never know either, not while we're alive, and the knowledge we obtain when we're dead can never be shared with those we have left behind to move on, to another world, a better world, or perhaps no world at all, and perhaps these are all the same."

At this everyone reared back in shock. The Rabbi smiled. "I know," he said. "Social *criticism* is never received well, particularly when the aim of social criticism is to charge people to make this world a better place. Olam Ha- Zeh is Olam Ha- Ba!" he said again with a mighty roar, "And if all we can offer it is duality, if we bring joy into it only at the expense of misery and vice versa, we have failed this world, which means we will fail the next world, too, because how would it be different? How can death make us wiser if we never let life make us wiser? What we must do to annihilate this awful, avoidable truth that we alone are responsible for making a reality, is first acknowledge is as truth, but never *accept* it as truth, because in spite of what we're taught, in spite of what the politicians would have us believe," at this again he made a covert look at Ben Yehuda, "it *can* be changed. We Jews are charged by the lord with the task of yet another world, the world called Olam Tikkun, the world restored, and we must do this because the world restored is both Olam Ha- Ba and Olam Ha- Zeh. The world restored is another one, not of a sad, obscure mixture of both joy and plague, but a place where all people take responsibility for the world and make an effort to cure it of its plagues. Alfred Tennyson said, 'it is better to fight for the good than to rail against the ill,' a message that I have tried to take to heart, but it is difficult, sometimes one can't tell the difference between fighting for the good and railing against the ill, particularly in this world of joy and plague that are so mixed together in a great grey area we can hardly tell the difference between the two anymore.

"Olam Tikkun is the ultimate world, it is the world of all worlds, it is much more important than Olam Ha- Ba, and the lord has put us on the quest to find it because it is the Earth's only known purpose, and always will be." As he finished this line he looked once more at Ben Yehuda with his searching gaze, then at last opened the Torah and had the cantor read from it.

Hadassah leaned over to Ben Yehuda. "What was that about?" she asked.

Ben Yehuda lowered his head and shook it doggedly. "It was about so many worlds," he said, "and that all of them need to be on my shoulders for me to do my job right."

The town of roof floor was strange. Dachboden was divided into two opposing sides and forces, the west and the east, just as all the world was divided, the west supposedly being more progressive and more normal, and the East being a great mystery westerners could never understand, with customs that were supposedly backwards, arcane and irrelevant. East Dachboden was a communist state, west Dachboden a capitalist one. And both thought the other side was so different, practically two different worlds carved out of a single city, but truthfully they were not. Both of them were part of economic systems that had taken over the system of government, that had crawled into the state, because so few politicians now realize economic systems and government are supposed to be as separated as church and state. The only difference was that in east Dachboden, the state owned everyone's property, and in west Dachboden every-one's property was owned by the bank, which, because of the extrem-ist lassez faire free market, was pretty much the state.

Both sides thought they were for the ultimate freedom, but really they were just two sides of the same slavery based on radically different ideologies, one another's obverse that was really like a reflec-tion, both were just a reversed, but exact image of each other. And either way, Juno Moneta was the ruler of the two sides- either way he benefitted from it. Either way he got all the money, all the chattel, all the property, because he was a dictator, and so he proclaimed *l'etat c'est moi,* I am the state, and he was the state, and the bank which was the state disguised, so he owned it all, he owned all of Dachboden and its people, he benefitted off of capitalism and communism, of the east and the west, it all belonged to him, both separate ideolo-gies which, nonetheless, carried out their plans similarly, both worlds that were so foreign to each other though they had so much in com-mon- the degradation, the fear and the eye of the surveillance camera staring back at them, trying to look in their thought to see if they'd thought anything against Juno Moneta, and anything against the economic systems he used to control them.

Dachboden was a strange town. Cara swore in this roof floor she could often hear people walking above her- always busy, always in a hurry, walking over her grave, her roof floor, as if it were noth-ing but another thing in the way of the success they were so hungry for and worked so hard for but still came sparingly along with good luck- by degrees, and never enough to justify the workload. But then Cara would look up and she would just see sky, but she swore she heard them, the people on the top of the roof floor trampling all over them.

Cara and The Poet were led to a small, roof leaking two bedroom apartment with cameras all over it. And they were asked to show their papers to the landlord, the local police office, the governor of the town, the maintenance staff of the apartment, the leasing office, etc., etc. The woman at the strange processing center had been right. You did not the ridiculously thick stack of your papers everywhere you go. Cara had to carry them in a large messenger bag, and the weight of carrying it everyday made her shoulders no longer symmetrical, the right one was always sunken in. She got a job at a bookstore. She quickly found that none of the books she liked to read were on the "approved reading list," so she stopped reading completely and at last, like everyone else, just numbly scrolled through Facebook almost all day, not caring that looking at it for so long hurt her neck and her eyes. Everyone in Dachboden was required to have a smartphone. It was obvious why. The smartphones had a tracking device in them, they were part of the carceral archipelago. So was Facebook. Cara knew she was being manipulated by this small device with its mind numbing most popular attraction, Facebook, but there was nothing else to do. She could not read anymore.

The Poet found life in the roof floor hard, too. She got sick almost immediately, and began to wither, which was no surprise, because a society like this needed The Poet to wither in order to maintain itself. But Cara took care of The Poet and consoled herself with the thought that that was why societies like this always eventually do die, because The Poet, no matter how much the times made her wither, never died. She was immortal in spite of the world that was always trying to kill her, to stifle her insolent voice, to not have to be reminded of her existence, to ignore her at all costs, no matter how loud she was… it wouldn't work, because she was immortal, whether the world liked her or not. Nature had made her naturally, and would keep her alive in spite of human beings and their distaste for her, because she was a part of nature, and nature does not allow the things it creates to die. Regrettably, this is why the psychopath is immortal, too, because nature made him to do constant battle with

The Poet, so The Poet will always be necessary. Cara only thought with sad regret that it seemed people were more accepting of the psychopath than The Poet, particularly in this awful modern world and its fatuous zeitgeist, which said it didn't mind dystopia at all, so long as it was technologically advanced Everyone in purgatory, everyone in Dachoboden, whenever one had a complaint, would smile wanly and pat you on the back and say "well, at least it isn't hell!"

Cara was exhausted after having to take care of a Poet that was dying inside her because she was dying in the society she lived in because it had done away with creative impulse. That's how they won people over in a society like this, they said 'let me rule over you completely, and I'll do you a favor. I'll get rid of the artists.' And for an artist to not make art is inimical to their very health and life. Cara noticed it more and more each day. Her wit wasn't as quick as it used to be, she didn't have as much to say, she wasn't nearly as interesting, she got dumber and dumber each moment of the day, and it was a survival mechanism, so she could fit into this society, conform to survive, as the doctor had said. And she was very sad because it seemed people liked her better this way. She wasn't as much of a threat, she wasn't so intimidating, she was just like everyone else who had borrowed all their speech all their words, all their language, from the "appropriate reading list,' from the category of non risqué, benign, inane and acceptable things to say. And the worse it got the more sick The Poet became, and the more sick The Poet became the more sick Cara was, their destinies being so indelibly linked. Cara was ashamed of herself. She had lost the ability to be an artist before she had even been able to create her *capo d' Opera,* the only reason she felt she had been put on Earth. So naturally, with no purpose and nothing meaningful to say anymore after a lifetime devoted solely to saying meaningful things, she became suicidal.

The job at the book store was numbing too. She was there all day almost every day, selling literary tripe to the few people who still read and only read garbage that was made solely for the purpose of entertaining people, not to make them think. Reading books in this world was the equivalent of watching very unartistic film. She had only one other co worker, a man named Kyle who always had a satirical look on his face, a man who was laughing at everything. He was the opposite of Cara, who was always weeping at everything, but the two of them came together because they realized their was not much difference between the two, it was all a tragedy and a joke at the same time, and laughing could be a form of weeping and weeping could be a form of laughing. Either way, she and Kyle were both different. Cara was hardly her usual perspicacious self, but she was still different. She realized she always would be, not matter what she did, no matter how much she conformed in order to survive, she would still always be different, and that was the tragic joke that had been made on her by nature, that she could stare at her smartphone, lose her wit, stop reading- she could do whatever she liked to try to be like anyone else in this world, but still she would be different, still there would be some kind of mark on her face that would demarcate her from the denizens of ordinary society, and also from society itself. She sighed as she thought of this.

She was at the bookstore, doing inventory, while Kyle was lazily sitting at the desk smoking a cigarette 'Men,' Cara thought to herself with disgust, bit she kept working and didn't bother him because besides The Poet, who was diminishing at the same rate as Cara's intellect was, Kyle was her only friend.

"You want a cigarette, Glaukopis?" he asked her dully from the desk. He had started calling her Glaukopis, which was the name of Athena's form as an owl, and was associated with wisdom. Cara liked the name but she didn't feel like it applied to her anymore.

"No time," Cara said tetchily, "there's too much work to be done."

"Why do you care?" Kyle asked.

"Because there's nothing else to do in purgatory except work. You're hardly allowed to think."

"Not so loud," Kyle said sharply. "The cameras."

Cara nodded at him dully and kept shelving books. She and Kyle were intimate, they had sex every now and then, on the rare occasions when they had the energy, and Cara found the mechanical nullity of purgatory was present in fucking now, too. They fucked the same way everyone fucked now, without passion, just to have something to do, just to pretend life was normal because you could still fuck, even with the camera in the room. There was no joy in it- Cara found it hardly different than the monotonous clicking and hum of a typewriter where the writer sitting at it was writing something very formal and constrained, something without imagination, like a manual.

"We're lucky, though," Kyle went on loudly, so the camera's would pick up the sound of him saying something that wasn't subversive at all to cover up Cara's gaffe about thinking. "That we're on the west and not the east."

Cara shrugged at him and he gave her a dangerous look. "Smoke a cigarette," he said again. "Take a break, I'll shelve."

She numbly did as she was told, but she was grateful for the cigarette. She got on her phone. There weren't even any news outlets anymore, all the news now she knew was propaganda, there was nothing but Facebook. This new world had completely banished her from the intellectualism she actually needed in order to survive, because she was a solitary creature, and really the only things you can do in excessive solitude without going insane is learn and create. Cara knew this well, and now she was not allowed to do either, because she was not allowed to learn, and you cannot create without learning. All she had to do with this surfeit of solitude now was scroll Facebook, and so it was no longer solitude but compulsive boredom, which drives all people insane.

Kyle shelves the books ad looked into the camera and said loudly, "Its better than Hell!"

They went back to Cara's apartment and had their mechanical, formal and not only loveless, but not even erotic sex. Kyle got on top of her and thrusted with awkward, spasmodic jerks, while Cara, with eyes wide open stared at the ceiling and tried not to look at him. It took him a long time to finish because this sex was so dispassionate, and Cara moaned occasionally but only out of pity. These days she only even had sex out of pity- pity for herself ad Kyle and all the hapless inhabitants of Dachboden. It was just a means to forget herself. She was forgetting everything recently. She had forgotten her keys, her I.D., and she had forgotten everything she'd learned, she had forgotten her precious *sittenlehre*, her morality, her character, she had forgotten every book she'd ever read. She had even forgotten how to make love. At last Kyle finished, but he did so without gusto, without even pleasure, he was simply taking care of a biological need, as if he had just eaten an unsavory bit of food just to survive, just because there was no other food. He dismounted and rolled over. Cara rolled over in the other direction, not facing him. He looked at her with rage, as if this were her fault, all of this, this world one could live in physically but which debased the soul, a world one could not live in mentally, because she was the closest thing to blame.

"You know, you can do more than just lie there, Glaukopis."

Cara didn't say anything but just shrugged with her back turned to him and pretended to go to sleep, though her eyes were wide open. Kyle grunted with his rage and kicked Cara's nightstand but she still ignored him. He then began to put back on his clothes, all the time inveighing against the woman next to him in his head. He lit a cigarette from the post coital anger rather than pleasure. He looked once more at Cara's back. He knew she was feigning sleep. At last he sighed. He did feel sorry for the girl, and he knew that was the only reason they slept together, because he pitied her and she pitied him, more than they pitied most people in Dachboden, because they were both different, they both had more trouble than most people having to lie to the cameras every day. He softened and put a hand on her shoulder. "It's ok," he said. "it's ok. It's ok," and he just kept repeating it. At last Cara looked up at him with a look of concern.

He sighed again. "I'm leaving."

"Ok."

He finished putting on his clothes and looked into the camera that had just watched him debase himself for pity, not even for love, and he said hollowly, emptily, as emptily as he had made love, "it's better than hell."

CHAPTER 3

The Nebulo

The immigrant sat at his lunch table at the high school and ate alone, watching the mass of white kids all eat with one another happily, make jokes, talk about sex they hadn't even really had, all of them with their clothes picked out so deliberately, many of them with parents that could afford to buy their popularity. The immigrant just felt lucky that his parents hadn't been kicked out of the country. He remembered the border. It didn't use to be quite as bad. Now it was much worse. He kept up with the news. He heard about the children in custody who weren't allowed to touch one another or play. He heard how things like English classes had been cut from them. He heard about how the ICE lost 1,475 migrant children, most of which were lost to the hands of traffickers. He heard about children who had died in custody because they weren't given medical care. And then the worst day, when the ICE, without the permission of congress, raided 2,000 immigrant families with the hopes of deporting them all. He remembered how scared he and his family were that day. His parents were illegal, but DACA, no matter how hard people tried to get rid of it, (the Supreme Court would not let them,) protected him for a little while.

America was perhaps the most difficult country to be from another country in. The immigrant remembered coming here as a child, not realizing the implications of it, because his parents were trying to escape Syria, luckily just before the travel ban. He didn't know he would have to go to America and receive an education that was practically irrelevant to him, and he would have to forget the education that had applied to him. He knew who George Washington was, the mass of white male American parents, but no one around him knew what a Qadi, a fitna or a fatwa were, it didn't matter to them, and it didn't matter much to the American educational system either. No one learned it, and it felt like it was verboten to speak of it, because people were afraid of it, people were afraid of him. He lived in a world now where people thought freedom of speech meant the right to be racist, and yet these were the same people who attacked journalists. And then the people in charge, they wanted him out even more than the kids in school, they tried everything they could to get him out, but the immigrant knew about them, too, with their long history of misprision and defalcation, and even other awful crimes like rape.

Kids at school always joked that he had a bomb in his back pack. This almost made him wish he did, but he knew it was wrong. If only they knew. If only the world realized he had travelled illegally half way around the world to escape men with bombs, because they had tried to drop one on his home. To be anti immigrant was to be racist. And to be an immigrant in the modern world was to always be at the mercy of the powers that be, which wanted to get rid of you- a whole nation he had to run to for protection and it felt this entire nation was hostile to him. He had no home now. His original home was war ravaged and hardly recognizable to him anymore, and his current home was a place where few people felt love or sympathy for him, and rabidly wanted him to go back to the home that had been viciously barrel bombed- these were his two options, stigma or war, so naturally, he had to pick stigma, and America itself resented him for it. And he was just a kid. Why should children have to be at the center of politics? Just because his skin tone was different and he had a heavy accent. That was the other choice, be at the center of politics or be at the center of a long, bloody civil war, and of course he had to pick politics, and of course America resented him for that.

If only they knew that if none of this happened, all of these cosmic accidents he had accidentally been caught in the storm of, if he had never lived in Syria, if he had never had to be an immigrant, he would just be a regular kid. He was a regular kid, but one with worldly experience even most adults (particularly in America) had, so he was forced to be well mature beyond his humble teenage years and so he was alone, because this education, this American culture, its customs and its *paideuma* did not apply to him, the ubiquitous norm did not apply to him. But it had always been like this. Children had always had to suffer at the hands of politics, because war was child blind- it could only see death, not that which it killed. These games of power adults like to play constantly, they couldn't see it was killing their children, either. And often no one cared if a child died if they were foreign. 'In war, they don't think of you as a child,' the immigrant thought, 'they just think of you as another enemy.' And now he was in America, and they thought the same thing, though ideologically, which in some ways was worse, because war was so rapid and so blind it barely had the time to recognize he was a child, but ideology, it could see him as a human being, it just chose not to. So he had to choose between being hated and murdered, and of course he had to choose to be hated, and America hated him more for that.

In this country, where ideologically no on thought of him as a child like any other, he was forced to no longer be a child, just as childhood was about to end anyway, but he did not get to cherish the final days of it, it had ended abruptly when the war came, and he hung on to it as long as he could, but he knew he would have to abandon it eventually and enter the cold, anxious and hostile world of adulthood. But adults were just like teenagers. They were all very cruel to one another. And he was an adult, not only in a teenager's body, but with a different skin tone, a heavy accent and a different religion. He had no hope of ever being accepted here, and he had accepted that, because the choices he had had to make, none of them were really choices. He was an immigrant, a toy in the hands of the political and historical machine, so with every decision he had to make he had no choice, he had to survive on the necessity of harsh reality alone, a harsh reality other people had made for him from their ignorant unkindness. He shook his head, finished his lunch and went to his next class. It's amazing the things some people have to survive.

Al Haifa resumed his position looking at the stars. He didn't have a joint right now, but it was still enjoyable, just the silence of it all. That's what he craved more than anything, silence. That's why he had started his little revolution, in the hopes that one day it could all be silence, no more sounds of gun shots killing protestors, no more bombs, no more disasters. Everyone had always told him it was just a dream, that it could never possibly happen. 'Lazy bastards,' he thought. They wanted it to be impossible so they didn't have to make the effort required to make it a possibility. He remembered something his college professor had always told him. His college professor had always called him a 'nebulo,' which was a Latin word that basic meant a drifter or a ne'er-do-well. It derived from the Latin word nebula, which meant cloud and fog. It meant his head was in the clouds and his mind was in the fog. That's how it appeared to the outside world, but really Al Haifa could see through the fog an image that was all too clear, and it was an image of desperation, hopelessness and fear, it was an image of mankind degraded, and Al Haifa did reside in the fog, in the obscurity of dreams, but it did not mean he could not see what was beyond the fog, and what was at his feet even as his head was in the clouds, it was just he preferred what was beyond these things. But still he looked out of the fog into the real world and he pitied the people who had to live in it- he pitied the people who were not like him, who had no dreams and were so Earth bound they were in a different fog- the fog of having to ignore the cries of the world to do the so basic tasks of paying the bills and getting the food on the table, people who had been made so Earth bound they could not only think solely of the Earth, but specifically their tiny slice of it, people who were so mired in slavery they could never see beyond being a slave. And Al Haifa wanted to liberate these people.

He had argued with that college professor so often. The man would call him a nebulo, and Al Haifa would say he didn't mind being such a thing. Then the professor would riposte back that he would always be adrift and alone, that he was living for nothing, that he could not possibly succeed and make a valuable contribution to society etc. etc. Al Haifa sighed and watched the static stars. He had to meet with the damned War on War people in a few hours. He didn't want to talk to them. He appreciated everyone's interest in politics and the act of making it more humane, but Al Haifa had only become a revolutionary because he had to. These kids chose to be because they thought it made them cool, they thought it made them edgy and informed, and they thought it made them good. If only they knew so few revolutionaries ever came out good, and they, who had chosen it almost out of boredom, out of the ennui of being a young white male American who is oppressed in no way and unconsciously realizes this has made them different from most of the world, and also not a profound as it. So they take up revolution like it is a hobby, and their outrage is so insipid because truthfully they don't know what they're fighting because they've never had to fight it before, they are just thrusting and parlaying at an invisible enemy they cannot even put a name to, like children with fake swords fighting the imaginary.

And Al Haifa could never hope to explain it to them. He knew that. People who haven't been through it, they can never hope to comprehend it. He lit a cigarette and stared more deeply into the stars, as if he were delving into them, as if they had the answer that had thus far eluded humanity, and that's what had invented politics, war and revolution, whatever the hell the difference between the three was. He remembered the college professor. "Most of the world isn't successful," he had told him. "And I have a hard time believing that most of the world are good for nothings like you call me. I have a hard time believing the elite few that have come upon success by accident are the good people of the world..."

"By accident?" the professor had said. "No one gets it by accident, people work..."

"Everyone works," Al Haifa had replied staunchly. "Only few get to see the rewards of this work...by happy mistake. Your sense of moral superiority isn't helping anyone, Professor, so it is not moral."

And then he had walked out of class and dropped out of college. It was the most liberating day of his life. That was the day he realized he was made for so much more than simply buying a house, getting a good job and having a family, the facile system of living college had tried to inculcate in him. It was the day he knew he had a great destiny that only a few people would ever understand, and that's why people called him a nebulo. He had thought of this prospect and realized all that it implied, greatness, but also loneliness, loneliness he would not be able to describe to the masses of human beings who did not wish to understand it and did not wish to empathize with it. But at the time he was young and a fierce idealist, so he didn't care. He didn't care that he would be lonely so long as he had a great destiny, because at the time, when he was nineteen years old, it felt like he could not live without one. He felt he had to have a great destiny otherwise his birth would have been a mistake and an accident and there was no reason for him to be on the Earth at all. Now, at age twenty eight, he still felt the same way, but with less enthusiasm. He knew he *had* to have a great destiny, but now, with age, it was just that- an obligation, another thing fate had chosen for him without asking how he felt about it, another thing just like college. But there were moments when he still carried the burden with pride. Every time a Palestinian told him he had given them hope, every time they won a small victory, because he knew small victories were what made up great victories. Yes, he was destined for something more, so much more than people thought he was because apparently he seemed so wayward and unimpressive, but he was right that day he had decided college wasn't going to help him achieve this great destiny- he *did* have a great destiny, even if this great destiny was just to be a nebulo.

Cara was at the bookstore, mindlessly putting approved literary garbage on the shelves and yearning for a philosophy book as if she were starving and it were a bit of food. Kyle sat at the desk, smoking and looking at his smartphone, as hey both did in shifts. They were both very impecunious, because the book store had so few visitors. Most people did what Cara and Kyle did. Most people read their smart phones, ignoring the tracking device within them, ignoring the fact that their bit of numb entertainment came at the cost of Juno Moneta always knowing where they were. Cara shelved the books and thought about The Poet. She was dying. She had taken her to a doctor and he said she was dying from exhaustion. Cara knew it was true. She was dying from the exhaustion of doing nothing, of slowly rotting away.

Cara knew she had to do something to save her, because if The Poet died she would as well, but there was something else in her, something that had always been in her mind and which the society she now lived in encouraged so much it had resurfaced again, after all the hard work Cara had done to bury it- there was something in her brain that told her to just let it happen, to just let both of them die because they were not relevant anymore and perhaps they never were- perhaps they had just tried to burn an indelible image into mankind and it was nothing but the most fallacious vainglory, and the image would fade no matter what, and now, when they had both lost their gifts, it wouldn't matter if they died, and maybe it never did. So why not just die? They were so miserable anyway, it wouldn't make any difference. It wouldn't be much of a transition from being the walking to dead to being the lying dead.

Kyle snapped her out of her reverie, thankfully, but these thoughts still trailed on after her waking existence, constantly nagging her, never being quiet or allowing her mid to be quiet. Now that she had forgotten how to think, she could only think about die, and she didn't so much want to die as she wanted to stop thinking about it, and if death was the only way she could accomplish that…'Christ,' she thought, 'this is worse than hell,' then she looked around desperately to make sure no one had heard this thought. 'Calm down Cara,' she told herself. 'It's bad here, but no one can read your thoughts, what little of them you have…'

"Your break is in five minutes," Kyle said to her.

She looked at him as if she had not understood him. He looked at her with a single raised eyebrow. "Your break is in five minutes," he said again.

"Oh."

He put down his phone, put his elbows on the desk and looked searchingly at her. "You know, I think you and I would actually be pretty close if it weren't for…"

"Weren't for what?"

"I can't say it. Suffice it to say that love has again come at the wrong place and the wrong time, in an environment where it can't flourish."

Cara shrugged. "I don't know," he said. "I think here it might be more important here than anywhere else. Love when it's a form of rebellion, that's when it's most powerful…"

"Shhh!" Kyle admonished, and lowered his voice. "Don't use the word rebellion. Do you want to get tagged?"

"Honestly," Cara said, without lowering her voice, "I don't care anymore. It can't be any worse than this."

"Than what?"

"Than this!" Cara said and gestured broadly, "this whole world, this routine, this lack of anything to think about, and at the same time too much to think about. It's driving me mad. It's all driving me mad, because we don't even have the freedom to admit we're in hell…"

"Shhh!" Kyle said again, panicked. "What are you doing?"

Cara looked directly into the camera. "This is just hell of another name," she said to it. A red light flashed on the camera.

"You idiot!" Kyle screamed. "You know what that red light means? It means you've been tagged."

"I don't care," Cara said again. "This is the first time I've felt alive in months. I'd rather be dead, Kyle, than go on living like this. It is against every moral fiber in my body, it is against my peace of mind, my will, my sanity…"

"Shut up!"

"It is against everything that really matters to me. The Poet is dying, and she's the only part of myself that has ever mattered."

"What are you talking about?"

"You're wrong, Kyle," she said calmly but Kyle reared back because he swore she had flames in her eyes. "We wouldn't have been close in the real world, because you're a coward," and then she left and slammed the front door behind her. Kyle gasped as the light from the camera went off again. It was illegal to quit your job in Dachboden, all over purgatory. Kyle wanted to run after her, but he didn't want to be tagged as well. He knew it would only be a moment before the police were here. What the hell was wrong with her? She found it hard enough to do her work, (her actual work, not the job at the bookstore,) enough as it was, how was she going to do her work now that she'd been tagged? But then, maybe the work would be more meaningful to her then, if it was forbidden, if it was illegal, if it was not on the "approved reading list."

It wasn't long before the police showed up. They came in swaggering, boasting with their movements of being some of the few people in the country that had power, but Kyle knew they were fools. They were Juno Moneta's puppets, too. He sighed. 'Cara is right,' he thought to himself.

"One of your employees has been tagged," the officer said gruffly.

"Yes, I know. She left. I don't know where she went."

"We'll find her," the officer said with a smile. "But just so you know this bookstore is under extra surveillance now. We'll have to search the place. Do you think she snuck in any books that weren't on the approved reading list?"

"No," Kyle said wearily, "I don't think she knew how to get hold of that."

"Still we need to search the place. Truthfully, she was tagged the first day she came here. We knew the day she came here she was odd, she and her sister. She behaved herself for a little while, but now…"

"She's been tagged this whole time?"

"Yes. Now, I have a team of officer's looking for her, and the ones with me here are going to search your bookstore. And I'll have to ask you a few questions."

"Sure."

The officer made himself comfortable. "You got any coffee?" he asked.

"I'll go get you some," Kyle said, and he went to the break room and made some coffee with his hands shaking violently. "Jesus Christ," he whispered under his breath, but he didn't want to divulge any further in front of the camera that was in the break room. He spilled coffee grounds everywhere and tried to calmly clean them up. "Jesus Christ," he kept saying. "Jesus Christ."

As soon as Cara had left the bookstore someone had stopped her at the door. They both looked ominously at the camera that was hanging down before them. The man had spoken in a harried, rough whisper, his voice sounding as if he had smoked a whole pack of cigarettes by morning then swallowed some nails. He had gently grabbed her by the elbow. "Come with me," he had said.

"Are you the police?"

The man laughed. "Not in the least," he said. "I heard what you said in the bookstore. That was very brave. Here, put this on," and he threw her a cloak and a wig. "It's a disguise. My name is Bernard. I suppose I do have a job similar to the police. I operate the cameras in Dachboden. I have disabled several of them in order for you to get free."

"What?"

"Put on the disguise and I'll lead you the way, the path where the cameras are disabled…Running the cameras isn't my real job… Hurry, girl, put on that disguise! Time is of the essence!"

Cara putt on the disguise. The wig was white so Cara stooped over like an old woman. Bernard had also given her a cane. He smiled at her. "You learn fast."

"So what is your real job?" Cara asked, and Bernard grabbed her around the arm to create the pretense that she was his grandmother and he was helping her get around. People in Dachboden kept their eyes down. No one really noticed many things anymore, they were too busy with their private grief that they could not speak aloud anymore, they were too busy in their heads, the only place they could mourn anymore. 'That's what Dystopia is like,' Bernard thought. 'Either your grief is too private or it is too public, and either way you are alone. That's how they do it, that's how all predators do it, and a tyrant is the predator of an entire nation. The easiest way to control someone, or a group of people, is to make them feel alone, and either way does it, living in a world where you're supposed to scream your grief on Facebook, or in a world where you cannot even tell your close loved ones about it. Both ways make you alone, and when you're alone you're easy to manipulate, rather than be united. That's what they do to individuality, too,' and he looked sideways at Cara, 'anyone who has the balls to say what's wrong with society, society turns them into a madman and a freak, so no one will listen to them. They are made alone for other reasons than why everyone else is made alone, so they are even more alone, because they are individuals, and are not made alone to be controlled, but made alone to go unheard.'

Bernard snapped out of his reverie. "I'm a samizdat publisher," he whispered to Cara.

"You're a samizdat publisher?" Cara asked and suddenly her eyes had lit up for the first time in months.

Bernard smiled down at her already with fondness. "You're a writer, aren't you?" he asked.

Cara looked at him warily. "How did you know?"

He shrugged. "It's easy to tell. You don't look like anyone else, you don't dress like anyone else, you don't sound like anyone else, you must be a writer."

Cara smiled at him in return. "We're almost there, " Bernard said and clutched to her more closely.

"Almost where?"

"Headquarters." He stopped in front of a camera to make sure it was turned off, looked around to make sure no one else was around, and knocked very loudly on the ground. The ground opened up. Cara gasped as Bernard once more asked for her hand. She looked down and there was a spiral staircase going into the ground.

"Come with me," he ordered lightly again, and Cara did as she was bidden. They climbed all the way down the spiral staircase, which had a pretty shaky newel that was hard to hold onto, and when they got to the bottom it seemed they were in a library. Cara looked around, and suddenly her eyes lit up again.

…In this library, there was Dostoyevsky, there was Fichte, there was Tocqueville, there was Wolfe, there was…She gasped for breath and grabbed the end of the shaky newel once more. She was overwhelmed. Bernard looked at her an smiled once again.

"Welcome to the unapproved book list."

CHAPTER 4

Glaukopis

The refugee sat alone in an attic in a very poor neighborhood in Germany. No one in the rest of the house, basically a tenements building with a few languages within its walls, spoke *his* language. He was surrounded by humanity from all sides, they were crashing in through the walls, suffocating his head, but he had nothing to do with them and they had nothing to do with him- all this humanity and him, alone, in the midst of it, and they had not a word to say to each other. He felt as if he lived life constantly in a terrarium, as a foreigner, while people who were also completely foreign to him stared in at him. They didn't know he understood "the Western world," no more than the western world understood him, and Europe was like an alien territory, the only place that let him in but so tiredly, it being a nation that was so history weary from its own crimes it accepted him as an obligation after an irrevocable mistake more than out of genuine pity, and much of the country still hated him, they just knew it wasn't as socially acceptable to hate him out loud now, but he saw the way they looked at him.

And this action of compensation was met with criticism from all over the world. Even the so called liberal politicians spoke against it as something impractical, and not an obligation of humanity. That was the problem with humanity these days, it had shirked its obligations to itself, and left itself unkempt and uncared for, like the refugees it spit on. It was five o clock in the morning. He had been up all night listening to the other tenants fight with words that were mere garbled sounds to him, just as his words were to them. But still he had to get up and work, or he would have to go back to battered Syria, where he had been a rebel because he knew death was better than what history in its unfolding now had to offer him and his people, and which he was still living through, though in a completely different world, a supposedly better world, who thought people from worse worlds were a stigma. He worked for only fifteen cents an hour, and very hard labor. He knew he was a slave, he knew he had jumped between worse and better worlds just to be a slave in both of them. He knew the whole worldwide system of capitalism that didn't even want any country to take him in could still use him for the cheap labor to make surplus value, and that was the price he had to pay for his asylum- political asylum always works that way for the anonymous people, for the people who don't have diplomatic immunity and pale skin.

He rose wearily from the makeshift bed he had barely slept in, with other strangers lying on the floor next to him. He knew he was basically homeless, in more ways than one. Syria was not home any longer, Germany had never been home, and this crowded, should be condemned building was no different than living in a homeless shelter s well. 'God,' he thought to himself, 'to be made homeless three times over.'

His back already ached from the poor night of rest and it cringed at the thought of his hard labor for fifteen cents an hour "job." But if he didn't he would be kicked out of Germany, and then he would be made homeless four times over, with no country at all. All that would be left to him was the lonely Earth. No one wanted that, except the tyranny that had so pitilessly wrenched away all of his homes.

Al Haifa rubbed his temples laboriously and sighed. He had a massive headache. He felt like his skull was finally going to cave in. He sat at the head of a large table and waited, his head in his hand, massaging his temples and drinking a cup of coffee as if it were a glass of water to a man that had been dying of thirst in a desert. The door finally cracked open. 'Good,' he said to himself. 'I'm tired of waiting. I want to get this over with…I feel weak. But I'm not allowed to be weak. Christ, I sometimes wish I was Ben Yehuda.'

The Ohio faction of the War on War group filed into the room raucously. Al Haifa inspected them quietly. None of them looked any older than thirty. 'The youth are getting old,' Al Haifa thought to himself. 'Slowly, but it's happening, and they're hanging on as desperately as they can to something that was never pleasant, not to them either- youth. Youth wasted in poverty and shitty nine to twelve hour a day service jobs that barely paid, in a ruined economy, then in a political crucible, and now they're losing youth, too, and they're trying to salvage it, the only thing they had over a world that had otherwise damned them, and now it's about to be gone, and a new youth will come forward. A new youth will come forward after the last youth wasn't able to leave its mark on civilization. It was not able to produce a great poet, a great politician, a radically discovering scientist. It wasn't able to produce anything, because the world wouldn't let them, their shitty jobs wouldn't let them, their parents wouldn't let them, the housing market wouldn't let them, Facebook and the smartphones they clung to wouldn't let them. The times had always been in a conspiracy against them, hoping they would fail, and they did as the times bid, they failed. And now they are…growing old. I do feel sorry for Americans sometimes.'

Al Haifa sat with his back straight against the chair and had to feign that he wasn't tired or ill, because if he did then history would only ever remember him as tired or ill, The kids sat around the table, many with Supreme hats on smoking American Spirits and all buzzing together in something that *did* have potential, even if the times wouldn't allow it, and Al Haifa realized, they had more than he would ever have, much more than his parents or his country would ever be able to give him, but they also had nothing. Al Haifa did pity them, and his headache began to diminish, and he grew taller in his chair, and he had the at once commanding but gentle presence he had always had but which he was never aware of. That was because it came naturally, because it wasn't an act, it was who he really was, and the War on War group, a group of kids who were now becoming no longer kids, but did not get the spoils of supposed success and security of growing older, were immediately cowed by him but in awe of him at the same time. 'A real revolutionary,' they all thought.

"Thank you for coming," Al Haifa started, and his voice was sweet and dulcet but also firm, intransigent, unbreakable. He was soft but he was strong. This was a good combination. "What would you like me to do for you."

Everyone looked to Manny. Manny fought the urge to roll his eyes but cleared his throat instead and began to speak, but truthfully Al Haifa made him nervous as well.

"We need protection," he said. "The Proud Brethren, they want to kill us."

"I know," Al Haifa said quietly. "And I will protect you, but unfortunately I do have conditions."

"We figured as much," Manny said stand offishly.

Al Haifa smiled at him gently. "I just want you to think a little bit more about what you're doing," he said. "If you keep up this way…you'll be remembered as terrorists."

"There is a point where terrorism is just fighting for liberty…"

"Whose liberty are you fighting for?" Al Haifa asked.

Manny blushed a little and squirmed a little in his chair. "Everyone's liberty," he said.

"You're attacking the wrong people," he said. "Ben Yehuda doesn't have anything to do with taking anyone's liberty, he's just a poor sod who's in the wrong place at the wrong time, just like everyone else, just like you. You think you are fighting for the liberty of all, but really you are fighting nothing. Nothing is the thing you are afraid, complete nullity, the arbitrariness of history. But it is as Manuel Sanchez said. The only way to fight arbitrariness is by not being arbitrary oneself. Cruelty is arbitrary, war is arbitrary, and I know you are warring against it, but this way you have just started another war. Terrorism is not the answer, it is not fighting for liberty, it is just answering violence and prejudice with more violence and prejudice. If I had done any of the things you have done, I would be vilified all over the world. Terrorism is what started the war in the first place. You are only reaping the seeds which you want to stop from growing…"

Manny's blush got deeper. "I didn't come here to be lectured," he said.

Al Haifa sighed. "No, and I did not come here to lecture you. You know, you and I are probably almost the same age. So I shouldn't treat you like a child, but I'm afraid your view of the world is still a bit childish. I've seen revolution, I've seen war, I've seen terrorism, all of them are awful, all of them, including revolution, are usually an insult to humanity. All of them are violent, all of them do not give a damn about innocent lives, they're not pleasant, Manny. But here in Palestine they're unavoidable. But you, you don't have to live like this."

"I have to do *something.*"

"I agree," Al Haifa said gently.. "I think everyone has to do something, and you're right, the people who don't think they need to do anything to redeem history, it is because they are the ones in power, because it is not their liberty that is being stolen. I appreciate your interest into my world, I really do. Not very many white people do have an interest in it. But you're going about it the wrong way. I am happy you want to help me and my people, but as you act currently, you're not."

Manny gaped for words but stopped. He didn't know what to say.

"Terrorism is arbitrary," Al Haifa said again. "It is just as arbitrary as war. Therefore it is war."

Manny glared deeply into the man's eyes. "Yes," he said, "and we are waging war on war, so that is a form of war."

"It is a form of digging yourself into a hole," Al Haifa said pointedly, "by burying yourself further and further into a grave of proliferation proliferating itself. If one makes war on war, then one makes war on war on war, and so you have it neverendingly, you make meta wars, you make wars within wars within yet even greater wars- you turn war only into a macrocosm whose microcosm reflects it."

Manny gaped. He hardly understood what this man was saying. He opened his mouth for a rebuttal but then quickly closed it He grappled to find something to say. "Well don't you hate hatred?" he asked and it came out more like a petulant whine, like the cavil of a child.

"No," Al Haifa said firmly. "I simply love."

"You're a saint."

Al Haifa chuckled lightly. "I'm sorry," he said, "I don't want to make an enemy of you, but I don't really want to be on your side either. However, I will protect you, because I know liberty is full of compromises, so I will compromise my morality a bit and help you, because I know groups like the Proud Brethren are what's destroying your country, but I warn you once again, be careful how you fight your enemy, lest you become your enemy," and with that Al Haifa gave Manny a very grave look, full of gravity and an intense seriousness that made Manny uncomfortable. Then Al Haifa changed the expression in his eyes to one of gentility and smiled at the boy. "I will talk to Sanchez. He will be able to find you protection. I know as soon as the press finds out they're going to hate Manuel and I even more than they already do, but I promised you I would help you in some way. But now, I have to mention my conditions.

"Yes," Manny said wearily and a little impudently. Al Haifa just kept his calm smile on him. "As I've mentioned, I want you to change your entire tactics, I want you to give up terrorism because they are already dying to call me a terrorist, and if I am supporting terrorists, I will feel thy are right. But you are as young as I am. I believe you can redeem yourselves. The other condition, I want you to leave Ben Yehuda alone. Like I said, he's not the problem. Sometimes he contributes to the problem, but he's not the problem…"

"Then what is the problem?"

"Something much greater than ourselves, but also much lesser. Something we foolishly created and now we must destroy without using any methods of destruction, because it *is* destruction, and as you cannot wage war on war, you cannot destroy destruction. You simply have to create something else, something that redounds to your better qualities, your will to build something up, not your will to tear it down, which is truthfully no will at all but a regrettable impulse."

Manny looked at him with a raised eyebrow. 'What the hell is this guy saying?' he thought. 'Is he already gone senile?'

"Why?" Manny said. "Why do we have to leave Ben Yehuda alone?"

Al Haifa sighed. "Because he's my friend," he said weakly. "Is there anything else I can do for you, or is this all?"

Manny glared at him again. "That's all," he said pointedly, and he and the rest of his faction got up to leave. Al Haifa stood up and gave them a half salaam. "Thank you for coming," he said, as though his job was also a service job, and these were customers.

Manny bowed back out of automatic politeness but as soon as he left the building he was enraged. Al Haifa had been one of his heroes, but now that he had met the man he thought he was an asshole, a disappointment because he was much greater than Manny thought.

Cara looked around in wonder. The unapproved book list was home. The Poet was already there sitting on the dirty ground, obviously hungry, poorly dressed and ragged, but being the happiest Cara had seen her in a long time. She didn't even look up from the book to greet Cara, but Cara didn't mind. She was anxious to get her nose in one of these books, too. A great, firm hand clasped her elbow. She looked up and Bernard smiled warmly into her face.

"That's not all that's down here," he said, and then he directed Cara through a door past the library and opened what looked like a small, frowzy office. Cara beamed. There was a typewriter on the desk. She was almost dizzy with happiness, feeling as if some cosmic force she would never hope to understand had delivered to her once more her sole purpose, after many months of it having been robbed her. To live without what you love is a dire thing. It is even easier to live without who you love, because everyone has to do that at some point, due to either separation or death, but to live without *what* you love, that is to live without something that's not supposed to leave you like other people are, and which is supposed to die with you, not before you. It was more faithful than a lover, more permanent than mortality- it was something we often lose throughout the dizziness of life's chaos, but which will always come back to us, so long as we want it to, so long as we do not forget it for much vainer things.

Cara looked at Bernard, eyes moist with inchoate tears. "Can I…"

Bernard smiled at her still warmly. "Of course," he said. "That's why I brought you here. The only condition is you have to let me read it."

Cara swallowed heavily. It had been months since she had written, she was probably garbage now, but it would be worth it just to do it again. She nodded her assent to Bernard's only condition and sat down at the typewriter, at once nervous and exhilarated, as she had been the first time she had sat at one of these impassive and commanding machines. She began to write:

"People think there is strength in evil, and that goodness is only softness, but they are so wrong- it is goodness' softness that makes it so strong. There is strength in softness and gentleness, because it is a fighting of a world that seems to be against it, and often it is not the most natural impulse in human beings. It is so strong because it has to be learned, and because the more soft you become, the harder the world will be on you. And to endure this and to still be soft, to still be gentle, to still posses the naivete that is your goodness, is to have passed the test of time. Bad things happen to good people, but only because they are the thing that makes them good. I believe you should be soft on yourself and soft on the world. If you have no humanity you do not deserve to be part of humanity. You should be soft in your heart but tough in your resolution, for evil, though it can mean power, is weak because power is weak and hollow, it means nothing. Evil is profound weakness, it is a violation of human will and therefore it is a violation of will power in general, because it is easy to will the evil, it takes actual strength to will the good when often all things are against your idealism. All things except truth, nature and reason, the only things worth adhering to. Evil is feeble mindedness, it belongs to people who cannot look too deeply into the hearts of men and see the value within them, though it is covered beneath all the corruption that has been made rife in the world because evil is so easy, because it is so lazy, and often in their imprudence people will to have no will. Evil is ignorance, evil is stupidity. I not only believe that the world can be changed, I believe it *must* be, because if it is not we will only dig deeper and deeper into misery and one day will no longer be able to deluding ourselves into thinking nothing is wrong with it. Evil is weakness, it is avoiding the problems of the world, which,inevitably, makes them all the more potent- ignoring the adversity of evil only makes it stronger. Evil, in the end, comes down to not possessing the strength to know the truth, and the next step that must come after knowing the truth, being able to *change* it, at least those truths that are the lies of evil men and their power, their power to destroy the world. Goodness is the power to save it. It is real power, divine power, not the power that is authoritarian and breeds in wealth, it is a power that breeds in poverty, amongst people who have nothing else but their sense of character, their morality, their softness that the world was unable to take from them…"

At this point Cara trailed off. She swiveled in her chair and looked at Bernard. "It was the best I could do," she said, as if she were making an apology. Bernard picked up the half filled piece of paper and read it. He looked up to her. "It's good," he said. "It could give people hope."

Cara bowed her head bashfully. "Can I tell you something, and will you promise not to call me crazy?"

Bernard's eyebrow lifted with curiosity. "I won't call you crazy," he whispered solemnly, as an oath.

"You found me for a reason," she said. "I do not believe in God, but I do believe in this force in the world which I can never hope to name, which leads people to the people that were destined for the, to the people who can either ruin or rescue them, and either way, for some obscure reason. I do believe there is a strange connection between the living and the dead. I'll give you some examples of what I'm talking about, because I know I'm not being that clear. There is an affinity among all artists, alive and dead, between artists you know personally and artists you've never met. I believe that unwittingly, unknowingly, the people you wish to emulate have a bond with you, and somehow, again unknowingly, can seek you out in times of desperation, even after they have died.

"My examples. One time I was feeling very low and I could not leave the house. I wanted to leave the house because it was becoming like a prison that the longer I stayed in became more prison like, but I could not leave. It took me an hour of severe mental training to finally get up and go out. I had nowhere to go, so I just picked some place. It was a thrift store. I am a big fan of David Bowie, he has inspired much of my art. In that thrift store I found an obscure video tape about him. Amazingly, it was a VHS and at the time, in my poverty, all I had was a VCR. I know this is a coincidence but it must be deeper than that. Another time the same thing happened- I was low and needed to get out. I went back to the same thrift store. There was a book by Tom Wolfe, another artist I admire. The book was called "A Man in Full," one of his lesser known novels, and in it he went into great length about the Stoics, particularly Epictetus. This lead me to read The Art of Living, and The Art of Living was a book I felt sent me on the right path in my life- it told me that wisdom and character takes an entire lifetime to build, that the effort never stops until the day you die, but as you go along you get better and better, wiser and wiser, and one day, though you can never stop building yourself, you still become content with the thing you're building. It taught me that happiness is not what we're told it is- success, renown, etc., it taught me you should actually live without these things because with them comes dissatisfaction, that is striving for a vain thing when really all you should strive for is goodness and the ability to live with yourself, to be content with who you are, though you never stop building them. And after I read that, I wasn't depressed any longer.

"I found these things because I had to, because it was necessary. I won't say they were given to me by god, believe they were given to me by the artists themselves. Again, I'm well aware that David Bowie and Tom Wolfe do not know of my existence and never will, but there is something in them, something that lingers on after death, that does. For lack of a better expression, I'll call it their 'artistic aura.' I think this artistic aura can seek out the artistic aura of other artists, whether one knows them or not, and even if one is living and the other is dead. I think this artistic aura seeks out other artists in pain."

Bernard smiled again and nodded his head almost enthusiastically. 'Why is this man always smiling?' Cara thought to herself, but only because she envied it.

"I don't think that sounds crazy," Bernard said, again with a solemnity that didn't match his smile. "It's funny about Epictetus," he went on. "The man was a slave and a prisoner all his life. He was at the bottom of society, and there were others. Hillel, Socrates, Homer, Jesus Christ. All these men were at the bottom of society. To be frank, they were *bums*. None of them had a Talent to their name, most of them were homeless wanderers, they were all at the very bottom of society, they were fucking *bums*," he said again. "They were at the bottom of society because they rejected society. They had nothing, they were no one, and yet they're some of the most famous men who have ever lived. They were bums, but they started a revolution in thought that history as long as it lives will never forget. And always they appeared in history when there was some war, or people were becoming more corrupt, or it seemed like the end of the world, and they rejected society because society's morals had been lost. They all offset the times they lived in. Without fighting, without really doing anything except thinking, they offset the war, the corruption, and the end of the world. Sure, they did not end the war, but Christ even said he did not come to save the world. They simply offset it. And these men, by doing nothing but thinking, offset it so much that while they could not end the war, they gave us the means to do so. These beggars, wanderers, what today we would call losers, they gave us the truth, and that truth remains on Earth even while they are in the grave, and it is worth fighting for."

Cara looked at him and simply nodded.

"And I can see them alive in you. Remember, geniuses are incredibly flawed human beings. " Bernard said, and looked at her seriously, no longer smiling. Cara became nervous but she nodded again.

Then Bernard relaxed again, smiled again, and took her little bit of writing off the typewriter. "Sign it under an alias," he said, "and we'll publish it."

Cara took the piece of paper and wrote: By Athena Glaukopis, Juno Moneta's sworn enemy, then next to it she drew a little cartoon of an owl with her face on it. She handed the paper to Bernard and he chuckled at it, then walked off with it. The Poet, at last removed from the book she was reading, poked her head in and looked deeply at Cara. Cara looked at her deeply in return. They both smiled. The Poet was not dying anymore.

CHAPTER 5

Ahavah

The Poet sat in her underground lair, reading what she could, trying to learn from the universe what she could. She knew that even though she was eternal, she didn't have very much time, so she was always working, and when she was not working she was not well. She was often alone, she was often misunderstood, and though in her youth she had lamented it terribly, now it was just a fact of life. It didn't bother her anymore. She realized it was her natural state. She knew she was lonely for a cause. She knew she was lonely for justice, peace and truth, all the noble things of mankind. That was why she was so misunderstood, because most people could not bear loneliness or causes- most people could neither live or die for nobility, and The Poet knew she would have to do both, that she lived lonely and misunderstood for a cause, and she would die for this cause, also in a lonely, misunderstood way. But because she was so difficult to comprehend, she would be interpreted for the rest of history. She knew that. That's why death did not frighten her. Death would really be her beginning. After she died, people would understand her.

She used to think that was too late, but now she thought the old cliché, 'better late than never,' and it didn't bother her anymore. But she was not looking forward to death either. She didn't think at all about the future. It was at once too near and too far away to comprehend- it was like a distant, unusual and foreign word, which, at one time, during the peak of one's erudition, one could define clearly, but now when after years and age taking hold and with it the withdrawal of memory, one looked at the word and got a vague presentiment of it, but one didn't know what it meant anymore. The Poet was growing old, and she was growing young. She had always been like that, she had always been old and young at the same time. That's why she knew she would not live long. The world would not let her, because the world had put immortality in her mind, and it could only be claimed with a death that was just as anachronistic as her life. Throughout all time she would exist, and she would always be placed in the wrong time simply for being placed in time. She knew she actually belonged in some distant place outside of it, to that future, to that once familiar word she could not longer define, to her early death and then her immortality.

But she wanted to live for as long as she could, because she knew she also couldn't die too early. All that time when she *was* dying, because she couldn't do her work, and all that time she had *wanted* to die, she did not actually die. The universe would not let her because she hadn't done enough work yet. She would die prematurely but she would also die at exactly the right time, because though she was meant to live forever, she was not meant to be alive forever. She was meant to die when at last she had said all she had to say. At one point she thought this actually would take an eternity, but now she realized that though the universe wanted her to do a lot of work, it didn't want her to work endlessly, though thought was endless, and she really could go on writing until eternity. There was always something to write about, there was always something to say. People don't realize it, but there is and always will be something to say that hasn't been said before. The day when there is nothing left to say will never come. The human race, like The Poet, will die first.

Ben Yehuda walked along the destruction and masses of desperate people wearily, like it were a chore. He felt guilty for it. Al Haifa would take this as a chance to show some humble but immense bravery that Ben Yehuda could not find within himself now. He then sighed inwardly as he thought Al Haifa was growing weary too, that, in spite of his outward humble but immense bravery, he was just like him, and they were both inwardly sighing at their *weltschmerz* because neither of them, both being in such a position where they really had such stake in the world and its future, were not allowed to sigh outwardly. And this having such stake in the world and its future was what had made the *weltschmerz* so strong. How then, could their world have a good future, when even the people who wanted to save it were tired of it. *Especially* the people who wanted to save it were tired of it. The *weltschmerz* was the first step to two different both winding and opposite roads- either eventually to true change, or to hopelessness and defeat. Ben Yehuda and Al Haifa only could hope it would lead to the first road, but Ben Yehuda comforted himself a little bit when he thought, either way, though it often didn't feel like it, it would be a destiny they chose. Ben Yehuda just prayed that they had the strength for the first road.

Tel Aviv had been bombed again. Ben Yehuda, still wearily, recited Tel Aviv's history in his head. Theodor Herzl, the inventor of the Zionist movement, had spoken of Israel as "the Altneuland," the old new world. The translation of this in Hebrew was Tel Aviv. And indeed it was the old new world. It was an ancient land, right in the belly of mankind's first civilization, and still it was always relevant. Ben Yehuda was tired of it being so relevant. Ever since its inception, it had been a crucible of international politics. His people had been expelled from it many times, and they had finally returned to it, but still they were the seat of international politics, even in the new world, in which Israel was still old. And now they wanted to make it the seat of the Holy Government. That made Ben Yehuda sick. The more he thought about it, the more he realized a government should never be deemed the status of holy. That was how the democracy in his country was failing. It was at once too old and too new, and things like that, they are built to last forever, much past the age of life weariness, and yet, also being new, are somewhat callow and inexperienced.

And the damned Holy Government. It had been America's hare brained idea of course. Ben Yehuda realized, America, which was just a new world, the once strongest republic in the world, due to its infancy, was flirting with the idea of a totalitarian regime. You could see it seeping everywhere into their culture. Intelligent people were getting less intelligent, more complacent. Media was becoming more artistic, but only a cabal of people knew this media and many of them were very inclusive and ostentatious about it. For more so called regular people it was hard to gain access to it. But besides that, movies, even ones geared towards intelligent people, were getting more idiotic, art was getting more idiotic, almost everything was aiming towards a mass dilettantism. There was an aggressive culture industry in America geared towards making people uninterested and no longer participating in politics. Ben Yehuda knew what was going on. He was lucky to not yet be alive at the time, but he knew well, he knew more than anyone should have to know, this was the beginning, this was the dipping one's toes in the water, this was the inception of mass political madness, this was how it had started the first time.

He walked amidst the wreckage, trying to console what people he could. He knew this was bad, He knew this meant the Knesset was only going to get more anti Palestinian, and he knew they would go after Al Haifa first. Why did he have to meet with the damned War on War people? That certainly didn't help his image in Israel, but Yehuda supposed Al Haifa didn't care. And he should rest easy. He knew part of the reason Al Haifa had met with them was to protect him. So many insurgents from all sides, so many different terrorists to worry about, and Ben Yehuda certainly disapproved of them, but he felt guilty. He could see why he had made them so angry. But no matter what he did he would make someone angry. That's politics. He wasn't sure why some men liked this power. He was trying everything now to get away from it, and it made him feel like a coward, but it also made him feel sensible. Cowardice, in many ways, was sensible. He scoffed to himself. 'That's why politicians are so pragmatic,' he thought, 'because we are scared. You have to be scared to want the kind of power we have.'

He strolled around aimlessly, looking at the destruction that was so routine here. 'The power,' he thought, 'and the fear, the cowardice, I can't tell the difference between the two anymore. Maybe there is no difference.' At last he grew tired and stopped walking. The press, the Knesset, some diplomats were following him the whole way, trying to reinforce his sensible cowardice, his power, so they could blame him for it later.

"Are you alright sir?" some faceless war congregant asked him.

"I'm fine. I just need rest."

The man simply nodded and walked away. Ben Yehuda grabbed a canteen of water and drank out of it. 'Damned desert,' he thought. 'The old new world, it's a fucking desert, a void, a pilgrimage you make to nowhere.' He drank the water greedily. He put his hand on the smooth rock beneath him and it burned his hand. He inspected it dully. There was a carving in it, some Hebrew letters, he, vav, he, aleph. Ahavah. It was the Hebrew word for love. Ben Yehuda wanted to look at it and laugh at first, but then something stopped him. He had never thought about the word much before. It was deliberately spelled to be only one letter different from the word Yahweh. He looked at it and a chill ran down his spine. It reminded him of what he thought of Al Haifa, that its bravery was humble but immense. It was just placed on a little rock on this earth, but somehow it rose to the highest heights. It rose up and with its humble bravery it was lonely but formidable. It rose up from the humility of its bravery and soared and it escaped the Earth, and the short sightedness of politics and history. It would always survive the bombing.

Cara and The Poet lived in the underground world of the Unapproved Book List for a while. And Cara, at last allowed to think again, read and wrote rabidly, like it were some kind of devotion, and at last her writing got good again. Bernard and the samizdat team published many of her short stories and critical essays, all under the heading of Athena Glaukopis, Juno Moneta's Sworn Enemy, and all with the little drawing of her face on the owl. Cara was shocked how many people were actually reading the samizdat publications. She got very secretive letters from people, people who were reading her writing. Compared to the whole of the population of purgatory and Dachboden, not many people were reading the samizdat publications, but considering that if one were caught with these writings the punishment would be life imprisonment or death, more people were reading them than Cara expected. She was relieved to find that people knew they were being held in mental slavery, and that they would risk their lives to end it, that they, like her, were willing to read in an underground lair just to read.

And the unapproved book list was a much larger organization than she had originally thought as well. Many people came down to this lair, going and coming, reading and writing. And Bernard told her there were actually many lairs, that the unapproved reading list was a network not only all over Dachboden, but all over purgatory. It made Cara sad that people had to risk their lives just to read a decent book, but the fact that people *would* risk their lives to read a book made her quite hopeful. That's how any form of despotism ends, if one is willing to give their life for thought. Cara thought it strange, she had never realized it before, but this she thought now, was what philosophy truly meant- it was a way of teaching people how to die for their principles. That was what she had learned from Socrates, from the Stoics, from Christ, from "the bum revolution," as Bernard called it.

Bernard was working on "The Bum Revolution," a philosophical treatise, while Cara, after a little more training, was at last able to start working on a novel again. But she also published about one critical essay a week. They went by mostly unnoticed at first, but finally they caught people's attention. They had not yet been noticed by Juno Moneta's administration or Juno Moneta himself, and Cara was relieved about that, but she knew it would not last long. She knew if she had the guts to call herself his sworn enemy, one day she would have to be his sworn enemy, and Moneta was not likely to be kind to anyone who threatened his tenuous (more tenuous than he even expected, and he did have a notion that it was tenuous,) power. But it was the truth. She *was* his sworn enemy, and the whole point of the writing was to fight him, so in order to fulfill her duty, her obligation to history, it would, in the end, have to be noticed by Moneta, and she would perhaps have to die for it, as philosophy told her she had to die for philosophy. It was basically dying for free will. That's all Cara wanted for herself was free will, and she realized, the only way she could have free will was if everyone had free will, and that was why she had never been driven towards authority, not for herself or for anyone else. This was why she would not be told how to live but also why she did not tell others how to live. People who thought philosophy was a teaching of how to live, people who thought it was so dogmatic as that, she realized were quite wrong. It was not a teaching of how to live. It was a teaching of how to die.

But these were extreme times, so that was probably why Cara felt that way. Maybe in normal times philosophy was simply a guide to wisdom and thought, but now, in these times, it was something one had to die for. And Cara thought that philosophy, though it was applicable through all times, was especially applicable to a totalitarian regime, that it was especially applicable when it had been outlawed and was no longer a simple matter of thought, but a rebellion. Every totalitarian regime had tried to crush philosophy, it was philosophy's biggest enemy and philosophy was its biggest enemy, they could not possibly exist together, and philosophy would have to win the battle each time, otherwise the world would be lost.

Cara was in a peculiar position now. Now she was in the middle of it, in the crucible. She was at once a philosopher and a revolutionary. She had heard the two don't go well together, that revolutions always ultimately fail because they are based on ideals. This made her sad, because that's how a Dystopia came to be, by getting rid of all ideals first, a process society almost looks forward to, because ideals are a burden, and it always works. Then when you try to fight them with ideals it always fails. But often history has no choice. In a regime like Juno Moneta's, a revolution, no matter how awfully it ends, is inevitable. And Cara only wanted to be a philosopher, but she knew part of being a philosopher was taking up arms against the things that told people not to think. Philosophy would be completely moot if she didn't.

But it was a sad position, and Cara felt it could only end in disaster. That's what history taught her, that through man's self destructive urges to rid themselves of the burden of ideals they create disasters that man only knows how to remedy with another disaster, cataclysm upon cataclysm, death upon death, and this is the foolish way we fought for life, but Cara, and The Poet too, in spite of their supposed genius, could not think of another way to do it either. Cara sat at her typewriter and smoked a cigarette. She was weary, sad and young. She was like most people, She had an optimist and a pessimist within her. The way she was different than most people is that the pessimist in her was much stronger, because, she realized, she had fed it so much more. But she had only done that because it always seemed more in accord with reality, and it broke her heart less. About the former she still didn't know whether she was right or wrong. Both of them, optimism and pessimism, seemed like a hallucination, and realism, whatever that was, seemed like something that the human mind, always dominated by perception, could never hope to understand. So Cara never knew whether to be happy or sad, and that was why she was sad.

Bernard walked lightly into the room. "You working?" he asked.

"Taking a break," Cara said tiredly, and gestured to the cigarette in her hand.

Bernard nodded. "Can I join you?"

Cara nodded in return and Bernard sat down across from her. "What's wrong, Glaukopis?" he asked.

"Nothing."

Bernard laughed and grabbed her by the hand. "You're a terrible liar," he said. "And I'm not going to lie, in spite of your vast intelligence and introversion, you are easy to read."

"Thanks."

"It is a compliment," Bernard said firmly. "It means you're not duplicitous. It means you're honest, so honest in fact I can see the honesty on your face. Now, tell me, what's wrong?"

Cara sighed deeply and dragged on her cigarette. "I don't think this is going to end well," she said.

"No," Bernard agreed, "probably not, but what choice do we have? You know we cannot live the way they want us to live."

"Yes, and we shouldn't have to either. No one should have to live that way, it's just…" but she could not find the words.

"You're not happier after the Unapproved Book List?"

"I'm much happier, but I'm worried. There's a storm coming. I can feel it."

Bernard shrugged. "Well, yes," he said, "there is. We all knew that. That's why we did all of this, because we know a storm is coming and we have to be armed. Any government like this, it is so tenuous. That is one thing I'm thankful for, a republic is so much stronger…"

"But how long is it going to take for us to be a republic again? We're going to overthrow Juno Moneta and his tenuous government and then there won't be enough time, there won't be enough time to build a government as strong as a republic. We'll have to replace it with another tenuous government, and it will be at least one hundred years before we can build a republic again. We'll become Juno Moneta."

"I can never see you being Juno Moneta," Bernard said, trying to sound reassuring.

Cara looked distrait at the block of concrete where there would have been a widow if they weren't underground. "This isn't even my world," she said. "I'm trying to fight for a world that is not mine, and which I don't belong in."

"Well, no one really belongs in purgatory…"

"And aren't we all going to move on anyway? Either back to hell or to heaven?"

"You're the one who said this is only hell of a different name."

"Yes, but I don't want to go back there either. I don't want to be in the afterlife at all. It's just as hollow as real life."

"Well, it was imagined, so it was based on life."

"I just want it to end," Cara said pitifully. "I'm so tired. I'm so tired of saving worlds I don't belong in."

"Well, which world do you belong in?"

"None of them," Cara said seriously, "I belong in a place that does not need redemption because it's nothing, and to me that's what the afterlife should be. Not more politics."

"Well, life was not what it should have been, so why would the afterlife be what it should? Besides, we all have a different idea of what any world should and should not be. None of them can meet all of our expectations, but I think it's agreed that no one enjoys living in purgatory as it currently stands, so it must be changed…"

"It's just a test, Bernard," Cara cried, "to see if we can get into heaven. And what's the point? What is heaven?!"

"Calm down," Bernard said gently. "You think about the future too much…"

"It's hard not to, when it's so daunting."

"The thought of heaven is daunting?"

"Yes, because the things people do to get to heaven…they are certainly things that belong in hell. And I've been through hell and I got out of it. And I did it without religion, without ideology, I did it based only on faith in myself, so I didn't destroy anything on my way out…"

"Really?" Bernard said with a wry smile. "I heard you shut down all of hell. Now it's time to do the same thing to purgatory. It is a long journey, and I know you must be tired…"

"I am. But not because I have to fight. I have always had to fight, that comes naturally. Having the odds, and even at times, the world against me, that is natural to me, that's just the way I was born and I cannot change it. What really makes me so tired is just how lonely it is. What really makes me tired is that I am the only one on my side, and that's the sole reason people call me insane, for being for myself and my own ideas instead of being for something supposedly higher. I am the only one on my side," she said again, "because my side is trying its best to be right, when everyone else and their sides of multiple people find it easier to be wrong. I am trying desperately to grasp and to hold onto the truth that is being buried under the sickness of the masses, the sickness of all these people and their sides that have many numbers in them, it is the sickness of people who belong. It is not a sickness I've ever been allowed to be a part of. I am the only one on my side, therefore I believe my side is reason, and reason in the midst of mass madness, is always deemed madness, because it is not the majority."

"It'll change," Bernard said. "History will remember you and your reason kindly, and the people on the side with many people on it, will be known solely for barbarism."

Cara scoffed. "What does it matter?" she said. "I'll be dead then."

CHAPTER 6

Daimonion

The Philosopher sat quietly at his table. It was a bit of a solitary life, being someone who was more dedicated to thinking than he was to talking- many people did not realize this meant he was genuine, or perhaps they did, and that was what frightened them about him so much. He said his life was solitary, he would never say it was lonely. It was in the past, until he got used to it, until he realized that when you prefer to think than speak, you must spend much time alone, but after awhile it wasn't lonely, once he finally stopped looking at people with their busy lives and their so called happiness and realized it would never be happiness, at least not for him. He liked to think more than he liked to speak, and that meant he had to live differently than most people. He had always wanted to live differently, he knew the prescribed life was not for him, but it was indeed a struggle at first, fighting against all the norms. The norms didn't seem to realize that he was not wishing his life on everyone, just on himself. He didn't care if everyone else felt more comfortable with the prescribed norms- the philosopher even understood that. It certainly was more comfortable, but comfort was not the ultimate goal of his life. In fact, he had to fight it a little bit.

Yes, it had been a lonely life at first, but once someone is given to philosophy for years and the old age sets in, loneliness becomes more and more natural, it becomes more and more real, and then at last it is the comfort he was initially trying to avoid. Now it was just a solitary life, and all the philosopher wanted was truth, and truth is something one must seek alone, particularly in these times, when the masses have abandoned it. All he did was read and write. He knew that one never really stops being a student, particularly someone who is studying philosophy. Philosophy was like so many other subjects that one could study for their whole lives and still not know everything about it. That's what the philosopher liked about it, that it gave him some thing to do for the rest of his life, and because he had chosen to live differently, once the world had left him alone, it gave him the gift of time- he had much more time than someone who lived the life of the prescribed norms, which demanded one stay so busy they didn't notice they were dying rapidly. The philosopher had more time on his hands, and though it meant he noticed death approaching a little more, still death was approaching more slowly.

He had himself, and, in the end, that had to be good enough. The approach to wisdom is long, lonely and can even be agonizing, but to people like the philosopher, nothing else was as fulfilling. All the learning, all the knowledge he hoped like an alchemist to turn into wisdom, like turning air into gold, had made him very depressed at first, particularly when he was young and at that point wise enough to see the world as it was, but still too naive to completely sacrifice his ideas of how he wished it were, but after awhile the more he learned and the older he got the more he became content. He was not happy, he knew too much for that, including the fact that happiness was something illusory, but he was not sad either, and that to him was wisdom, this state of what appears to be indifference but is really acceptance, acceptance of the fact that one can have their ideals, and it is noble to fight and even die for them, but that one cannot conform the world around them, particularly when everyone had different ideals.

So philosophy lead him down the road of accepting which ideals could be fought for, and which were completely lost on the world. He still believed the world could be changed. He would always believe that- he would always believe it was not the world that was refusing to change, but the short sightedness, ignorance and avarice of it inhabitants that was refusing to change. And the hardest thing to change is people. Sometimes the philosopher thought it was actually a sin to try to change people. He simply wanted them to be less self destructive, he simply wanted the to see the potential they were wasting on far less noble things. But he knew not everyone could be like him, and in fact the world was not meant to be like him. He was an antidote, therefore he could only be very sparse, therefore so few other people were like him, but he was an archetype which throughout the ages, though it had dwindled, had endured and remained an integral part of time and its human bred successor history. Some things were still sad though. The philosopher noticed that the more he and his kind became a dying breed, the more philosophers dwindled, the more they were needed. Their antidote was more portent than ever now that it hardly existed. He had always been a dying breed, in spite of his immutable eternity, and now he and his kind were almost extinct. He was desperately holding onto what little remained of himself, his truth and his wisdom and his antidote, in a time where people were relieved to think that at last it was dead, that the people who impertinently shouted to them "think more!" were at last dead, and now there was nothing to make them doubt their comfortable ignorance.

'This is how it happened the last time,' the philosopher thought. 'There is a storm coming, and I don't know how we're going to fight it, when people like me, our voices have at last become completely silenced.'

He sighed. At least he was getting old. Maybe he wouldn't live to see how it ended, but still he thought about the world that is handed down to children once their previous generation has destroyed it, and then children try to fix it, then become adults and destroy it as well. He didn't want this cycle to continue, and yet he didn't want the human race to die either. That was one of the points of philosophy, to preserve the human race, but to preserve it in dignity, in wisdom, truth and antidote, instead of the barbarism it had lead itself to believe was preservation but which was really destroying it.

The Philosopher had himself, and that's all he would ever have. That's all anyone would ever have, so one had to make oneself believable, one had to make oneself true. One had to listen to the Daimonion. So many people didn't. So many people were able to remain false to themselves by completely ignoring themselves, by never listening to themselves, only listening to everyone else, to the prescribed norms the philosopher had tried so hard to get away from. Even in old age, when one accepts loneliness as solitude, and then solitude as wisdom, it did still sometimes hurt. It hurt to be so very different from most people. But he had no choice. It was who he was. He had at once chosen to be like this but was also born this way. He had chosen to live outside of the prescribed norms but something told him destiny also made him do this, that it was a choice he had but no choice to make. And this predestined choice, it was the very essence of free will. That and the ignorance most people chose instead.

Sanchez sat on the ground at the Freedman's cemetery in Washington and stared at some nondescript bit of wall. There was a beautiful sculpture towards the left of him, called The Path of Thorns and Roses, but other than that it was a modest memorial, much more modest than it should have been, because it was, essentially, a potter's field. That's how slavery ended, in a potter's field with a modest memorial. All one gets from a martyrdom like that, a martyrdom they didn't even choose, is a nice sculpture over your mass grave, a melancholy piece of art for a melancholy piece of history, in a solemn place, a place to bury strangers, a place to bury people who were forced by history to be strangers, who were marked by prejudice to come and go into this world unnoticed, and to be commemorated as an anonymous mass- there is a class system even after you die. If you were forced to live as a stranger, as people are only ever forced to be strangers, no one walks into loneliness, (and particularly the facelessness of being another in a multitude of the victims of history, willingly,) you are also forced to die as a stranger. Only the people with the big money get the nice graves.

Sanchez was in D.C. again, hoping once more to talk to the president about the issue of Mexican slavery, so it didn't end like his current surroundings, as a solemn potter's field. But this place was solemn, he liked that about it, and he could feel the strength of the dead that were under the grass on the other side of the memorial- they had become free, against all odds, with their own ingenuity. They had to do what few people in America understood now- they had to *fight* to become educated, just like many Mexican slaves had to do now, while the rest of America treated knowledge like it were something impertinent and irritating, they didn't know the destitution, the degradation of being prohibited it. Sanchez was once a slave, and he remembered it with clarity every day. It had started so called subtly at first, with his parents working well below minimum wage, then their children working for nothing. That was the horror of America now- we were now leaving a worse world, with less opportunity to our children than a better one. The process of time through the generations has reversed, regressed and delineated into this glaringly noticeable entropy that most people deny. And the Earth was getting so much hotter, and Sanchez was waiting for the dead to come out of their unmarked graves.

He walked around a little bit more. There were two placards on the ground, they said "the grave of a child," next to another two placards that said "grave of an adult." Sanchez shook his head wearily. 'There is still a class system after you're dead,' he thought to himself, 'and still a false system of authority we cling to even though it has failed us for thousands of years.' He walked through the gate of the memorial and stood outside and smoked a cigarette. He had to be at the White House in an hour, to speak to the president, to ask him to do what was all too possible but which frightened people so desperately, to end the false system of authority we cling to though it has failed us for thousands of years. The institution of slavery, like any other institution, which is corrupt in its very nature, like any other institution, ruled by the false holy so they can fulfill their wickedness and spread it like a sickness all over the Earth.

He smoked the cigarette slowly, trying to savor every second of it, dreading when he would have to go back to the white house. The president was an asshole, and Sanchez knew he thought of him as a potential threat, so he would never be inclined to be friendly towards him. Many people wanted Sanchez to be the president, and he didn't know how he felt about that. The president had demanded that politics make Sanchez corrupt, and Sanchez knew he would eventually have to meet these demands, the demands of the world, that you conform to its corruption or live a lonely existence, the existence of a stranger. Sometimes Sanchez actually thought this was preferable. Perhaps it was better to have no one except your dignity. The thankless work, the thankless life, the only person who rewards you is yourself, and this is more sincere. This annihilated arrogance and puts self respect in its place, even when no one else respects you, even when you are alone in the world and are a beggar. Sanchez looked warily to the side, to the busy street. There was an old woman staring at him from across the sidewalk. She was in mourning clothes. She walked up to him, grabbed him roughly by the wrists, putting her crone like face as close to his as she could, smiling and revealing a mouth without teeth. She squeezed his wrist with friendliness but also with a strength that crushed Sanchez' hand.

"Go into the house of mourning," she said, "for it is a house of love." And then she evaporated into thin air, just like the rest of the strangers. Sanchez often thought the strangers were better at loving. Maybe a life without love teaches you to love more copiously, maybe one knows the value of it much more when it is denied them. It is like when people in the midst of intense suffering turn their eyes to God. They have never known God's love, they have been deprived of it their whole lives, and that is what taught them to love God. God loves the suffering, and He will make man suffer in order to love them more. Sanchez thought about a life without suffering. It seemed facile and utterly senseless. That was the problem with the other politicians. They did not know how to suffer, so they did not know how to love, and in a position such as theirs, with the world somewhat in their hands, it is the most important position in life to know love and let it guide you. So many philosophers and politicians thought it was supposed to be a job that had nothing to do with love, that was built only on cold, hard logic, but Sanchez thought that was what caused the world's turmoil, the fact that it was controlled by people who had abandoned love for power. But perhaps it is true that you can't have both.

Sanchez looked around rapidly. Ghosts, ghosts everywhere, particularly in this city, where the ever hanging potential, the sword of Damocles that hangs over politics' head, where mass murder can be signed on a bill. Sanchez got in his car. Only a couple of blocks from the White House was K street, a street infamous for underage prostitution, among mostly gay and black teenagers who cannot read or write. Next door to power is always poverty, that's what the power feeds on like a louse. Ghosts, living ghosts everywhere, who were killed by the government as soon as they uttered their first breath. More strangers walking the loneliest street in the center of the world, more people who had loved and suffered, and done both equally, at many times being unable to tell the difference between the two.

It would be a long drive to the white house. Sanchez knew what was waiting for him. The president had already told him he could end Mexican slavery but only at a high price, the price of Sanchez' lonely dignity, his ever alone sense of self respect, as real self respect always is. He didn't know what this awful compromise would be, but Sanchez, after many years of so dangerously mixing politics and idealism, could not be shocked by anything. He knew how low these men could often go. So he drove slowly to the white house with dread. The traffic was murder today, and Sanchez was glad. He was just like everyone else, he just wanted to slow the inevitable, and make a painstaking diversion to death. He looked around him, the big city with its in turn anxiety and isolation, booth of them at the same time. Such a large mass of people, all of them from different parts of the world- different languages, different religions, it was easy to lose oneself in all of them. With so many people, one became alone enough to even become a stranger to oneself. Still, Sanchez couldn't give up this city, with its profusion of diversity, because he could not give up the idea that he could save them all one day. He could not give up this idea because if he did he would want to die. He already did want to die, because the task he had charged himself with, which he felt was in accordance with what God, if He existed, would want him to, was so difficult, and met by resistance everywhere. Power resisted it with all its ersatz might, and even some of the people Sanchez wanted to save resisted it in the habit of weakness.

Sanchez knew only a few things. He knew that superiority is not something that could ever truly exist, nature does not allow it, and that those society likes to tell us are stupid, are usually much smarter than us. It all made him sick, it had always made him sick, it was a disease, and he did not suffer from the disease but the symptom, which was much more lonely. But it was nice sometimes for one to be alone with one's self respect. That was the only natural way to forget the world, and it is also the best way to remember it, to know its suffering and to know its one's duty to alleviate it as well as one can. Sanchez thought he had picked the wrong game with politics, which was a resistance against empathy, but Sanchez had thought it would be the easiest way to help people because it was the position with enough power to make it easier to help people. He still believed this was true, it was just something politicians were happily indifferent to, that which power had made them forget. Sanchez almost envied them. It is easy to envy the people we hate, and the lifestyles that we are so against.

But it didn't matter. Sanchez didn't care what degrading thing they were going to make him do. If corruption were the compromise between politics and progress he would take it. He would do anything to free his people. The only thing he was sad about was that he wondered if he could still be an idealist afterwards. But then again, idealism had only ever made him suffer. He was envious of the people who weren't idealists, the people whose lifestyle he was so staunchly against. Idealism had made him suffer, but the idea of a life without suffering- it sounded facile and senseless, just as senseless as suffering. And yet he wanted to alleviate the suffering of others. He got a strange thought. What if taking away someone's pain is taking away their stake in life? Still, he felt no human should have to suffer more than another human, particularly not based on anything so ridiculous as color or currency. His ideas had existed for untold generations, they would always be a part of the world and life itself, and yet they still were strange to people, they still were unwelcome.

The traffic was moving too fast It always was like that. Time was like an adolescent who was fighting its parent humanity for inventing it, when it knew it was not natural. It was never on the side of man, it works against us. But Sanchez knew, there was no point in trying to delay the inevitable. There was no point in fear. It only made the suffering more acute, adding mental anguish to the physical. He got to the white house much quicker than he wanted to, but he got there and tried to abandon fear, the fear that soon, in order to keep his ideals alive, he would have to kill them. He got in and the president was waiting for him.

"Sanchez," he said with an oily, smarmy smile. "Sit down."

Sanchez nodded and sat.

"I think we have a solution for your little problem, the matter of Mexican slavery, but I tell you, it's not going to be pretty."

"I thought as much."

The president ignored this remark and lit a corpulent cigar, looking the perfect picture of relaxation, the perfect picture of relaxation as everything was going to hell. "We'll have to suspend the writ of habeas corpus to get the bill through that will free the slaves…"

"That's unconstitutional."

"Do you want your people free or not? Trust me, many unconstitutional things have been done for less noble enterprises."

Sanchez swallowed heavily. "Yes," he admitted, "that's true," 'Like the war you started,' Sanchez thought to himself, but knew better than to say it.

"So you'll sign it?"

"*I* have to sign it?"

The president shrugged. "Well, it's your campaign. Sign it and then we can get the bill through the house and senate."

"You just want to tarnish my name," Sanchez whispered under his breath, but the president heard him.

The president laughed. "Yes, a little bit,"" he admitted. "But you know as well as I do that politics is a competition, and however you try to revolutionize it it's not going to change. I do want to tarnish your name, but not so much because I perceive you as a threat. You are a threat, many people see you as a beacon of hope, but I know in the end you'll be too idealistic for the people. In a way, I'm helping you Sanchez. I'm knocking you down from the realm of the Gods back to humankind. And people will be more comfortable with you now. The people don't want a president who's so much smarter than them, and they particularly don't want a president who's more noble than them either. To the people, Sanchez, your idealism is just a passing fad. They will get over it when they realize it's not ancient, practically dead and noxious enough to be generally accepted by a majority, which everyone except lunatics want to be a part of. I so want to tarnish your name, but not because of the election next year. I want to tarnish your name so you won't be so perfect, so you'll be like the rest of us, the majority…You'll thank me in a few years when you're part of this majority and you realize its opposite goes nowhere, that it is just a dream."

Sanchez was seething. "It's not lunacy that makes one wish to not be part of the majority, it's bravery," he spat.

"Only a lunatic would want to be that brave."

Well then, I'm a lunatic."

The president lifted his brows. "So, you're not going to sign it? You're going to leave your people to slavery?"

"I'll sign it!" Sanchez screamed as if in agony, then hung his head and stared listlessly at the ground. The president laughed at him ruthlessly.

"Atta boy," he said. "The bill is being proposed tomorrow, be in congress around eight…"

"You bastard," Sanchez said with his head still hanging, his face red with anger. "Goddamn you," he said with balled up fists, tears coming out of his eyes, "goddamn you and all you people who invidiously think aspirations are delusions."

The president just snorted. "You're doing the right thing, Sanchez," he said in a dead pan, mirthless voice. "You can leave now."

Sanchez gave him one last glowering look, fists still balled up, still shaking. "Are you happy now?" he asked the president. "I've become a whore."

The president laughed raucously, cachinnating without mercy, as if it were all a joke.

Meanwhile, in Dachboden, Kyle had become used to not having Cara in his life. He worried about her constantly, and he could never speak his anxiety. He realized that was what the yoke of tyranny was, when people are no longer allowed to express their madness, and have to keep it locked within, growing more and more mad until the insanity without words eats their heart and they are forced to die without having ever been able to express the thing that very well could have been wisdom, if it had ever been nurtured instead of crushed and repressed inside the barrier of isolation that tyranny delimits between the people and the government.

And he was growing insane. He hired another person to work at the bookstore, and they fucked too and it was even more loveless and degrading than sex with Cara, who he was at least fond of. But there was nothing else to do. There was nothing else to do in this miserable world but fuck miserably in front of a camera with someone you were not allowed to feel a connection with because you were not allowed to feel a connection with anyone in this administration. That was the easiest way to control a person was to isolate them. Any tyrant knew this. That's why tyranny happens so easily, because it is easy to isolate people, especially in masses, which are easy to brainwash: a tyrant can tell them their isolation is simply the right thing to do. Loneliness can at times be the right thing to do, but never isolation, particularly not isolation for the sake of the state, which is necessarily an unholy thing, you are not meant to worship it. Once it bestows on itself the status of a God it is immediately a tyranny.

But Kyle kept eking out this isolated existence because he still hoped to see better days come, and because he was too broken now to even commit suicide. That would be too rebellious. He was scared to be tagged even beyond the grave. So he just kept numbly scrolling through his phone and having loveless, dispassionate sex with people he barely knew, because he barely knew anyone now. He barely even knew himself. Though his biggest fear was of being tagged, he often felt Cara, wherever she was, was happier than him. Perhaps it did pay off to be a rebel.

Failure is the most difficult and best road to success. If you cannot fail, you cannot succeed, because failing is much harder, and can often mean a little more, though both of them mean barely anything. I have no respect for a successful person who has never failed. A successful person who has never failed is merely a result of nepotism. Juvenal said "the most successful people have been exiled a few times," the most successful people are those who are first called an enemy of the people. The enemy of the people is the people's best friend, though they don't know it. The enemy of the people is really the savior of the people, they are just the enemy of the system that has become master of the people, and which, the people think, they cannot extricate themselves from in order to survive. The enemy of the people is always remembered fondly. The enemy of the people saves the people by having the strength not to follow the modus operandi of conformism that people are so afraid to leave behind, and in a totalitarian system such as ours, rationally. An enemy of the people, or, in other words, a savior, does not give a damn about survival, particularly if survival comes at the cost of who they are- particularly if society means being degraded to the most abject conformism, where one can barely think, let alone speak.

I am not the enemy of the people. I am Juno Moneta's sworn enemy, and if the people can no longer tell the difference between themselves and Juno Moneta, thereby thinking because I am the enemy of Juno Moneta I am the enemy of the people, that only proves that I am even more needed, that an enemy of the people is more necessary now than ever, simply because they would be deemed as such, just because a pundit and a demagogue has told people who to hate and fear, so they will not be able to determine who they hate and fear themselves- in other words, so they do not learn the most valuable part of education, to hate and fear him. The effects of fascism in the modern world has been so far reaching. Even many of my friends I considered intelligent fell under its sway, because they could not extricate themselves from social media and its conspiracy theories, so they could not extricate themselves from the means of control, from the propaganda brainwashing, from all the blatant lies that have been strategically placed and festered on the internet. The only reason I wasn't one of them is because I read books, books that told me this could happen again, that it is constantly a possibility, and books which taught me to look for the signs and the symptoms. Basically I studied history and learned from it, instead of passively and hopelessly accepting it as some kind of inevitability. That's the only reason I myself did not fall under the sway of Juno Moneta as well, simply because I read books, and reading books made me strong enough to be an enemy of the people.

I beseech you to follow my lead. Pick up books that have been criminalized. Risk going to jail for it, because this, though dangerous, is also freedom, and there is no point in living without freedom. I'd much rather be executed than not be able to think anymore, because though some peo-

ple wish to be lifted of the burden of thought, they do not realize thought is the essence of freedom, and to live without freedom is to be a walking corpse. That's what Juno Moneta wants for us, and he has simply deluded us into thinking it is our best interest. Because I read books I was able to think. Because I was able to think I was free. Please follow my admittedly humble example. I am well aware no one wants to be me, since I am an enemy of the people, and everyone knows how difficult that life is. It is much easier to vilify me than to join my side, which, for most of my life, has been practically singular. That was what made me free, though. It is true freedom is a lonely road, but there are many things to be feared much more than loneliness. Loneliness, in fact, can be a refuge. It can be a refuge from insanity. It can be a refuge from mass hysteria and absurdity. It can be a refuge from the many things that are to be more feared than loneliness. But must people don't like it because they know it is not a refuge from death. But I would take death over this insanity, this mass hysteria and absurdity. Death is not to be feared. What should be feared in its place is a death like life. That is much worse than just simply death, and that is what Juno Moneta has degraded us to,..

Cara stopped there for a moment and rotated her head around her neck. So few people knew this was actually very hard work.

"Already done?" Bernard asked.

"No, just taking a break."

"Let me read it."

Bernard read the text with his archetypal smile plastered on his face. Cara looked away. It was hard to watch someone read your writing. It is like standing naked before some judging scrutator. But Cara supposed that's why she had become a writer in the first place, to stand naked before a world that wanted to damn her, but which wouldn't be able to because of her honesty.

Bernard looked up at her, still smiling. "You're getting better," he said.

"Thank you."

Bernard put his feet up leisurely on the desk. "Athena Glaukopis," he said teasingly, "enemy of the people."

Cara giggled in spite of herself, and Bernard looked at her sideways.

"You have very grand plans for yourself, don't you?" he said.

"Yes," Cara admitted a bit shyly. "I always have. I couldn't help it. Every time I learned about some great hero or martyr from history I couldn't help but to want to be them. I *have* to be one of them someday, otherwise I'll feel like I didn't live up to my full potential, otherwise this amount of intelligence mixed with rebelliousness that I have been gifted with will be a total waste."

"You will some day," Bernard said assuredly. "You have a flame in you…I've never seen it before."

CHAPTER 7

Erizein

The Patient sat as patiently as she could in the waiting room. Sometimes it only took a matter of minutes, but usually it took hours, and yet if you were fifteen minutes late you had to reschedule. The patient felt as if the doctor's time was valuable and hers wasn't. But it was hard, when so many people were sick. American capitalism had made an industry of making everyone ill- by making unhealthy things so accessible and also the only form of relaxation- they had made an industry of sickness, first by making everyone ill, then by forcing them to pay to be ill. And it was the poor, the people who really could not pay, that were made to pay the most, as they were the ones who were made the most sick. That's how capitalism worked, it made the few rich by making the mass impecunious and in debt for their illness, and the fact that it had seeped so thoroughly into medicine was disturbing- it meant now more than ever one had to pay to live. It meant that capitalism had made an industry of living as well as dying.

The word "patient," comes from the Latin word *patiens*, which means suffering. Capitalism made money out of suffering, and the doctors made money out of waiting. Patience derives from *patiens*, as well. It was the suffering of having to wait, the suffering of slowly having to wait for an expensive death that would be then dumped on their children after death. The patient remembered once when she had seen a funeral procession with a post office vehicle right behind it. It had made her smirk with a cynicism that was not natural to her.

It made her think "I don't care that you have gone into your grave, you still have bills to pay."

The patient was in years worth of medical debt. Her first surgery had been 30, 000 dollars, and now, each visit with the doctor, was ninety, and she had to come once or twice a month. And she was on SSI, which only gave her eight hundred a month. She was drowning in the debt of sickness, the largest debt in America. All so the Kapporeth Health Corporation could become more wealthy. The town of Kapporeth was very poverty stricken, so there were hospitals everywhere, the only mansions in the area, also looking over the ghetto where people had to flock to the hospital so begrudgingly, because they knew it was a glamorous expense they would always owe. The patient's brother was an addict. The heroin problem was particularly bad in Kapporeth as well. They had put her brother in rehab only for two weeks, that was all his insurance could pay. Within only a month he relapsed. Then she saw on the television the story of an addicted celebrity. He got to live in a sober living clinic for two years, and he was clean. The patient remembered thinking with a cynicism that was not natural to her, and which, regrettably, was the truth- she had thought: "You spoiled bastard. You get on drugs because you have the money for them, then you recover because you have the money to be healed as well, while the rest of us get on drugs because we are too poor for anything else, then we cannot afford the healing. We have to die for our addictions instead, then pay the bill for this death."

And she was a drug addict too, but she was made an addict by the doctor. These pain pills, she needed them often, and before she knew it she was just like her brother, as addicted to the only temporary cure as she had been the sickness- the sickness of poverty, the sickness of being sick in order to make an unseen other richer than her family, which being plagued first with poverty, then with plague, could ever dream of being. 'people,' the patient thought to herself. 'They want everything but they still want the right to complain about it. It's only the people who have nothing that are thankful for it.'

Manuel Sanchez woke up blearily on the airplane at the pilot announcing they were going to land soon. Sanchez looked out of the window. He saw a brown, dilapidated Earth beneath him, and a mass of clouds, something which everyone saw something different when they looked at it. And people, in their intense fear of loneliness, would always try to get you to see what they see, but Sanchez knew this was a pointless exercise. You have to hold on, you have to hold onto what you see in the world, whether it be dismal or joyful, and not let anyone else tell you to see it a different way, because we are humans, and that means we cannot help to look at things, and we cannot help to judge the things we look at. It's possible that what everyone sees is wrong, and that was how Sanchez looked at the world, and he staunchly held onto this thing that others called nihilism because this nothingness was all he had of the world, and it was the closest he could get to truth. He knew people wanted him to see something different. He knew they wanted him to see the incredibly vague idea which was all the majority could comfortably agree on, written in clichés written in blood, refusing to see the darkness even as it spread all over the Earth, and condemning anyone that truly knew it. And one does not choose to truly know it. It simply finds some people and takes them under its sway, making it so they have to look at the world a little differently than the vague idea that was presented them all their lives in order to survive. Sanchez knew this well. That was why he would not let anyone take away his nihilism just as much as he would not let people take away his idealism, because it was strange, but they were both related. Each needed the other to survive, and Sanchez needed both of them to survive as well. And people wanted to destroy them equally, because they were taught by their vague idea that they were both a form of rebellion from the vague idea which everyone needed to belong.

The plane landed slowly. Sanchez had been riding in planes for years now but still he never got used to the landing. But there was nothing to fear. Nothing should be feared at all, even nothingness should not be feared. That was all Sanchez knew for sure, this was his worldview that differed from the vague idea because the vague idea was made in the image of fear and all it had taught people to do was fear, especially nothingness. That was the sole reason it was invented. They landed in the town of Kapporeth. A baby was screaming.

Sanchez looked around at Kapporeth. A small town, like any other, with nothing in it, but this was the seat of the health corporation. Sanchez supposed because the area was poor, and there was more sickness to exploit. He breathed heavily, tried to ignore the infant and walked out of the plane.

He was going to meet with the head of the Kapporeth Health Corporation today, to try to end its ban on abortion. He did not have much hope, but he knew he had to do it. There was, at the very least, that writ of mandamus the president had told him about. And as much as Sanchez dreaded it, habeas corpus was suspended, and the bill to free the slaves was going through the house and senate. Some things were going his way, thought the way he had to go about it was inimical to him. He thought of a poem he'd read. Ovid. He couldn't remember the exact quote, but it was something like, "oh the games of love that I hate, but have participated in all of them.' That was how Sanchez felt, that love should not be a game, but politics and the corruption of the world had made it one, and you had to play to win- you had to play a ridiculous, imbecilic game with no rules in order for your love to win, in order to merely express your love, and apply it to the world. That was not what Christ meant. And it disgusted Sanchez, but he had to play, he had to do things that would disgust himself, he had to be disappointed with himself. In this world, he was not allowed to love simply anymore. He had to love as part of a competition now.

He stopped at the airport food court and got some Chinese food, he had the time, and then he left for KHC's main hospital in Kapporeth, to speak to a representative. He was tired and he wondered what sick game they would make him play, what kind of disgusting thing he would have to do just in order to love. When he got there an entire board of representatives were waiting for him. The hospital did not surprise him. It was the only sign of wealth in the entire town, a disgusting amount of wealth, belonging to something that had played the game of love and won. That was the worst part of the game, Sanchez thought, that it is usually won by people who do not love at all, but merely pretend to, while people like him, those who really loved, always lost. That was because he was wise enough to know love was not supposed to be a *kriegspiel,* but no matter how much he hated it, no matter how much he railed against it inwardly, he had to follow the bent of the world, he had to play the part given to him, the part of a lover amongst those who have forgotten love for wealth, having won the game. He was a loser amongst millionaires.

One of the representatives gave him an unctuous, disgusting smile. "Sit down please," she said. Sanchez nodded and sat.

"We are pleased that someone as famous as you, Mr. Sanchez, is interested in our hamlet."

"Well, you are the seat of the Health Corporation, which, lets face it, is the seat of the Holy Government."

The woman's once smarmy face now went stone. Sanchez smiled at her ribaldly and relaxed in his chair.

"What do you want?" the woman asked.

"You know what I want."

"Yes, an end to the ban on abortion."

Sanchez nodded.

"Well, I' sorry but we just can't do that. We have the votes…"

"Actually, you don't. You know your bill, highly unconstitutionally, was only put to vote in a few states, all of them gerrymandered…"

"That's not…"

"And it passed only through the senate, not the house, and yet you still made it law…"

"Well, didn't you sign a bill to suspend the writ of Habeas Corpus?" the woman said bluntly. "Isn't that unconstitutional?"

"I had to do it," Sanchez pleaded, "for my people."

"I'd say none of us is innocent, Mr. Sanchez."

"No, not anymore," Sanchez admitted miserably. "Not since the Holy Government made us flout the laws of this country and live in fear. We are under a totalitarian regime, we are in a dream world where nothing makes sense anymore, and now that the government is holy, law isn't anymore. And you help them."

"You help them too."

"How much do you charge someone without insurance for a surgery? What is the size of the bill you give a man who is just been shot after you save his life?"

"It all depends. We're the wealth in this country, Mr. Sanchez, we do what we have to do."

"You are the oligarchy in this country. You are the capitalists in this country. You are the evil of America."

The woman chuckled and smiled. "We're just keeping up with the times," she said. "I suggest you do the same if you hope to survive."

"You don't merely survive. You make millions off other peoples survival, you tell them they can only survive by paying you."

The woman shrugged. "There are many institutions one has to pay for to survive…"

"No one should have to pay for institutions that are not helping them anymore. No one should have to pay for institutions that are actually exploiting them…"

"We save lives."

"Do you know how many women have died this year from back alley abortions? How many doctors have committed suicide in jail for having to perform them? I'd say you're selective about which lives you save. I say you save some lives and simply forget about others. And the cost it is to have your life saved. So many people can't afford it. You forget about them, too. That is not charity, that is an industry that does charity when the price is right."

The woman chuckled again and Sanchez balled up his fist. "Well, what do you expect from an industry? We don't hide what we are. We call ourselves the Kapporeth Health *Corporation*, after all."

"It is supposed to be charity…"

"Life can't be free, Mr. Sanchez."

"Well, you shouldn't make death just as expensive."

She scoffed at him again and Sanchez glowered. "You're right," she said. "We are the Holy Government, which means we are society. You cannot destroy us. If you destroy us you destroy everything."

"You're destroying lives…"

"We're saving them, it just isn't free. Nothing is free, Mr. Sanchez, not even charity anymore."

"This is not charity," Sanchez shouted, his face a tumescent red. "This is a bureaucratic scam you call life, that you call society."

"We want you to leave, Mr. Sanchez," the woman said. "We are firm in our resolve. We believe abortion is murder."

"I believe you, who let people die in the name of charity, simply for being poor, are murderers. I think it is not only my people that are in corvee, but this entire nation, and it is because of institutions like yours, that cure illness by first creating it, and exploiting poverty by making that as well. " Then Sanchez got up, still shaking, grabbed the table that the woman was sitting out, and threw it over. The woman screamed and just barely ducked out of the way. Then Sanchez did this to every table, he threw the all over and they all looked at him like he was a raving lunatic, his face the still tumescent red, and then he opened the door and looked back at them once more as they were scrambling for their so called order. He shook his head. "There must be a higher authority than the Holy Government," he said, "that can judge bastards like you," and with that he walked out, having castigated the money lenders in the temple.

Kyle woke up wearily. He had to be in the book store in two hours, but he didn't intend to go today. There was a woman lying next to him who he didn't even know. To have a stranger in your bed- at one time it was thrilling, but now it was part of a routine like so many others that was death like, that was a trance one put oneself into to convince oneself that they are alive, and they will not die for a while, but after the first few strangers in the bed, he realized death was everywhere, rolling around in the sheets with them laughing while they were parroting moans, making false sounds of pleasure, and that was the reason both of them were in the bed. Some people find the best way to escape death is to confront it- with booze, with drugs, with sex with some anonymous junky and then waking up the next day faintly and half heartedly worrying if one had contracted a venereal disease from it, but such rational, almost responsible thoughts did not last that long. One could drown them in more booze and more reckless insanity. One could shut them up easily with this lifestyle. That was the only thing that was attractive about it, being able to mute your social conscience.

Kyle got up and poured himself another glass of gin for the hangover. Like so many other people who lived this life, he thought he was being a rebel, but really he was giving up to the very society he was trying to escape by living in its underbelly. Really he was just where Juno Moneta wanted him to be- too cowardly to either live or die, doing neither and doing nothing but only making the most half hearted attempt at suicide and an even more half hearted attempt at living in the midst of this prolonged and feeble suicide. It was not rebellion at all, it was allowing this tyranny to do with his brains what it wanted to do: turn it into simple, atavistic instincts, with all the reasonable, higher thoughts muted by ebriety. Kyle at last got out of bed and stoically wrote a note and put it by his bedside, ignoring the woman who was still sleeping next to it He wrote a note that said simply- 'I cannot do this anymore for one reason: My soul will not leap past my brain.'

Then he set the note on the night stand, grabbed the gun from the drawer, stared as defiantly as he could into the camera, but he knew he still looked weak and he said, "this is hell of a different name," and then shot himself in the head.

I am not the enemy of the people. I am Juno Moneta's sworn enemy, and if the people can no longer tell the difference between themselves and Juno Moneta, thereby thinking because I am the enemy of Juno Moneta I am the enemy of the people, that only proves that I am even more needed, that an enemy of the people is more necessary now than ever, simply because they would be deemed as such, just because a pundit and a demagogue has told people who to hate and fear, so they will not be able to determine who they hate and fear themselves- in other words, so they do not learn the most valuable part of education, to hate and fear him.

Juno Moneta read this with his jaw slowly dropping by turns. "Who the hell is this?!" he demanded. "Who the hell is this 'Athena Glaukopis?'"

"That's what we're trying to figure out, sir," a servile and degraded man said from the corner.

"This obviously hasn't passed through the approved writing center."

"No, sir. We believe there is some kind of Samizdat publisher we didn't know about."

"Samizdat publisher!" Juno Moneta cried with fear. "What is this kladderadatsch? My sworn enemy! Well, if she wants to be my sworn enemy, I will treat her no less than such! Christ, it's happening, the day I knew would come. There's a revolution coming. I do not like this intellectual opportunism. I don't even particularly like intellectuals…To be honest I've always been a bit frightened of them," then Juno Moneta paused, his hand shaking. "What am I saying?" he asked. "I'm the leader of all of purgatory. I am not afraid of anyone," but he did not sound sure of himself at all. It sounded like he was afraid of many things, and that was why he had wanted to become a dictator in the first place. He thought the power would vitiate the fear, but it had actually only heightened it. He had replaced one fear with another. He had become a dictator out of the fear of not having power, and he remained a dictator out of the fear of losing it. Either way, fear actually ruled his life, and that was why he had made the people of purgatory so afraid as well. He had spread his fear across a nation, and this he called leadership. Really it was just an illness he had never been brave enough to endure alone. He wanted the entire world to suffer from it as well.

"Don't worry, sir," the servile and degraded man from the corner said. "This is only a camarilla of outcasts, they certainly don't speak for the entire nation."

"This is how it all starts, though," Juno Moneta said with shaking hands. "These intellectual opportunists!" he spat again. "Why can't they just leave authority alone? They call us bullies, but they're trying to take everything from me! Bastards!" And then he shoved with his right arm everything off the desk. He looked around wildly. His hired hand tried to stay calm. He was frightened of Juno Moneta as much as Juno Moneta was frightened of "intellectual opportunists." But now that the hired hand really looked at the man he had to call sir for all these years, as he saw him shaking with a mixture of anger and fear simply because he had an enemy, the hired hand realized he was actually quite weak. He was actually quite weak, and yet he determined the fate of their entire world. 'Why do we let men like this rule us?' he thought. This weak man had so much power over him. This weak man could ruin his entire life- in fact, his life constantly hung onto a tenuous thread that bent at the caprices and vagaries of this weak man. The hired hand had been taught his whole life that power was strength. That's why he was a hired hand. But now that he had grown older and gotten such a close inside view of power and the world, he realized he was sorely lied to. Power, particularly absolute power, is actually profound weakness. The strong actually have no power at all, not in the traditional sense of the term. The strong actually live on the streets in obscurity and have to fight for their every meal. The strong are the people who are at the mercy of power. The hired hand shook his head sadly. That's what's so fundamentally wrong with this world: the strong are at the mercy of the weak.

"Intellectual opportunists!" Juno Moneta screamed again. "Damn them all!"

"What do you want me to do, sir?"

"Find out who this awful bitch is, and have her killed."

"Yes, sir."

Juno Moneta grabbed his zippo from his pocket and burned Athena Glaukopis' letter. "And anyone else who gets caught reading this letter," he said, "they will be sentenced to execution as well."

"Yes sir."

"You may leave now."

"Yes sir."

And now Juno Moneta was alone, the thing he feared the most. He began shaking again as he grabbed for a cigarette, then called on the intercom another servant to bring him coffee and lunch, just to hear a human voice in this very brief time of being alone, but they always felt interminable. He had always felt, since he was a small child, that if he was left alone for a moment he would be left alone for eternity. He would never let his mother go, he would never let anyone go. That's what a tyrant is, someone that won't let you leave. The woman came and brought him coffee and lunch, because she knew when he said he wanted it he wanted it immediately, a man like this would not wait, particularly when he was bored. He took the victuals from her and grabbed her by the hand, pretending he had the thing he had always been lacking, affection, and that's why he never let anyone leave.

"Oh, Cassandra," he moaned in a falsely plaintive voice. "It is a pity. It is a pity you can't own the world without destroying it."

Echoue

Manny sat staring at his phone screen absently. People were moving around him, stirring, but he had such an easy way out, a way to disengage his attention whenever he wanted to. At least it was just the phone now. It used to be heroin. He missed heroin at times, like all recovering addicts did. He missed the thing that made him not give a damn about politics. He missed the thig that made him not give a damn about the world. But as soon as he had quit the drug he became political again. He had always been like that, but he was like so many other people of his generation- he was political but he never understood politics, and he had not researched it as thoroughly as he should had.. He was meme political, he blasted his politics on Facebook everyday, and that was where he got his news. That was what he was doing right now, trying to seem edgy, relevant and important and up to date in the most cowardly way. He had only ever fancied himself a revolutionary, and he was fortunate enough to live in a world where people do not delve deeply enough into each other than to see people for anything than what they so half heartedly pro-claim they are, so he was a revolutionary. He was lucky there were not too many people around to deeply analyze him, because they, like he, were too absorbed in their telephones, their meme politics, to really care. So Manny said he was a revolutionary and everyone believed him, because they were too lazy for doubt.

He was many things he did not even know he was. He was a Blanquist, which meant he believed revolution should be set up by a cabal of people and unbeknownst to the masses, so he was an oligarch. He was a Lassallean, he believed in impeding so called intellectual opportunists and he believed in a centralized democracy, as if that's not a contradiction, so he was a tyrant too. And he did not even know what aa Blanquist or a Lassallean were. He didn't know his beliefs had already been tested by time and proved wrong. He had learned nothing from history because he had barely studied it, and here he was trying to make it. Here history was, at the mercy and in the hands of the most facile pseudo intellectuals, who, no matter how insane they were, were an easier pill to swallow than the real intellectuals, who by now had been turned into circus freaks and for the radicalism of reading books were made chandalas and had no real stake in the world anymore. And of course the people Manny though he was fighting for, the poverty stricken proletariat, also had no voice in this. It was a *froschmauskrieg*. It was a battle between ersatz intellectuals and idiots. And those were the modern politics of America.

Manny was very selective on who he allowed in The War on War group. It didn't matter their race or sexuality, but they had to be "cool," they had to follow the hijinks of his cold, disengaged pseudo intellectualism. They had to be the cabal of hipsters. They had to have long hair and smoke American Spirits and have Wiz Kahlifa tattoos and not be too passionate about their so called revolution. They had to be blasé and bored. They had to be on their phone all the time. They had to be just like him. Fortunately almost everyone in America was just like him now.

He didn't realize he was his own enemy. He didn't realize he was fighting himself, and that he was not going to win.

Cara sat reading in the library. The day she knew would come had come. Juno Moneta had proclaimed her his enemy as well. Her writings were circulating everywhere, first in Dachboden, but now in all of purgatory. Anyone who was caught with any literature by Athena Glaukopis was to be sentenced to death. Cara was at once flattered and alarmed that people were still reading it. She didn't want anyone to die merely on account of her, but she supposed that this was how it worked, that anyone who was a friend of hers was also Moneta's enemy, and perhaps they had reached the same conclusion she had, that there was no point living without it, without intellectualism and its natural rebellion, which was the first thing to be suppressed when a tyrant came along and was also the first step to ending his tyranny. But often Cara wondered what everyone wondered- she thought, 'I believe I am fighting for the good, but what if I am completely wrong? What is there is no good at all? What if really I am just fighting for nothing, against nothing?' It was a disturbing thought and she had it often. She had the same problem with this thought that she had with many thoughts, 'Is this truth or just my despair?' It was often hard to tell the difference between the two. And what if despair was truth? That was a disturbing thought, too, and what if all these disturbing thoughts were truth? And maybe truth was just like despair. Maybe it was nothing at all. Maybe the search for it was just looking for another abyss within an abyss. What if it was just another escape that lead nowhere? What if it too were a lie? Or perhaps there were no lies, and therefore, no truth. She hoped all these thoughts were seen merely through the bias of despair, and she prayed this bias was not truth.

Bernard snapped her out of her reverie. He noticed the ponderous look on her face. "You alright?" She merely nodded.

"The telecast is ready for you," he said, and he handed her the owl mask she was supposed to wear as they recorded her. They were making broadcasts out of her now, too. So Cara put on the mask, because that's what this revolution was to her- it was her wearing a mask, playing a role that history the great director had assigned to her more than she had assigned to herself, and having to be something she was not sure she was, but which she had merely proclaimed herself to be in a moment of passionate thoughtlessness. 'This is no different than love,' she thought. 'I have to become the hallucination of myself to give people hope.'

She walked into the unapproved book list's makeshift newsroom, sweating underneath the mask, anxious beneath the delusion of herself that was giving people this hope she hoped was not false, but which she herself could not feel. But she had to be strong. She had to be strong for the people. She had to be strong for the mask. The cameras started rolling.

"Good evening, Purgatory," she said through the mask, speaking through a voice masking mechanism as well. Then she got right into it. "The disturbing thing about today's world, about our particular tyranny, and what makes it different from the tyrannies of history, is that it does not produce propaganda, it merely convinces people that *truth* is propaganda. This people were willing to believe all too readily. People want truth to be propaganda and they want propaganda to be truth. This makes everything, especially truth, the hardest thing in the world, simple. That's the appeal of Moneta's particular fascism, that it makes the truth easy. But an easy truth is always a lie, and when the government is built on a lie, that means everything is built on a lie, that means our lives, having become so inextricable from Moneta's politics, that govern everything we do, is a lie. Nothing will make someone more depressed than living a lie, particularly when one realized it, and those who do not realize it are only lying to themselves more, they are only even more comfortably deluding themselves on top of society's comfortable delusions, they are even more lost than those who know.

"Those who know are closer to the truth, therefore they are closer to not living a lie any longer. Antonin Artaud called Van Goh 'the man suicided by society,' and that's what the society Juno Moneta has built on lies is trying to do to us- he is trying to get his insane suicide to suicide us. He is trying to make us live such a lie that we will not be able to live anymore. He is particularly trying to do it to those of us who are different. More regular people are able to live a lie, they almost feel more comfortable doing so, but unusual people, what makes us unusual is we have to find a life that's close to the truth, to the extent that this is possible, and it *is* impossible in the current society, which has made life itself a lie. This is when you know the time you live in is madness, when death seems more truthful than life. I only feel sad that perhaps it has always been that way, throughout time. I do not know if it is just because we have made life a lie and death truth or if it is true, that life is a lie and death is truth. I don't know. I think perhaps neither are either, and that's the truth. See, it is by no means simple.

"And there are incredibly dangerous things we will do not to think about it. We have bartered our freedom from escapism. We knew Juno Moneta would make everything a lie, and we elected him to escape the truth. We helped him build the society that would suicide us, that's what he was to us, he was a means of assisted suicide, all our historical and political destruction is. And while we're doing this, we can lie to ourselves and say that we are living, not that we are simply working on dying, making life far too easy, making truth too simple, giving up. It is a national sickness. I saw it on Earth, too, which is really in the same position as purgatory, and neither are quite different than hell. But they both have the potential to be heaven, so long as we will let it, so long as we don't bog it down in the falsehood of our escapism, our laziness and ignorance which not only abets cruelty, but often even turns into cruelty. We must fight all our impulses of over simplification, because it is an impulse not only to lie, but to be lied to. This is Athena Galukopis, Juno Moneta's sworn enemy. Good night."

The cameras turned off and Cara batted away the microphone that was dangling in front of her face. The cameraman, a man named Steve, went up to her. "Cara," he whispered in her ear, "what the hell was that about?"

"If you didn't understand it I don't want to waste both our time explaining it to you."

"*No one* is going to understand that."

"I disagree. It won't be many, but then again, not many are risking their lives watching our program."

"Well, lets not push away the few followers we have by being just as strange as those who hate us say we are."

Cara took off her mask and flung it unceremoniously on the floor. "Is this just a broadcast to you?!" she cried. "Is all you care about our number of viewers?"

"Well, what the hell is the point of broadcast if you have no viewers?"

"We'll have the ones we need. The people who don't understand what I just said, they will not understand our cause at all."

Steve simply shook his head, lost for words, and walked away with an irascible heave from his chest. As he was walking away The Poet came up to Cara.

"That was good," she said. "You're becoming more and more like me everyday."

"That explains why I become more alone everyday."

The Poet smiled at her patiently. "You know what Ibsen said, 'The strongest man in the world is the one who stands the most alone.'"

"No one wants to be that strong."

"No," The Poet said, "they don't. but you are. It was like everything else. It was just something that happened to you…"

"I had no choice in the matter…"

"Well, like you said, no one chooses to be that strong, or to be that alone. That is what experience has done to you, but it means only one thing- that you have learned from it."

Cara hung her head. "You," she whispered under her breath, "I am becoming more like you, each day stronger and more alone. All I've learned from you, Poet, is the art of having no discipline over my thoughts."

"You have your creativity," The Poet said patiently, "that I gave to you. That is how you discipline your thoughts. I know how it is. When you're not writing you have no control over them. But that's just part of the process. You drown in thoughts all day until it is time to sit and write them down and then you still cannot trammel them, but you can organize them. But still you need the chaos for the order."

Cara looked at The Poet ingenuously. "Did I sound like a raving lunatic?" she asked.

"No. Not to me."

"And are you the only person I sound sane to?"

"Perhaps."

"So I only sound sane to myself. This writing, it is just talking to myself."

"And by talking to yourself you have made a dialogue to the world. Don't worry so much. You were good. It doesn't matter if

Steve liked it or not. By standing on your own the way you do, well, that's the best way to get people on your side one day…"

"You mean after I'm dead?"

The Poet sighed. "Yes," she said. "Do you know why you stand so alone? Because you are the future, and because you are the future, you are history. You are too far behind and ahead to keep up with the world. You will be forgotten initially so you can be remembered again, just like the future, and just like history. Both have to fight for their existence the same way you do. We all have to fight in order to become a memory, in order that we can still exist after we cease to exist. And the best way to do it is to stand alone. Whatever stands alone is hard to ignore. People think the masses are hard to ignore, but an individual is even harder to ignore, particularly by history, which many people don't realize, is a manifesto of the individual just as much as the masses…"

"I don't want history to be my manifesto."

"I don't think you have any choice. Particularly if the future is your manifesto."

"Why do they have to be the same?" Cara asked pitiably..

The Poet shrugged. "Because, in the end, all of time is history. In the end, all of time is a memory."

"A memory of war, slavery and genocide…"

"And also a memory of you and all the people like you, who fought to put an end to such things. Also the memory of individuals, who, by looking to the future, tried to ameliorate history. You are in doubt now, but you will be proud of yourself one day. You will find that the seemingly dubious truth that you fought for, really is truth, or the closest a human being can get to it, and you will die peacefully, having left the memory of history's future."

Cara tried not to roll her eyes. She didn't believe a word of it. How could someone like her, be someone like that? But she supposed what she had supposed almost her entire life, as soon as she found out she was unusual: "If no one else is going to do it, I might as well."

CHAPTER 9

Al Isra

Al Haifa sat down in his somewhat squalid kitchen and read by the dim light. He was thumbing through a few pages of the surahs, the passages of the Quran. He did not believe in any God and he never would, but he admittedly found religious texts soothing at times. They were well written, after all. It was people who had ruined God, not God who had ruined people. All these wars, including the one Al Haifa was in, all amounted to the same thing- "my culture is better than years. My God is better than yours." And Al Haifa felt all cultures, all worship, had failed the God that was there idol and which they had used as the vision of their supposed supremacy, what they used as the driving force of imperialism. They all thought God meant one thing- to take over the world, to rule people. They all thought it meant that to have a God meant you had to be a God. Al Haifa didn't have a God, and so he felt no need for power. And so the whole world looked upon him as a loser whose revolution would be short lived and would fade into the background with the general noise of war, of people trying to spread their God all over the Earth.

Christianity often made Al Haifa sad. Christianity had started out as such an underdog, and then it became the imperial religion of the world. It had destroyed paganism just to become a pagan. This monotheism, this act of having only one God, it only made people feel as if there should be one culture, too, that everything should fall under the ubiquity of Americanism and its God. It had won. It had taken over the world. Al Haifa was happy to have no God because it meant he did not have to rule the world, something that had never been enticing to him, perhaps because he had never believed what he was told to believe. He did not want to take over the world, he wanted the opposite. He wanted thee world to be as it naturally was—without these facile rulers who were never profound enough to realize they were ruling nothing, and when at times they got the faintest inkling of this truth, they would pull on the reins even harder, they would choke the nothingness they ruled over with an even more iron grip, and force nothingness even more into submission, but Al Haifa knew it was all an illusion. The world is nothing and nothing is free. Nothing cannot be anything except free. That's the thing people mourn so much. That's the reason they had invented God, and under His aegis, tyranny.

This was what Al Haifa was trying to fight. He did not want to rule the world, instead he wanted the world to be in its natural state, unrulable. But he supposed it already was. It was not the world these people ruled, it was its people, which they had to settle for in the world's absence. *That's* what Al Haifa was fighting against. He was fighting against so many shortsighted people who, when they had heard about God, wanted to imitate Him. They did not know they were mocking Him, and if God did exist, he could not be a tyrant such as them, because He or She or It, whatever God was, if there were a God, had made the Earth and the universe that engulfs it nothing, and nothing is always free. So the world is free, without a real ruler, and therefore, probably, without a God. That was Al Haifa's logic. Something that had been created this free could have only created itself. And while he was fighting for its freedom it felt like so many more people were fighting against it, trying to escape it, and using God as the holy excuse for this cowardice, for this fear of the unrulable.

In spite of Al Haifa's lack of religion, he had never been a rakehell like everyone had expected him to be. Still they did not find him moral, because his morality was different than theirs. His morality depended more, as Shakespeare said, on the quality of mercy rather than justice. His morality didn't involve uniting the most deeply at someone else's exile. His morality came from within himself, instead of the nebulous, abstract realm of a sky people didn't understand,

and an incredibly simplified version of creation. So he was an outcast for prescribing to his own morality instead of the *de rigeure* morality borrowed from a book people did not understand, written about a God they did not understand, and calling themselves moral because they didn't understand morality, and this ignorance was supposedly just. Just, not merciful, so Al Haifa could never subscribe to it.

He scrolled numbly through the surahs. He got to Al Isra, the night, Muhammed's long night at the Dome of the Rock. This was something Al Haifa could understand. He supposed every prophet at some point had to face an Al Isra, a very long night, full of delusions and temptations, full of the loneliness of someone who is different trying to make the hard decision between remaining human and leaving the world. Prophets are not immaculate, as history stupidly remembers them. They all face the night, the incredibly long night, a metaphor for the dark depression each potentially god like person experiences when they are not sure if they truly want to be god like. Al Haifa didn't think of himself as a prophet, particularly when he had no religion, but he understood Al Isra. His whole life had been like a long night. His whole life had been spent in a dark corridor looking for the dimmest candle so he could make sense of it all, trying at once to leave temptation but also to remain human, and then realizing that is an impossible task, that one day he would have to be more than human if he expected to still walk this world but no longer be of it. But Al Haifa always wondered, you go through this long night, perhaps for years, and what happens after it? He knew the Quran was wrong, that it did not end in divinity, so what did it end in? What happens when it's over? Do you just go along with your life, halfway enlightened but still with the touch of darkness inside your soul, trying to pretend you did not see what man is not supposed to see, trying to still fit in with other humans who are blessed enough in their lack of curiosity never to know this night, and just go on with the unusualness of knowledge, alone in the light you had fought so hard for?

He sighed and put the Quran down. He supposed that was what it was like, until you stumble and fall completely by chance and wind up in another Al Isra, and repeat the whole process over again.

All of this until death. Regular people are spared this. He supposed that was why he had been alone all this time. It was terribly hard to meet someone when you didn't belong to anything. He didn't even belong to the long night. And he knew a sad fact about love- well, it wasn't so much about love, it was about the human inadequacy that always fails love: he knew that when you truly suffer with somebody, it is easy to separate. The closest thing to blame is who you have suffered with. That was what he had learned from love, that he was a blind benighted idiot and he was alone in the long night, that he could not take someone else to be in it with him. That would be too ruthless, and Al Haifa wasn't like that.

But it was a strange thing. After all the long nights Al Haifa had been through, and even how strange it had made him in the so called real world, he was a man, who, by necessity, moved on so quickly it often didn't even feel like it happened. His long night, though still in memory, barely existed to him, because it was a memory that was one hundred years old, belonging in a different world, and happened to someone who wasn't even him. He felt like his long night was at a time when he was not born yet. It was something he read in a book or saw in a film. It was almost someone else's memory, accidentally placed in his head. It had happened in a dream like state, so one day Al Haifa was able to write it off as only a dream. He wished only that he didn't feel the same about the world of the living he returned to. But that's what trauma does. It makes you a stranger to both existence and non existence. It makes you believe in neither. But, at the very least, the one merciful thing about it is that eventually you become a stranger to it, just as much of a stranger as you are to the regular ennui and routine of life once you are lucky enough to return to it. It was hard to be a stranger to almost everything, but it was good to be only half acquainted with the past. Al Haifa even felt he didn't have a past at all. He was here for every little moment, and he, being at last solemnly resigned to reality, gave them a fond farewell as they left, then forgot about them, waiting for the next moment.

Cara sat in her makeshift bedroom and avoided the typewriter like it was the devil. She had been writing so much, she was exhausted. Her little anonymous pamphlets had turned out to be very popular, in spite of her supposedly strange broadcast. Steve had calmed down, everyone had calmed down, But Cara was tired. She was tired of living underground. She wanted to see the sun again, but she knew the sun meant exposure and death. Bernard knocked quietly on her door, and she wearily answered it.

"What's going on, Glaukopis?"

"Just taking a break."

Bernard smiled at her once more ad sat down. "No, I didn't meant that. What's going on with you?"

Cara lit a cigarette and put her feet up on the desk, trying to be relaxed. "You know," she said. "There never has been a single revolution I believed in."

Bernard chuckled and tried to relax as well. "The only revolution I've ever believed in was the bum revolution…"

"And you made that one up."

"No I didn't. It's history, like every other revolution was bound to be. That's the sad thing about revolutions, they're unforgettable but they rarely work in the end." He scoffed. "They're just like a bad love affair. The only revolution that really took hold was the Industrial Revolution, which abetted capitalism and damn near reverted us back to slavery." He sighed. "I often feel like the world is more pliant to corruption than idealism. Idealism it fights tooth and nail."

"You don't think the bum revolution was effective?"

He shrugged. "I don't know. But I believe in a lot of things that haven't been effective *yet*. I'm still looking towards the future."

I am trying to, but sometimes I feel like if we continue on the road we're on, there won't be much of a future left."

"That's *why* I look to the future. That's why I'm a dreamer. That's why I'm an idealist. I will attempt to cure the sickness, but if I can't, the least I can do is not suffer from it." He paused for a moment. "Do you believe in Christ?"

"Sometimes. Do you?"

"Well, no matter what I think of religion, he was a big proponent of the bum revolution. At the very least, I believe in His message, and I believe in what He died for."

"What did He die for?"

Bernard smiled. "The same thing He lived for- love. That's the only thing worth both living and dying for."

The bum sat at the bus stop, his hands shaking violently as he picked a cigarette butt off the ground. He had been a homeless man in Kapporeth for a very long time- he thought he had seen everything, but he had never seen this. He heard about it on the news almost every other newscast, bit he never thought it would literally happen in his home, but he considered this for a moment and realized the Earth was his home, so it *had* been happening in his home all this time, but this time it was directly in his back yard, if only he had a back yard. Kapporeth had a lot of historical districts because it was an old place and it was proud of how old it was, more than it would be of any progress it made, which, due to its age, people hoped it would be immune to. One of the historical districts was called the Olorisha District. It was a place that the bum had panhandled in often, including tonight. But tonight it had been the site of a mass shooting.

The bum could hear the gunshots echoing in his skull and there was nothing else in his head. He could hear the screams, the terror, and besides that his head was empty, it had been drained by the loud sounds of a desperate and screaming tragedy. Only a few months ago Kapporeth was the site of a KKK rally, one which the local government had spent six million dollars on. The bum shook his head with ponderous sorrow that made his head feel heavy even when it was empty of everything but screams. Kapporeth could no longer be so proud to be old.

It was strange. Life seemed to be at a standstill, but it was still going on. The Earth was still turning blindly because it didn't know how to do anything else. A small speaker was at the bum's head at the bus stop and it played a slow tune. The bum listened to the tune, hoping it would drown out these sounds in his head, but the song was too soft and too sad and too beautiful. Its soft plea was not loud enough over the sounds of bullets and bombs. No one could hear it over all that noise. But the bum could hear it. The bum could hear it and he felt all the profuse love in his soul surge up so painfully, in agony of his body, and in sorrow of having been so failed.

The bum walked across the street from the bus stop to the record store adjacent to it. He got the bottle of black spray paint he kept in his knapsack and wrote in crude graffiti on the wall, "My city is dead."

CHAPTER 10

Vates

Gershom Ben Yehuda sat and watched the television with horror in his eyes and was grateful for a moment that he was not an American politician. There was the shooting in Kapporeth, then one in Texas. The shooting in Texas was motivated by anti immigrant sentiments, as most of the domestic terrorists attacks in America had been that year. And what was more horrifying, the president told everyone, and made many people believed him, that it had nothing to do with white supremacy, but was the fault of the mentally ill. Ben Yehuda's jaw was slack with the numb shock of it. Another scapegoat of history. As if the mentally ill didn't barely have a voice in America as it was, now all their voice would be crushed out, grinded down to nothing, them supposedly being the fault of mass terror in the country. The president, by saying it was a problem with mental illness, had completely diverted people from realizing it was white supremacists. And Ben Yehuda realized, people who believed that, it was because secretly in their heart they were white supremacists. And so many people believed it.

"America has gone insane," Ben Yehuda said aloud to no one through gritted teeth. He knew it had happened before, many times in history, but still Ben Yehuda was not sure how it was possible, how so many seemingly good, nice people could bend to hysteria like that, how so many regular, functioning members of society could swallow down propaganda so easily like it was but a small placebo pill, how people could just parrot such an awful opinion because a man in power had said it and for some reason it was easier for them to believe than the truth. The president just manipulated people's hate, and used it to distract them from the truth- he was so popular because he gave the people what they wanted: he gave them an excuse, he told them it was alright, fair, even reasonable, to despise the unusual. He allowed them to hate freely what they had always hated secretly. He told them their irrational fears were all justified. And in this way he had a choke hold on America, poisoning it with its own once more clandestine unreason, as if he were extricating all the bile in our hearts and using it to dissolve the world into one large, propaganda swallowing, truth despising idiot who was glad to abandon facts for the joy of being told their inner cruelty was just.

Ben Yehuda just didn't understand how this happened. He didn't understand why evil had such a more enticing sway on people than good, simply because evil allowed them to remain ignorant. He knew what the Sefir Yetzirah had said, that evil exists for the sake of free will, but only human beings can be evil, because only human beings have free will. It was a dangerous and sad thought, but he thought perhaps, if evil was part of the bargain, and people's free will tend to bend towards it because then they could shirk it, free will, and thereby, human beings, should have never existed.

'What is wrong with us?' Ben Yehuda thought. 'We blame insanity so we can continue to be insane. Of all the things we've made, the only good one was art. We're idiots. We're cruel and stupid, both out of a cowardly need to belong at all costs, certainly at the cost of convictions. We're monsters.' He hung his head and turned the television off, not wanting to hear anymore. It was sad to him how easily people became brainwashed, how they almost waited for it readily in hopes it would lead them to believe in something without having to go through the pain of believing in something. But Ben Yehuda supposed it was hard, when throughout all time evil had used the same rhetoric as good. Still, he was sad. This was a confusing and overwhelming time. All of the revolutionary artists were growing old and dying, and no revolutionary artists from the younger generation were taking their place. That was because the world today demanded that one not have time for art. The world demanded today of the younger generation that they work in a minimum wage service job for the rest of their lives, fifty hours a week and simply come home to the television and the social media websites, too drained to do anything else but to, at the end of the day, drain all their intelligence and talent into mindlessness.

Ben Yehuda hoped there was someone out there who wasn't living that way. He had envied America for years, but not anymore. They were destroying themselves almost in mockery of their once prosperity, and now using their ease, their comfort that much of the world would probably never know, to be self destructive, to throw away everything they had in a still relatively young nation. Ben Yehuda supposed the impulse was always there, in every nation, but he'd never seen a people accept it so gladly, almost greedily, because it would abet the mindlessness they were taught to accept as reality and which they had deluded themselves into believing they enjoyed. They were a nation of barely paid labor slaves, and mental slaves as well. He had never hated America, he thought they had wanted to help him, and now he thought sadly that they only wanted to help him at the expense of hurting someone else, and that's how they dealt with allies.

Ben Yehuda drank his coffee numbly, getting to the stage in aging when nothing about the world could shock him again, and he hoped it remained that way, for something to shock him would have to be truly awful, even more awful than the things he coarsely accepted now as not surprising. And that made him apprehensive and paranoid, because in this state of knowing the world so well, he also knew that the world wanted to shock those who had the hubris to think it could not disturb them anymore, that at any minute, at any time in history, in the right social crucible, it was thinking about the unthinkable, getting it ready for people like him who could not even imagine it as either a possibility or an impossibility. He shook his head with weighty sorrow. 'These people,' he thought, 'who have accepted hysteria so easily. They are the real mentally ill ones.'

Cara sat with her back against the wall, reading a book almost painfully, in discomfort of body and the discomfort of mind she always felt. She put the book down for a moment and stared at the wall and thought about herself, as she always did, and inevitably, when she thought about herself, she thought about everything. 'I can't stand myself,' she thought to herself. 'So much of myself I have not chosen. So much of my personality is involuntary. Who I am is mostly compulsive. Very little of it have I wanted for myself. I wonder if everyone is that way, or if its just me, and if its simply because I'm insane. Maybe everybody else gets to be exactly who they want to be. But I doubt it. I feel like you can only decide who you are to a certain extent. Nature and nurture takes care of everything else that free will cannot extend itself to, and that's personality, and therefore, human nature.'

She put the book down wearily and tried to close her eyes. All this time in the afterlife, she hadn't been able to take her medication. She had to see hell with even more deranged, naked eyes than usual. She felt sad, sick and strange. Everyone else took pills and they were intoxicated. She had to take pills to remain sober. And all these months without them, having to be dragged through hell and then this cold, impersonal world called purgatory- she often wondered if she had hallucinated the whole thing. Most people took pills and became intoxicated, when she *didn't* take pills she had no idea anymore the difference between reality and illusion, they both bled together as one at last in her mind. She had to take pills to live as people normally do, naturally, not thinking too much whether reality is illusory or not, and being certain that the life they are living is real. The sad thing to Cara is she wasn't sure this was not an illusion as well. At times she felt the chaos of her unmedicated mind, where there was no difference between reality and illusion, was closer to the truth. But no one could possibly live that close to the truth without being destroyed by it- truth that naked would make someone an empty hull, a husk with eyes that look at nothing and see everything, but which cannot move or speak. Being that close to the truth was being in hell without being able to express it any way. It was catatonia. It was being in hell and not even being able to write down what you saw. That's why even writers have to have comfortable illusions. When you see the void bare you cannot do anything except stare into it. You cannot do anything else. It will not let you. It punishes you for having revealed it, (if only to yourself, because it would be incredibly unkind to reveal it to anyone else,) by not allowing you to act anymore, by not allowing you to see anything else. It strips you of both reality *and* illusions, so as a human being you are left with nothing. Cara didn't know if it was insanity or an extremist form of sanity and if both were the same, but either way, it is unlivable. She had to take pills to go on with the life, perhaps illusory, known as reality, and at last have the comfort everyone else is born with naturally, of not having to look so deeply into it to see if it were illusion or not, because when she did look that deep, she realized illusion and reality were the same. And this fact she would never unlearn. She would know it forever, but at least she didn't have to live in its unlivable truth anymore. At least she could put herself at a comfortable distance from this fact and call that reality, even if it wasn't truth.

But she hadn't taken in her medication all in the afterlife. The afterlife doesn't make you pure. It doesn't make you sane, in fact, one cannot tell if it is real, just a dream, or a prolonged hallucination. That is why death mercifully made us unconscious of it, why with death we no longer feel, because eternity could not be as confusing as the brief cataclysm of life with its vaudeville madness, its extreme haste, its overwhelming spectacle that one cannot draw themselves away from, and once they do, they see life has flown away. It is a winged creature. It is frightened and fleeting. It is free but it is too quick to be really seen. And we within this life, we do not have wings. We are wedded to the ground, so of course we cannot keep up with it. We cannot fly away with it. We cannot forget it even as it mocks us with its roaming freedom that we cannot match, by flying away. But of course because it is so free it can only fly away into oblivion. Cara knew this. And once it does fly into oblivion, that is when we are at last able to catch up to it. That is when we are finally as free as it.

But Cara didn't feel that way in this afterlife. She felt like the prisoner of a dream. It was not that much different than life. She tried to close her eyes but then she heard the voices again. She heard Bernard's voice but could not find him anywhere. He kept calling her. "Glaukopis," he said softly. "You have no choice but to save the world, because you are its prisoner."

"What the hell does that mean?" Cara called, but no one spoke back. She tried to relax a little more in her chair and close her eyes, but she kept hearing voices, all screaming in competition to be heard until they were a meaningless din, and none of them could be heard over their own desperate palaver. 'It's alright,' Cara told herself. 'It's just a dream, and my dreams don't mean anything. They're just here to mock me.'

"You have to save the world because you're alone," Bernard's thin, disembodied voice said in the air.

"If I save the world," she whispered back in return, "Will I finally not be alone? If I save the world, will myself at last go along with it?"

Bernard's voice laughed at her caustically, a dream mocking her. "Are you kidding me?" he called. "Once you save the world you'll be more alone than ever! Everyone will hate you because salvation is so much harder than being damned. You will go on with your life, constantly doing the right thing, and as you do it getting more and more alone."

"Oh well," Cara sighed. "I suppose I shouldn't even ask about myself anyway. Myself can always answer myself, even at a time like this. That's all this conversation is. I suppose I should think only of the world, and forget myself."

"That's your problem," Bernard said. "The two are the same to you. When you are sick the world is, and when the world is sick you are. So you do want to save it to save yourself. You have become so wrapped up in it you do not know anymore where it ends and you begin, because secretly you know, and that is why you are so afraid, that really you don't begin until it ends. Your whole personality, your whole self, you're just a post apocalyptic dream. You're an antidote to the future, but an antidote no one would ever use, because the world's problems are your problems, and your problems are the world's problems. No one wants to live like that. Even you don't like it. You cannot swallow your own antidote, either, you can't swallow yourself or the future you are trying to ameliorate, because the truth is, the reason you relate to the world so much, is because you are an insoluble problem too."

"And that's why I want to save the world?"

"Yes."

"Will it ever happen?"

"I have no idea, not even as a hallucination can I see the future. The future is in thin air, as always, no one being able to grasp onto it. It flies and we don't."

"Can you read my thoughts?" Cara moaned desperately and wearily.

"I am your thoughts," Bernard's voice said emphatically. "That's all this is," he went on, "is your thoughts taking on a life of their own. You can't help it when you have such an imagination. Sometimes you mourn that your thoughts are dead, always dead, right after you have thought them, and so you bring us to life, to compensate for all the dead things in your mind. Face it, your head is a mausoleum."

"Isn't everybody's?"

"Yes, but you mourn yours. You mourn your head. Most people don't do that. Most people place all their dead things in there and just go on. Bu you, you brood about it, and in that way you keep things that should be dead, that *want* to be dead, alive. And then you get trapped in it on days like this and the thoughts become more alive than you are. You just have to passively accept them as all these foolishly resurrected things start to overwhelm you. That's what's different about you, that's what makes you so odd. You're too sensitive, and you pay too much mind to the dead."

"I'm sorry," Cara said weakly.

"Don't be sorry to me," Bernard's voice said. "It's you who suffers from yourself."

"I want to save the world," Cara whimpered pitiably. "But I don't know if I can. It's not my world."

"Don't feel so alone. It isn't anybody's world."

"Is that why it can't be saved?"

"You tell me," Bernard said. "You don't belong to anyone either. Can *you* be saved?"

"I've saved myself many times. I've done it all alone. I've been ill alone and I've healed alone."

"Perhaps the world is the same way. It has to do everything alone too. It's alone in nothingness. That's your problem. You're too much like it. You mirror it. Most people can go about their day and think that just because Earth is alone they don't have to be…"

"Well, I don't like to fool myself like that."

"Exactly. That's your problem. You won't delude yourself, and that's why you suffer from yourself. Without some helpful delusions, you have no antidote to you, and *you*, who in your quest to save the world have become so much like it, have no antidote for the earth either. So you exits like this, just as alone as a thing you want to save because you believe if it becomes less alone you'll become less alone. And that's why your delusions are not comfortable like most people's. That's why your delusions frighten you. Do you know why your delusions frighten you so?"

"I'm sure you'll tell me."

"Because they could become real."

Cara snorted. "They already have. My delusions, they've become the world."

"Well, maybe you need to extricate you and your loneliness from it a little bit."

"But if I do, will I be able to save it?"

Bernard's voice sighed a bit. "That is the unanswerable question, I suppose."

Then Bernard's voice at last died down and Cara tried to shut her eyes again, hoping it was all over. Someone reached over and tapped on her shoulder. She tried to ignore it, but then she heard The Poet's stentorian voice call her. "Cara!" she screamed. "You can't ignore me!"

Cara looked up at her and withheld the scream. The Poet had suddenly turned into Deiphobus. She was horribly mutilated, an arm lost, her face already becoming *vermoulu*, worm eaten, and there was a maggot in her eye. Cara tried to scream but nothing came out. The Poet touched her with the hand that was remaining and said to her, "Don't worry. I am the vates, I am the one who can see the future, I am the one who can see the truth, though I can only see both in glimpses, being hardly aware of them once I have found them, me being in something of a trance when I come to know things that I'm not supposed to know. Kind of like you are now..."

"Are you dead?"

"Always, but it doesn't matter to me. Ego ii, I ii."

Cara knew what she said. 'I go on.'

"Well tell me," Cara said almost impatiently. "What is the future?"

"When you divorce yourself from the world that cares not a whit about you even though you wish to save it, you feel even more alone. You are alone with it, you are even more alone without it."

"I already know this. This has all happened to me before..."

"And obviously it is happening again."

"Bernard tells me to remove myself from the world, you tell me to remain wedded to it..."

"I want you to remain in it."

"Well, I can't really live anywhere else. Even when I'm dead like you I'll still remain in it."

"Ego ii."

"Yes," Cara said tetchily, "you go on, but what about me?"

"You do not go on with me, at least not you as you know yourself. You go an as me. You go on as the world remembers you, someone who attempted to save it, someone who could not live with or without it while the world could do both in regards to you. But it will remember you, just not as you are. It will remember you as me."

"Well, you are my better half, even mutilated as you are."

The Poet laughed. "Yes," she said, gesturing to her missing arm. "I am only a half. And still, ego ii."

Cara was about to respond to her when she felt something hit her very hard on the head, like a club. Everything went black immediately, but The Poet's words she could still hear in he head, as always. "Ego ii, ego ii," kept repeating in her head even as she lost consciousness. It lingered on.

Ben Yehuda sat once more uncomfortably with his wife Hadassah in the Synagogue with the strange new Rabbi. They were doing a service especially for the victims in America. The Rabbi got onto the pulpit and cleared his throat, his hands trembling a little bit. "100 people in America die everyday due to gun violence," he said.

'100 people a day?' Ben Yehuda thought to himself. 'Jesus… That's a war.'

CHAPTER 11

Die Irrenhaus

Ben Yehuda sat with Yasser Al Haifa, feeling both calm and divine in the man's almost mystic presence, feeling as if, with Al Haifa's help, he could do some real good in the world that had so far only begged him to do harm. But he didn't want to do what people wanted him to do anymore. He didn't want to be the slave of the Knesset anymore. The only reasonable people he knew were Al Haifa and the unusual Rabbi that made everyone uncomfortable with his too abstruse and eloquent speeches, about things beyond which an easily uncomfortable understanding *wanted* to reach. Ben Yehuda did want to reach it though, but there was still cowardice keeping his hand back, keeping his mind reared like a horse under reins, preventing him from at last touching the long face of the infinite, of trying to study its misunderstood beauty. He was beginning to think misunderstood beauty was the most beautiful kind, because it was alone. Beauty alone is such a painful sight to see, the profound and universal sense of loss you feel looking at it *is* beauty. Ben Yehuda was beginning to learn this, but still there was something, the part of his mind, which, like the people who felt uncomfortable with the new Rabbi, told him to stay wading in the shallow water, warning him constantly if he kept looking at this misunderstood beauty he would become a misunderstood beauty himself, and be alone. Power already denoted loneliness, but a lack of it, or having a power people cannot explain, surely that was worse. Power in the regular sense at least was an aegis. But still Ben Yehuda wanted to shed it completely, and throw himself head first into the great unknown, because he thought it was both foolish and brave. And this brave foolishness was the essence of intelligence, that misunderstood beauty that serves mankind unendingly though the average man despises it, looks down upon it, is threatened by it, and made uncomfortable by misunderstood beauty because they hate the strange and they hate beauty, particularly if it is not the average, mass produced industry type of beauty, but real beauty. It makes them just as uncomfortable as the strange, it makes them just as uncomfortable as the intelligence that selflessly made their lives so comfortable in spite of their obloquy.

"We need to speak to Sanchez again," Al Haifa said abruptly, bringing Yehuda sadly back to reality, and the politics he could not escape, that no one can escape, no matter how stupid they try to remain.

"You think so?"

"No other American politician is particularly fond of us. They used to be fond of you, until you made that speech about gun control…"

Ben Yehuda smiled and Al Haifa chuckled with him. "I'm proud of you," Al Haifa added.

"It is nice finally not to be liked," Yehuda said. "I feel free now. People who are disliked, disapproved of, they're free. To be well liked, particularly by the public, that is to be a slave. And I don't want America's approval anymore. I want my own approval."

Al Haifa smiled at him brightly. "That's all you need. Now, tell me, how does it feel to be free?"

Ben Yehuda mused for a moment. "It's wonderful but it's strange. It's strange because it takes an incredible amount of strength, and it's wonderful because I never thought I had that kind of strength, but it is a strength marked by loneliness. It is the strength of being alone. Most people don't want to be that strong. I never really wanted to be that strong, either. Well, I did, but I always knew it was just a fantasy I had of myself. In real life, being that strong, it's much harder. People don't thank you for it…"

"In the end you thank yourself for it."

"Yes, but it is an incredible labor. I think the strong often wish they were weak. It's not kind the things life does to people in order to make them that strong. And, as I said, my new found strength is the strength of being alone. It is the strength of being unusual myself, as unusual as my strength, it is the strength of not belonging anywhere. I've never had that before. I've been so passive and eager to please my whole life my cowardly inobtrusive self just fit into anything, but now I don't." He chuckled for a second. "With this new found strength called freedom, I don't think I'll be able to be a politician anymore! Politicians are chained to many things by nature, and now that I am not chained to anything, I do not feel chained to politics anymore, but I still feel chained to the dying world I live in and hope to alleviate it. And people!" he laughed again. "people are going to hate me for that! People are going to hate me for my freedom, my strength!"

"They envy it."

"But they do not want it."

Al Haifa smiled his youthful, wry smile. "You're right," he said. "They envy it, because it is freedom, but they don't want it because, as you said, it involves being alone and strong, and the alone and strong don't belong many places. They envy it because they know deep down it truly is strength, strength they are not capable of, but also strength they don't want to try, if it means not belonging anymore, if it means, as you said, their 'cowardly inobtrusive selves fit into anything.' They can't give that up, not even for freedom, because it is freedom's opposite. They can't give it up because it is too comfortable, and because they do not know themselves well enough to seek their own approval, their own thanks. They have to get it from an inane community."

Ben Yehuda mused a little more. "I know it's going to be hard," he said, "but I'm glad. I would not give up my strength and my freedom for anything, not even love. Now it is the *donnee* of my entire life's work."

Al Haifa laughed at him fondly. "Gershom," he said, "it is love. It's going to be unusual. The two of us with our freedom and strength, though we are hated and envied for possessing a thing people don't even want, still right now we are the cynosure of politics, the cynosure of the world stage. I suppose that can happen. I suppose you can be famous for how alone you are."

Ben Yehuda shrugged. "I guess when you're that alone history remembers you better than other people."

Al Haifa sighed. "I'm sure anyone in that position would happily trade. To have no loved one except the world…"

"Don't you think that's the position we're in?"

"You have Hadassah."

"Yes, but she doesn't understand. How could she, though? She's not a political figure, she's just waiting in the background to make me tea and put me to bed. I did that to her. You know, she's incredibly smart, but she bends to the Knesset easily. She doesn't want this to end, being a political wife. I suppose it has leant her more power, too." Ben Yehuda sighed. "She's so normal," he groaned, "like I used to be. She was meant to be a political wife. And I, I keep getting stranger and stranger, the more I know of politics. It's a terrible thing we do to women. We put them on this short thread and attach them to us, and that's how they exist. Then, for even the most impulsive vagary, we decide to cut the thread, they don't exist anymore. At least that's the way we try to make it. Once we leave them we try to make them as obscure as possible. We make them feel they can only have stake in power if its's our power."

"Do you love Hadassah?"

"Yes, very much, but I'm afraid I've turned her into nothing but a scrim, a backdrop for the stage I'm on. I wonder why she doesn't resent me. But she just accepts it as natural because of how normal she is. She's much more suited for politics than I am."

Al Haifa dully inspected his nails. "You're going to be in a lot of trouble for speaking so casually to me in this way."

Ben Yehuda merely shrugged.

Al Haifa lit a cigarette. "Sometimes I think perhaps it's not so bad to be as alone as I am. I mean, you have a wife, and you are alone. You have a wife, and you are misunderstood. Perhaps with love it doesn't change. Perhaps if you're an outcast in the universe you're doomed to be an outcast in love as well. And I don't know which one is worse. I don't know if it's worse to be alone alone or alone together. I guess you suffer either way. I guess you're lonely whether you're too far from people or if you're too near them. If you're too far from them, they cannot hear you so they cannot understand you. If you're too near them, they can hear you so well, you're so loud, that they don't understand you. Either way, I've always felt with people, with lovers, in the end, I had to be silent. That was the only way I could be, not understood of course, but at least accepted. 'Oh he's just quiet.'"

"I don't know which one is worse either, Yasser, but I suppose it is meant to be like that. I think maybe loneliness and love are a scale and they are meant to be equal."

Al Haifa shook his head. "Why do we have to be so different from nature?"

Ben Yehuda shrugged. "Nature made us that way. I suppose she wanted a rebellious child. You know, you can get lonely without a rebellious child."

"But nature never punishes us. She wanted a rebellious child so as not to be lonely and then she neglected this child…"

"Well, that's why the child is rebellious. Because she's lonely but she also doesn't give a damn. You want nature to punish you? You do believe if she punishes you that means she loves you? Well, she doesn't. Many people have stayed with someone they don't love just not to be lonely."

"That bitch," Al Haifa said emphatically. "She invented us just to use us as little more than a loveless diversion from loneliness, as if we are nothing but a casual lay."

Ben Yehuda shrugged. "She wanted to create something that would naturally rebel against its creator. You're simply doing what nature bids when you are so frustrated with it."

Al Haifa sighed, put out the cigarette he had just finished smoking, and immediately lit another one. "I just don't understand it anymore," he said mournfully. "I feel like history, no matter how much we try to escape it, still seeps into our personal lives, that it actually *governs* our personal lives, even though we made our personal lives as a deliberate diversion from it, so we could think there was something that affected us more than history, but it's not true. History rules over our personal lives like mars rules over war. We invent the personal life to think there's something more meaningful to us than history, that history doesn't impact us, that our little casual love affairs and promotions and social circles are more important, that the macrocosm cannot swallow up the microcosm, when really the microcosm is simply the macrocosm's puppet, when really our personal lives are just a dim reflection of history. I tell you, the more deaf we become to history the louder it gets. The more we try to shirk its responsibility with useless palaver and *cicalata*, the more rampant the devil becomes. We cannot blame nature for that. *We* invented that. The only reason I'm so politically active is because I have no personal life, so I have nothing to distract me."

Ben Yehuda shrugged, "Maybe we believe love is more important than history."

"Pah!" Al Haifa scoffed. "Are you kidding me? Most personal lives do not consist of love. They consist of play acting at love. It's all a stage, the macrocosm and the microcosm alike- the microcosm is just a stage with not as many supernumeraries, so one can more easily be the lead actor upon it."

"You're being very cynical. People do really fall in love, in spite of history, and it is the best defense against it..."

"But history kills it every time. The microcosm is too tainted by the macrocosm for love to survive in it."

Ben Yehuda scoffed himself. "You don't have a personal life," he said. "You have studied personal lives *and* history from a distance, through books and strange foreign films. You think it's all a Russian novel!"

"People are affected by history," Al Haifa said sternly, "no matter how much they try to delude themselves into thinking they are distant from it."

Ben Yehuda sighed and settled more into his chair. "I do agree with that," he admitted.

"And I think today history affects us more than ever. Technology these days is a tool of history, of politics. It offers convenience at the price of alienation, and people accept these terms. And I know, the easiest way to control even one person, and now whole nations of people, is to alienate them."

"You're right," Ben Yehuda said, "but you need to not think about it so much. It's obsessing you."

"I just feel like the last sane person left in the world. And I have to stay sane, even if I'm alone in it. There's so many people trying to make me insane. They offer me companionship at the price of delusions, and some days it is an attractive offer, but I have to stay sane in order to change the things I want to change. I have to stay sane in order not to be an idiot. I have to stay sane not to compromise my entire hexis, all my convictions, all that's important to me. So I have to be alone."

"That does sound hard."

Al Haifa sighed. "Are you religious, Gershom?"

"Yes," he admitted timidly, "I am. I take it you're not?"

"No," he said, "I'm not. To me religion is just like communism. It is a beautiful theory, one that can only retain its purity in the written word. In practice it is a war."

Sanchez watched the television numbly. His bill had passed through both the house and the senate. The Mexican slaves were free, and at last Habeas Corpus was reinstated. He wanted to sigh with relief, but he knew he did not have time for that. On the television a manumitted slave was smiling and holding a sign that said "Viva La Sanchez!" Sanchez smiled briefly in gratitude, but he did not feel like a good man, he felt like a man who was simply sad and people mistook his plaintive deportment for goodness. He wanted to celebrate this new found freedom, but he knew too much about history and too much about reality. The freed slaves had a long way to go. It would still be a war for a while, a war that the Mexicans had never wanted to fight, against an enemy they never even considered their enemy, even when they enslaved them, against a people who they were merely trying to stand side by side with, in proof that they were worthy of equality. Sanchez sighed. People shouldn't have to prove that. All people are born deserving of equality.

But at least one battle was temporarily won, before it became the long battle ahead. He believed in his people though, and he knew they would make it. This is a battle that is destined to be won, though it takes almost centuries of fighting, still, nature is in favor of it, though she never makes anything easy. Sanchez scoffed. 'no,' he thought to himself. 'It's not nature. It's human beings, in retaliation of nature, in discord and spite of the freedom she has created, it being the only thing that is natural to her. He shook his head as he thought about the news. 'The camera,' he said to himself. 'It certainly captures the soul of man. It is the only thing now we have to remember ourselves by, and it is just like a mirror. It is a reversed image. It sees differently than the naked eye sees just as every naked eye sees differently. It is based on vision, and not even human vision. It is an illusion, and it is how we record ourselves, it is how we make a souvenir of ourselves. It is how we remember all our wars, our genocides, our mass rapes, our political gaffes, our crimes and inadequacies. It teaches us that all we can do to alleviate tragedy is simply to remember it, to make it a part of history. We let it remain like the bones of a saint, but we do nothing to prevent this saint's martyrdom. We remember, we recall, we do not prevent. And even our memory is not that great. It needs the bulky appurtenance of the camera. It turns even tragedy into an illusion. It makes war a cinema.'

He got up for a moment and he mixed himself a drink. Rum and coke was all he had. He mixed the drink and watched the news with silent studiousness as he mixed the drink. 'It's a time capsule,' he thought. 'When mankind is dead, and whatever next group of voyeurs comes to dig into the past, they will see our entire story in the television set. It will be the tomb we will lock ourselves into. And these new people they will see a small mixture of sad fact and then after that an overwhelming enfilade of farce, of advertisement and fantasy. They will be like us. They will hardly be able to tell what's real or not either, especially once everything is behind glass and screens. In the television, in the phone, in the camera, that is where we have buried ourselves and along with it our entire experience, the whole of our knowledge about the world, a mixture of sad fact and then after that an overwhelming enfilade of farce, delusions and illusions created by the soft glow of the glass and screen which one dies in.'

Sanchez scoffed to himself. 'I should have been a poet,' he thought, 'and not a politician. Perhaps I could have saved the world much more by renouncing my stake in it.' He sat back down on his lounge chair, feeling like the perfect picture of the average American, as brought to us by the camera- someone who sits in reclining chairs with a mixed drink and watches television while the images of people in the rest of the world were images of people being tear gassed at protests, being raped, being bombed as civilians, tumescent from starvation, burying their dead in mass graves in the moment's ceasefire: they were what the average American saw as he sat in his recliner with his mixed drink, as he watched the television. 'What has the camera done to us?' Sanchez thought. 'It is the madhouse we are all locked up in. It has replaced our imagination.' He supposed it was because creative evil seems to be the easiest way to be creative. Creative good has always been less popular. It is not as easy to portray on a television.

'I get weirder and weirder,' Sanchez said to himself as he continued his long inner soliloquy. 'The more alone I am, the more I read, the more I engage in lonely intellectual activities, the smarter I get, the more alone I get. But I don't mind. I would so much rather be alone and aware than ignorant and in love.'

CHAPTER 12

Vorago

Cara woke up sleepily and looked around her. She was in a prison cell. She did not know if she was imagining it or not, but she was glad *something* had knocked her out, so she could sleep for a moment, and mercy as it rarely did for her, allowed her to forget her dreams. But then she woke up and she was dreaming again. She could only pray one day she would forget it, when she woke up from hell and purgatory, into whatever dim or vast horizon awaited her after that. She was not allowed to have much hope now, though. Her mind would not let her. Her mind had taught her hope only ends in disappointment. The things she learned from depression were a mixture of truth and cynicism, and when she was not depressed all she could do was try to extricate the two, try to tell which from which, and when she was unable to, she became depressed again, and had to start the whole process over. It was like building something one had to destroy the moment they made any progress on it, because to finish building it would mean to be dead.

She kept hearing voices, everywhere someone shouting and accusing her. She trembled on the half caved in prison bed. Then she heard it again. A man crooning out of the darkness, 'Now tell me who's that writing? John the revelator." Cara covered her hands over her ears to try to block it out, but that never worked. She should know better than that by now. She should realize delusions are *loud*, much louder than truth that is a bit more humble, a bit more sad and self regretting. Truth itself is a philosopher. "Tell me who's that wrrittinggg? John the revelator, wrote the book of the seventh seal!"

Cara heard a knock on the outside of her cage. She looked up with timid fear and saw it was only Rhadamanthus and The Poet.

"What's happened?" she said. "How can I tell you're real?"

Rhadamanthus dropped for a moment his saturnine and satirical attitude and looked at her with softer than usual eyes. "Its ok sweetie," he said gently. "We really are here."

"What's happened?" Cara asked again, completely vulnerable, completely naked to fear.

"Well, honey," The Poet said cautiously. "Juno Moneta found out about the unapproved book list."

"Where is Bernard?"

"I'm sorry, Cara, he's been executed. They've all been executed. They want to execute *you* publicly, but we're here to break you out."

Cara groaned. "I want to die," she said, "but I'm already dead. So what's next?"

"Ego ii," The Poet responded stoically.

"Come now, baby," Rhadamanthus said, still gently as he broke the lock on the cage. "It's time to get out of purgatory. You've been in the middle for too long."

"Where will I go from here?"

"Heaven," the Poet responded calmly. "But you must go through one more trial first."

"No," Cara whispered pitiably. "No more trials."

"It'll be alright," The Poet said and linked her arm in Cara's. "Follow Rhadamanthus," she gently ordered and Cara did so. She was still psychotic and she rambled all the way.

"We are God," she said through some unfiltered, unrestrained cynicism, trying to find truth in her own hebephrenic nonsense. "That's why we're so cruel. And all God wants is forgiveness. All He wants is for us to forgive *Him*. He made us out of atonement. He did not realize we were another sin. And now we have to forgive Him and forgive ourselves as Him. All we can do is forgive. We cannot escape the sin of creation..."

"Who's that writing?" Rhadamanthus began to sing.

"Where are we going?" Cara asked.

"To the town of Vorago," Rhadamanthus said.

"What's that?"

"It is the most destitute, war ravaged town in purgatory. It's named after a Latin word which means chasm, abyss, etc. It derives from the Latin work Vorare, which means to devour."

"How will it not devour me?"

"Well, the void has devoured you before, you made it."

"I didn't want to go through this again."

"In Vorago, there is a labyrinth. You must get through that in order to make it to heaven."

"Oh great!" Cara cried sardonically. "A void and then a labyrinth! You're telling me the only way to get to heaven is to become lost?!"

"Yes," Rhadamanthus said sternly. "That is exactly what I'm telling you."

"God," Cara said, and started shivering. "Will You ever forgive me for being lost? And will you ever forgive Yourself for making me lost? Can I forgive You and You forgive me?"

"I thought you were braver than this," The Poet said to her in a mild excoriating tone. "You're making me ashamed. You're not living up to me."

"How can I be brave when I'm lost?"

"How can you not be brave when you're lost? Do you think you're going to make it out of the labyrinth any other way?"

"It's hard to be brave when you're losing your mind."

"We'll you have to be, otherwise your mind will become lost and you along with it. Bravery is the clew. Bravery will get you out of the void and the labyrinth."

"Bravery," Cara whispered, as if it were a word she had half forgotten. Then she thought about it for another moment and remembered. "Bravery is what got me into all of this. I've been brave for so long, I just want to take a break and be a coward again. Fighting everyday, fighting the dangerous parts of my mind and then on top of that fighting the times I live in that wants me to indulge in all my darker motives, it gets exhausting. It's hard not to bend at all. Luckily I have certain convictions that prevent me from doing many things my zeitgeist almost demands, but still. I am very tired. I don't want to fight anymore, just for a moment."

"Well, I'm sorry Cara," The Poet said emphatically. "But now is not that time."

"Will there ever be a time?"

"Death. You can stop fighting when you die."

"Then what's to motivate me to fight death? Death is my cowardice, I suppose. Life has demanded too much bravery from me."

The Poet put her hand on Cara's shoulder. "It'll be fine," she said. "Of course everyone is afraid of the void and the labyrinth. Both remind people of life once it becomes too bare, but you have experience, you've done this before…"

"And it made me brave, and bravery made me lonely."

"You were lonely when you were a coward too, when all you longed for was love and death. You see a little bit more in the world than just these two things now, both which have eluded you, and both which you burrow in when you're afraid. Ah, here we are. This is Vorago."

Cara looked around. It was the most destitute place she had ever seen. There were large craters in the ground everywhere from bombs. People walked around homeless and mutilated, making small firs in the streets to keep warm. Many of the houses had no roofs, and even if they did, were too dilapidated to live in. Cara looked around and saw a large sign in one of the windows of the house that was *sans toit*. It said 'Juno Moneta 2030.' Cara scoffed with a mixture of disgust and pity, the two feelings she felt most often when from a distance viewing the human race as if she were not past of it, which often she felt she wasn't, but when she sat and thought about it, no matter how different she was from most people, the two judgments she passed the most on herself were disgust and pity as well. And who did she think she was, that she could judge mankind? She supposed someone had to do it in the stead of God's absence, but still, it didn't matter. Her judgments were all moot. They could not change humanity. They could not change a war ravaged Vorago from voting for the man that had war ravaged them. All of Cara's disgust and pity was wasted, wasted on humanity and herself, because no matter how hard she tried, she could not extricate the two and she could not refrain from judging them, from analyzing them. She supposed it was better than condemning people. She didn't understand it though. People hated her disgust and pity, tried to think it was not relevant, and scorned her judgment while they ran into the arms of whoever had condemned them.

She sighed heavily as she walked through Vorago. This was something she had seen with the comfortable distance of her television, she had never walked directly in it. It was different seeing it firsthand. Such an enormous wave of pity mixed with helplessness came over one so they could not feel anything at all. It made you feel so much at one time that you could only process the enfilade of emotions vaguely, and in the end you could not feel, you just felt like you were watching yourself, and you were someone else, feeling. It was mostly due to the helplessness. The helplessness often engulfed the pity, so one abandoned pity for helplessness, and then with helplessness came forgetfulness. One just moved on and accepted it as a tragedy one could not solve. One could only solve minor tragedies, the big ones which we have created, are somehow out of our hands. So Cara walked through this human desolation already completely numb to it, already desensitized the very minute she had seen it, because it was history, it had already happened and it was over. One could only mourn it now, and people only ever mourn these things vaguely. Cara felt sad and ashamed. Actually being in it, she still kept herself at the comfortable distance she did when she saw it on TV. One had to survive. She looked at all the maimed and homeless. They looks like they were too tired of feeling to go on doing it for very much longer either. The callousness one adopts as a survival instinct, it's what allows these things to continue, it's what makes history keep going.

At last they reached their destination. It looked like a prison. There was barbed wire around the gate of two large, imposing doors and a sign above them that said 'The Palace of Entrails: Trojaburgen.' It was the only thing in the entire place that went completely unscathed by the war. It was some kind of sacred but forbidden temple, something people worshipped simply because they feared it. It was no different than Juno Moneta. A man looked at her stolidly and then he and the other guard slowly opened the doors. Cara had never been so nervous in her life. She felt like this was the defining moment of her future. It was a responsibility she could not get away from, unlike the responsibility of helping people like the ones in Vorago, which she and helplessness could easily shirk. 'It is a responsibility,' Cara told herself, 'and you need responsibility. All people do. Without responsibility there is just the void. If you don't take up responsibility it means you are depressed. That's all depression is, having realized the void beneath responsibility and therefore no longer being able to accept responsibility. Depression makes it so you can't do anything, then you get depressed from doing nothing, from having no responsibility, and then you are incapable of responsibility even further, and then you get more depressed, are more incapable of responsibility, are more depressed, etc. And everyone looks down on you for it. Responsibility, because it covers the void, is holy in our world. Holy *Anagke,* the thing that keeps us from realizing there is a certain truth in depression, in the inability to be obligated anymore. So I must not become depressed. I must accept this as an obligation. It is only strange that my responsibility is the void. I suppose that is the middle ground, though.'

She clenched her fists, breathed heavily one more time, and entered the labyrinth.

The guard looked at her sideways. "Follow the clew," he said. "But be careful. It is so thin it is almost invisible."

"We'll meet you on the other side," The Poet said. "I'm sorry we can't go with you."

"It's fine," Cara said stiffly. "It's my responsibility." She went into the labyrinth and she thought how strange it was the way burdens were assigned, completely arbitrarily, but she supposed her burden suited her. She thought, in a masochistic way, she had almost chosen it. Almost. It just found her the way all burdens randomly find their victims, it was just that in the end it contributed largely to her personality. She wondered if all burdens were like that, or if it was just hers. She felt spoiled. Most people in the world, their burdens were historical, like the people of Vorago. They would probably do anything to trade burdens with her, to have the burden of simply visiting the labyrinth instead of having to live in it. But she supposed we all lived in it, just some of us more comfortably than others. For some of us it is practically hidden. For some of us we don't even know we inhabit the palace of entrails. Some people inhabit the palace of entrails as kings and queens, and they are put in such luxury in the midst of the confusion they do not even see the confusion. The rest of the people in the palace of entrails were beggars. Cara, as always, was somewhere in the middle. She knew the confusion, the sorrow, the horror existed, and she did want to alleviate it but she did not suffer from it herself. Her burden was to simply know it, not to live it. A burden many people would happily take, unlike in America where even that burden is shirked. That's the ultimate sin of luxury, when one finds they can do without knowledge, when one finds they are in wealth while being in ignorance. Cara wondered if these people, who did not know the world and did not have to partake in it, had any burden at all. This was given just as arbitrarily. Many people suffered from horror, some people suffered from the mere knowledge of horror, and some knew neither, and did not suffer at all, and all three of these states were doled out blindly by destiny- the only pattern that seemed to emerge were that the first two were given punitively to the strong of character, the last as a reward to the weak of character. But Cara supposed what made one have a strong character was their burden, so people without one would always have a weak character. And they lived in the largesse and indolence of a much aspired to ignorance- they are still rewarded for it, this minority that is happily not suffering with the rest of the world, nor even acknowledging the suffering.

Cara sighed inwardly. The modern times were sad to her. These days people refused to believe the things they enjoyed were evil. She walked through the labyrinth. The guard was right, the clew was practically invisible, but she could see its dim glimmer in the light, this thin, tenuous strand of bravery that was all that could get anyone out of the labyrinth, this very little bit of meaning in a world that was otherwise a senseless maze. Such a small, hardly visible thing, and it was all anyone had to hold onto. Cara tried to follow the clew, losing track of it easily as she always had, and then she made the mistake of looking up. Above her was an Ascapar sized haruspex looking into the palace of entrails to read the future. Cara almost screamed. She was a Lilliputian compared to this person, this person who could look into destiny, while Cara only had a thin clew. This Brobdingnagian seer that towered over her life and her future, she scared her more than the labyrinth. She looked down just to escape the intimidation of it all. She looked down and she could not find the clew anymore, while the towering prophet looked into the entrails she was so enmeshed in and interpreted something so distant and hardly conceivable as destiny, trying to figure out in advance who got what burden, and what burden was on humanity. She did this and Cara felt like an ant, something that belonged to a large mass of indistinguishable creatures as she got swallowed up by them, as she drowned totally anonymously, without notice, in the entrails the haruspex was interpreting. Cara wondered with fear and confusion, how was it that this destiny could assign her this burden, when she was too small to even be seen by it, when it didn't even realize her existence. She wanted to run from it, but it was too large, too all encompassing- it was everywhere. Every where she turned in this labyrinth she could see the seer looking in on her without even noticing she was there, but getting enough of a vague presentiment of her to determine her future. For once Cara did not want to know the future. This haruspex, even if she did determine fate, even if she *was* fate, even she was just guessing. That's what made the universe, and how the universe determines itself, by taking a totally blind chance, which, in the end, turned out to be inevitability. Cara wondered then what was the point. What was the point of anything at all, when everything was not predetermined, but determining itself every second, and only by a foggy notion, and this was fate?

She tried to ignore the seer and looked desperately for the clew. She could not find it for several moments until at last there was a little ray of sunlight that penetrated the labyrinth ad left a small but bright glint in the ground that Cara knew was the clew. She found it and decided not to look at the seer anymore, just as the seer wasn't looking at her She decided the seer wasn't looking at anything at all, that she was just staring into nothingness and picking out of that an arbitrary pattern in nullity. It was a pointless exercise. It was more meaningful to search for the clew. 'Thank God I am a detail oriented person,' Cara thought, 'and I can always see the small.' She followed the thin wire all through the looping of these architectonic intestines, the weaving road with so many meandering paths that all lead to nothing, and only one of them lead to an exit. 'It's life,' Cara thought to herself with horror. 'The palace of the entrails is life. That's all it amounts to, a web of offal.'

She followed the clew and lost it several times, but she supposed that was inevitable. She supposed that the seer she decided she must ignore if she expected to live had unwittingly made it that way, on accident. Everything was an accident. She supposed that was life too, just an accident with purpose, a purpose you have to find in the depths of the winding offal, very small and only slightly glinting, but you have to hold onto it as well as you can, so it can be an accident with purpose instead of pure accident, so fate can justify itself, and thereby, one justify their existence. The slew was easy to lose, especially for people like Cara, who are overwhelmed by the totality of the labyrinth, who cannot help seeing the whole, and realize it is radically other from human beings, and we, it's little parts, barely exist in it. She thought how much easier it was for people who did not take a panoramic view of the labyrinth, and just kept their nose to the clew. She desperately wanted to be a person like that right now. She thought the only way to survive this was to be other than who she really was, to create her own whole that was different, better than the mumping and poor postured, insane writer. She knew what she had to do. She would actually have to be The Poet to get out of this.

But The Poet was blind. How could The Poet see the ever evasive clew? Perhaps she could see it better than everyone. Perhaps it was not something you had to look at, search for through vision, perhaps one simply had to feel it, perhaps that tiny thread was somewhere in Cara, and perhaps it was easier to see inwardly. Perhaps it was part of the supersensible world, not the sensible one. She closed her eyes, she became blind. At least this way she could not see fate. She closed her eyed very tightly and began to see a thin white line travelling forward. She followed it. She began to panic because it moved forward the whole time, and the labyrinth was almost infinitely curved. The clew was like time, moving forward even though matter was bending it along with space, along with the curves of the labyrinth. Cara realized it only appeared to move forward. Something, the seer maybe, and entirely on accident, was trying to make it easier for her to get out of here. So she followed the straight line even though she felt herself turning and twisting in the labyrinth. She for a moment felt at peace. She felt she was simply some flotsam moving passively with the ocean, and in her mind, though she knew it was an illusion, the ocean moved in a straight, finite line, instead of being so expansive and crashing its torrential waves in all directions, as far as the horizon.

Life was so unusual, and the things that governed it. It was no wonder most people had decided not to think about it, and in many ways, Cara was doing the same thing by following this straight line in her own imagination, instead of looking around at the totality of the labyrinth and the giant seer above it. She realized that her quest in life was somewhat foolish and doomed. She wanted to make peace with language, something else that had been used as an organon of hate. But she could not dream up any other quest, any other fate. Language was the only hope she had. It had been used as an organon of hate, but it could also be used to castigate this hate, to drive it out with the rest of the irrational and delusional- language was different from everything else that had been used as a tool of war, it could also be used as a tool to destroy war- it could be used as propaganda and it could be used as the antidote to propaganda. Language had two sides. Violence only had one.

She thought of this and the clew became brighter, easier to see in the midst of the blindness. Something swelled within her, a roaring crescendo like the ocean beating a man against a rock, and something strange within her, an alien voice that was still her own, though she had never heard it before. 'There's so many depths to the universe and to the planet Earth,' Cara thought, 'and there are even so many depths of myself. There are even things about myself I do not know yet. Everything is so complicated. Everything, if you look at it with inward focus, is infinite. The clew is infinite and I am along with it, since we move in a straight line in the labyrinth.' The voice then told her to open her eyes.

She did. She looked around. The Poet and Rhadamanthus were looking up at her smiling. She had made it out of the labyrinth, with the infinity that rested within her. She had done it, she had escaped the palace of entrails in blindness. She had acted just like fate. She went to move towards The Poet and Rhadamanthus but suddenly all she could see was a blinding white light.

PART 3

Heaven

"*Each Heaven is also a prison,*"

Ralph Waldo Emerson

Ideel

Ben Yehuda woke up in bed sore after a troubled night of sleep. Sometimes the transition from sleep to wakefulness was not an easy one. He groped around in bed but he did not know what for. Immediately he felt a deep sense of anxiety that grew in the pit of his stomach. Today was the day he met with the American president and the Knesset about making Israel the seat of The Holy Government. He didn't want to do it, all for his friendship with Yasser Al Haifa. If he made Israel the seat of The Holy Government, the Palestinians would certainly be screwed, and Al Haifa would never speak to him again. He didn't know if he could bear that. He loved Al Haifa. He reminded him of himself when he was younger, but so much braver. His memories of being in the Palmach were so distant now. They seemed to be the memories of someone else, someone who still lived inside him but which he had drowned with the hardness of reality, someone who was much more naïve and much more honest. He felt like a coward again. He knew if he didn't do it, he would be met with disapproval from his entire nation. He forgot the glory of being someone who was disapproved of for leaving behind opinion and instead taking up the moral right, and now could only remember the pain, the loneliness of it. That lingered much more.

He groped around some more on the night stand to find his glasses. He looked over for a moment at Hadassah, who was still sleeping, unconcerned. She was lying flat on her stomach, and Ben Yehuda briefly rubbed her shoulders lovingly while at the same time not trying to wake her up. "Oh, Hadassah," he whispered under his breath. "Our love will never work, because we'll never be able to leave this world." Hadassah groaned sleepily and rolled over.

Ben Yehuda suppressed a sigh and got out of bed. This was the worst thing he had ever done, being in politics. He'd never wanted to die more in his life. Working in the Palmach was better. Perhaps, he thought for a moment, it does make you more happy to do what you think is right, rather than what people want you to do. Though it denotes struggle, in the end I think you can more easily accept yourself. And perhaps it's better to be accepted by yourself than the damn Knesset, the damn president of the United States and the bloody nation of Israel. Again he wished he could be Al Haifa, though life was probably much more unkind to him, that was why he was authentic. Ben Yehuda thought he only ever flirted with the idea of authenticity, as if it were a nice dream, but not something that could be possible. Again he felt himself burying his already deeply buried youth under the cynical pragmatism of what people deluded you into thinking was reality when you aged.

An aid knocked on the door. "Prime Minister," she said, "The U.S. President has just arrived and the Knesset is gathering."

"Thank you, Alice. I'll be there in a moment."

He sat on the bed and put his hands in his face. He would meet disapproval wither way, either from himself or from a large portion of the world, and he didn't think either would be easy to live with. If only it were arbitrary, if only it weren't in his hands. He stopped for a moment. In an odd way, when you really thought about it, arbitrariness was more fair than anything. Arbitrariness was nature's justice. But he realized human beings could not rely on that solely, that would be acquiescing to fate completely, abandoning the little bit of free will fate gave us. He could not leave all his problems to destiny, because arbitrariness, even if it was the world's fairness, would often assign sorrow and powerlessness with its blind justice. It was only fair because it brought it to everyone. But it was noble to take control of the very little things you could. He could not use destiny as his divine cop out. He had to make a decision. He had to utilize his free will, his own sense of justice, which, unlike nature's, *could* truly be based on the right. It only made him sad when he thought that most people's very sense of justice was arbitrary- it swung back and forth with whatever was the current popular opinion. He didn't have to be that way, though. Oh, if only the notions of good and evil weren't possibly arbitrary as well. He did believe in an absolute good though, and he knew there was an absolute evil, he had seen it everyday, he had known it since he was a child. He was as certain of its existence as he was certain of the existence of the absolute good, because the absolute good *had* existed, incarnate in rare human beings, and even if it was a minority, it was worth fighting for. The minority is always worth fighting for. A person standing completely alone, they usually were the good. He believed a person standing alone possessed much more goodness than if you lumped humanity all into one mass. Goodness was lonely, like its two paths to it, wisdom and truth.

And ben Yehuda desperately wanted to be good. He looked at Hadassah. Would she still love him as a solitary creature, a singular figure? Slowly she roused from sleep and looked up at him.

"Is it time already?" she asked.

"Yes, it is."

"What are you going to do?"

"I'm going to stand up for Al Haifa and the Palestinians," ben Yehuda said timidly but proudly. "I'm not going to do it. I'm not going to have Israel be the seat of the Holy Government."

"Why?" Hadassah asked, astonished. She had never seen him so resolved before.

Ben Yehuda smiled wryly and enigmatically, as if sharing a secret with himself. "Because I'm a idealist," he said.

Cara awoke in an entirely white room. She panicked for a moment, thinking she was in some kind of solitary confinement, when she saw a thin but robust looking woman sitting next to her bedside and smiling cloyingly. "Welcome to the superstructure," she said.

"The what?"

The woman smiled more widely. "You're in heaven," she said. "You're lucky, usually we don't let sick people into heaven, but we were touched by your long ordeal..."

"You don't let sick people into heaven?" Cara asked with disbelief.

The woman shrugged. "Now that you're in heaven, some things are going to have to change. I understand that you have been to hell. Don't tell anyone your experiences there. We try to keep heaven sorrow free, that's the whole point of it…"

"So you have to ignore hell."

"Yes. We know you have knowledge of the darker side of humanity, we don't want you to share it."

Cara sighed heavily. "You have to know the dark side," she said, "if you ever hope to understand God. If you don't know the dark side, you don't know how so many have suffered, you completely forget about them…"

"And that's exactly what I want you to do."

Cara's mouth went slightly agape. This woman, she had seen many like her. All of these people when she met them vaunted cruelly to her 'my road is happy,' while Cara tried to rebut, 'Well, my road is deeper,' and they looked at her as if she were completely insane, eyebrow lifted, an expression on their face that clearly said 'why would that be a good thing?' Cara thought about all the people she met in hell. She had to know the dark side to keep them in memorium, to remember what she'd seen, to know the disease that haunts so many people- to surpass it she had to not forget it. And she realized, The Poet, the philosopher, the bum, the prisoner, the slave, the soldier, the refugee, they were all the same person. They were the human race.

"If you must know the dark side," the woman went on, "please keep it to yourself. People here don't want to know."

"It's an awful lot like Earth," Cara said absently.

"Oh no," the woman said. "It is nothing like Earth. We made sure of that."

Cara looked at her emptily. This whole time, during all the afterlife, all she had endured here in the land of the dead…It seemed no different than life to her.

"I'll give you a tour," the woman said brightly. "Once you're in heaven, you'll be happy."

"If I'm happy," Cara asked, "will I still be able to be profound?"

Again, the woman looked at her like she was insane. "What do you need to be profound for?"

Cara sighed. "I don't know."

CHAPTER 2

Ashe

Cara walked around heaven. It was almost the same temperature as hell.

Cara fanned herself frantically and looked at her tour guide. "Why is it so hot?" she asked.

"Well, people like it warm. Look around." Cara looked around. There were people swimming in pools, longing in deck chairs drinking pina coladas, everyone was enjoying the blistering heat. Everyone here was retired, bored, and would be waiting for death if they weren't already dead. "Supposedly it's so hot because there's a large hole in the ozone layer," the woman went on, "but nobody here believes that, and we don't think about it. Besides, everyone likes it warm."

"What do you think about here?" Cara whispered under her breath.

"That's a good question," the woman said, having heard her. "And you'll need to learn the answer. Obviously you can think about whatever you want to- one can't help their thoughts, but there's certain thoughts you can't discuss here. Anything of a grim or depressive nature, anything about politics, unless everyone in the room agrees, and you certainly can't talk about hell or purgatory. The whole point of being here is to forget those, and Earth too. That means you can forget about politics, forget about war. It truly is a wonderful place."

Cara didn't say anything. So far heaven seemed like a somewhat more mild combination between hell and purgatory, the blistering heat, the ennui, and not being allowed to speak about things. Cara realized this was a place that if one became depressed in, they would have to be depressed alone. Her whole life she had hated Earth and wanted to leave it, and now she wanted to go back there more than anything, although it was not much different than these places that were mirrored in its image, and not the other way around. How could death be so much like life? Cara decided the driving force of everything on Earth and beyond was ashes, that it was not fire that drove us, but its death, that it was the stale ennui of dwindled passion that kept all human beings going, everyone living off a memory, everyone, like her, feeling nostalgia for something that was no different than their present lot, but which time had dressed these ashes as roses. And she hung her head thinking about that, realizing she would never be able to speak about it here. Heaven can make you nostalgic for hell.

"Can I write?" Cara asked.

"So long as the writing is uplifting."

'So long as the writing is cliché,' Cara thought. Cara didn't understand why people found clichés so comforting. She found many of them were even more hopeless than the things she wrote, but they were a kind of hopeless that told people, 'rest easy, because you cannot change the world. It is ok to do nothing.' People liked hopelessness so long as it was anodyne, and it allowed them to have a lazy will power. Her road was deeper. Her road ran underground, in marriage to obscurity and in love of the obscure. Many people could not even see her road, because they did not look too deeply at the world they were treading on. We tread on the world, we deform space and time, is that all we are here for, to run a course of destruction on the universe? Were we created because nature is a masochist, or just bored? Is that all we did? In spite of all our learning, all our art, which no matter how important it was ran on the road underground as well, where only the few who had also buried themselves could see it, that was the bulk of what we did, destroying the place that had so unwittingly inhabited us, and destroying each other along with it, destroying everything, trying to bend the world. The crusades never ended. The middle east was so beautiful, and then someone had set a vast collection of bombs there, of civil war and civilians being attacked by terrorists and soldiers alike. The middle east, the land of

God, was a land of war. But everything was like that. Everything that was supposed to be beautiful was a horror, religion and love alike. And heaven.

Cara was finally directed to a mansion where she would be staying with The Poet. The Poet was waiting for her. Cara noticed she still didn't have eyes. She looked to the woman, "You can't do anything for her?"

The woman shrugged. "Well, at least she can't see any evil."

"Sure," Cara said laconically, and the woman left and Cara sank into the couch. She looked at The Poet.

"I don't think we belong here," she said.

"I don't think anyone belongs here. It's just like hell."

"And Earth," Cara said stiffly. "I guess no one belongs anywhere. Why didn't I fit in then?"

"I suppose you more obviously didn't belong anywhere, for some reason."

"Because I was aware of it," Cara said plaintively. "If no one belongs here, why do people not feel as strange here as I do?"

"I think it's natural to some people to not belong anywhere. And that's why they belong, because they don't rebel against it too much."

"Or think about it too much."

"Perhaps you could think about it less."

"How can I?" Cara stormed, "when I don't belong so much I cannot even belong with everyone else who doesn't belong?"

"I don't know," The Poet said. "Perhaps it's the opposite. Perhaps you do belong on Earth and heaven and hell and that's why you're an outcast."

"I don't like it here," Cara said callowly, almost throwing a tantrum like a child.

"Well, you're not meant to be here forever. You aren't meant to be anywhere forever, not even in the afterlife."

"So the afterlife isn't even eternal?"

"No kind of life can be."

Cara stared blankly at the empty television screen. "Life and death," she said slowly, through gritted teeth. "They're so similar. And now I'm in heaven, a place where I'm not allowed to be sad."

"Do you want to be sad?"

"I want the right to be. I fought for that on Earth, too."

"You're not supposed to fight for anything here."

"That's why it's not a real heaven."

The Poet shrugged. "Well the words 'real heaven' are an oxymoron as it is."

"Has any of this been real?"

"Has it been real to you?"

Cara paused for a moment and thought. "Parts of it have been, and parts of it have been pure fantasy. Many of the things I saw in hell, they seemed real, and purgatory was so much of a fantasy it was a hard reality, it being a society built up on delusions, and there was no truth behind any of these delusions, and that was realistic…I don't know. My whole life I've had such a hard time telling the difference between reality and fantasy as it is…"

"Well, they're very close."

"But this one, heaven, a world where they think sadness can't exist…that's just pure fantasy."

"Do you think sadness is necessary to life?"

Cara sighed and dragged on her cigarette desperately. "Unfortunately, yes."

"Well, this is the afterlife."

"And I think it abides by the rules of life, of reality, and just as heaven can't exist on Earth, I don't think heaven can even exist in heaven. There is something rotten in the state of heaven, something its hiding. Heaven is a hypocrite. I can draw the same metaphor for it as Christ did for hypocrites- it is a marble sepulcher, it is beautiful on the surface, it is beautiful where the artist invented it, but like so many other things the artist invented, beneath it is a rotting decay. It's a fantasy and fantasies are made on lies. Fantasies are made on hypocrisy."

The Poet chuckled lightly. "You never believe someone when they say they're moral, do you?"

"Not when their morality consists of ridding the world of sorrow by cordoning it, then ignoring. I've been the victim of that 'morality' all my life."

"Well, most people are not like you," The Poet said almost sardonically. "They don't treat love as if it is a game of solitaire."

Cara shrugged. "Well it is true that no one wins."

The Poet smiled at her gently. "There's a bar in here," Cara added. "Would you like a drink? Sorrow is not allowed here, but alcohol is. Sorrow is not allowed here but its false antidotes are."

"Yes," The Poet said gloomily. "I see why you think that is hypocrisy. I suppose hypocrisy really is just the none too subtle art of lying to oneself, and trying to apply this lie to the world…but I don't think it can be helped."

"Why is that?"

"Because the devil is much older than Christ. I'll have a seven and seven please."

Cara nodded even though The Poet could not see her, and then she went to the bar to make them both a drink. "Well," Cara spoke from the bar in the kitchen. "Christ will always be young, that's part of who He was, so that His message would always be new. The devil's message is ancient, and our conscience, because it will renounce itself easily, listens to it a bit more easily. It's older and louder. Christ's message is fresh each generation. It will always be virginal. People find it hard to deal with something that new, that original, that young. And it's also eternal. People are not used to that. People are not used to something that is so new being forever and somehow still always being new. It seems to be contradictory."

The Poet didn't respond but nodded her head in the other room, even though Cara could not see it. After a minute or so Cara came back with the drinks. She handed the seven and seven to The Poet gently, who had to grope around for it for a moment.

"Do you suppose people drink here because they're happy?" Cara asked.

"I suppose people drink here because they're bored."

Cara tried a weary smile, but her face would not support it. If it weren't for The Poet she would feel so alone, and yet she was alone because of her. "I guess that's the one good thing about depression," she said sadly, "it prepares you for death."

"Well, don't waste your life preparing for death."

"Yes," Cara said, and sunk back into the couch with the drink in her hand. It was true heaven was comfortable, but it was a little bit too comfortable. One could so easily waste away here, and it was a wonder to Cara that this was what most people wanted. "Many people see it that way, but still, I don't want to be frightened when I die."

"You've traded fears," The Poet rebutted seriously, "You were afraid of being afraid of death so instead you chose to be afraid of life."

Cara sighed. "Well, what do you want me to do?"

"I have a feeling we won't be here long, so I want you to return to life, and forget about death for a little bit."

"How can I now that I've seen it?" and tears were streaming down Cara's face."

"You've seen many things you had to forget. Just think of it as another hallucination."

"But I know it's not a hallucination. Death is very real. It's so real you can't imagine it. How am I supposed to pretend that it's a delusion?"

"Death is not a delusion, but the love of it is."

"I don't love it, I just feel there's no point in hating it. If I hate it it will only come sooner. And how can one be alive and be indifferent to it? I just have some strange silent respect for it, and try not to be too intimidated by it. But I cannot go through life pretending it doesn't exist. Too many people die for me to do that."

"Just hold more respect for life," The Poet said emphatically. "That's all I ask of you. You want to get out of here don't you?"

"I do, but when I go home, what will I go home to? Yet another dystopia. I've been from dystopia to hell then back to dystopia and now I am in Utopia, and it feels non existent even while I'm here. It doesn't seem anywhere near as real as the horror…and the horror doesn't even seem that real either. I have put a wall between me and it, and it does still climb over the wall, particularly when I'm off guard, but this, heaven, utopia, I will have no memory of it at all, because nothing happens here, because it is just a dream, and not even my dream, someone else's. I am living in someone else's dream, while in the meantime my dream is laying in abeyance on Earth. Utopia will not sink into me the way hell did. Good memories are the hardest to hold onto. The mind remembers most what you beg it to forget. Good memories it seems to think are inane. Good memories don't stick because happiness is fleeting, therefore the recollection of it goes too, it flies with time. But I don't think I'll have many good memories here. I feel more like an alien here than I ever did on Earth. Just some inane memories of someone else's dream, someone else's dream I didn't belong in." She sighed once more and wiped the tears out of her eyes. "I hate my mind," she whimpered. "I really do. There are so many questions in it, so may more questions than there will ever be answers."

The Poet heard her quiet sobs and wrapped a very strong arm around her. "It has to be that way," she whispered. "There have to be more questions than answers. If the two ever equal out it would be detrimental to the human race, because the human race would stop wondering. I know sometimes that sounds attractive. Wondering can be quite painful, but if we stop doing it, there will be no answers at all."

CHAPTER 3

Amathia

Cara managed to get some alcohol induced sleep and woke up with a hangover. She walked outside to take the trash out. The sun was blaring bright and scalding hot and she had to turn away from it. Her neighbor was mowing the grass and he stopped the lawn mower to look at her.

"Howdy neighbor!" he called.

Cara managed a weak but friendly smile and said hello to him.

"You look sick, you alright?"

"I have a bit of a hangover."

The neighbor than turned stony and glared at her. "You're not supposed to drink enough to get a hangover here," he said icily and sanctimoniously.

"Oh," Cara said in her usual flat tone when someone had made her angry but she didn't want to express it. "Well, I'm sorry I'm new here."

The neighbor softened a bit at that. "You know, some people can drink and drink and never get a hangover. That's ok here. But you can't get a hangover. No one is supposed to be sick here. Nice weather we're having, right?"

'It's hot as hades,' Cara thought to herself, but she smiled and nodded in mock agreement. Then she felt bad about herself. The one thing that was any good about her is that she was brave enough to be herself even in worlds where everyone was supposed to be whatever the ruling institution deemed them to be, and now she had given that up too, for heaven, so people in heaven would not hate her the way people on Earth had hated her. 'Damn the white man,' she thought to herself, 'and how he keeps his hegemony over the Earth by infecting the world with the disease of the most inane conformism, of so called normalcy. I don't want to give into that.'

"It is a bit hot, though," Cara added. The neighbor gave her a final glare and then kept mowing his lawn. Cara smiled mischievously to herself and finished taking out the trash. By now she realized she had to be an outcast, at the risk of completely losing herself, and she had lost herself so many times, and each time it had been incredibly difficult to find herself again in the mess she had buried herself in, she wasn't willing to do it again. It is when we lose ourselves that we turn to evil, Cara realized, and she had found herself for the last time, she thought. If she lost herself once more she would be gone forever, and go through life forever more being a stranger to herself, after she had gone through the incredibly operose task of getting to know herself, who was even shy with the self. She would not allow that *vericundia* anymore. She had worked too hard to convert herself from shy to brave, so she would not stop being brave now. She would not become a coward even if cowardice was awarded with paradise. Cowardice in the past had been too painful for her. Cowardice meant regret. Cowardice meant damaging love, then giving it up. Cowardice meant giving up emotion, cowardice meant electing to stop feeling. Cowardice meant selling your soul to the devil. Cowardice meant no longer being an artist. Cowardice, being fear, ended only in hate. It was the sole reason the world was ruined. Cowardice was the banal insanity, it was a direct path to evil. Bravery, on the other hand, was the cure to insanity, though it meant standing alone. There is sanity in the solitude of ideas.

It is brave to be alone in sanity when society has lost its mind, though you will be labeled a Pariah, a radical, a lunatic. But Cara couldn't imagine being called anything else. After all this, all she had been through, seeing hell and purgatory and not conforming to their madness, she was not about to give up in the final leg of the challenge and conform to the madness of heaven. This banality, this so called moral ennui, it was a form of madness, it was just madness with all the passion drained out of it. And if that really was sanity, Cara did not like sanity. She thought, if this was sanity, that sanity was another form of madness, the madness of overly loving oneself, at the exclusion of the world. She went back into the mansion, into the air conditioner. At least that part was different from hell. The Poet had still not gotten out of bed, though it was almost noon. Cara sighed. She knew The Poet was dying here as well, just as she had been dying in purgatory, and if The Poet died Cara would be in bad straits. She would not die if The Poet died, something much worse would happen. She would go on living without her, the only reason she had ever found to live. This had happened to Cara before. She had abandoned The Poet to cowardice before, to the banal madness that was tainting all of heaven, and she really had been dead, dead and still living-that's what cowardice does to us. And one cannot live that way for long. If one is alive and dead, eventually they have to choose one or the other. Cara hung her head in shame when she thought of how she had chosen death first, before, in the end, she at last became brave and chose life. But she supposed it had to be that way. She supposed she had to know the misery, the depression, the madness of cowardice before she could choose the sanity of bravery. She had always been like that. She had always been skeptical of people's definitions of light and darkness, so she had plumbed the darkness first, just to see if it was what the church had told her it was. It was and it wasn't. It was certainly dark, but Cara realized all prophets had been there, and for them same reason she had, out of the same skepticism. It was just something some people have to do.

And Cara was still the same way today. She was skeptical that heaven was really a paradise. How could it be, when it was killing The Poet? Cara mused for a moment about making herself a drink, but she didn't want heaven to throw her back into the deep chasm of alcoholism that cowardice had almost drowned her in. She felt like the afterlife, the entire time, was trying to test her, trying to see if it could make her insane again. But Cara was always a little bit insane. That was the price she payed for her sanity. She was shocked for a moment when she heard a knock on the door.

She went to the door and opened it tentatively.

"Howdy, neighbor!" someone said again.

"Hello," Cara tried to say in a friendly tone but it just came out groggy.

"So, you're the new girl in town? We wanted to welcome you!"

"Oh," Cara said, surprised. "Well, thank you."

"I'm having a party on my yacht at four today, feel free to join!"

"Oh, ok," Cara stumbled out laconic speech. "Sure, I'll be there. Thanks for offering."

"No problem. We like to make everyone feel welcome here. Everyone is happy in heaven. If you're not happy in heaven there's something wrong with you."

Cara gulped and managed another weak smile. It was true, there was something wrong with her. The neighbor left and she shut the door. What was wrong with her, she thought, if she could not be happy in heaven? All this time she had felt her inability to fully grasp happiness was realism, but now she wondered if it was delusion. She supposed no one in the world would ever know. She just new her attitude was less accepted, and she also knew this didn't necessarily mean it was wrong. But there is no incorrect or correct way to see the world. People thought objectivity was optimism, and subjectivity pessimism, but that was simply because no one did see objectively or subjectively in an entire objective or subjective way. We always twisted it to some mood, and abstraction was deemed horror and the more usual was deemed the good. And Cara did not know if this was true either. It was true that horror was abstract, or at least we necessarily perceived it that way- if we perceived it any other way it would overwhelm us- horror was abstracted in mental self defense. So then Cara wondered if it really wasn't abstract at all, we just made it that way to handle it better, and if that was so, the fact that horror was made an abstraction was what continued to make it so possible, if people could only look at it so dimly, if people had made it man-ageable to perception. The more we abstract something doesn't make it any less real. In fact, Cara thought it only made it all the more real, that the things we don't allow ourselves to feel are the most real, the most harrowing, the most painful even if we are ignoring it.

Cara hung her head. She always felt the tragic was more real than anything else, and she didn't know if this was something wrong with her or if this was truth. Perhaps truth was an illness, an illness only the few suffer from. She did feel sick inside, since she did not know how to be happy. Happiness to her was the biggest abstraction of all, that and love, them being two things that could never be defined and therefore each individual has their own definition of. 'One man's trash, another man's treasure,' Cara thought, 'and one man's heaven another man's hell.' It was all the same to her anyway, every layer of the threefold afterlife. She gave up the little amount of restraint she ever had and made herself a drink. She would go to the damn yacht party, she decided. Maybe it wouldn't be so bad. She walked upstairs and went past The Poet's room. She was in bed, coughing and blowing her nose. Cara had always thought The Poet was some mythical entity, much greater than her, but now she realized how shockingly they were the same person.

To be sick in heaven, what did that mean, if it meant anything?

Eventually The Poet got out of bed, though she was very sickly. Her hands shook as she poured herself a glass of orange juice and coughed raucously. Cara looked at her with raised eyebrow. "You know," she said, "You're not made for death."

"Neither are you, my dear," The Poet responded back fondly, and gently pat Cara on the cheek. "But perhaps no one is. Perhaps we are all meant to live more than we are meant to die, though the latter is certain as well."

"Are you dying?"

"I don't know. But I've come to realize through this journey, this whole time I've been in danger because of death, you will not let me die. You know if I go then so will your will, and you have finally gotten to the point in life where you hold onto your will fiercely, because you know without it life is hardly livable. I am proud of you, Cara. You have learned from the past. You know how to utilize your insanity now. I feel safe with you now, because I know at last you will not give me up., perhaps only because you've given e up before, and you remember how painful it was, but still, perhaps that had to happen. Perhaps you had to go through that, the lack of will, to come to understand how important will is. When you were depressed you thought you didn't need it anymore."

Cara smiled. "Yes, I'm glad I learned, the hard way, of course, but that's the way I am. I think learning anything easily is almost a sin."

The Poet chuckled. "So, do you want to go to this damn yacht party?" Cara asked.

The Poet shrugged. "We might as well."

So in a few more hours Cara and The Poet headed to the marina and found the appropriate yacht. It was easy to find because it was named 'Thanks a Yacht.' Cara and The Poet both rolled their eyes, but boarded anyway. The people looked at them strangely. They were unfamiliar in a world where everything had to be familiar. The neighbor who invited Cara pulled her aside. "Who is that woman with you?' he asked.

"My sister."

"Why doesn't she have any eyes?"

"Someone gauged them out in hell."

"Well, we don't want that. Tell her to wait on the pier. I don't want her condition upsetting anyway. That's a horror, and we do not allow horror here. Besides, it seems like she's sick, too, and we don't want any sick people here either."

"Are you serious?"

"Why shouldn't I be? Tell her she can't board. Why were you in hell anyway?"

"Some people are in hell by accident."

"No they're not. Only bad people go to hell, sick people."

Cara turned red with anger and walked towards The Poet. "It's ok," The Poet said. "I overheard. I want you to still go."

"What? Why?"

"I want you to see what we're dealing with."

"I think we know what we're dealing with."

"Go. I'll wait for you."

Cara rolled her eyes but acquiesced. "Alright," she said, "whatever you want," and she returned reluctantly to the people on the yacht.

"What's your name?" someone asked her.

"Cara."

"How did you die?"

"Isn't that a bit of a morbid subject?"

"How did you die?" the person asked again, seriously.

"I didn't," Cara said. "I'm just visiting. Here, I brought you guys a bottle of whiskey…"

"You're just visiting?" the man asked. "So you don't really belong here?"

"No one does."

"Everyone does," the man said stiffly.

"Except me? I am not dead," Cara said sternly, "but I am here because I owe death something. Death taught me the value of love. I know, life should have taught me the value of love, but I'm a very strange person, so death taught it to me. I see things a bit differently."

"Are you insane?"

"No," Cara said emphatically, "I honestly don't think I am, It's just that sometimes a person can be so different from you that they are merely perceived as insane. That happens sometimes, to some people."

The man squinted his eyes at her while he puffed his cigar and everyone on the yacht stared at her strangely. "I don't understand you," he said.

"My point exactly," Cara countered and sat down while she placed the bottle of whiskey heavily on the table.

"This is my yacht," the man said. "It is my birth right. What's your birth right?"

"I don't have one," Cara said.

"Why not?"

"Because I don't believe there is any such thing as birth right."

The man squinted at her again, and in his downright eyes Cara could see disgust. "You are strange," he said. Cara just shrugged. For the rest of the party she didn't speak much. The rest of the inhabitants of heaven drank just as much as her. In fact, the bottle of whiskey did not last long. They all drank copiously and managed not to seem intoxicated as they did it. That was the trick in heaven- you could drink as much as you wanted so long as it didn't intoxicate you noticeably, so long as it didn't give you a hangover, so long as it didn't make you sick. In other words, one could be an alcoholic in heaven so long as they were a high functioning alcoholic, and this of course they did not believe was alcoholism.

They talked about the most mind numbing things, and in circles. Cara couldn't get a word in. All their talk was arrogant, too. All of it was about what promotion they got, what new appanage they had added to their house, what achievements their kids had made at school- Cara felt sorry for the children. The children were just another prize awarded them, the children were just another example of how successful they were- Cara doubted any of these people looked at their children as small, confused and alone human beings who desperately needed love, but rather looked at them as another appanage to the mansion, as something that needed to be made head boy at the finest prep school just to sustain their parent's image. Their children were nothing more to them than yet another undeserved *trouveille* in a lifetime of undeserved *trouveilles*, because they were cold enough to forget about bad luck, about misfortune, and so were rewarded for their callousness with the success that came easy to them, since they would never participate in a success that was operose, that was difficult, because they would not take part in a struggle. Cara sat there and brooded and deeply hoped their children would rebel. They probably would, if it was as Cara suspected, and they needed love desperately. All rebels do. Rebellion itself is just a cry that there's not enough love as was promised, as we all would deserve if only we allowed ourselves to.

Everyone gathered around to take snap chat photos. Cara rolled her eyes. Social media had been used as a tool in hell and purgatory, she wasn't surprised it was used as a tool in heaven, either. All three were a means of control. These people were just the type that enjoyed being controlled, particularly because of the reward that was given them for this control- laziness. They took a photo of the large yacht and all the expensive alcohol and all their sickening, teeth too white smiles, and put the caption 'It's a hard knock life for us,' on the photo.

"That's barbaric," Cara whispered under her breath.

"What was that?" someone asked.

"Nothing."

"So, Cara," someone else said, "What do you do?" that was the requisite question among these people, that and 'where did you go to school?'

"I'm a writer."

"Ah, that's neat. Did you go to school for it?"

"No."

"Maybe going to school for it would help."

"It doesn't," Cara tried to say genially, but her mock friendliness was running out. "Do you mind if I smoke?"

The owner of the yacht cut in. "A cigarette?" he asked.

"Yes."

"You'll have to get the hell off this boat if you want a cigarette."

Cara's mouth hung agape. "But that other man smoked a cigar…"

"Cigars are ok. Cigars are a sign of wealth. Cigarettes are a sign of addiction and poverty. They're low class."

"You guys have drank almost four bottles of champagne and whiskey, plus all the pina coladas, you don't think that's a sign of addiction…"

"These are also signs of wealth."

"Let me get this straight…if an addiction is a sign of wealth, it's ok, but if it's something you've seen a poor man utilize…"

"If you want to smoke a cigarette you'll have to get the hell off of this boat," the man said again.

At last Cara completely dropped her mask of cordiality. "I'll do so happily," she said. "I'd rather smoke a cigarette, I'd rather have a 'low class' addiction, than be on this damned boat any day!"

"Really?" the owner of the boat said. "You'd rather be among the sick than the wealthy?"

"I'd rather be among the sick than those who scoff at sickness," Cara said finally.

"Then you have chosen your side."

"Yes, I have."

CHAPTER 4

Aubade

After that no one bothered Cara and The Poet anymore. They were quickly branded as undesirables. Cara sighed into her coffee. She felt like she was on the side that was right, that she was merely a minority because she was intelligent and therefore more capable of understanding morality, but then other times she felt maybe she was anti social, contrarian and cold. She vacillated between this often, this 'I am not sick, I am just different,' and then 'perhaps I really am sick.' Perhaps she had romanticized exile, and fooled herself into thinking it made a person great. Perhaps the people in heaven had the right to hate her, perhaps she really was cold and unfriendly. She sighed once more. No matter what, there was always something wrong with her. No matter what she was always weak and addicted. No matter what she was always alone and so she had put aloneness on a pedestal, she had made it something noble out of cowardice, out of the fear of trying to escape aloneness. She wondered if it were her the whole time, that people had never alienated her like she felt they did, and she just simply did it to herself to form this idiotic image of herself, the writer in exile in heaven. How absurd it all seemed now.

The Poet was lying in bed again, dying once more. The Poet was the same as Cara, happiness only made her sad as well. 'What the hell is wrong with us?' Cara thought. 'How can someone's immune system be so adverse to happiness? I suppose it's the damn skepticism again, the damn intellectual, haughty skepticism that unravels everything looking for the evil inside, just to shove it in people's faces, to say 'see, I told you this was not paradise, just hell disguised,' this damn skepticism that tells me everything is a lie, including happiness. I am an outcast in heaven. That says a lot about me…Christ, I am so weak…' Cara heard a stirring upstairs so she started to walk toward it. Someone was playing a guitar. 'Oh,' Cara thought blankly. 'Rhadamanthus.'

"I sold my soul to the devil," Rhadamanthus crooned as he violently strummed the guitar, "because the devil told me if you ain't got a soul, you can't get the blues/ And the devil was right/ But now I got the blues/ Cuz I ain't got not soul./ Now I got the blues, cuz I can't get the blues."

"You are a good writer," Cara said to him softly.

"You too, kid."

"So, while I'm here, am I going to meet…Him?"

"God?"

"Yes."

Rhadamanthus chuckled. "Na," he said. "I ain't even met Him. You don't get to meet Him. Human beings, even after they're dead, can only perceive Him in parables. To meet him naked, face to face, without a story, without anyone writing it, it would be a lot like that void you stared in, and I imagine you wouldn't be able to look away. You think people think you're strange now, Jesus."

"So that's it, huh?" Cara said. "I get to meet the devil but I don't get to meet God."

"Sorry kid."

"Why?" Cara asked. "Why does He reward the people here and not the people in hell?"

"No one knows," Rhadamanthus said. "I'm not even sure God knows why."

"Do you think He exists?"

"By hearsay. None of us will ever meet Him, none of us will ever know Him, but we have overheard Him at times, we can hear whispers of Him in nature. People like you perhaps can see Him better…"

"I can't see Him at all."

Rhadamanthus chucked at her gently and put a hand on her cheek. "You live in a world where most people disassemble this world first with the parts, then with the whole. And you are the opposite. You see the whole first, and then the parts come vaguely into view within it. And that's why you've been lonely. Most people want only the parts. Most people are actually frightened of the whole. The whole is the other, the whole is strange, the whole is mysterious, and the whole demands a certain amount of bravery the parts don't. And that's why you are the way you are, Cara. That's why you can speak for human nature even though you are so different from most human beings."

"That's a simpler explanation than I thought," Cara said, "but it makes sense." Cara chuckled for a moment. "Why do people say you are a cruel God? I think you are actually quite gentle."

Rhadamanthus smiled. "I am," he said. "In my whole. But in the whole everything is gentle, because in the whole everyone is merely misguided, misunderstood, like you. You know this and have seen this and that is why you are so forgiving to human beings. That is the most important thing wisdom, which is the analysis of the whole, teaches us, to be gentle with people, because no one deserves their fate. Not even the people in heaven. Does that answer your question for you?"

"Yes," Cara said.

"We can never meet God," Rhadamanthus said. "We can only ever try to understand Him. And that means understanding the whole. That means being gentle with people. You see the whole, and the next rational step is to forgive it."

Cara nodded. "Take care of The Poet," Rhadamanthus said. "I think it's gotten to the point…She needs you just as much as you need her. Your journey is almost over…"

"At the end of the journey…Am I going to die."

"Of course. Everyone does. But you've already seen death. I doubt you're frightened of it anymore."

"No, of course not. But I still think I don't understand it."

"Perhaps you aren't meant to understand it. To understand it, one would have to be in a very dark place first. You already have understood death, and you forgot that understanding so you would be able to go on living. That is what I recommend you continue doing right now. You have to forget this knowledge. You have to forget you have understood death, that you have seen the void, that you have walked through the labyrinth…"

"How the hell am I supposed to forget those? Come to think of it, they were the most defining points in my life. They made me who I am."

"You can be who you are and forget what made you who you are, particularly if, like you, you were made by some kind of trauma. I have tried to teach you the lord's aseity, now I guess I have to teach you death's aseity. Everything in the world has aseity, that it borrowed from God. Everything simply just is. And nothing, too. So why not forget death and nothingness, even if they have marked you? They are just like everything else, they are just like you, they are just like God, they just exist. Forget what made you. That is the easiest way to stay sane. Forget death which turned you into a philosopher but first made you long to die, forget nothingness for doing the same thing, and then, after that, forget even God, because perhaps he did the same thing, too. Your wisdom so far has been longing for an experience that is not meant for you yet. To understand death too early is no prize. You think you're lonely now. I know you want to understand everything, but perhaps some things in their aseity are meant to be abstruse, perhaps we are not meant to understand death. I don't really think you can understand death until you die, no matter how hard philosophy tries."

"So then there is no point to philosophy, if everything simply is."

"I didn't say that. We can understand things in their aseity to a degree. That's what philosophy is for. But I tell you, we are not meant to understand death. We are not meant to understand death and we are not meant to understand God."

"Maybe that's why I've confused the two."

"Maybe. Confusing the two was probably your attempt to understand them, but did it work? Did longing for death really make you wiser?"

Cara sighed her reluctant concession. "Only after it was over," she admitted.

"Exactly," Rhadamanthus said through gritted teeth. "If you must look back on these things you have to do it as a philosopher, as someone who is merely studying these phenomenon, not as someone who has actually been through them. Think of philosophy as something to distance you from yourself and the thing you are contemplating, so if you think of death, you can have it as a barrier between you two."

"Is that really the purpose of philosophy?"

"No, but it is something about it that is helpful. You can't contemplate these things- nothingness, death, God, without some productive telos in mind for its end, to think of them just to think of them, to mirror their aseity in thought, that will make you go mad. You should know, you've already done it. I'm simply trying to stop you from making the same mistake twice. You know you were incredibly lucky to come out of it. Next time you might not be so lucky."

"It wasn't luck, it was work…"

"But do you think you have it in you to do it again."

Cara, whose shoulders were raised in her hostility, lowered them and looked into Rhadamanthus' eyes. "No," she said, "I probably couldn't. It was a year long dream, and I don't remember exactly how, what happened to make me do it, but one day I just woke up. I woke up to realize that if I kept living in a dream I would die. But I have one question. I know you're right, I know it's very important to not let that happen to me again, but then why am I going through this ordeal? Why is life or fate or God or whatever is doing it always testing me, always putting me in situations that might send me back to that? Why, if I succeeded finally, am I still constantly being tested?"

"I don't know, Cara. Depression has taken a particular liking to you, because you used to give in to it easily, but now that you fight it, it wants you even more. Misery doesn't like to lose people. It will probably hunt you for the rest of your life, because at one time you were the perfect victim."

Cara sat on the floor next to Rhadamanthus and lit a cigarette. "You want one?" she asked.

"Sure."

Cara handed him a cigarette and they both sat down and puffed in silence. Cara began to cry soundlessly. Rhadamanthus looked at her and raised an eyebrow, also soundlessly asking what was wrong. "I've never felt so alienated since I entered heaven," Cara said through her quiet tears. "...Christ, the only place I fit in was hell! What does that say about me?"

"And you didn't really belong in hell either. I've known people like you. Not many, but they still come, people who are too wise to live, and too wise to die. I can see how that would be a sad predicament."

"I should have never done it," Cara said. "I should have never wanted to look into heaven and hell. I should have never allowed myself to be misery's perfect victim…Now that I have, now that I've broken the seal, now that I've tasted suicide, the taste will never go away completely. I will always know it."

"I'm sorry, kid, but it's too late to go back. You just have to learn to live with it. And I know it's a cliché, but maybe it did happen 'for a reason.' Maybe once you learn to live with it you will also learn to live."

Cara finished her cigarette and got up. "I'm gonna go check on The Poet."

Rhadamanthus smiled. "You know what's the best way to keep her alive?" he said.

"What?"

"Write."

Cara smiled and sank back into the wall. It was so confusing sometimes being one of the people Rhadamanthus spoke of, who recognized the whole more than the parts. It meant she could love easily the whole, she could love all of mankind, but it was difficult for her to love individuals. Even the ones she really did love she wasn't particularly good at loving. She could love the whole because it was an abstracted thing, because it was something she was a part of, but she often felt she wasn't part of the people she met, that she was very distant from them. She hated herself a bit for this. She hated herself for preaching compassion and love when she could only love the vague idea of humanity, and not its individual members. And she knew when she died this would be something very few people would understand. If she ever did get recognition for her writing, she would be remembered as someone who could only love within the bounds of creativity, someone who had a golden heart when they were writing, but a cold one when they were doing anything else, and Cara supposed it was true. She could not live up to her own abstracted love of the whole human race. She could love the whole in all its flaws, but not the parts, because of her strange attitude and her strange mind, because writing had taught her to love the whole, art had taught her to love the whole, but still nothing yet had taught her how to love people as an isolated phenomenon, as they were when they abstracted themselves, separated themselves from the whole. And Cara had done this herself. By loving the whole she had put herself outside of it. By loving the whole she had made herself a stranger to it, from analyzing it instead of passively moving within its framework like most people did, barely even realizing it was there even a it operated their lives.

Cara looked to Rhadamanthus. He was playing guitar and singing again, he was playing his aubade to the world, his mournful serenade for the world had turned him into a judge and a revelator, someone who had to love humanity in their own cruelty, who had to love it by being fierce and critical of it, and many people did not realize, in his seemingly harsh judgment, that he forgave those he judged much more than he forgave himself for judging them. Cara put an arm around his shoulder as he continued his song. She understood him, and he understood her, and that was the closest that two people like them could get to love.

Rhadamanthus smiled up at her and continued his song, his manifesto about the horrors of both feeling and then no longer being able to feel, something Cara understood all too well.

CHAPTER 5

Exile

Cara awoke the next morning, for once not hungover, ready to go to the council meeting. She had received an invitation to it the day before, and she decided she'd go. It was the first thing she'd been invited to since the disastrous yacht party, and this was something she'd be more interested in. That was the one thing she liked about heaven, that there were no politics, but often she wondered if that were true, and there actually were politics in heaven, they just went completely ignored. Then she shook her head at herself. 'There I go again,' she thought, 'looking for something wrong,' but she knew nothing ever was as it appeared to be, except a very small amount of people and they are outcasts. Cara wished there wasn't this duplicity in everything, that in everything visible there was something underneath it hidden, something very beautiful or very ugly, depending on who the person is pretending to be. She wished the world could ever be honest about itself, and didn't always have to be wearing some mask for protection from censure. Cara would prefer to just accept censure. It was better than the burden of a persona. And she felt like heaven was wearing a mask as well. In fact, she felt like heaven was a particular anomaly that haunted our time. She felt heaven was just the mask, there was nothing else underneath it. 'Oh well,' Cara though, 'I suppose that's honest, too, I suppose that's being honest about the fact that one is a lie.'

So she wanted to go to the council meeting to see if there were politics in heaven. She just wanted a glimpse of the world that paradise ignored, because it was the world she was from, and she belonged to it because of its struggles. In a world that was supposedly struggle free, Cara just felt moot and senseless, there being no meaning to discuss, no people to save, no code of honor to stick by, no important worldview, nothing for a writer to do at all. She had chosen her side, they had said. She had chosen to be with the sick. She had chosen to be with the people who never had the luxury of a mask, time and history's constant victims, alone back on Earth. She got dressed and ready and walked the block to the town hall. Heaven was a small town. Heaven was a suburb. Heaven was a place where people like her were not allowed. Heaven itself was a mask, the mask people wore when they were pretending to be good, and because there was not much underneath them, because the mask was only hiding nothingness, they actually believed they were good too.

Cara reached the town hall quickly and sat down in the back where no one could see her. It didn't work. Everyone there was staring at her, and they all avoided her. She got the back of the classroom all to herself, because since she had chosen the side of the sick she was now the plague, an imaginary plague, she was actually an antidote, but many people avoid the antidote like it is the plague because they prefer the plague, they have adjusted to it, and there's a certain amount of complacency in it that as comfortable. That was the sickness of heaven. That was the sickness that was socially acceptable. That was the sickness that was popular opinion, the mask the protected one from censure. Cara was used to censure now, though, and she even thought there was some dignity in receiving it, that there was some dignity in being a condemned thing, in being treated like a disease when one is really a cure. But perhaps that's how the antidote worked in the end, first by having to martyr itself, first by being stigmatized, crucified, first by being the butt of some great universal obloquy, first by being treated like a sickness. Cara knew how it went. She knew that liberation was actually quite painful.

The council began and Cara pushed herself back deeply in her seat in the back of the room. It was mostly mindless business, almost completely about which structure didn't look pristine and so they would get rid of it. Then of course a structure that didn't look pristine was Cara. A tribunal that called themselves the Vehmgericht took over the council. They called themselves "the exile tribunal."

"For our next order of business," the head of the Vehmgericht said, "the exile of Cara Weisman." Everyone snickered and turned their heads to look at her. Cara remained calm.

"First we will give her the right to defend herself, though our resolve is mostly made up. Ms. Weisman, it is said you were hostile at a yacht party, why is that?"

Cara stood up and cleared her throat. "I simply thought it hypocritical that they could drink and smoke cigars but I could not smoke a cigarette."

The head of the exile tribunal snickered. "Hypocrites," he said, "is that what you think of us?"

"Yes." Everyone in the room gasped, but both Cara and the head of the tribunal did nothing, the head of the tribunal merely smirked and Cara kept a firm face of stern resolve.

"Why?" the man asked. "Why do you think we're hypocrites."

"Because you have an exile tribunal in heaven. But it's more than that. I want to ask the council a question, if I may."

"I suppose you may."

"By a show of hands," Cara said, "how many of you have ever doubted, when you were alive, that you would go to heaven?"

No one raised their hand, but an officious woman in the crowd cried "Well, why should we ever doubt it?"

"There," Cara said to the head of the tribunal. "That's why I think you're hypocrites, because you have never doubted that you would go to heaven, simply because of your status in life. You all have been cold to anyone who's not like you. You all have been the deciding factor in who is allowed to be loved and who isn't. You all have exiled most of the world, and still, no matter what, you have always thought you were the divine. You have never once come to a moment of painful conscience and thought, 'what if I don't make it, what if I'm not good enough to be allowed entrance into heaven?' like almost everyone else in the world has. In fact, you have actually made most people feel this doubt, and what's worse, you made them feel this doubt, this doubt that you have never been forced to feel, was justified, simply because someone had made a mistake, simply because they did not lead the life of opulence, the heaven, that was given to all of you, and which you have never had to doubt, thinking of it as your birthright. I don't understand it, I don't understand how anyone could live like that, completely assured they would go to heaven. Most people have not been that lucky. How can you be holy when you allow people to have so much less than you? How can you be holy when you declare yourself holy, with no humility, when you are not declared holy by others, but by yourselves, and the society that blindly made you fortunate? How can you be in heaven, when you never wondered if you would go to hell?"

The head of the Vehmgericht looked at her agape, then resumed his smug expression. "Well, we are in heaven, aren't we? So I suppose we had no reason to doubt."

"I'm in heaven, too," Cara said firmly, "even though you people have told me not only here, but during my whole life on Earth, that I was going to hell. That's why I think you don't belong in heaven. Anyone who tells someone else they belong in hell does not belong in heaven. But yes, you are still here, but that's only because in our confused world people readily believe the merely assertorical. You saying you're good is merely assertorical, because you think of goodness as a birthright too. And in this world when you so violently assert something about yourself it is believed simply out of intimidation, and also because it provides the luxury of not having to look too deeply at people. That is the lie that your goodness was. Your goodness was an appearance, and people accepted it and believed it only so they didn't have to think too much. That's your legacy. And you did it too. You asserted to yourselves that you were good so much that you believed yourself, too. You lied to the world and you lied to yourself, you were just lucky that these two things were easy to be deceived, because they wanted to be deceived, yourselves and the society that always catered exclusively to you, both of you wanted to believe it was true, that you deserved it, because then the world would make a little more sense, but I repeat again, it is a lie. And if this is a lie, I believe so is heaven."

More gasps from the crowd. Someone yelled "Get her out of here right now!"

The head of the tribunal at last dropped his smug mask to reveal his anger, but he kept calm, though his face was red with indignation. "Is that all you have to say, Ms. Weisman?"

"Yes."

"Fine then, we will take a vote. All in favor of Ms. Weisman's exile?" Everyone in the room raised their hands. Cara didn't mind. The judge felt comfortable enough to smirk again, having won, as he always did. "We sentence you to exile," he said to Cara proudly.

"And where exactly am I being exiled to?" Cara asked.

"Earth," the man said sternly. Cara smiled. At this moment she was so happy, she was so happy she was returning to the place that she belonged, the place that she belonged because everyone was an exile on Earth, in exile of the universe. And, she realized, it was the only place where The Poet could live. Therefore, it was the only place that she could live. The afterlife was for the birds.

Cara, The Poet and Rhadamanthus were pushed off the surface of heaven. Rhadamanthus laughed the whole time, as he usually did, and strummed on his guitar "Kicked out of heaven," he crooned, "cuz I'm a judge in hell. But I ain't got the blues. There's a place for everything and that's the place for me, at the bottom of a well."

It was a slow fall, as Cara knew it would be. She had to hold onto The Poet in her blindness, as she had to hold onto The Poet her whole life, for The Poet was a Sisyphean labor like any other, but she was the only labor that could ward off the insanity, that could ward off the death that was always waiting in the wings of Cara's skull- The Poet was the tenuous balance of Cara's mind, and she had to hold onto because she was easy to lose, and every time Cara had lost her she had lost herself along with her, so she had to hold on desperately, she had to hold onto The Poet even more tenaciously than she had to hold onto love, and that was what Cara felt was sick about her, but she supposed it was the same thing. She supposed when she desperately grasped to The Poet when they were falling from the sky like some devil or some apocalypse, that she was grasping onto love, just a different kind of love, one that was more distant, more cold and more painful, the love of the whole, and the love of love which was her fragile sanity as well as her delirium as she plummeted from heaven back to Earth. Earth was the only place that would accept such an anomaly as her, she knew that now. That was what was good about Earth and that was what was awful about it, that it would accept any anomaly. It would accept an anomaly like her, one with a misguided but good, and at the bottom, gentle heart, but it would also accept an anomaly such as Putin, Stalin, Sisi, Hitler, who had all found ways to live without the heart at all, who lived without confusion, and therefore lived without reason and without any feeling for their fellow man, either the parts or the whole, they simply wanted to blow up the whole thing. Nature accepted both of these anomalies equally, passively and indifferently, but unfortunately, people generally accepted more the latter anomaly, they accepted it as something that was part of reality, more than they accepted Cara and her chasm of a heart, haunted as it was with the ghosts of idealism, because this they believed was a fantasy. Cara shook her head as she thought of it. "And people think I'm a pessimist," she said under her breath.

They finally fell through the dark plumbs of space and started slowly to reach the Earth. "Are we almost there?" The Poet asked, nervous.

"I think so," Cara responded. Rhadamanthus just kept laughing.

"I don't think I'll see you girls again," he said. "I think I must return to hell."

The Poet turned around and faced Cara with her eyeless visage. "I don't think you'll be seeing me either," she said. "I'm going to resume being something that is merely inside of you, no longer a humanoid prosopopoeia that exists in the physical world. I will again be yet another ghost that has haunted you all your life, and as long as you're alive, always will. I will continue to be the ghost which if ever stops haunting you will make you die."

"It's fine," Cara said. "That's only natural."

"Here it comes!" Rhadamanthus yelled as Earth approached "Goodbye ladies! It's been a hell of a time!"

Cara and The Poet embraced quickly as they made the final fall, while Rhadamanthus, still laughing, fell even further. Cara closed her eyes as they fell faster, her ears popping from all the sound that was inundating them, but she heard things that comforted her. She heard babies crying, she heard men and women laughing, some moaning, and the last thing she heard was the great swell of the sea as at last she opened her eyes. Everything went black for a moment, and there was a sharp ringing in her ears from all the sound. She looked up slowly. She was in her tine apartment, sitting at the chair by the desk with the typewriter sitting on it, having gathered dust from waiting for her for so long. She looked around blearily. The Poet was still there.

"How do you feel?" she asked.

"Better. I never related to this world, but it turns out I relate to the afterworld even less. There is one thing I have in common with Olam ha Zeh. It has a lot wrong with it, and so do I. All this time I thought I was an exile here, and it turns out I fit in here like a glove. Everybody does because nobody does. I am very glad to be back here. I didn't know the value of it before. That was my fault."

"What's better here?"

Cara sighed. "I don't know, but there is something. This place is war ravaged, desperate and starving, but there's something about it that's the best place in the galaxy. Probably because it is the only place in the galaxy, but until we find better this is what we have got. And I don't think we can look to the impassive stars for a better world. We have to make the world we live on a better one, because it is the only one, that is why it is so unique and that is why it is so alone, it is the only one, the only possible lover, and I have found that things that singular are always troubled, but they are also exceptional, they can be remembered, they can change the world. The world can change itself, with our help. We can make it the extraordinary thing it really is, though we can never make it any less alone, at least we can make it talented. At least we can remember it as an artist, and, if we do our job right, not a failed one. I think this is why nature created human beings, for this task, to make the Earth go down in cosmic history, so one day we will be the best world not by default of being the only world, but really the best world, once we come to accept it truly is the only world so we *have* to make it the best world."

The Poet smiled at her. "Write this all down," she aid. "Write everything down, every little thought you have, or it will be wasted in thin air. I'm going to go back inside you now. There I'll have eyes again, but before I do have a question for you."

"What's that?"

"What did you learn from the other world?"

"Only what I just told you. Besides that, I learned nothing from death." Cara smirked almost cruelly and then said. "It didn't change my worldview a whit. Now that I've seen the afterlife, I *especially* don't believe in it."

Imprisonment

Cara awoke the next day and everything around her was plastered with the veneer of normalcy, like a layer of dust that covered the abstraction and the decay, the senselessness underneath. Again Cara felt like an alien, moored in a world she had once known well but was now a stranger to. No one really comes back from the afterlife, not even her and The Poet that had now returned inside of her. She didn't know if this ghost within her was the veneer or what the veneer was hiding, the decay. She supposed poetry was a sign of aging, and now that she had seen death before the end of life she certainly felt anachronistically old. She came back to a world that was in every way the same, but like in some parallel reality, with little changes only an overanalytical person like her could see, but once she saw them, these details of minutiae, the parts in the whole, the abstractions within the abstraction, the machine within the machine, the decay beneath the veneer of normalcy, it became like a huge detail, like some obvious, overpowering thing in the room that could not be ignored. That's why life had always been hard for her, she could not ignore the things she was supposed to ignore.

She sat down and wiped the thick layer of dust off the typewriter, to reveal the machine within. Complexities within complexities, all to make the simplified whole that was in rebellion of its abstruse parts, trying to hide them within its normalization, its ubiquity. She began to type, all she could do left, The Poet inside her still screaming, the ghost still haunting, her still being alive. '*Amusa,*' she wrote, 'it means *against the muses*, and I think it's where the word amusing comes from. Amusement, entertainment, everyday it murders the muses, and as the muses are murdered so are ourselves- when we let our minds decay we decay along with them. When we go against the muses we go against ourselves, we cheat ourselves to the devil, we sell our soul, we give into numbness, to passivity, we lose our divine fire, we give up the part of ourselves that is eternal as if the whole time it were a nuisance. Human beings have given up on the only reason to live, and have accepted in its place the diversion of making life a game- we have turned ourselves into players, and at the end of the day when we are tired of the yoke and tutelage of playing we simply watch other people play in our stead, and that is how we live our lives now, first as begrudging participants but then in idle hours more happily as voyeurs. We are against the muses, we are against inspiration, we are against the new idea and instead want the same idea repeated ad infinitum- we have abandoned the new for the familiar, we even want innovation to be familiar, a taste of the things we already know, but altered enough to be supposedly unique. That is the new and absurd goal of mankind- to never have to learn anything new, so one can erroneously assume they know everything, that there is nothing else to learn, and the rest of life is a dragging on of what we were taught initially, with no variation, as if all we ever had to learn was already learned in childhood, and adult means learning nothing else hence, and that's maturity.

'But nature does not operate this way. Nature is the muses, and she speaks the truth by using only a few human beings to speak it for her, as a medium, as a puppet, but it is better to be the puppet of truth, who are the minority, than the puppet of lies, who are the majority...'

She stopped here and jumped as she heard a sudden noise. It sounded like someone knocking on the door, but loudly. Soon she realized it was someone kicking the door in. She ran and grabbed a knife from the kitchen, but when the door broke down there were The Holy Police waiting for her. She dropped the knife and held up her hands.

"*Still*," she said. "The Holy Government really holds a grudge."

"How did you do it?" the holy policeman said, pointing a gun at her. "Where did you run away to?"

"How did *you* do it," Cara asked in return. "How, after all this time, did you find me again?"

The holy policeman pointed to the camera that was hanging over Cara's desk.

"Shit!" Cara screamed. "I forgot. The goddamn cameras!" The goddamn carceral archipelago, *amusa*.

It wasn't long before the holy police completely swarmed her and she was taken in chains, to the prison within the prison, freedom only being a bad joke around here, a parody, a mask that people wore, a simple diversion.

Cara spent two days in prison, in a solitary cell, receiving meals three times a day by cold guards who had learned for their own mental ease to think of people like her as not human, just another dog they had to feed. Cara was restless and growing insane. That's what solitary is for, to drive someone insane. *Quos vult perdere, mentat.* And Cara was already an easy target for insanity. She only felt lucky that she had been alone much of her life, that made it easier. She was used to a solitude that bordered on madness. It was as if she'd been training for this moment her entire life. She used her fingernails to make little drawings in the walls, even though the sound it produced was horrible, she had to do whatever it took, whatever it took not to end up delusional or catatonic. Most of her fingernails had broken now because of this process, so she started to scratch herself deeply with her now blunt fingernails and paint the walls with blood instead. It's terrible sometimes, the desperate things some people have to do to stay sane. To many people these things seem insane themselves. But Cara knew this was erroneous, she knew this was the opinion of an eye untrained to understanding, the general opinion, the popular opinion, the one that didn't understand on purpose. She could live without such an opinion now, or at the very least she no longer gave a damn about its obloquy towards her. So many things she had gotten used to, and learned to ignore. She supposed she was just like everyone else that way, but she had different things she needed to get used to, and different things she needed to ignore. In fact, she had to ignore the things most people were taught to pay attention to, and pay attention to the things most people were taught to ignore. That was her desperate sanity. She had to be herself to stay sane, she had to be unusual to be sane- to a degree, she had to be a little bit insane to stay sane.

She understood this even if not many other people did, but it didn't matter. She decided it was more important to be understood by yourself than others. The guard thrust his nightstick on the bars of Cara's very small window into this small world and she jumped and quickly tried to hide her blood paintings. She looked around with stark confusion. It wasn't time for a meal.

"Visitor!" the guard called harshly then walked away again.. Cara smiled happily to herself. "I have a visitor?" she whispered breathlessly under her breath, as if she were in love. "I wonder who it could be…Rhadamanthus, maybe…"

In a few minutes more the guard came back and opened the door with another man standing with him. Cara was quite shocked to see who it actually was.

"Manuel Sanchez?" she cried.

Sanchez came in and sat down on the padded ground. He looked dazedly at the small painting on the wall in blood as Cara was desperately trying to hide her self inflicted wound from the guard, then he looked at the fingernail etchings and he smiled at her gently. "You've been keeping busy in here," he said.

"I've learned it's more important to stay busy when you're alone than when you're with others."

The guard looked in at the cell. Sanchez, very intuitively, put his back against the wall and covered the blood painting. The guard nodded tacitly and left them alone.

"Thank you," Cara whispered.

"I just hope I didn't ruin your painting."

"I just hope you don't have to keep the faded red of it on your back like the marks from a whipping."

Sanchez raised an eyebrow at her but ignored the comment. "I've been to law school," he said, "I'd like to be your defense in the trial."

"I'm getting a trial?" Cara said, surprised.

"Yes," Sanchez said. "No matter how hard The Holy Government tries, there are some staples of the law it cannot erase. Unfortunately, you will be tried by the Holy Government itself, as if this were some international crime."

"The Holy Government," Cara said slowly. "A part of me was always hoping they were a myth..."

"Well, they are in a way, but their dominion over us is very real."

"I can't believe I missed this place," Cara whispered.

"What was that?"

"Nothing. I feel so adrift, adrift between life and death, not sure which one I am more loyal to."

Sanchez grasped Cara by her hands. "Are they giving you your medicine?" he asked.

"No."

"I'll raise hell about that. I've decided that's what I'm here for."

"Yes, me too."

"And besides, I don't mean to be rude, but we're going to need you to be a little more coherent than this for the trial."

"I understand," Cara said. "I want you to know I'm not completely out of my head, though."

"No," Sanchez said ingenuously, "I don't think you are. I don't think you've ever been completely out of your head. I don't think anyone in the world has ever had that luxury."

Cara smiled at him. "I could always tell you were good," she said.

"I can tell you're good, too. Our souls seem to seek each other..."

Cara laughed gently. "A politician and a prisoner," she said, "I don't think that's ever happened before."

"Still," Sanchez said, "we're very much alike."

Cara looked at him and smiled as a quick stab of desire, of ever unfulfilled *sehnsucht* briefly stabbed her heart with an acute pain, then immediately became dull to the point of non existence as it always did, love being nothing but a rapid memory that almost at once faded into the background of routine and daily ennui, that one looks back on one day with wisdom as nothing more than a passionate folly, something someone can do without in the insensate lusterless solemnity of old age. Sanchez saw her brief look of passion and saw with more alarm how quickly it faded back into the numb insanity of a prisoner, as if it were something she was not allowed anymore. How can one love without freedom?

Sanchez cleared his throat nervously as he looked into the eyes of instantaneous fire that quickly turned into two dead coals and he had to look away from her. He didn't know why, but he felt that in many ways he had failed her. "I'll get you a trail date as soon as I can." He smirked at himself painfully for a moment. "I'll enact the writ of habeas corpus, the very thing I suspended only months ago." He put his back into the wall again, into Cara's blood. "This damned profession," he continued, "it doesn't allow anyone to not be a hypocrite."

"The world doesn't allow anyone to not be a hypocrite," Cara corrected, "because in order to ensure the good, one must first do terrible things. That's just the way it is."

She spent another two days in solitary confinement, until at last the guards let her out and put her in a normal prison, if such a thing existed. Cara found the cell to be the same. She had looked all around the world, at every dialectical extreme, and she had found them all to be the same thing- life, death, love, hate, freedom and imprisonment, they were all just subtle variations on the same thing, and they all had death at their core. Everything had death at the core, that's why everything was the same. She did not speak much to her fellow prisoners. She felt as sorry for them as she felt for herself, and that had been her problem her whole life, that she looked at herself and as soon as she looked at herself she saw the world, and she could do nothing but feel pity for both, as the two were inexorable though ridden by separate illnesses, in the end they were the same, too. In the end they both had death at their core, that's why Cara felt sorry for them, herself and the world that followed quickly after this self, so one could easily get lost in it, such a close chase, one could not tell which runner from which. And that's what they both were, runners, who as they ran away from time ran straight to it, inevitably.

Cara spent a couple more days in the general prison, still she did not hear anything else from Sanchez. At last the day came when the guard rudely hit his nightstick against the bars and said curtly once more, "visitors."

Cara was so excited she did not notice the plural of the word so laconically spoken. She waited for Sanchez with almost girlish, naïve delight, but her face quickly darkened when instead she saw a crowd of ten boys all with the same gelled, asymmetrical haircut, sporting tattoos and sucking insouciantly on vape pens. "Who are you?" Cara asked.

"We're the Kapporeth faction of War on War."

Cara sat on the dirty, hard ground of her prison cell floor, with a loud, graceless thud in embittered disappointment. The man, the ringleader of all these identical men, continued. "We're her to offer you our support," he said.

"What's that going to do me?"

"We are protesting your trial."

Cara sighed and ran a hand through her hair. "I appreciate that," she said, "but please don't do anything violent."

The man's face also darkened, quickly became hard. "Is that all you know about us?" he asked. "Is that all we're known for."

"Yes."

Rage spread on the man's face like a blush. "I'll have you know we have the support of Yasser Al Haifa…"

Cara waved him away flippantly and Manny stopped short in his sentence. "Bitch," he hissed at her.

"That's fine," she said. "Many men like you have called me that, among other adjectives, like 'Crazy,' 'Fat,' 'Angry,' 'Homely,' and things like that. I'm used to it by now."

"You're a writer, right?"

"Yes, how did you know?"

"When you disappeared, after you wrote the essay that destroyed the confession booth, there was a news website that published said essay."

"Oh," Cara said, indifferent.

"It was good," Manny said. "I liked it and when I read it I thought I would like you, but now that I've met you, not at all. You're just like al Haifa, you're out of my grasp, you're all the things I merely pretend to be, but I am loved more for my pretending."

"I know," Cara said.

"Well I won't let you forget it." He paused for a moment "Aren't you around my age too?" he asked.

"Yes," she said. "I'm twenty eight."

Manny shook his head. "And a writer. So strange. You represent us, but you're nothing like us."

"I know," Cara said again.

"You are *saepe noster,* almost one of us, but you're not one of us."

"Most of the people you supposedly defend are probably nothing like you," Cara spat with vehemence.

"Well, we're not going to defend *you*. Too bad for you. We could have really helped you."

Cara laughed almost cruelly. "'War on War,'" she said. "Yes, that's how you rid hypocrisy, by perpetuating it further. You have not saved or even changed the world, you have just added to its chaos."

Manny shook his head again, as if at a child who would never understand the complexities of such a mature mind, as if Cara had no idea what she was talking about, as if because she was a madman, the truth she spoke could be written off as madness as well.

"You are *saepe noster,*" he said again. "you are almost one of us, but you are not one of us, and you never will be. Therefore we can't defend you."

Cara smiled her madman's desperate, misunderstood and easily mistaken for evil looking smile at them. "Do you honestly think that still bothers me?" she said.

Die Prozess

"Nothing could be decently hated except eternity," – Giuseppe di Lampedusa

Cara spent a few more days in the numb sameness of prison and then at last her trial was decided upon. She would be tried by The Holy Government itself, in The Holy Court. The Holy Government was already wrathful that it was unable to attain Israel as its seat, with Ben Yehuda's new found idealism, and Cara knew they would want to take their wrath out on her. She was hopeful, though. She had Sanchez. She believed in Sanchez.

The prison escorted her to The Holy Court in a van without windows so she couldn't see how to get to it. She smirked to herself. 'This is just like the mental hospital,' she thought, 'all of these divine institutions, all of authority, it is just a desperate cry for power in a madhouse.' When they got to The Holy Court the guards escorted her inside still in chains. They did not take the chains off. They directed her to sit in a chair in the middle of the courtroom. Cara looked around. It looked like any other courtroom, but there were paintings of Christ on the ceiling, in poor imitation of Michelangelo. It was a mixture between a court and a church. Cara did believe justice was holy, but not this justice. She found it strange that in a religion whose main prophet's entire hexis was based on unconditional forgiveness, that so many people thought of it as a religion of punishment and guilt. She realized in The Holy Court they did not

worship Christ, they worshipped condemnation, because condemnation made them feel like God.

Cara sat in the chair and waited for the judges to convene
and she looked desperately around for Sanchez. She got the guard's
who was still standing next to her attention. "Hey," she whispered.
"Where's Sanchez."

"Manuel Sanchez has also been arrested," the guard reported
robotically, another slave to authority, another slave to condemnation, even if it wasn't his own.

"So I'll be defending myself?"

"Yes."

"As usual," she whispered. "Always defending myself, and
apparently I'm not very good at it, because it never changes anyone's
minds. Maybe I should stop defending myself. Truthfully, in the end
and the beginning, I think the sentence has already been passed."

The guard ignored her and looked with his usual stoic expression at the wall. He was the man with the whip who was waiting
under the wings of another man with a whip, the man that possessed
the whip for him. That was authority.

At last the main judges of The Holy Government slowly filed
in like a funeral procession. 'The Holy Government,' Cara thought
to herself, 'something we have been taught for years to fear but
which we have never seen. Now I truly get to see it.' And The Holy
Government was as she'd expected it to be. It was an oligarch of a few
elderly Caucasian men with dry, stony, rigid and piously peremptory
faces, all trying to appear solemn so you could not see how cruel they
were, but Cara knew this veneer of piety, of solemnity, was awfully
thin. Beneath it was the writhing hypocrisy, the decay, the feeling
that one was of the best brand of people simply because it was easier
for them to follow and to break the rules, having made them. Cara
tried to conceal the look of hate she had for them. They had turned
the world into a frightened penitent sweating and screaming and
bending on his knee as he scourged himself, thinking the whip was
his own, so deluded by these people he did not realize it was them
that put the whip in his hands, it was them he was praying to out of
fear, not God. That was all they had made of the society they sup-

posedly wanted to fix. They had only wrecked it further with guilt. People like The Holy Government, they teach you to be guilty for the wrong things. They teach you to feel guilty for loving instead of hating. They teach you to feel guilty for your body and your mind instead of the war. They teach you to feel guilty for being born and dying instead of being eternal. They teach you to feel guilty for being sick instead of being healthy and castigating the ill. They teach you to feel guilty for all the things that are out of your control, instead of the things that are within your control, and that was how they controlled us, by assigning us a guilt for inevitability, therefore, a guilt that could never be assuaged.

The judges sat down and the guard locked Cara's chains onto the chair before their intense scrutiny. It was an army of scrutiny Cara was facing alone now, but she didn't care. In front of these men, she refused to feel like a criminal. She had known her whole life that they were the real criminals, and thus came her lack of respect for the law, but only the law that was cruel and senseless, only the law that was consecrated lawlessness, only the law of criminals like these. The head judge cleared his throat and thus the proceedings began.

"Cara Weisman," he said, deliberately ominously, "you are charged with destruction of Holy Government property, resisting arrest, sedition, treason against The Holy Government, and for breaking the Holy Government's law of lack of incalcitrance. How do you plead?

"Not guilty," Cara cried as if to God, with her head held high, incredibly proud of the fact, in a world that wanted her to feel guilty for the most harmless peccadillos, she did not feel guilty.

The judge saw her pride and glared at her. "Very well," he said. "We will be doing the questioning today, The Holy Government itself. Did you deliberately break a confession booth?"

"Yes, I did."

"How did you do it?"

"I wrote something a machine could not understand."

"Why did you do it?"

"To prove that human beings can still do that."

"Excuse me?"

"I wrote something a machine cannot understand. I wanted to prove to the world that human beings can still do that, and I wanted to prove to myself that I could still do that, so I knew I was still human."

The judge sneered at her. "That's a recalcitrant thought," he said.

"Is it, or is it just human? Even Montesquieu said one cannot be punished for their thoughts."

"It's a different era."

"It's an era gone backwards, where hundreds of years of the study of law have been spit upon and devolved."

There was a quiet gasp among the jury, and the judge glowered. Another man from The Holy Government piped up. "That is certainly a recalcitrant thought," he said.

"Yes," Cara acquiesced, "it is. But recalcitrant thoughts are often truth. That's the problem I have with the law. You get rid of recalcitrant thoughts, you get rid of truth. That's what a tyranny tries to do."

"Do you just want to get executed?" the first judge cried, exasperated.

Cara shrugged. "I don't want to be executed, but I don't mind if I do. I want people to hear my words and dare to have recalcitrant thoughts again. I want people to hear my words and dare to search for truth again, even if it is against your laws. That is something I don't mind dying for."

The judge sneered at her again. "You think you're so brave," he said, "but you're just foolhardy. Your quest for so called truth is mere effrontery."

"Perhaps," Cara admitted. "Only time will tell. As for the present I think I'm doing the right thing, and that just has to be enough, since I can never know the future."

"Fool," the judge spat at her. "I'll tell you the future, you will be hanged! Who and what do you think you are? Do you think you're some kind of a martyr?"

"Only time will tell," Cara said again. "I am an atheist, though," (more quiet gasps of shock in the jury,) "and I have always been attracted to atheism because it is a religion that is forgiving enough not to require martyrs. But perhaps times have changed. Perhaps now atheism is so suppressed that it does need a martyr. Perhaps you, this tribunal, have made it so that atheism needs a martyr. It is sad. That was the thing that was so pure about atheism. That was the thing that was so pure about nothingness, that it did not require a sacrifice, but there is truth in nothingness, and now that people have tried to forget truth as if it were only a bad memory, now I suppose nothingness does need a sacrifice, because we are back in the darkest of times, the times when people, since they are denied the right to live for the truth, have to die for the truth instead. I do not know if I'm a martyr if it is as you say, I am just a foolhardy idiot, like I said, that's up for history to decide, but I will say, I have not always felt this way, but in these times, I am willing to die for no God just as in the past people were willing to die for God. I will die for my lack of religion like they died for their religion, because my lack of religion has been violently oppressed, just like every religion has. And regrettably that's something people have to give their lives for, and I agree, foolishly. It is noble to die for one's God, it is noble to die for one's country, and, in present times, it is noble to die for one's godlessness, but in the end, one is simply dying in a war- one is simply dying because human beings are greedy, callous and in the end, afraid of all the things they refuse to even try to understand. All martyrs, all soldiers, though they have died nobly, as an antidote to that which killed them, simply died as a sacrifice not to any of the Gods, or even to the nothingness I tout as the truth, but to man's folly."

The main judge glowered at her, his rage, his hypocrisy, surfacing completely now while under this stare Cara writhed and withered in her *hexenstuhl*, waiting for his sentence, waiting for the world to further vilipend her.

"Is nothing sacred to you?" the judge spat as he whispered.

"Only the truth."

Another man in the tribunal piped up. "Why did you become an atheist?" he asked.

"For a simple reason," Cara said. "It was the masses who murdered Christ and then it was the masses that worshipped him. I'm an individual so I did neither. I'm an individual," Cara repeated, "that means I don't worship anything, therefore I don't kill anything."

"Then you are entirely ineffectual," the judge said.

"Perhaps, but I'd rather be ineffectual to this world than try to ruin it. I don't want that stake in it- I don't want the stake in the world that is the world's destruction. I'd rather come and go quietly, but judge, believe it or not, I have not done nothing in my life. There are actually many other things one can do besides worship and kill."

The judge ignored her and stared at the list of charges dully. "You plead not guilty," he said.

"Yes sir."

"And yet you admit you committed the crime."

"Yes."

"Explain this."

"I submit to the court that it was not a crime at all, and that's why I'm not guilty. It is not a crime to write something a machine can't understand, it is only an exercise in humanity, one we have largely forgotten. I just wanted to remind the world of it. See, that's what I do. Since I do not want to take part in the world's destruction, since I do not want to worship and kill, I am simply here to *remind*, to remind the world of some of the essential things it has forgotten in its hysteria to become a slave."

"I don't give a damn what you're here for," The judge not too solemnly pronounced. "So, you wrote something a machine could not understand, and thereby you destroyed the machine. That's destruction of Holy Government property. Therefore you are guilty."

Cara shrugged. "Better to destroy a machine than a man. Better to condemn a machine than a human being."

"You have only condemned yourself."

"No, *you* have condemned me, and you will pay for it one day…"

"Are you threatening me?"

"I'm just saying, *resurgam*, I shall rise again."

"Only Christ could ever rise again…"

"And with him, his ideas. That part of me shall rise again. You can execute me now, but some people will remember my words and they will follow. I did not change the world but I have opened the path for others to change it, a lonely road, I know for sure, but you should know, as long as mankind exists so will the few that are brave enough to take this road, and this minority will crush you in the end. You will find you have always been powerless, and thus your lust for power. You will learn there is strength only in the rare, and the rare will someday tear down your wretched empire, and they will do it in my name, to avenge my blood, because they will know, I am not guilty."

"You are guilty!"

"I am not guilty. I am one of the few people in this world brave enough to be not guilty."

The judge banged his gravel and screamed. "Execution!" he cried. "The sentence is execution!"

"*Resurgam*," Cara whispered again. "And as I rise again, you shall fall."

"You insist that you are not guilty," the judge whispered in a sibilant hiss, "but *I* proclaim you guilty. And in the end that's all that matters to people."

Cara smiled at him wryly. "It's not all that matters to me,"

Cara was returned to the prison and her execution was put in order almost immediately. Cara didn't mind. She'd rather die than be a prisoner. The judge of The Holy Government knew this, and that was why he killed her, not out of mercy, but out of having the chutzpah to prefer death to enslavement, which was the biggest crime against any autocrat, including The Holy Government.

Cara was returned to her solitary confinement and she smiled. 'I guess one dies as they have lived,' she thought. She only wished she could speak to The Poet again, but she knew that would be the part of her that would not die in the execution- in fact, if anything, it only strengthened The Poet. The Poet was a thing the world was constantly trying to kill, but could not. That would be that part of her that would do the *resurgam*, and one day, Cara and her kind would win the battle against the masses and their delusions, this Cara knew for sure. The truth is always known in the end, and even becomes louder the more we try to ignore it. The truth would one day prevail indefinitely, and that was the day Cara would still wait for patiently in death, that would be when she rose again. She was certain it would happen someday, and she was glad to die for it, even if, in the end, she was dying for man's folly, she was dying for man's folly to replace it with the truth someday.

It wasn't long before the guard came and got her and lead her to the spot where she would die. She gave him a happy smile and he glared at her as he took her away. The judge had only given her what she'd wanted, death instead of a life without liberty. The guard didn't notice that on the wall Cara had left a poem in her own blood. These would be her final words, not even spoken. The blood on the wall said,

> Heaven, hell, purgatory,
> A wise man wants none of these,
> And yet without them nothing exists.
> That is the divine tragedy.